WINTER DUTY

WINTER DUTY

A NOVEL OF
THE VAMPIRE EARTH

E. E. KNIGHT

A ROC BOOK

ROC
Published by New American Library,
a division of Penguin Group (USA) Inc.,
375 Hudson Street, New York, New York 10014, USA
Penguin Group (Canada), 90 Eglinton Avenue East, Suite 700, Toronto,
Ontario M4P 2Y3, Canada (a division of Pearson Penguin Canada Inc.)
Penguin Books Ltd., 80 Strand, London WC2R 0RL, England
Penguin Ireland, 25 St. Stephen's Green, Dublin 2,
Ireland (a division of Penguin Books Ltd.)
Penguin Group (Australia), 250 Camberwell Road, Camberwell,
Victoria 3124, Australia (a division of Pearson Australia Group Pty. Ltd.)
Penguin Books India Pvt. Ltd., 11 Community Centre,
Panchsheel Park, New Delhi - 110 017, India
Penguin Group (NZ), 67 Apollo Drive, Rosedale, North Shore 0632,
New Zealand (a division of Pearson New Zealand Ltd.)
Penguin Books (South Africa) (Pty.) Ltd., 24 Sturdee Avenue,
Rosebank, Johannesburg 2196, South Africa

Penguin Books Ltd., Registered Offices:
80 Strand, London WC2R 0RL, England

First published by Roc, an imprint of New American Library,
a division of Penguin Group (USA) Inc.

First Printing, July 2009
1 3 5 7 9 10 8 6 4 2

Copyright © Eric Frisch, 2009
All rights reserved

RoC REGISTERED TRADEMARK — MARCA REGISTRADA

LIBRARY OF CONGRESS CATALOGING-IN-PUBLICATION DATA:

Knight, E. E.
Winter duty: a novel of the Vampire Earth/E. E. Knight.
p.   cm.
ISBN 978-0-451-46274-9
1. Valentine, David (Fictitious character)—Fiction. 2. Vampire—Fiction. 3. Kentucky—Fiction.
I. Title.
PS3611.N564W56   2009
813'.6—dc22   2009001125

Set in Granjon • Designed by Elke Sigal

Printed in the United States of America

To John O'Neill,
who keeps the heroic dream alive

Dies iræ! dies illa
Solvet sæclum in favilla
Teste David cum Sibylla!

—Requiem Mass
usually attributed to Thomas of Celano, c. 1200

CHAPTER ONE

The old Jackson Purchase, Kentucky, November of the fifty-fifth year of the Kurian Order: Summer and winter contest the season, with fall waiting on the sidelines as though waiting to determine a winner.

Gloriously warm, some might even say hot days give way to chill nights of thick dew and fogs. The trees cling to their leaves like bony old women chary of nakedness, and the undergrowth remains thick and green or brown.

A line cuts through the growth, trampled and torn into a furrow that circumnavigates only the biggest trees. A stranger to Kentucky of this era might conclude a bulldozer had gone on a rampage, but to natives the furrow is instantly recognizable as a legworm trail.

Capable of eating their way across country at a steady three miles an hour, or doubling that if the riders chain the jaws and scythes shut and prod them along with pokes to their sensitive undersides, the giant yellow caterpillarlike creatures provide a ride smoother than any wheeled conveyance. Especially considering the broken-up state of many of Kentucky's roads, cracked when the New Madrid fault went in 2022 and exploited by new growth.

The trail ends at a camp.

The two worms huddle next to each other in the cold, contracted as tightly as their segmenting allows. One would almost say "unhappily," were the odd, segmented creatures capable of anything as prosaic as happiness or its antonym. Their skin is never more reminiscent of old fiberglass attic insulation than this late in the year, when new winter growth turns the outer layer into tufts and tatters.

Each of the worms bears a pair of curious wooden yokes across its back, projecting from its sides like yardarms of a sailing ship. Each pair supports full hammocks, two to either side of the legworm. A few more walking wounded limp here and there in the camp, bringing food and cleaning those in the hammocks under the supervision of a blue-uniformed nurse. The nurses look exhausted, having spent the day walking up and down the back of the beast with the practiced air of a circus performer, plunging a hook into a fleshy yellow tuft to drop down and check on a patient, offer water, or adjust a towel hanging so as to keep the sun out of the wounded soldier's eyes.

The rest of the camp not on guard cooks, bakes, or sleeps dead-deep and dirty. There's always too much to do in a hospital train.

A thin strip of woodland and a slug-shaped marsh sit beyond the farthest picket, where a pair of figures lies on their bellies just below the crest of one of the low rolling hills of this quarter of Kentucky where it falls off toward the Mississippi River. Their prone bodies are pointed, like a pair of compass needles, at another camp, smaller in numbers but more spread out in size—a careless campsite, more interested in avoiding one another's smells and sounds than organization or security.

The watchers are male and female, though it is hard to tell by their hair or apparel. If observed from anywhere but atop them, they might be mistaken for a couple of dropped bundles of laundry. The female's long brown overcoat is so patched that the fabric takes the appearance of a camouflage pattern. A thin, freckled face and a fringe of knife-cut red hair can just be made out behind the bug eyes of a pair of mini binoculars. Her longer, leaner companion carries more weapons and gear. He's clad in an odd fusion of weaponry, pebbly leather, and slate gray uniform that looks more like the overalls a utility worker might wear, with thick padded knees and elbows. He's worn-looking from scarred face to pocked and scratched bootheels. In contrast, clean and silky black hair covers the back of his head in a luxurious fall down to his shoulders.

Her binoculars sweep from campfire to sentry, from thick-tired four-wheel vehicle to tent to trailer. She's counting, assessing, calculating risk and threat potential.

His unassisted eyes remained locked on a huddled group of figures in the center of camp. They're neither tied nor restrained; instead they sit behind a staked-out square of construction pegs and red twine, eating hockey puck–sized biscuits the color of gravel from a freshly opened box. Mothers have mashed and soaked them in water for their children; the others either break up the rations with fingers or bite into them, depending on the condition of their teeth. One of the stronger captives, a hulk with a pair of gloves over his ears serving as elephantine earmuffs, wrestles a heel of bread from a weaker, old man with a neat goatee. Their guards do nothing to intervene. It's gone all too soon, save for a few biscuits given up by the older specimens behind the string to the mothers and children.

It's hard to tell exactly what the watching man may be thinking; he keeps his face a careful mask. But a careful observer might note that he's blinking more than his companion as he watches the huddled captives try to feed their children.

†

David Valentine suspected his eyes were glittering red in the dark, like eyes reflecting a camera's flash in old pictures of wedding guests. The night vision he'd had ever since becoming a Cat came with some odd side effects. It was a gift of humanity's Lifeweaver allies in their war against the Kurians, but a double-edged one. While his pupils could open as wide as if under a pharmacological effect to let more light in to the sensitive, and multiplied, rod-shaped cells beneath, that also left him vulnerable to headaches when exposed to sudden glare and color vision that was a little off from what most people experienced.

Though the tears interfered with his vision, Lifeweaver-improved or not.

His light-thirsty eyes watched the strangers' nighted camp. The sky might have been a pane of glass between Earth and the stars, and the moon would be up in a couple of hours, when it would glow like a searchlight.

They'd been lucky, oh, so lucky. Both parties had approached and camped without cutting each other's trails, and only his train had bothered with a proper reconnaissance.

His wounded and their caregivers were settling down just on the other side of a low hill and a stretch of soggy woodland between.

A meeting engagement, then. Whoever found out the most about the other fastest would have the advantage. No sign of scouts discovering his wounded, or he suspected he'd see more action in the camp.

"Who do you think they are?" he asked the woman next to him. Alessa Duvalier had trained him in the business of operating in the Kurian Zone.

"Poachers. Nomansland trash."

All the layers of clothing made them look like bloated ticks. A ratty undershirt covered by variegated flannel with a windbreaker over that, and then an old military gear vest with ponchos in assorted configurations pinned back but ready to rearrange if the strangely warm fall rain started up again.

Headhunters returning from a successful raid, probably bound for Memphis or Nashville. The Kurians had few scruples about stealing population from one another's territories. Human rustling could make a person rich.

In this case what the raiders were doing was a little less dangerous. They'd probably rounded up people displaced by all the fighting in Kentucky in the summer and fall, or perhaps caught escapees from some Kurian principality or other making a run for the Free Territory across the Mississippi.

Twelve poachers. Plus two kids and the women. That he and Duvalier could see. Maybe more in the tents or out of camp hunting or on errands. They were old-school with their transportation: a gas ATV, a few motorbikes, tough-looking mules and llamas, a knot of sleek brush ponies, and two trucks towing big horse trailers for their captives, riding like livestock on the way to the slaughterhouse.

Damned if he'd see them driven into those carts again.

But twelve. A job for a company of soldiers.

Or a small, very careful team. He had one of the best Cats in the business lying next to him. She'd volunteered for the operation in Kentucky last summer. He still wondered why.

Duvalier lowered the binoculars. The wide, light-hungry pupils turned on him. Valentine picked up a faint glitter in the darkness, like polished copper reflecting flame. "You're thinking about those scruffs."

Slang for future aura-fodder. Anything to keep from thinking of them as someone who might be a brother or a daughter.

"And if I am?"

"Will you at least let me go in first and shave the odds?"

Of course his orders said nothing about rounding up strays. He had to consider that if it went bad, his wounded could end up driven to the Kurians south or north of here.

The rewards in return for the risk didn't amount to much. The people who had the guts and resources and luck to make it to the Freehold often needed years of education before they were more of a blessing than a burden. Without someone to schedule every moment of their lives, they wandered like lost sheep or were taken advantage of by hucksters and con artists.

Their kids, however, took to the Free Territory like famished horses loosed in good pasture. The ones with memories of the Kurian Zone often made the best fighters in the Cause. They accepted the discipline and regulation and privation without complaint. They soon learned that the Quisling thugs who'd robbed and bullied everyone under their authority ran like gun-shy rabbits when put up against trained soldiers. Even more, the Reapers, instead of being invulnerable avatars of the local dread god-king, could in fact be hunted down and dynamited out of their holes and killed.

Colonel Seng, who'd led Javelin across Kentucky in the most skillful march into enemy territory Valentine had ever experienced, had once been one of those children.

The Free Republics could use another Colonel Seng.

But twelve. Plus two kids and the women.

He couldn't do twelve. Not all at once, not without running too many risks of a mistake. Duvalier might be able to, but it would take her all night in her methodical manner. But perhaps he could stampede them.

Two paces away, Alessa Duvalier lay swathed in her big overcoat with her sagging, flapped hunter's cap pulled down low. You had to look twice to be sure there was a person there rather than an old, lightning-struck stump.

Her eyes sparkled red, alive at the thought of cutting a few throats. Duvalier had a personal grudge against all Quislings. She'd selected Valentine years ago to become a Cat, tutoring him in sabotage, sniping, assassination, intelligence gathering—all the variegated duties that covert operations in the Kurian Zone entailed. They still bore faint, matching scars on their palms that sealed the odd bond between them, a strange blend of mutual respect and an almost filial blend of conflicting emotions.

"They'll send out scouting parties in the morning, sure as sunrise," Duvalier said.

"Bound to cut the legworm trail," Valentine agreed.

"We could nail the scouts headed our way."

"Which might draw more trouble, if this is just an advance party of a bigger operation," Valentine said. "Besides, it won't help those poor souls in the trailers."

Duvalier's mouth opened and shut again. "Let's skip the usual argument. I know you'll just pull rank anyway."

Valentine answered by stripping off his uniform tunic as she muttered something about crusades and hallelujahs and saving souls.

"We'll need someone good with a rifle," Valentine said. "Just in case they don't bite."

"That old worm driver, Brian something-or-other—he has that scoped Accuracy Suppressed. He hit a deer on the run with it. His kid's always carrying it around."

They ended up bringing the son—his name was Dorian—forward. The father came along as spotter. Dorian's father claimed the boy was just as good a shot, with better eyes. He'd already seen action that summer and been blooded at what in better times would be called the tender age of fifteen at the river crossing where Valentine had taken out a company of Moondaggers with a handful of Bears. Dorian's swagger showed that he considered himself a hardened veteran.

Valentine could just remember what it was to be that young.

He outlined the plan and had Dorian repeat it back to him.

"Steady now, Dorian. Don't pull that trigger unless they throw down on me, or I signal. And the signal is . . . ?"

"You hit the dirt," Dorian said, even though they'd already been through it once.

"Remember to check your target. I'll be moving around a lot in there. Can do?"

"Can do, Major Valentine."

†

It felt good to run. Valentine enjoyed losing himself in his body. Idleness left his mind free to visit the nightmare graveyard of his experiences, or calculate the chances of living to see another Christmas or summer solstice, or think about the look on the old man with the goatee's face when his fellow prisoner ripped the heel of bread right out of his hand. So he escaped by chopping wood, loping along at the old easy Wolf cadence—even the rhythmic thrust of lovemaking.

Though the last left him feeling vaguely guilty for not being attentive enough to the woman.

Since they'd said good-bye to the Bulletproof legworm clan after the battle across the river from Evansville, he had nothing but memories of Tikka's vigorous sensuality and the musky smell of her skin. They could be revisited at his leisure. Now he had work to do.

He had the sense that their affair was over, her curiosity, or erotic interest, or—less flatteringly—the desire to cement good relations between Southern Command's forces and her clan being satisfied.

†

He crouched in a bush, watching the young sentry, who seemed to be watching nothing but stars and the rising moon.

Valentine checked his little .22 automatic, which he usually carried wrapped up in a chamois with his paperwork. Over the years he'd had cause to kill with everything from his bare hands to artillery fire, but he'd found a small-caliber pistol more useful than any other weapon. It was quiet, the rounds were accurate at close range, and you could carry it concealed. With the lead in the nose etched with a tiny cross so it would fragment and widen the wound, it did damage out of proportion to the weight of the round.

He wondered if the Kurians' death-machine avatars, the Reapers, felt the same electric nervousness when they stalked a victim.

Of course, in a meadow like this, in open country, Reapers did not stalk, at least not for the last few dozen meters. They acted more like the big, fast cats Valentine had seen loose in the hill country in central Texas, covering the distance in an explosive rush that either startled their prey into stillness or made escape futile.

Of course, in the city it was something else entirely. Urban Reapers were the trap-door spiders of many a ruined block, striking from a patch of overgrowth, a pile of garbage, or a crack in the ceiling. But he doubted these headhunters worked the cities. Too much law and order, even if the bad law and order of the KZ.

He turned his senses to the camp, trying to get a sense of the rhythms of the headhunters.

They were singing. Three of the men were passing a bottle, falling out and joining in the tune between swigs, taking turns improvising rhyming lyrics in old-style rap.

The sentry sat in a tree overlooking the bowl-shaped field and soggy patch, within hallooing distance of the camp.

The safety went back on the little .22, for now. Valentine guessed why they put the youth on watch. Young men had good eyesight, especially at twilight. He'd probably be relieved by a veteran for the late shift. The boy was alternately yawning and chewing on bits of long grass root, glancing back toward the camp for signs of his relief.

Valentine balanced the chances of the young man doing something stupid against the possibility of using the kid to get into camp armed with some bargaining power. If Valentine just approached the poachers, they'd have him facedown in the dirt until they secured his weapons, at the very least.

Valentine wormed his way up to the trunk from downwind, using a mixture of crawling and scuttling during the sentry's frequent glances back to look for his relief.

The relief sentry started his walk uphill to the lookout tree, holding a heavy, swaddled canteen by its strap.

Valentine loosened his sword and pocketed the automatic, grateful that he hadn't had to use it. He shifted to his submachine gun, double-checking the safety.

The boy, anticipating his relief, clambered down from the scrub oak. Valentine slipped up behind.

Valentine moved quickly, clapping a strong left hand over the kid's mouth and elevating the kid's wrist to his shoulder blade with the right.

"Don't crap yourself, kid. I'm not a Reaper. But I could have been. I want you to remember that when we get back to your campfire sing-along. I could have been. What's your name?"

"Trent. Sunday Trent," the boy sqeaked.

"Sunday? Like after Saturday?"

"Yes, sir."

"Knock off the 'sir,' boy. I'm not some local trooper you have to polish. They call me the Last Chance."

Valentine couldn't say why he picked the name. One of the Moondaggers had called himself that. An emissary sent to deliver threats and ultimatums, he hadn't intimidated the Southern Command's troops—the quickest way to get their backs up was to start making demands and informing them they were beat.

Valentine thought of tying the kid's hands—he had spare rawhide twine in a pocket, as it had lots of uses around camp—but settled for looping his legworm pick in the back of the boy's pants and prodding him along with the haft. Less aggressive that way and it kept Valentine out of elbowing distance in case the boy made a gesture born more of desperation than inexperience.

Being careful about others' actions as much as your own was how you stayed alive on Vampire Earth.

"Sunday, I need to talk to the boss of— What do you call yourselves, a gang?"

"Easy Crew, sir. Blitty Easy's Crew."

"Which one's Blitty Easy?"

"The one with the tall hat, sir."

Valentine thought of giving the kid a poke the next time he said sir.

"Call me Chance, Sunday."

"The one with the hat, Chance bo— Chance."

The use of names was relaxing the kid a little.

They met the relief sentry on the way, a man with no less than nine Old World jujus around his neck, a mixture of car manufacturer iconography and bandless watch faces. Valentine recognized a Rolex and Bulova dangling from gold chains. Valentine remembered some of the decorations as Gulf Coast Reaper wards.

"Keep your mouth shut, Sunday," Valentine said.

"That watch post has blind spots right and left," Valentine called. He kept Sunday Trent between himself and the sentry as they passed.

The relief looked distinctly unrelieved at the news.

"Hollup!" the relief called belatedly.

The camp was contracting like a turtle tucking in its limbs for the night. One of the poachers guided a captive to a tent, his hand firmly on the back of her neck. She didn't struggle—a pregnancy was a guarantee of life in the Kurian Zone, both as proof of fertility and for the sake of the new member of the human herd.

The gunmen stood up at Valentine's approach, swapping eating utensils for guns and clubs.

"Easy now, Easy Crew," Valentine muttered. "Just relax, Sunday. All I want to do is talk a bit."

Sunday led him into camp and people gathered, naturally curious about the stranger. Weapons were readied but not pointed.

Sunday pointed out the leader of the headhunters.

Valentine had to admire the big man's sartorial taste. From the dirt pattern on his extremities, Valentine surmised he drove the ATV. Valentine hadn't seen a beaver hat since New Orleans at least, if not Oklahoma, and this one had a lush shine to it that spoke of either recent purchase or tender care.

"Careful, tha, with that gun, stranger," Blitty Easy said. Everything on him looked bright and expensive, from the silver tips on his shoes to the diamonds fixed to the skin in the place of one shaved eyebrow.

"I'm here to talk, not shoot," Valentine said.

"Even shooting off your mouth can be dangerous around me, Injun Man," Blitty Easy said. "What's the matter, we grab somebody's heir? You the big tough man they sent to get him back. No, her back."

"I think bigger than that. I want the whole bunch. Leave the bonds. I want to present them wrapped up like a big bouquet."

Blitty Easy laughed. "You talk pretty big for a man with nothing but a dumb kid in his sights. You can shoot him if you like.

Serves him right for letting himself get snuck up on tha in that tree."

"What direction you going, Sunday?" Valentine asked, poking the kid in the lumbar with the barrel of his gun.

"South. Mem—"

"Shuddup, Sunday," Blitty Easy said.

"South," Valentine said. "Good. You won't have to circle around to avoid us; you can just keep on track."

Blitty Easy stood up, thick legs holding up a stomach that jutted out like a portable stove. Not flab, exactly, but the heavy center of a powerful man.

Valentine walked Sunday around the circle of onlookers. Each took a step back as he approached and held his right fist cocked so his brass ring was at eye level. The circle of men and guns around him widened and spread and thinned as though he were rolling dough.

They eyed the submachine gun at his hip. Carrying a quality firearm like that openly marked one as either a tool of the Kurian Order or someone operating outside it. Easy's Crew maintained their well-armed independence by living on the fringes of the masquerade of a civilization beneath the towers.

Deadly as his weapon was, some would say the brass ring on his finger was the deadlier weapon. It was the mark of Kurian favor. A wearer was owed respect, for the fear and favor of the Kurians hung about the ring's owner like a king's mantle.

"Who do you think you are, threatening my crew?" Blitty Easy barked.

Valentine held his brass ring high. "Who am I? A man tested by the only law that lasts—that of the jungle. I speak three Grog dialects and have a foot pass for half the tribes west of the Tennessee and Ohio. I've watched Twisted Cross tubs open, ridden the cannonball St. Louis to LA, and flown with Pyp's Circus. I've sailed the Caribbean and the Great Lakes and Puget Sound, humped hills in Virginia and Baja, tickled lip from Albuquerque to Xanadu. I've won a brass ring and the power to put you all in unmarked graves. I'm your last chance, Blitty Easy."

Easy had a good poker face. "Why you bothering with us, then, Mr. Big Shot?"

"The Old Folks are interested in Kentucky right now. They don't want to see another state fall to the guerrillas. We're on our way to talk some sense into the more friendly locals. I thought my goons would have to forage for heartbeats, but you went out rounding up strays and did the job for us."

"We get paid for them?"

Valentine would have happily bought the lives, had he or his column had anything the brigands would accept.

"Payment is you just hand over your collection without going in the bag with them. My Old Man likes keeping brimful on aura when traveling, and they're not particular."

"He's bluffin'," someone called from behind Valentine.

Valentine whirled. "Kiss my ring and check it out. I don't mind."

A brass ring on its rightful wearer accumulated enough bio-electric charge to tingle when you touched your lips to it. Valentine found the sensation similar to licking a battery. His brass ring, fairly won in Seattle, was legitimate enough, and he usually kept it with some odds and ends in a little velvet bag along with a few favorite hand-painted mahjong pieces. Though he'd lost his taste for the game long ago, they still made useful tokens for sending messages to people who knew him. The only tarnish about the ring was the mark it had left on his conscience.

Valentine could tell the crew was impressed, even if Blitty Easy still looked suspicious.

"Or you want to test me some other way?" Valentine said, drawing his blade.

"Regular Sammy Rye, with that blade," Blitty Easy said.

"Steel without the talent to back it up's just so much butter knife," a man who smelled like cheap gin said, two younger versions of himself flanking him.

Valentine inflated his lungs and let out an unearthly wail. An imitation of a Reaper scream had worked once before, a dozen years ago, several hundred miles north in the hills of western Illinois. It might work here.

Movement and a bullet crack.

Valentine's reflexes moved ahead of his regrets.

The camp exploded into noise and motion, like a tray of ice cubes dumped into a fryer.

He knocked Sunday flat.

No rhyme or reason to the rest. The fat was in the fire and he had to move or burn. A hand near him reached for a chest holster to his right and he swung his sword and struck down in a sweeping blow. A shotgun came up and he jumped as it went off, spraying buckshot into the men behind him, turning one's cheek into red mist and white bone. A poacher put a banana-clipped assault rifle to his shoulder, and then his hair lifted as though an invisible brush had passed through it, and he went down, a thoughtful look on his face as he toppled.

Valentine rolled free, dropping his sword and reaching for the little submachine gun he'd carried across Kentucky twice as he ran out of the firelight. With a shake, the wire-frame folding stock snapped into place and he put it to his shoulder.

A bullet whizzed past, beating him into the night.

The poachers had pitched their tents in a little cluster, and he moved through them. A shaggy back with a bandolier—he planted

E. E. KNIGHT

a triangle of bullets in it between the shoulder blades, moving all the while, zigzagging like a man practicing the fox-trot in triple time.

Tent canvas erupted and Valentine felt hot buckshot pass just ahead.

Move—shoot, stop, and reload. Move—shoot, shoot; move—shoot, stop, and reload.

Blitty Easy's Crew was shooting at anything that moved, and Valentine was only one of several figures running through the night.

Turned out the twelve and then some could be taken without too much of a risk.

These weren't soldiers; they were brigands, used to preying on the weak. They popped their heads up like startled turkeys to see where the reports of the sniper fire came from and received a bullet from Dorian's rifle. Pairs of men moved together instead of covering each other—Valentine cut two down as they ran together toward the machine gun pointed impotently at the sky.

Valentine saw a figure with long hair running, dragging a child. *Please, Dorian, don't get carried away.*

There was only one headhunter Valentine wanted to be sure of. He wasn't that hard to find; he made noise like an elephant as he ran through the Kentucky briars and brambles.

Thick legs pumping like pistons, Easy made wide-spaced tracks for timber.

A brown-coated figure rose from the brush as he swept past. She executed a neat thrust under his shoulder blades.

The fleeing figure didn't seem to notice the quick poke. Blitty Easy pounded out three more steps and then pitched forward with a crash.

Duvalier kicked the corpse and then waded through the brush to Valentine, sniffing the beaver hat suspiciously as she passed.

"That was a good piece of killing," Duvalier said, wearing that old fierce grin that made Valentine wonder about her sanity. She lifted a coattail on one of the bodies and wiped off her sword.

An engine gunned to life and another shot rang out. The engine puttered on, but he didn't hear a transmission grind into gear.

"This might be nice for winter." She tried the hat on. The size made the rest of her look all that much more waifish, a little girl playing dress-up. "Smells like garage gunpowder and hair oil, though."

They covered each other as they inspected the camp. The only one left alive was Sunday. He looked around at the bodies, shaking like a leaf.

"They said it was good money," Sunday said. "Easy work. Easy work, that's what they said. Easy crew. Easy work. Get rich, bringing in rabbits."

Duvalier put her hand on her sword hilt, but Valentine took her elbow.

"He's just shaken up. We can let him go."

Valentine turned on the boy. "You load up a couple of those llamas and go home to mother, boy. Kentucky's harder than it looks."

They circled around away from the bodies and checked the trailers and the prisoner pen.

"We're turning you loose," Valentine said to the captives. "We're heading west, all the way across the Mississippi. Any of you want to go that way is welcome to file along behind under Southern Command protection."

A few gasped. One young girl, no more than six, lifted one chained-together leg as though asking for assistance with a fouled shoelace.

"There's got to be a bolt cutter in one of those trucks," Valentine said to Duvalier. "See if you can find it, Smoke."

He turned away and flipped the maplight switch on one of the running trucks, a high clearance pickup with the cab top removed and replaced by an empty turret ring. One of Easy's Crew leaned back behind the wheel. If you looked at the side of his head that wasn't sprayed all over the hood of the open-topped truck, it appeared as though he was sleeping.

"You want us bringin' our supplies, Cap'n?" one of the captives asked.

Valentine looked at the captives' rations. Blitty Easy's Crew fed their captives on the cheap, as you'd expect. Hard ration bread. Sticks of dried legworm segment divider—interesting only as chewing exercise—and sour lard, with a half-full jar of a cheap orange mix that tasted like reconstituted paint chips to drink. Though it did sanitize water. They'd be better off cooking the poachers for food, but of course Valentine couldn't suggest *that*.

It took a while to get them organized, to distribute loads on pack animals. He'd send a patrol back for the vehicles.

As he walked back toward Dorian's sniper perch with Duvalier, he refilled his submachine gun's magazine from a heavy box of 9mm rounds he'd found in one of the locked glove compartments. It had yielded easily enough to a screwdriver.

"What was that?" he demanded of Duvalier once they were out of earshot.

"A darn good killing," Duvalier said, showing her teeth.

"I said I'd make the first move," Valentine said. Was he more angry at the killing, or orders being disobeyed?

"You screamed, Val," Duvalier said. "I thought you were calling for help. I gave the order to fire. What's your malfunction, David? They were just border trash."

"Major, if you please."

Duvalier rolled her eyes heavenward.

"Just doing my duty," Duvalier said. "You even remember what yours is? We're supposed to fight them in as many places as possible, the 'fire of a thousand angry torches' or however that speech by the former Old World president went."

The mood passed, as it always did. Valentine was more vexed at himself than Duvalier. At least she had the guts to admit she liked killing.

Valentine took his mood out on the food snatcher wearing the stolen gloves as earmuffs. He got to arrange the bodies and see that each one's face was faceup but covered by a shroud of some kind.

†

Valentine felt better as they gathered Easy Crew's collection of aura-fodder and vehicles and brought them into camp. A sergeant gave the usual recruiting speech as they broke camp the next morning. Anyone who wanted to join the fight would head back west to the new Southern Command fort on the banks of the Ohio guarding Evansville from the Kentucky side. They'd have an important job right off, getting the vehicles back with the guidance of a detail from the sick-train.

They ended up with two. A fifteen-year-old boy with a lazy eye and a widow of forty-one who'd learned to use a rifle as a teen in the Kurian Youth Vanguard.

"I quit when my mom got sick in her uterus and they stuck her in a van," the volunteer explained. "Mom was right smart, could have been useful a hundred ways if they'd let her get operated on and recover."

Of course Sergeant Patel, the senior NCO back at Javelin, could make soldiers out of odds and ends of human material. There was always more work than there were hands.

More aura for the trip home. A prowling Reaper would spot

their psychic signatures from miles away, even in the lush hills of Kentucky. He and Duvalier would have to team up every night and sleep in their saddles.

†

Four enervating days later Valentine had his wounded across the Mississippi. The Kentucky worm drivers turned homeward, their sluggish mounts willing to move only in the warmest hours of the day no matter how much pain they inflicted with the long, sharp goads.

The Kentuckians would stay on their side of the river. Valentine felt guilty saying good-bye and wishing them luck, they'd pushed their worms on through the cold until death was assured for their mounts. Without a group of others of their kind to coil with, in a knitted cocoon to protect the fall's eggs, the frost would take them like delicate fruit.

"These two are goners, I think," Dorian said as they made their good-byes. He'd been quiet ever since shooting six of Blitty Easy's Crew on that wild, clear night.

"We'll compensate you and your father somehow," Valentine said, signing an order and tearing it off from his dwindling sheaf of blanks.

"Wish they could give me back that night. The one with the shooting."

Valentine felt for the young man. Dorian had stepped across a terrible threshold far too young.

"You followed orders and did what had to be done, Dorian," Valentine said. "Better than thirty people are going to live to a fine old age because you're a good shot. Remember that."

The youth nodded dumbly, and his father nudged him back toward the high saddles.

Duvalier embraced him with one of her characteristic hugs, half handshake and half lover's embrace. She nuzzled the bristle on his chin.

"I'll see that they get back all right. Any orders for me back in Henderson?"

"Be careful. I think if the Kurians move on us, it'll be from the Ordnance. You could check the rail lines up that way."

"Can do," she said.

"I won't be gone long. I'm just going to give my report, see about supply and replacement, and return."

She slipped away as though bored with the good-bye, and Valentine returned to supervising the river embarkation.

Javelin had left Southern Command with bands playing and people cheering and tinfoil on their heads.

Its wounded returned under cover of darkness, hauled across the Mississippi in some of Southern Command's Skeeter Fleet—twin-engined outboards ready to make wake at the first sign of trouble.

No crowds met them on the western shores, just a deputation from Forward Operating Base Rally's commander at the edge of the Missouri bootheel.

Colonel Pizzaro looked incredulous when Valentine announced that he'd been returned with fresh from a hard-fought victory in Western Kentucky. Valentine handed over a sealed report to Southern Command from Colonel Bloom, now in command of what was left of the expedition to the Appalachians.

"Don't be stingy with the steaks and beer," Valentine said. "They walked a hard trail. They deserve a few luxuries with their laurels."

Pizzaro cleared his throat. "Tell me, Valentine. Don't hold back. How bad was it over there? Papers are playing it down or calling it a catastrophe."

"Could have gone better," Valentine said. "But it wasn't a disaster. We've gained allies, just not where we expected. I'd call it a major victory for the Cause."

"He's a good man, but kind of an oddball," one of Pizzaro's staff said to a corporal in a voice he probably thought too quiet for Valentine to hear. "Always full of fancy ideas about working with Grogs and stuff."

Pizzaro snorted. "Victory? Not according to the *Clarion* headlines. Or are you aiming for a nice long rest somewhere quiet with lots of watercolor paint?"

"It was a win for the good guys, Colonel."

"You're selling that at headquarters?" Pizzaro asked. "I wish you luck."

CHAPTER TWO

*S*outhern Command Mississippi Operational Area Headquarters, *the second week of November:* The architects who designed the Mall at Turtle Creek in Jonesboro would still recognize their structure, though they'd be surprised to see some of the renovations caused by war and necessity.

One of the anchor stores has been hollowed out and turned into a vast machine shop for the repair and renovation of valuable electronics, and the rest of the big box stores serve as warehousing. The smaller shops have been converted to training classrooms, meeting areas, offices, break rooms, a medical center with a pharmacy, even a kennel for the bomb sniffers and guard dogs. Only the food court is still more or less recognizable; if anything, it is a little more interesting, thanks to cases displaying unit histories, photographs, and citations. And some of the hardy palms planted inside by the builders have survived the mall's looting, deterioration, and restoration.

Most of the exterior doors have been welded shut, of course, and netting and silent antiaircraft guns dot the roof. Barbed wire encircles the parking lots scattered with buses, trucks, and staff four-wheelers and motorcycles ready for use and dispatch.

Of course, the polished floors are patched and the ceilings are being rebuilt in some areas to repair minor earthquake damage the mall received in 2022.

David Valentine, having passed through the security station and visitors' lobby taking up the old bookstore, idles with a yellowed copy of French military history on an upholstered chair that smells like cigars and mildew and body odor, his thumb smeared with ink for an ID record and his bad leg stretched out where it won't interfere with passersby. He had enough pocket money for a bagel and a glass of sweet tea at the little café for visitors waiting to be met.

He fights off a yawn as he waits.

On the other side of the old store, security staff search and inspect those passing in and out of the headquarters, not a yawn to be seen. The Kurians have their own versions of Cats.

†

The ink had dried and the last crumbs of the bagel disappeared by the time General Lehman's adjutant appeared. The staffer might have been a living mannequin of crisp cotton and twill. Valentine felt scruffy shaking hands with him. All Valentine had managed in the washroom was to comb his hair out and wash his face and hands.

Perhaps it wasn't the chair that was so odiferous after all.

"You can just take that book if you like," the adjutant suggested. "It's all Southern Command library. I'm sure you know where to drop it."

"Thanks for the tip," Valentine said. Not that he needed it. He'd visited the quiet library and reading room in one of the mall's old stores to unwind after the quick debriefing he'd undergone on his arrival yesterday afternoon. Three paperbacks, one with a duct-tape spine—the illustration of the dripping-wet bikini girl on the cover reaching up to undo her top did wonders for circulation—were already stuffed into his duty bag beneath the reports and Javelin correspondence.

They'd talked about Javelin, good and bad. When Valentine gave them his assessment for the addition of Kentucky to the United Free Republics, his interviewers had exchanged a look that didn't strike Valentine as promising.

And he hadn't even begun to describe what he had in mind for his Quisling recruits.

He saved that for the end, and they told him to take it up with General Lehman the next day.

There was another wait outside Lehman's office, and Valentine switched to American history, a biography of Theodore Roosevelt. He was experiencing the Badlands with Roosevelt after the nearly simultaneous deaths of his mother and wife when Lehman's staffer summoned him.

When Valentine finally stood before the general in command of the eastern defenses, he was surprised to see a pair of arm-brace crutches leaning against the desk and the general's right leg encased in plaster and a Velcro ankle brace on the left.

"Bomb beneath my command truck," Lehman said. "Flipped us like a flapjack."

He looked paler than Valentine remembered, thin and strained.

"Let's hear it, Valentine," Lehman said. "Don't spare me; I know I sent you out there."

Lehman dipped his little silver comb in the water glass and commenced cleaning his drooping mustache in the methodical fashion a cat might use to clean its face. It was whiter and less bushy than it had been a year ago at the planning sessions for Javelin. Cover Lehman in dust and denim, and he'd pass for a cowhand straight off a Texas ranch, but he had precise, machinelike diction, weighing each vowel and consonant of his sometimes cracker-barrel phraseology. Valentine had heard that as a junior officer he'd been in signals, communicating with other Freeholds around the world.

"Should really make you a colonel, Valentine," General Lehman said.

"What about the confirmation vote?" Southern Command was allowed to run its own affairs within the confines of its budget— and parts of it even made money by engaging in civil engineering projects or restoring machinery—but promotion to colonel and above had to be approved by the UFR's legislature.

General Lehman nodded. "The *Clarion* would get in a huff and their chickens in the legislature would squawk in tune and the whole list would probably be voted down. They've had a field day over Javelin. You understand."

"I do."

"Of course, there's no reason we can't pay you like a colonel."

"Under the assumed name," Valentine said. Technically, David Valentine was a wanted man and couldn't draw pay, civilian or military. Not that it would do him much good if the pay increase went through. Few colonels got rich, despite their pay-draws twice that of a major. A colonel was expected to spend most of it on entertainments for his command, and most also gave generously to families of the command who'd lost fathers or mothers. A private who was good at scouring arms and medical supplies and selling them back to the Logistics Commandoes could do better.

"There is one promotion I'd like you to make," Valentine said. "I'd like Sergeant Patel—his name is all over those reports—made a captain."

"Shouldn't be a problem. I've heard the name. Wolf, right? Twenty years or more."

Valentine noticed there were archival boxes all against the walls, and two locked file cabinets hung open.

"Moving to a new office, sir?" Valentine asked.

"That's one way to put it. You didn't hear about the election, then?"

Valentine didn't follow politics when he was in the Free Republics, beyond what filtered in to mess hall chatter and newspaper articles.

"There's been a change, as of the first week of November," Lehman continued. "President Starpe lost. Adding Hal Steiner to the ticket didn't help as much—"

"I'm sorry, General. Hal Steiner? From down south near the Louisiana border?"

"Yes. Of course, you've been out of the UFR. Sorry, it's all anyone's been talking about here. Steiner a friend of yours?"

"I met him as a lieutenant."

"Yeah, he's the one who helped keep all the Archangel forces hidden down in those swamps. The Concorde Party made a big deal about Steiner coming out of the KZ and treating Grogs like people, and between that and the bad news out of Kentucky and the Rio Grande, the New Federalists were plastered. Anyway, old DC is out and Thoroughgood is in. Once Lights's sworn in, he'll nominate Martinez to take over Southern Command, and I suspect the legislature will approve, though the Texas bloc will be voting against him, of course, because of the bad feelings about 'seventy-three.'"

A piece of Valentine's brain translated the political farrago.

Archangel, of course, was the operation that ousted Consul Solon and the Kurians from his brief hold on the Ozarks. In the chaos following, Southern Command seized much of Texas and Oklahoma and a patch of bled-dry Kansas.

The United Free Republics, after a messy birth, had divided into two parties, the Concorde and the New Federalists. Other than their slogans—*Liberty and Justice through Thoroughgood* for the Concorde, *Starpe Can't Be Stopped* for the New Federalists—he didn't know much about platforms and so on, though the perpetually dissatisfied *Clarion* supported Thoroughgood through its editorial page and its reporting.

"Old DC" was a nickname for President Starpe, not because of some connection to the old United States capital, but because he earned the nickname Danger Close as an artillery spotter during the tumultuous birth of the Ozark Free Territory. He'd infiltrate Kurian strongpoints and called in artillery fire literally on top of himself. His opponent, Zachary Thoroughgood, was a scion of the Thoroughgood family, owners of the Thoroughgood markets and a several hotels and casinos in Branson. They also controlled a brewery that produced a fine spruce-tip ale that Valentine's old CO in Zulu company had been fond of as well.

Valentine had first heard of Thoroughgood as a prosecutor who busted up criminal gangs operating from the borderlands and then for improving electrification and water supply across the UFR as a legislator. Thoroughgood's friends and constituents called him "Lights," and Valentine had heard him called "Lights, Camera, Action" here and there, for he was famously photogenic and traveled everywhere with a photographer.

As to the "Texas bloc," Valentine knew that in the legislature there were constant fights between the representatives from the old Ozark Free Territory and the newer regions. Rules of seniority favored legislators from the Missouri and Arkansas areas.

General Martinez, of course, was an old enemy. Valentine had put Martinez on trial for the murder of a pair of helpful Grogs who'd followed him up from the Caribbean. Valentine had always suspected Martinez had, if not an entire hand, at least a pointing finger in his own arrest after the fight in Dallas that led to his exile from the UFR.

Lehman got up and dug around in a pile of newsprint next to a bureau with liquor bottles lining their little rail like spectators. He tossed down a copy of the *Clarion*.

STARPE STOPPED, read the headline.

"I suspect there'll be changes once Martinez takes over. I won't be running the Mississippi front and parts east. All these boxes and such, they're not me getting set to move out; they're from the new broom coming in. There's been a suggestion of malfeasance on my part over Javelin. Preservation of evidence and all that."

"How could you know it was all a setup? They fooled Brother Mark."

Lehman chuckled. "You've changed your opinion of him, then? Back when we were organizing Javelin, I got the impression he was a stone in your hoof."

"He grows on you. Even the men are starting to confide in him. He's like the grouchy instructor nobody likes but still remembers ten years later."

"Soon I'll be a memory here. If I don't get retired, I imagine I'll be checking locks on empty warehouses and filing reports on other reports that'll end up going into my superior's report. General Martinez and I don't piss in the same direction on any number of things, starting with Kentucky. He penned an editorial for the *Clarion* about Javelin, Valentine. Of course, all the paragraphs featured the word 'fiasco' with the same arguments, but then the *Clarion* only has two tunes in their hymnal. Everyone around here's tight as a turtle's ass with the soup pot bubbling."

"What are our chances of getting some reinforcements into Kentucky? Garrison and training duty, until they can get themselves organized."

"Somewhere on the short block between Slim Street and None Boulevard, I'm afraid, Major."

Valentine stood up. "Whatever's being said about Javelin, it wasn't for nothing. Kentucky's come in on our side, more or less. The Moondaggers, the ones who bled Kansas dry, they've left bodies scattered from the Ohio to the Tennessee."

"That was just the first wave, son. The signals and intelligence staff thinks something's brewing in the Northwest Ordnance. Beyond the usual dance of reinforcements for the river crossings, with armed rebellion just across the river and over Evansville way."

Valentine wondered about Evansville. Technically it had been the extreme southwestern tip of the Northwest Ordnance, which encompassed the old rust belt states of Ohio, Michigan, and much of northern and southern Indiana. (The central part of the state organized itself with the other great agricultural Kurian principalities in Illinois south of Chicago.) "All the more reason to send us at least something. Without their legworms, the clans in Kentucky lose their mobility and flexibility."

General Lehman leaned back in his chair, staring at the ceiling as he drummed his chest with his fingers. "Maybe they won't have any more luck in those hills than we did."

"A fresh brigade could make a big difference in western Kentucky. The old legworm clan alliance can take care of their ridges. With Evansville as a supply base, they have hospitals, fuel supplies, machine shops, factories. There's even a company that produces tents and backpacks."

"I hate half measures, Major. The way I see it, we either pull out completely or go all in and shove every chip we can scrape together across the Mississippi. I'd like to argue for the latter, but we're in flux right now."

"I've got an ad hoc battalion of Evansville volunteers—I guess you'd call them. There's more than that in western and central

Kentucky. We could put the brigade back together and have near a division."

Lehman's comb went to work again.

"But right now, in Evansville, all you have is what's left of Javelin and your volunteers."

"The Kentuckians chased down the Moondaggers before settling in for the winter. Their legworms have to hibernate, remember. But the Evansville volunteers have the know-how for mechanized operations."

"Yes, the staff briefed me on that. You're proposing a sort of French Foreign Legion for ex-Quislings, am I right? They do a little bleeding for us, and in six years they get a new name and citizenship in the UFR. Quite a scheme."

"I realize I may have exceeded my authority in recruiting local support."

"That's what you were assigned to Javelin for: local support."

"To hear you tell it, my locals won't have anything to support much longer."

"All in or pull out, Valentine. I'm sorry to say it, but all in is just not in the cards this year. That leaves pull out."

"Can I at least get some matériel for my Quisling recruits? They're walking around in black-dyed versions of their old uniforms and using captured Moondagger guns. Not the best of rifles—they're mostly bolt-action carbines with low-capacity magazines. Fine for smoking out rebellious townies; not so hot when you're trying to bring down a running Reaper."

Lehman opened a notebook on his desk and jotted down a few words. "I'll see what I can do. I know some huge rolls of blanketing or bedding has shown up recently. Guns will be tougher."

"What about my offer to the Quislings, sir? Can you give me something in writing to back it up?"

"I'd be proud to. But honestly, Valentine, I don't think any of 'em will be around to collect. They'll either quit on you or be killed."

"Do you know something I don't, General?"

"It's been my experience that the top-level Quisling officers are excellent. Well trained, intelligent, motivated, cooperative. Their soldiers are brave enough. They'll stick where our guys will pull out a lot of the time. But you know as well as I that it's the quality of the NCOs and junior officers that define an army. I've not seen the Quisling formation yet that has outstanding sergeants. They're usually the best bullies and thieves in uniform."

†

Valentine swung through intelligence next. He had to place a call and be signed in by the security officer at the duty desk in the hall.

A corporal escorted him to Post's office. The corporal didn't even try to make small talk.

Valentine walked through a bullpen of people at desks and occupying cubicles, passing maps filled with pins and ribbons and whiteboards covered with cryptic scrawls on the walls, and arrived at an office beyond. Post these days rated his own adjutant, and Post's office was just beyond his adjutant's. There was no door between Post's office and his adjutant's, just a wide entryway.

Valentine knocked on the empty doorframe. Post beamed as he entered. There was a little more salt to his salt-and-pepper hair and a good deal more starch in his uniform, but then headquarters standards had to be maintained.

The last time Valentine had seen Will Post, his friend was lying in his hospital bed after the long party celebrating the victory in Dallas and the retirement of the old Razors.

Post sported a lieutenant colonel's bird these days. Even better, he looked fleshed-out and healthy. Valentine was used to seeing him thin and haggard, tired-eyed at the Chinese water torture of minutiae involved in running the old battalion, especially the ad hoc group of odds and sods that had been the Razors.

When Valentine had first met him in the Kurian Coastal Marines, his uniform bore more permanent sweat stains than buttons. Now he looked like he'd wheeled out of an award-banquet picture.

"Hello, Will," Valentine said, saluting. Post, as a lieutenant colonel, now outranked a mere major—especially one who usually walked around Southern Command in a militia corporal's uniform. Valentine felt embarrassed, trying not to look at the wheelchair. He'd seen it in pictures, of course.

"Good to see you. What happened to your ear?"

Valentine had left a hunk of lobe in Kentucky. If he could find the right man with a clipper, he should really even them up, even if it would make him look a bit like a Doberman.

"A near miss that wasn't much of a miss."

"Sit down, Val," Post said. "I was just about to order sandwiches from the canteen. They have a cold-cut combo that's really good; I think there's a new supplier. Cranberries are plentiful now too, if you're in the mood for a cranberry and apple salad. Our old friend Martinez has made some commissary changes already." He reached for his phone.

"I'll have both. I've an appetite today."

Post, in his efficient manner, had seen Valentine's discomfiture and acted to correct the situation.

While the Enemy Assessments Director-East called down to the canteen, Valentine glanced around the room. Post's office had two chairs and an odd sort of feminine settee that in another time and place would have been called a fainting couch.

"How's Gail?"

"Good. She does volunteer work over at United Hospital. She's good with me, with the wounded. She says she only does it to forget about what she went through, but she could just as easily do that by sitting in a corner slamming tequila. Which is how I met her, way back. Except she was reading."

Post's desk had too many file folders, reachers to help him access shelves, coding guides and a battered laptop to have much room for pictures. He had citations and unit photos—Valentine recognized the old picture of himself and Ahn-Kha on the road to Dallas.

Ahn-Kha. Probably his closest friend in the world other than Duvalier, and the big golden Grog wasn't even human. He was leading a guerrilla band in the Appalachians, doing so much damage that both sides were mistaking his little partisan band for a large army.

He'd seen that same shot on his visit to Molly and her son, ages ago. Ever since he'd brought her out of Chicago as a Wolf lieutenant, they'd been family to one another, with a family's mix of joys and heartbreak.

Odd that Post and Molly should both like that photo. Of course, the only other published picture of Valentine that he could remember was an old photo taken when he became a lieutenant in his Wolf days.

What Valentine guessed to be a map or recessed bookcase stood behind heavy wood cabinet doors complete with a lock. Nearest Post's desk was his set of "traveling wheels."

Valentine looked at the biggest picture on his desk: a family photo of his wife, Gail, and a pigtailed toddler. "I didn't know you had a child."

Post brushed the picture's glass with a finger, as though rearranging Gail's short, tousled hair. "We tried. It didn't work. The docs said they found some odd cell tissue on Gail's, er, cervix. Something the Kurians did to her in that Reaper mill, they think. We more or less adopted."

"Good for you."

"There's more. It's Moira Styachowski's daughter."

Valentine felt a pang. "I didn't know she had one."

"She's a pistol. Only sixteen months but we call her the Wild Thing. Jenny's all Moira. We were godparents, you see. And when that plane went down . . ."

They looked at each other in silence.

"Sunshine and rain, Val."

"I didn't know you two were that close."

"After you were hurt at the tower in Little Rock, we sort of hit it off. She found time for me while I adapted to rolling through life."

"You are rolling. A lieutenant colonel."

"I get a lot done. I'm more or less desk-bound."

Valentine wondered how much Post was leaving unsaid.

"Something to drink?" Post asked, opening a minifridge. "I have water, lemonade—er, wait, limeade this week—good old Southern Command root beer, and that awful cocoa—remember? I can order coffee. I don't keep liquor in the office. Best way not to give in to temptation is to make it physically difficult."

"Any milk?"

The bushy, salt-and-pepper eyebrows went up. "Milk? Sure."

The food arrived on a tray, under shining covers, reminding Valentine of the amenities of the Outlook resort he'd visited, and partially destroyed, in the Cascades.

"Major David Valentine, drinking milk," Post said, passing a carton. "You getting an ulcer?"

"I'm surprised I don't have one. No, I acquired a taste for it out west, oddly enough. It's . . . comforting. Ulcer or no."

"You acquire one here. Anyway, East is more my area. Speaking of which, you owe me a serious Kentucky debriefing. Between you and the Green Mountain Boys, it sounds like you cracked the Moondaggers. What's left of them are back in Michigan, licking their wounds and singing laments."

"I'm not so sure it was us. They tried the 'submission to Kur's will' routine on the wrong set of locals. In Kentucky you can't just wheel into a legworm clan and drag off the sixteen-year-old girls. Those guys know how to make every shot count, and while you're driving around the hills, they're humping over them on their worms."

"Well, we're celebrating here. Those bastards painted a lot of Kansas soil red. We call the area west of Olathe the Bone Plain now."

Valentine remembered all the little towns he'd seen, crossing that area with Duvalier. Strange that the Kurians would shed so much blood. Living heartbeats were wealth to them.

They talked and ate. Post impressed Valentine all over again with his knowledge of Kentucky. And Valentine was grateful to forget about the wheelchair.

"Did Lehman give you the bad news?" Post asked.

"What's that?"

"Javelin plus the operation against the Rio Grande Valley. Southern Command is probably going to pull in its horns for a while. No more offensives. It's all about 'consolidation' and 'defensible resolution' these days. *We've won our ramparts back, let's be sure they never fall again,* and all that. We're going back on the defensive."

"That doesn't do much good for those poor souls outside the walls," Valentine said.

"We tried our damnedest. You should see all the workshops. There are more tires and artificial limbs than shoe soles. You remember Tancredi, from the Hill? He's there. He's got it worse than me—he's wearing a colostomy bag. Our generation's used up. I think younger, stronger bodies will have to see the rest through. We need a rest. You need a rest."

Valentine admitted that. He was so very tired. He didn't mind the stress of fights like that one against Blitty Easy's Crew. You aimed and shot, lived or died. It was being responsible for the lives and deaths of the men under you that wore your nerves raw.

Valentine was begining to think he wasn't cut out for that kind of responsibility. But then, if he didn't do it, you never knew who might take the controls. If you were lucky, someone like Colonel Seng or Captain LeHavre. But men like General Martinez rose farther and faster.

He covered the noisy silence with a sip of milk.

Post waggled a pen between his fingers. Optical illusion gave it a rubbery flexibility. The pen stopped. He gave the old turning-key signal Valentine remembered from their days conspiring together on the *Thunderbolt*. Valentine rose and closed the office door.

"I'm probably breaking enough rules to merit a court-martial here, Val. They've got you on the books as militia, sure, but that's about the same as civilian under our regs."

Valentine shrugged. He'd let go of the career long ago. He enjoyed the freedom of being outside the normal chain of command.

"A friend brought in your report, and I made a temporary copy and read it first thing. All these proposals of yours about aid to those ex-Quislings out of Evansville and eastern Kentucky? It's not going to fly. I doubt it'll even hatch, to tell you the truth. We're about to undergo a 'reallocation of priorities.' As far as Southern

Command is concerned, Javelin was a disaster, and the less said and done about what's going on on the other side of the Mississippi, the better."

Lehman had given him the same impression, if not so directly worded.

Valentine shrugged. "We've friends in the legworm clans. We can operate as guerrillas. I'm only looking for a gesture of support. Some gear, boots, and a few boonies to train the men."

Southern Command's trainers of insurgent or counterinsurgent forces no longer wore the old US Army green berets. They'd taken to simple boonie hats, usually dressed up with a brown duck feather for NCOs, a larger eagle quill for officers.

"Not my area. I'd say take it to your friend in special ops, Colonel Lambert, but she's under a cloud right now. Investigation pending court-martial. Gross neglect of duty—Martinez is making her the scapegoat for Javelin. That giant staff of his has quite a few Jaggers."

Jaggers were Southern Command's military lawyers.

"Any more good news?"

Post spun, tossed his sandwich wrapper in the regular garbage pail. Security refuse went into a locked box with a slot at the top. "Lots. Well, not so much good as puzzling. We're getting odd reports from the underground, both in the Northwest Ordnance up in Ohio and the Georgia Control—they're very influential in Tennessee."

"I don't know much about the Georgia Control, other than that it's based in Atlanta. They make some great guns. Our guys will carry Atlanta Gunworks rifles if they get a chance to pick one up. Remember those Type Threes?"

Post nodded. "Good guns. 'A state run along corporate lines' is the best way to describe Georgia Control. Every human a Kurian owns is a share. Get enough shares and you get on the board of directors. Here's the odd feature: They let people buy shares too. By people, I mean brass ring holders, so I use the term loosely."

Valentine had to fight the urge to touch the spot on his sternum where his own brass ring hung from its simple chain. "I picked one up a couple years back. It comes in handy."

Post chewed on his lower lip. "Oh, yeah. Well, you know what I mean. Anyone who's served in the Coastal Marines is half alligator anyway.

"But back to the chatter our ears are picking up. Here's a helluva tidbit for you: Our old friend Consul Solon's on the Georgia Control board of directors. Would you believe it? Five years ago he's running for his life with Southern Command howling at his heels and half the Kurian Order wanting to see him dead for fucking up the conquest of the Trans-Mississippi, and damned if he doesn't wash up on a feather bed. The guy's half mercury and half Ralvan Fontainbleu."

Valentine chuckled. Fontainbleu was a nefarious importer/exporter on *Noonside Passions*, the Kurian Zone's popular soap opera. Valentine never did get the soap part, but operatic it was. Fontainbleu ruined marriages and businesses and sent more than one good man or woman to the Reapers. Oddly enough the drama was fairly open and aboveboard about the nature of the Kurian Order, though it towed the Church line about *trimming the sick branch and plucking the bad seed*. Fontainbleu was the particular nemesis of Brother Fairmind, the boxing New Universal Church collar who wasn't above busting a few heads to keep his flock on the straight and narrow. Valentine hadn't seen an episode since he returned from the Cascades—odd how he could still remember characters and their plots, relationships, and alliances. The desire to check up on the story plucked at him like a bad habit.

Back to Post.

"I had a feeling we hadn't heard the last of former consul Solon. What are the underground reports?"

"Scattered stuff. You'd think with Kentucky in turmoil the Kur would be grabbing pieces off of Ohio and Tennessee, guarding bridges and invasion routes, putting extra troops into the rail arteries north through Lexington and Louisville. But it's just not happening. To the north, the Ordnance has called up some reserves and shifted troops to support Louisville or maybe move west to hit your group at Evansville. But as for the usual apparatus of the Kurian Order, we're getting word of churchmen leaving, railroad support people pulling out. . . . If anything, they've pulled back from the clans, like they're a red-hot stove or something."

"Their troops in Evansville revolted. Maybe they're afraid the infection will spread."

"I'd like your opinion on that. What's Kentucky like now? Every legworm rider who can shoulder a gun shooting at the Kurian Order?"

"Nothing like that. The Moondaggers came through and just tore up Kentucky and hauled off any girl they could grab between fifteen and thirty. Really stirred the locals up. The place is in flux now; hard to say which way it'll go. They might just revert to their old semi-independence, as long as the Kurians don't aggravate the situation."

Post knitted his fingers. "We were hoping the Control was pulling back to more defensible positions and assuming there's a new Freehold being born."

"I don't think much will happen until spring," Valentine said. "That's the rhythm of the legworm clans. They settle in close to their worms for the winter until the eggs hatch."

Post nodded. "I wish I had more. You know the underground.

They have to be very, very careful. What they get me is good; there's just so little of it. Kurian agents are——"

"Dangerous," Valentine said, rubbing his uneven jaw. The fracture hadn't healed right. A reminder of his encounter with a Kurian agent working for the Northwest Ordnance when he'd found Post's wife in a Reaper factory called Xanadu.

"Yeah," Post agreed. "I wonder how many we have in this headquarters. We tend to win the stand-up fights. Yet more often than not, they figure out a way to make it seem like a loss. Walk down the street in Little Rock——"

"And one out of two people will agree that Texas and Oklahoma were defeats," Valentine said. He'd heard about the famous *Clarion* war poll just after the Kansas operation, repeated endlessly in articles and opinion columns since. That had been the last operation he and Post had shared—a blazing offensive that tripled the size of the old Ozark Free Territory. But it just gave the *Clarion* more cities to report bad news from. "So what do you think I should do?"

"Get as many as you can back across the Mississippi," Post said. "We can use them here."

"And leave the legworm clans hanging? They threw in with us in Javelin."

"They might be all right. The Kurian Order needs that legworm meat for protein powder and cans of WHAM."

They exchanged grimaces. They'd both eaten their shares of WHAM rolls in the Coastal Marines. WHAM was a canned "meat product" produced in Alabama, filled out with bean paste, and sweetened with an uninspiring barbecue sauce to hide the tasteless, chewy nature of legworm flesh. *Three tastes in one!,* the cans proclaimed. The joke with WHAM is you got three chews before the flavor dissipated and you were left with a mouthful of something about as succulent and appealing as week-worn long johns. It went through the digestive system like a twenty-mule-team sled. *Three chomps and run,* the cook on the old *Thunderbolt* used to recommend.

It was a staple of Kurian work camps and military columns operating far from their usual supply hubs.

"There has to be some good news," Valentine said.

"Full list and details, or just bullet points?"

Valentine poured some more milk. "I need cheering up. Give me the full list," Valentine said.

"I won sixty bucks this week at poker," Post said. "It's a short list."

Valentine tossed back the rest of the glass of milk. "I think you're right about that ulcer."

Post's advice was absolutely correct. Javelin hadn't worked. It hadn't died; in a way it had won, dealing a deathblow to the vicious Moondaggers. But it hadn't worked out as planned. Give it up and move on, the way you folded when you drew into a promising poker hand and came up with nothing.

Except the pieces were scattered across Kentucky along with his bit of ear, and they included a big, hairy Golden One named Ahn-Kha; Tikka, brave and lusty and vital; and the former Quislings who'd put their lives and the lives of their families into jeopardy by switching sides. Southern Command had run up a big bar tab in blood.

†

The next day Valentine sat through a second series of debriefings with Southern Command personnel and civilians whose professional interests included the function and capabilities of the Kurian Order. He was questioned about political conditions of the legworm tribes and the organization and equipment of the Moondaggers. He even had to give a rough estimate of the population of Kentucky and the Appalachian towns and villages he'd seen.

He had to watch his words about the Kurian manipulation of Javelin's COs through a mutt they'd picked up named Red Dog, the strange doubt and lassitude that temporarily seized even as aggressive a woman as Colonel Bloom, who was back with what was left of Javelin in Kentucky just south of Evansville. It sounded too fantastic to be true, but he did his best to convince them.

Finally, a researcher from the Miskatonic queried him again about the flying Reaper he'd seen.

"You sure it wasn't a gargoyle?" she said as Valentine sorted through sketches and photographs. They had one sketch and one blurry, grainy night photo of something that resembled what he'd seen. She had the air of someone used to talking to soldiers who'd seen bogeymen on lonely watches.

It had been wearying, answering questions from people who weren't interested in his answers unless they fit in with the opinions they'd had when they sat down in the tube-steel office chairs. Valentine let loose. "I've seen gargoyles, alive and dead. They're strong and graceful, like a vulture. This was more spindly and awkward. It reminded me of a pelican or a crane taking off. And it wasn't a harpy either. I've seen plenty of those snaggletooths up close."

"Yes, I know." Valentine thought he recognized his thick Miskatonic file in front of her.

"So do you have a theory?" he demanded.

"The Kurians made Reapers by modifying human genetic code. They could have done the same with a gargoyle."

All very interesting, but he wanted to be back with his command.

†

His last stop on his tour of headquarters was Operations Support. General Lehman had come through with logistics: There was a barge on the Arkansas river being loaded with supplies for his new recruits and to replace the most vital matériel used up in the retreat across Kentucky. Valentine would accompany it back to Kentucky.

He picked up mail—presorted for the survivors of Javelin. Valentine wondered what happened to the sad little bundles of letters to dead men and women.

The mail had been vacuum-wrapped in plastic to protect it from the elements, but it still took up a lot of room, especially since the locals used all manner of paper for their correspondence. The mail office had a variety of bags and packs for the convenience of ad hoc couriers such as himself, and Valentine just grabbed the biggest shoulder bag he could find. Judging from the waterproof lining and compartments, it might have once been meant to hold diving or snorkel gear.

He made a trip to the PX and picked up some odds and ends: Duvalier's favorite talc, a bottle of extra-strength aspirin for Patel, and a couple of fifty-count boxes of inexpensive knit gloves. If there was one thing Valentine had learned over the years of commanding men in bad weather, it was that they lost their gloves, especially in action. He liked carrying spares to hand out.

†

Valentine needed peace, quiet, time to think. He caught an electric shuttle and wandered into Jonesboro and found a café by the train station—a family-owned grill with three gold stars in the window. He learned from photos and boxed decorations inside that they'd lost two sons and a daughter to the Cause.

He pleased the owners by ordering eggs accompanied by the biggest steak on the menu rather than the Southern Command subsidized "pan lunch." The steak was sizable and tough, but his appetite didn't mind, and the cook had worked wonders with the sautéed onions. The young waitress—very young waitress, make that; only a teenager would wait tables in heeled sandals—chatted with him expertly. Almost too expertly, because he didn't know any of the local militia outfits, and his equivocal answers made her wrinkle her trifle of a nose. How many single, lonely young uniformed men did she wait on in a month? He tried not to stare as she sashayed back and forth with iced tea in one hand and coffee in the other.

Whether she was family or no, it would be unseemly to ogle the help under the eye of the mother at the register clucking over her regulars like a hen and the muscular father behind the grill. He couldn't think with her friendly pats on the back of his shoulder as she refilled his iced tea, so he paid his bill—and left an overlarge tip.

The little park in front of the courthouse beckoned, and he was about to take a bench and read his mail when he heard faint singing. He followed the sound to a church where a children's choir was rehearsing and grabbed a pew at the back. Women and a few men sewed or knit while their kids screeched through the Christmas hymns.

Valentine watched the kids for a few minutes. Typical Free Territory youth, no two pairs of jeans matching in color or wear, rail thin and tanned from harvest work or a thousand and one odd jobs. You grew up fast here on the borderlands. So different from the smoothed, polished, uniformed children of the elite of the Kurian Zones, with their New Universal Church regulation haircuts and backpacks, or the wary ragamuffins of the "productives."

The boys were trying to throw one another off-tune by surreptitiously stomping one another's insteps or making farting noises with their armpits in time with the music; the girls were stifling giggles or throwing elbows in response to yanked ponytails.

The frazzled choral director finally issued a time-out to two boys.

Valentine thought better on his feet, so he remained standing at the back of the church, shifting weight from one foot to the other in time to the music like a tired metronome.

Pull out or go all in for Kentucky? Pull out or go all in for Kentucky? Pull out or go all in for Kentucky?

✝

Valentine spent an evening enjoying a mock–Thanksgiving dinner with William Post and his wife, Gail. She looked strained by Valentine's presence—or perhaps it was the effort involved in cooking a turkey with the sides.

Jenny resembled her mother, white-haired and delicate-skinned. Maybe Valentine's imagination was overworked, but she crinkled her eyes just like Post when she smiled. The little three-year-old had two speeds, flank and full stop.

She was shy and wary around Valentine, standing in the protective arch of Post's legs, but she ate as though there was a little Bear blood in her.

The two old shipmates talked long after Valentine cleared the dishes away, Post had sorted and stored the leftovers, and Gail and Jenny went to bed. Valentine told the whole story of Javelin's trek across Kentucky, the sudden betrayal in the Virginia coal country, the Moondaggers and the strange lassitude of first Colonel Jolla and then Cleveland Bloom. He described the victory at Evansville, where the populace had successfully revolted, thinking that deliverance was at hand.

Valentine chuckled. "The underground was so used to parsing the Kurian newspapers and bulletins, assuming that the opposite of whatever was being reported was true, that they took all the stories about a defeated army being hounded across Kentucky to mean it was a victorious march along the Ohio. When the Kurians called up whomever they trusted to be in the militia to guard the Moondaggers' supply lines from the Kentuckians, they acted."

A cold rain started down, leaving Valentine with an excuse to treat himself to a cab ride back to the base's visiting housing. Post asked him to spend the night, but Valentine declined, though the accommodations given a corporal of militia couldn't match up to Post's cozy ranch-style. If he spent the night, they'd just be up all the while talking, and he wanted to get back to the logistics and support people about more gear on the alleged barge.

The "cab" showed up after a long delay that Post and Valentine were able to fill with pleasant chitchat. They shook hands and Valentine turned up his collar and passed out into the cold, rainy dark.

The cab was a rather claptrap three-wheeled vehicle, a glorified motorbike under a golf-cart awning that had an odd tri-seat: a forward-facing one for the driver, and two bucket seats like saddlebags perched just behind. The rear wheels were extended to support the awning and stabilize the vehicle. They reminded Valentine of a child's training wheels.

Valentine buckled himself in rather dubiously, wishing Post had offered him a drink to fortify himself against the cold rain. Another soldier, a corporal, slouched in the seat with his back to Valentine, his backpack on his lap and clutching the seat belt white-knuckled as though his life depended on it.

"Don't mind sharing, do you now, milly?" the driver asked.

"No. Of course not."

He gunned the engine, and it picked up speed like a tricycle going down a gentle grade. Valentine wondered why the other passenger was nervous about a ride you could hop off a few seconds before an accident.

"Of course you don't mind. Cheaper for both; gotta save fuel and rubber. Speaking of rubber, if you've a mind to expend one in service, I know a house—"

"No, thanks."

"I'm taking the other corp. It's right on the way."

That accounted for the nervousness. Worried somebody he knew would spot him. The awning wasn't like a backseat you could slump down into and hide. "Bit tired, thanks."

"Suit yourself. It's clean and cheap. Only thing you'll go back to the wife with is a bangover."

"A what?"

"Like a hangover, only your cock's sore instead of your head."

Valentine wondered what percentage the house gave the cabbie.

They pulled up to the house, a big old brick foursquare in the older part of town. Most of the houses here were vacant, stripped skeletons with glass and wiring removed, metal taken right down to the door hinges. The one remaining had either been under constant occupancy or been restored—Valentine couldn't tell which in the dark. It had a pair of friendly red-tinted lights illuminating the porch. Candles flickered from behind drawn curtains.

Seemed a popular place: A party of four was just leaving—

Valentine felt a sharp tug and his windpipe closed up. He realized a rope had been looped around his throat, and he was jerked out of the seat backward.

A quick look at looming figures framed frostily against the red porch light of the house. They had on ghoulish rubber Halloween masks. Then the ground hit him, hard.

The tallest and heaviest kicked him hard in the stomach, and Valentine bent like a closing bear trap around his neck. He opened his mouth to bite, but someone hauled at the rope around his neck, pulling his head away hard.

"David Valentine. You murderous, traitorous bastard. Been looking forward to this meeting," one of the masked men said.

"You hauled my little brother all the way across Kentucky to get him killed," another kicker put in.

Something struck him hard on the kidneys with a crack. "Few more officers like you and the Kur won't need no army."

Valentine roared back an obscenity and tried to get his hands up to fight the rope pulling his neck, but two of the attackers closed, each taking an arm above and below the elbow.

"All your idea. You and that dumb bitch from headquarters," an accuser continued.

"Cuff him good—he's slippery," someone with a deep voice advised from the darkness. He was too far away be delivering punches and kicks.

Or maybe his vision was going and it just seemed as though the voice was coming from a great distance. There were painful stars dancing in his vision like a faerie circus. Valentine felt kicks that might have just as well been blows from baseball bats, so hard were the assailants' boots.

"You've made enemies, Valentine. Now it's time to settle up."

The rain stung; it must be washing blood into his eyes.

"We don't like criminals walking our streets, bold as black."

They took turns punching him in the face and stomach.

"Grog lover!"

"Renegade."

"Murderer!" The last was a crackling shriek.

They added a few more epithets about his mother and the long line of dubious species that might have served as father. Valentine's mad brain noted that they sounded like men too young to have ever known her.

"You bring any of those redlegs into our good clean land, they'll get the same. Be sure of that."

"Hell, they'll get hung."

"Like you're gonna be—*huck-huck-huck*!"

"C'mon—let's string this fugitive from justice up."

They dragged Valentine by the rope around his neck. He strained, but the handcuffs on his wrists at his back held firm.

The old street in Jonesboro had attractive oaks and elms shading the pedestrians from summer heat. Their thick, spreading boughs made a convenient gibbet above the sidewalk and lane.

The noose hauled Valentine to his feet by his neck. His skin flamed.

Valentine knotted the muscles in his neck, fought instinct, kicking as he strangled. The rope wasn't so bad; it was the blood in his eyes that stung.

Vaguely, he sensed that something was thumping against his chest. An object had been hung around his neck about the size and weight of a hardcover book.

One of them wound up, threw, and bounced a chunk of broken pavement off his face.

"Murderer!"

"Justice is a dish best served cold," that deep voice said again.

They piled into the little putt-putt and a swaying, aged jeep that roared out of the alley behind the red-lit house. With that, they departed into the rain. Valentine, spinning from the rope end as he kicked, bizarrely noted that they left at a safe speed that couldn't have topped fifteen miles an hour, thanks to the odd little three-wheeler.

Valentine, increasingly foggy with his vision red and the sound of the rainfall suddenly as distant as faint waterfall, looked up at the rope hanging over the branch.

For all their viciousness with boot tips and flung asphalt, they didn't know squat about hanging a man. And he'd purposely kicked with knees bent, to give them the illusion that he was farther off the ground than he actually was.

He changed the direction of his swing, always aiming toward the trunk of the tree. The rope, which his assailants had just thrown over the thick limb, moved closer to the trunk. He bought another precious six inches. Six inches closer to the trunk, six less inches for the rope to extend to the horizontal branch, six inches closer to the ground. With one more swing, he extended his legs as far as they'd go, reaching with his tiptoes, and touched wet earth.

The auld sod of Arkansas had never felt more lovely.

Valentine caught his breath, balancing precariously on tiptoe, and found the energy to give himself more slack. He got the rope between his teeth and began to chew. Here the wet didn't aid him.

His blood-smeared teeth thinned the rope. He gathered slack from his side and pulled. He extracted himself from the well-tied noose and slumped against the tree. There was a wooden placard hung around his neck, but he was too tired to read it.

Even with the rope—standard Southern Command camp stuff, useful for everything from securing a horse to tying cargo onto the hood of a vehicle—removed from his neck, Valentine could still feel the burn of it. He swept his hand through the gutter, picked up some cold wet leaves, and pressed them to the rope burn.

They might come back to check on his body. He lurched to his feet and staggered in the direction of the door of the bordello.

He missed the porch stairs, rotated against the rail until he tripped over them, and went up to the door on hands and knees. Blood dripped and dotted the dry wood under the porch roof.

His head thumped into the doorjamb.

"He's made it," someone from within called.

He didn't have to knock again; the door opened for him. He had a brief flash of hair and lace and satin before he gave way, collapsing on a coconut-coir mat and some kind of fringed runner covering shining hardwood floors.

"He's bleeding on the rug. Get some seltzer."

"Lord, he's not going to die on us, is he?" a Texas accent gasped.

"Uhhhh," Valentine managed, which he hoped she'd interpret as a "no."

"What if they come back to check on him?"

"They told us not to come out. Didn't say anything about us not letting him in," another woman put in. "He made it in under his own power."

"They still might do violence, if'n we help him. Toss him in the alley."

"Hush up and quit worrying while we got a man bleeding," an authoritative female voice said. "I've never refused a gentleman hospitality in my life and I'm too old to change now. You all can blame me if they do come back. Don't think varmints like that have the guts, though, or they would have watched till he was cold. Alice-Ann, iodine and bandages."

Valentine blinked the blood out of his eyes. The women were of a variety of ages and skin hues and tints of hair, mostly blond or red. He counted six, including what looked and sounded like the madam—or maybe she just catered to the certain tastes in experienced flesh. A gaunt old man moved around, pulling down extra shades and closing decorative shutters with a trembling arm. The doorman? He didn't look like he could bounce a Boy Scout from the establishment.

"Before you throw me out, could you please get these handcuffs off? If you don't have a key, I'll show you how to do it with a nail." The speech exhausted him more than the trip to the door. He put his head down to catch his breath and managed to roll over on his pack.

"Are you kidding?" a fleshy older woman said, showing a brilliant set of perfectly aligned teeth. "In this place? Standard equipment, hunneh."

They helped him up and took him back to the kitchen and performed first aid at the sink. Valentine embraced the sting of the iodine. It proved he was alive.

When he had stopped the flow of blood from face and lip, he looked around the homey kitchen. Baskets of onions and potatoes lined the floor, rows of preserved vegetables filled racks in the kitchen, and bulbs of garlic and twisted gingerroot hung from the ceiling, fall's bounty ready for winter.

The madam introduced herself as Ladyfair, though whether this was a first name, a last name, a stage name, or a title, she didn't say.

"There's a little washroom just off the back door, next to the laundry room and past the hanging unmentionables," the madam said as Valentine rubbed his free wrist. "You just make use of it. There's a flexible shower hose. Just the thing for a fast cleanup."

Valentine, feeling a little more human, realized he stank. An unpleasant presence was making itself felt in his underwear.

It's not just an expression. They really kicked the shit out of me, Valentine thought.

When he came out, a towel around his waist, he glanced into the front parlor and noticed that the porch light had been turned off. A thick head of hair looked through the heavy curtains from the edge of a window.

Valentine rubbed his sore neck. The attempted hanging wasn't so bad; the pain was from the hard jerks from the rope during the fight. He wondered if he had whiplash.

They presented him an old pair of generously cut khaki trousers and some serviceable briefs. "We have a little of just about everything hanging in the basement," Ladyfair said. "You'd think we were a community theater. We do everything but produce Shakespeare."

"I'm surprised you haven't. The Bard had his bawdy side."

"You just come back now when you're up to it. You seem like a better quality than that rabble, and a smart business is always looking to improve the clientele. Seeing as that disgrace took place right on my front lawn, I'll offer you a freebie when you're feeling more recovered."

"I appreciate you taking me into your house."

"Oh, it's not my house. We're a limited liability partnership, young man. Quite a few make that mistake, though. I suppose I'm the old lead mare of the house, though I'm still very much involved on the cash generation side of things. There are some that have learned to appreciate a woman without teeth."

She winked.

Bordello co-ops. What will they thing of next? Valentine thought.

"Then I'm grateful to the whole partnership. Novel idea."

"Not really. I'm surprised. Your necktie party insisted you were a fan of professional gentlemen's entertainment. Said you used to visit a place called the Blue Dome. They said it was only fitting that you get hung up on the doorstep of a whorehouse, so to speak."

Valentine shrugged. "I don't suppose you could give me their names," Valentine said.

"You'll remember we haven't even asked yours."

"David will do," Valentine said.

"Well, David, if you want names, nobody gives a real name here. You should really hurry on. Mr. C, our banker and lawyer, is removing the rope from the tree, but if they come back . . ."

"Were they Southern Command?"

"They were in civilian attire but had fabric belts with those clever little buckles our heroes in uniform wear. One of them was drinking and kept talking about General Martinez and about how things are going to change for the better once he gets in, so I suspect at least some of them were."

A prettyish young "entertainer" came into the kitchen with the placard that had been hung about his neck. "You want this as evidence?" she asked with a strong Texas accent.

It was an ordinary wood bar tray, much ringed and weathered though carefully cleaned, with black letters burned into it:

David Valentine,
Condamned Fugitive
Law and Order Is
Coming Back to the UFR

Whoever had done it hadn't bothered to pencil out the letters before setting to work with the wood burner. "Back to the UFR" was rather crowded together.

"David Valentine," Ladyfair said. "It sounds rather dashing and romantic, as though you should be riding around in a cloak, holding up carriages with a pistol and donating the booty to the peasantry."

Valentine probed his teeth, checking for loose gum line or a broken crown.

"I am fond of novels when idling in bed or tub."

Valentine wanted to keep the sign just for the interesting spelling of "condemned." Might make an interesting memento on his office door. Maybe they'd summed up his life better than whoever would write his eventual obituary—if he died where people noticed such things. Condamned.

"I've troubled you enough," Valentine said. "I suppose you've lost a night's business because of this. If you'll let me know what the clothes and bandages cost, I'll come by tomorrow to repay you what I can."

"Nonsense. Here's a card. If you do find those rowdies, give us a jingle. We'll give them a little law and order when we testify in court. Dumb sons of bitches didn't wear those masks when they were in our parlor waiting on you. I'd like to be able to point them out in court."

"Cheap too," the young Texan said. "Kept complaining about not being able to run a tab for their whiskey."

Valentine inspected his reflection in a little mirror next to the kitchen doorjamb. He'd probably have some horizontal scarring on the right side of his face to balance out the long vertical bullet furrow long since faded on his left. The asphalt had been sharp.

Well, he didn't have much keeping him in the United Free Republics anyway. Besides, he had mail to get back to Kentucky.

He might as well abandon the guise of a militia corporal; it wasn't doing him any good. He'd return to Kentucky in the leathers of the Bulletproof clan.

CHAPTER THREE

*B*ackwater Pete's on the Arkansas River, the third week of November: Pete's is the informal abode of the river rats—the brown-water transportation flotilla of Southern Command and the sailors of the quick-hitting, quick-running motorboats of the Skeeter Fleet.

Pete himself is long dead, killed during Solon's tenure for theft of Trans-Mississippi Combat Corps property and smuggling supplies to "guerrilla bands" during the Kurian occupation. His widow followed him to the Reaper-gibbet soon after (hardly a word had to be changed in the indictment or the sentence), but his brother survived Solon's occupation of Arkansas and rebuilt the old riverside bar.

Built of ancient gray cypress beams the color of a January cloudbank, part dockyard, part trading post, part gin mill, and part museum, Backwater Pete's is an institution. A new brown-water sailor who first sees the fireflies of tracer being exchanged at high speed while bouncing down the Mississippi comes to Pete's for his first drink as a real riverman. Newly appointed boat commanders and barge captains fete their crews there, and retiring master mechanics say their farewells beneath the pink and lavender paper lanterns and sensually shaped neon.

The bar is decorated with grainy pictures of boat crews as well as old Sports Illustrated *swimsuit models and* Playboy *centerfolds, immortal icons of wet-haired desire. Wooden models of famous Southern Command river craft—mostly pleasure or sport or fishing boats and tugs converted to carry machine guns and old rapid-fire twenty-and thirty-millimeter "bush guns"—rest on a little brass-railed shelf above the bar. The traditional mirror behind the bar is more a mosaic of shards now, having been broken in so many brawls and patched together with colored glass it now resembles a peacock splattered against a wide chrome bumper.*

Most newcomers say it smells like tobacco, recycled beer, sun-baked sweat, and mud fresh from a swamp where eggs go to die. The regulars wouldn't have it any other way.

On that warm night of a quick-fading autumn the bar saw a stranger. His clothing set him apart immediately: thick blue-black leathers that looked too oddly pebbled for cowhide but not stiff as snakeskin. He wore a small machine-gun pistol in a big soft holster across his midriff and a straight-bladed, sharkskin-handled sword across his back. Vambraces like a motorcycle rider might wear guard his arms, but odd bulges running up from the wrist suggest they might be offensive as well as defensive.

For all the weaponry, the high military boots with their lace guards snapped over, the scar descending from his right eye and fresh bruising to the left, and the long black hair tied back so it's out of his eyes, he doesn't look like he's after a fight. For a start, he looks tired: the haggard, leeched-out look of a man who has undergone prolonged stress. Then there's the odd hang of his jawline. A humorous tip to his jaw gives him a slight, good-humored smile.

"Cat. Or maybe a Bear," one of the grizzled river rats says to his companions dressed in more typical attire of soft white trousers and light canvas jackets, sockless in their rubber-soled boat shoes. They don't make room for the newcomer at the bar, river rats being as fiercely territorial as any Dumpster-diving rodents.

"What'll ye think a Hunter wants here?" a man with a patchy youth's beard asks.

"Someone to push up into a length of trouble," the oldster says, unaware of just how right he would turn out to be.

†

According to Southern Command tradition, Backwater Pete's served the best tequila on chipped ice in the Trans-Mississippi Free Republics. Not being an expert on tequila, Valentine opted for rum and tea, a concoction he'd grown used to during his sojourn in a Kurian uniform with the Coastal Marines.

The rum was of good quality, all the way from Jamaica. Valentine reread his accumulated mail over it while his mind subconsciously absorbed the rhythms of Backwater Pete's. A man in a bar had a choice to be alone, even if he could smell the sweat and engine oil on the man next to him, and he'd dumped his six new companions at a Southern Command billet-flop.

They were all the reinforcements he was getting, and he didn't like the look of them. Hatchet men sent to decide what was worth saving and what was worth discarding, plus one young doctor and an ancient nurse.

He savored his mail like a gourmet meal. The aches and pains from last week's wounds were forgotten in the excitement of mail.

He opened the one all the way from Jamaica first, wondering what tortured route it had taken to get to the UFR. Probably landed by some friendly smugglers on the shore of Texas, probably on the same boat that brought in rum, coffee, and fabric dyes. The Dutchmen from the Southern Caribbean were good about that sort of thing.

There was a picture of Amalee, dated six months ago and stamped by Southern Command's mails in mid-October, probably on the same boat that made the rum runs. She had deep copper skin and her mother's wide, bright eyes. She would be seven now.

Seven.

Nice of Malita to write. The letter was mostly of Amalee's doings and development and included a clipping from the Kingston *Current*, describing the exploits of Jamaica's "Corsairs" off the coast of Cuba.

Nothing from Hank in school—Valentine had made a call to make sure he still was in school. He was just getting to be that age where a boy notices all the interesting ways nature arranges for girls to be put together.

Molly wrote him as well. He had three letters from her, increasingly worried as the months of last summer went by.

He found a dry piece of bar and penned her a reassuring reply.

There was one more letter to write. It had to be carefully phrased. Narcisse up in St. Louis would have to tell Blake that there wouldn't be a visit this year. He'd have to see about sending a Christmas present.

It was hard to read Blake. Valentine still didn't know if Blake had strong feelings about him one way or another. Blake was always interested in new stuff. Was a visit from "Papa" a break from his usual routine and therefore a source of happiness, or was it more?

Valentine shouldn't have been this tired. Maybe he was slowing down with age. He hadn't bounced back from the beating he took outside Ladyfair's little cooperative. Served him right for continuing to wander from office to office and warehouse to warehouse, hunting up help for Kentucky and his old stored gear and their resident ghosts and memories.

David Valentine even had the dubious honor of a trip back to Southern Command's new GHQ at Consul Solon's old executive mansion atop Big Rock Hill to plead Kentucky's case with the outgoing commander in chief. One way or another, much of Solon's late-model communications gear survived or could be easily repaired, and old "Post One" didn't lack for office space and conference rooms.

The southern half of the hilltop, the old final trenches and dugouts, had filled in and greened over since being churned to mud by big-caliber rounds. The consular golf course was back in operation, and the red brick of the former college a beehive of clerks and radio techs. New, giant radio masts had sprouted both on Big Rock Hill.

They had stared at his cuts and bruises and listened politely but briefly. A few made noises about thanking him for his efforts in Kentucky. He endured another quick debriefing where he told the same story he told in Jonesboro with the same outcome.

It was time to take them back to Kentucky.

His efforts in Jonesboro and Little Rock hadn't been completely in vain. They'd given him the hatchet man team of "replacement" NCOs and a shipping manifest of matériel being loaded on a barge, though how Southern Command thought he'd get a barge all the way up the Ohio to Evansville was the sort of detail they had been vague on. When he asked, they said someone was "working the problem" and he could meet the barge at Backwater Pete's.

The manifest looked promising. Uniforms, or at least fabric to make uniforms. Cases of weapons. Explosives. Even recreational and educational materials for the new recruits.

Even more reassuring was the vessel and captain listed on the manifest. Whichever logistics officer they'd put in charge of "working the problem" knew his or her business.

†

Valentine had last seen the barge tied up on the Arkansas when Consul Solon was still running the Trans-Mississippi from his network of numbered posts. Valentine led his six new charges to the foot of the gangway and called up to the anchor watch.

"Permission to book a travel warrant?" Valentine asked the rumpled deckhand on watch, rubbing sleep from his eyes. The deckhand sauntered off to get the captain.

Captain Mantilla may have changed since Valentine last met him during Solon's brief hold on the Ozarks and Ouachitas. Valentine's memory of the man had diffused like a rewetted watercolor. But as the captain approached, Valentine noted the mat of hair and the quick, flashing glances that weren't suspicious, just indicative of a busy man with a lot on his mind—yes, it was him.

He stood there in gray overalls bearing a camouflage moiré of grease stains and a formerly white but now weather-beaten ivory skipper hat riding the back of his head as though bored with the job. Thick bodied with a bit of a pot, he still looked like a fireplug with a seven-day beard and a couple arms hanging off it.

"Have to ask my passenger," Mantilla said. "I expect she won't mind."

"Passenger? Since when do passengers give orders to captains?"

"Her charter." Mantilla jerked his thumb over his shoulder.

Valentine was shocked to see Dots—Colonel Lambert, officially—looking lost in a big patrol coat and a hat with the earflaps turned down, and fiddling with her dunnage as if deciding what to have handy and what to store below.

Valentine wondered if she was traveling not so much incognito as low-key, a simple officer looking for transport. Probably on her way to meet a Cat and a Bear team looking to raise hell in Mississippi.

"Sir," Valentine said, saluting. "I'm told this boat's headed for the Mississippi."

"Valentine!" Lambert said, brightening. "Not going back already?"

"Afraid so. Javelin needs these replacements. You'll take priority, of course. I'll go on once he's dropped you downriver."

Lambert cocked her head. Her usual brisk manner was gone; she looked like a traveler who'd missed a bus. Little fissures explored her formerly vital, cheerleader-smooth skin from the corners of her eyes and mouth.

"I think we're at cross purposes, Major. I'm joining your command. I'm headed to Evansville as well."

"Is there a new . . . operation?" Stupid words—she no doubt had to keep quiet.

"No, I'm joining up with what's left of Javelin. I suppose you haven't heard. My whole command was moved under one of Martinez's staffers. They were going to stick me in an office routing communications where the only decision I'd ever make is what to have for lunch. So . . . I volunteered to go to Kentucky."

"As what? If you don't mind my asking."

"I don't mind at all. They need a new full colonel out there to act as CO. No bright young officer wanted the job—Javelin's a dead end as far as Southern Command is concerned. I'm not so sure. Thought I'd be the one to be out there for a change."

Lambert had run a sort of special forces unit dedicated to helping allies in the Cause. Kentucky was the second trip she'd sent him on, and whatever had gone wrong in the wooded passes of the Appalachians wasn't her fault. "You've nothing to prove to any of us."

"The coffee on this tub's surprisingly good," she said. "I think the good captain has connections in every trading port on the river.

Let's hit the galley and get some. Tell me more about these Quisling volunteers you recruited."

"I have some support staff looking for passage too. And mail, of course," he said, patting his oversized shoulder bag.

"That bag's a heavy responsibility," she said. "If the captain doesn't mind cramming a few more in, I won't object."

They asked Mantilla, who shrugged. "Fuck it. Cook will be busier, is all. I'm fine with it, ma'am," Mantilla said. "Your people do their own laundry and use their own bedding. I'm not running a cruise ship."

Valentine joined the chorus of "thank you, Captain's" from his charges.

"All you headed up to Evansville?" the sleepy mate asked.

"Looks that way," Valentine said.

"Tough run. Not many friends on the Ohio."

"Maybe I'll make some new ones," Mantilla said.

†

Last-minute stores of fresh vegetables came on board, and with no more ceremony than it took to undo mooring lines, the tug pushed the barge downriver into the narrow, dredged channel.

Valentine now knew why Mantilla's crew were somnambulists when they tied up. They worked like furies when the boat was in motion: throwing sacks of mail and unloading crates to shore boats along the run practically without stopping, nursing the engines, hosing windblown fall leaves off the decks, cooking and snatching food, and, most important, checking depth with a pole on the doubtful river. Mantilla's barge and tug was big for the Arkansas. Most of the river traffic was in long, narrow flatboats with farting little motors that sounded like fishing trollers compared to the tug's hearty diesels.

Valentine, feeling guilty for just watching everyone work, eating of their galley but toiling not for his bread, checked the matériel Southern Command had scraped up for his operation in Kentucky.

As usual, the promises on paper didn't live up to what waited in the barge.

There was plenty of material for uniforms: soft gray felt in massive, industrial rolls.

"I know what this is," Lambert said. "We took a big textiles plant outside of Houston."

"We'll have to sew it ourselves."

"It's light, and it keeps you warm even when you're wet. They use it for blankets and liners."

"What's it made out of?"

"Polyester or something like it. Everyone's talking about the winter blankets that Martinez is passing out made out of this material. But they're not talking about how he acquired them."

"What's the story?"

"Stuff comes from a fairly high-tech operation—a factory with up-to-date equipment and facilities. We captured it intact outside Houston. The ownership and workers were only too happy to start cranking out material for Southern Command as their new client. General Martinez wouldn't have any of it, though. He had them work triple-shifts cranking out fabric, and then when they'd burned through their raw materials, he stamped the whole product 'Property of Southern Command' and shipped it north. Factory never got paid and owner had no money to buy more raw materials, so it's sitting empty now instead of making clothes for Texans and selling uniform liners to Southern Command. But Martinez got close to a million square yards of fabric for nothing."

The weapons were painfully familiar to him: the old single-shot lever action rifles he'd trained on long ago in the Labor Regiment. They were heavy, clunky, and didn't stand up to repeated firing well. The action tended to heat up and melt the brass casings, jamming the breech. But it was better than nothing, and it threw a big .45 rifle bullet a long way. They'd be handy for deer hunting, if nothing else.

The guns kept turning up like bad pennies in his life.

"Don't look so downcast, Valentine. Check the ammunition."

Valentine opened a padlocked crate.

"Voodoo Works?" Valentine asked, seeing the manufacturer.

"Pick one up."

Valentine knew something was different as soon as he lifted up a box of bullets. He raised an eyebrow at Lambert.

"Yes, it's Quickwood. Testing found that the .45 shell was less likely to tumble and fragment. Only a couple of thousand rounds, but if you distribute the Reaper rifles to your good shots . . ."

She didn't have anything to say about the explosives Valentine uncovered next. They'd loaded him up with what was colloquially known as Angel Food, a vanilla-colored utility explosive that was notoriously tricky to use. The combat engineers used to say working with it kept the angels busy, thus the name. You could handle or burn it without danger, but it was quick to blow when exposed to spark. Even static electricity was dangerous.

For preserved food there was a lot of WHAM. Probably captured supplies taken off of Quisling military formations and now being repatriated to its native land. The WHAM had probably logged more time in service than many of his soldiers.

As to the training materials, they were mostly workbooks on reading, writing, and arithmetic: useful to many of the lower-level workers who escaped the Kurian Order functionally illiterate but not particularly useful to his troops.

For entertainment they had cases and cases of playing cards with the classic depiction of a bicyclist.

Valentine lifted one of the boxes and opened it. Inside, the cards were wrapped up like a pack of cigarettes.

"Strip poker?" he asked Lambert.

"Stakes aren't worth it, not with your face looking like that."

They laughed.

Valentine would have found it hard to put into words to say how relieved he was Lambert was joining them in Kentucky. She was the sort of person who did a good deal without drawing attention to herself. He'd come across an old quote from one of the Prussians, von Moltke something or other, that perfectly described her: *accomplish much, remain in the background, be more than you appear.*

But had she ever stood under shellfire before? History was full of leaders who were fine organizers but couldn't face what Abraham Lincoln called the "terrible arithmetic" of sacrificing some men now to save many in the future.

To be honest with himself, Valentine had a little trouble with his sums as well.

Later that night, as he fell asleep, he felt a slight, ominous tickle in his throat.

†

Valentine, thick-headed and sneezing on the flatboat trip downriver with his new charges, observed that you could mark the deterioration of civilized standards the closer you drew to the Mississippi by the signs along the Arkansas' riverbank.

He liked leaning on the rail, watching the riverbank go by. Mantilla had put them all in oil-stained overalls even dirtier than his crew's and beat-up old canvas slippers with strips of rubber sewn in for traction.

"Only because it's not barefoot weather, unless it's a sunny day," one of Mantilla's crew explained.

Back in the better-served counties with functioning law enforcement, there were polite notices not to tie up or trespass, bought at some hardware store.

Farther down the river, you had hand-painted boards up.

KEEP OUT! THIS MEANS YOU!

or

I'M TOO CHEAP FOR WARNING SHOTS

Then closer still to the Mississippi, the ownership left off with writing entirely and sometimes just nailed up a skull and a pair of crossed femurs at their jetty.

They left the last of the gun position and observation posts guarding the mouth of the Arkansas River at night and turned up the wide Mississippi with all hands alert and on watch.

Mantilla's men were experts with paint and brush and stencil and flag, and within a few minutes they had transformed the old barge with Kurian running colors.

Valentine stood on the bridge, drinking the captain's excellent coffee with Mantilla. They had a shallow draft, so the captain kept close to the Kurian east side as part of his masquerade. There were monsters on the river six times as long as Mantilla's little craft.

"You should have a little honey for that cold. Honey's the best thing. Colds are a real *suka*."

Valentine accepted some tea and honey. As usual, he was in for another surprise. The tea was rich and flavorful; it made much of the produce in Southern Command taste like herb-and-spice dust.

"That's Assam, all the way from Sri Lanka," Mantilla said.

Valentine wasn't even sure where Sri Lanka was. To change the subject, he inquired about the dangers they might face on the river, motoring right up through the border of two warring states.

"It's a sort of truce at midchannel," Mantilla said, pacing from one side of the bridge to the other on the little tug. "Nobody likes to make a fuss, sinking each other's river traffic. The sons-of-whores military vessels will chase and shoot right and left, but the coal and grain barges pass without too much trouble. Of course, the Kurian captains are smart enough to do a little trade with our little luggers; a few tons of coal or steel given up here and there for a quiet run between the Kurian Zone and the UFR is a small price to pay. The bastards would rather pay up than fall in the *schiesse* with our side."

"Chummy."

"We stay on our side; they stay on theirs. Most of the time. Your little venture into Kentucky broke the rules. Our Kurian friends can't allow that to stand, you know. They'll strike back."

"It had better be with something better than what they've used so far," Valentine said as the Mississippi unrolled like a blue-green carpet in front of the little barge. "The Moondaggers were vicious, but they weren't much in a stand-up fight against people who could shoot back."

"They were supposed to take you quietly into custody. After a few culls, the rest would be exchanged back to the UFR in return for some captured Texas Quislings or some other property the Kurians wished not to lose. Your little rebellion in the Ozarks is getting too big for its britches."

"Our little rebellion. You're on our side."

"Very much so. If I speak strangely, it's only because I know of other rebels in other places and times."

The "and times" comment put Valentine on his guard. How much did he really know about Mantilla? What did the captain's name mean in Spanish again? Was it a cloak or covering of some kind?

Valentine wondered how Mantilla, a river captain, knew so much about the fighting. You'd think he'd spend his time studying depth charts and dealing with customs clerks and patrol boat captains.

With the usual methodical lucidity he had during illness, he thought the matter over in the glorified closet that served as his cabin. He didn't like being played, but unless Mantilla was an unusually cruel gamester, he didn't think he was being toyed with. Instead, the barge captain seemed to be trying to let him in on a secret without saying so directly.

He went to bed wondering just who, or what, their captain was. If he was, say, a Lifeweaver, why would he be doing something as exposed and dangerous as traveling up and down the rivers of the former United States—and perhaps into the Caribbean and beyond as well?

The other possibility was that he was a Kurian who had gone over to the side of his estranged relatives, the Lifeweavers, to help the humans, but that made even less sense.

There was a third option. Valentine had heard rumors, long ago in his days as a Wolf, from his old tent mate that there was supposed to be another kind of Hunter, another caste beyond the Wolves, Cats, and Bears. Of course, it hadn't been much more than rumor. His old tent mate had claimed that it was something the Lifeweavers tried to effect in humans but that didn't work out; they all went mad and were locked up in secrecy.

Then again, Valentine had met an old resistance leader in Jamaica who'd been modified in some way by the Lifeweavers. She'd seemed sane enough, even if most of the rumors about her were insane. She'd offered some insight into his future.

She'd turned out to be at least partially right.

Valentine didn't know how there could be such a thing as precognition. There were so many variables to life. He'd seen too many lives lost by someone being a step too late or a step too early.

He quit thinking about Mantilla. As long as he got them safely to Evansville. Or to the mouth of the Tennessee in Kentucky, even. Past Paducah.

He woke up to gunfire.

It alarmed him for an instant. The familiar crack put him atop Big Rock Hill and running through the kettles of south-central Wisconsin and in the dust of the dry Caribbean coast of Santo Domingo and with the punishment brigade on the edge of the minefields around Seattle, not sure of which and remembering each all at once in dizzy, sick shock. Then he remembered Lambert had told him that Mantilla had said she could practice with her rifle up by Missouri bootheel territory.

He put on his boots, grabbed a piece of toast, and went up on deck to watch.

Lambert, dressed in some washed-out, sun-bleached fatigues, was firing her rifle from the seated position, looking down the scope through a scratched and hot-glued pair of safety goggles. Valentine had seen the rifle's cheap cloth case when he came aboard and wondered what she had in there. He recognized the weapon: It was one of the Atlanta Gunworks Type Threes he'd become familiar with when Consul Solon had issued them to his ad hoc group posing as Quislings on the banks of the Arkansas. They were sought-after guns in Southern Command, basically an updated version of the old United States M14.

Lambert looked like she had one rigged out for Special Operations. It had a slightly longer barrel with a flash suppressor and a fine-looking optical scope, as well as a bipod that could fold down into a front handgrip. The plastic stock had a nice little compartment for maintenance tools and a bayonet/wire cutter.

The bayonet was a handy device. It had a claw on the handle that was useful for extracting nails and the blade was useful for opening cans or creating an emergency tap in a keg.

But he knew the weight and length of the weapon all too well. Lambert, for all her determination, found it an awkwardly big weapon to handle.

She was using it to pepper pieces of driftwood, old channel markers, and washed-up debris lining the riverbank. She clanged a bullet off of what looked like an old water heater.

"You're a good shot," Valentine said.

"It's hard to be a bad one with this thing," she replied, putting her eye back to the sight and searching for a target. "I wish it wasn't so goddamn heavy, is all."

"Try mine," Valentine said, offering her his submachine gun. It was a lethal little buzz saw, with an interesting sloped design that fought barrel-rise on full-automatic fire. Perfect for someone Lambert's size. He'd carried it across Kentucky and back.

Valentine looked at the serial number on Lambert's gun. Something about the stock struck him as familiar. An extra layer of leather had been wrapped around the stock for a better fit on a big man. He'd last seen this gun outside Dallas—

"This belonged to Moira Styachowski," Valentine said.

"Yes," Lambert said flatly.

"She gave you her old Number Three?"

"No. Colonel Post gave it to me. I wanted his advice on a good field rifle. He said something about Kentuckians knowing a good long rifle for three hundred years and counting, and that if I got desperate I could probably trade it for a working truck, optics being precious in the borderlands. I am thinking about trading it, though. It's a great heavy thing."

Post knew his guns. Odd of him to give Lambert too much gun. He'd made a present to Valentine of his first .45 automatic. Valentine had lost it, of course, but had replaced it with a similar version at the first opportunity.

Lambert fired off a few bursts with the entry gun, ripping up a blackened old post for a dock missing its planking.

"That's more my size," she said.

Valentine considered a lewd comment about a small size having its advantages in ease of handling, but decided against it. Lambert wasn't a flirt and had been his superior too long for it to feel right, even as a joke.

They each fired off a pair of magazines. The Number Three wasn't quite as handy as the Steyr Scout Valentine had gone west with, but the optics were better and it had another hundred meters on the carbine. It was a weapon that could serve equally well as a sniper rifle and a battle rifle. Valentine wouldn't care to use it for house-to-house street fighting, but for the woods and hills of Kentucky it was ideal.

"Want to switch permanently?" Valentine asked. "I'd love to get my hands on an old Number Three."

"Will said to sleep with it, or you'd steal it," Lambert said.

"Unless it has sentimental—"

"I'm teasing, Valentine. Will said I should trade it if I found something better. I like your gun more. But are you willing to—"

"Only if I'm not breaking up a love triangle between you two and the rifle." Valentine instantly regretted the words. Stupid thing to say.

"I think he'd be pleased as anything if you carried it," Lambert said. "He thinks you hang the moon, you know."

"Only by standing on his shoulders. While he bled," Valentine said.

The cheery intimacy evaporated.

"Let's shoot," Lambert said.

"Ever fired a gun in battle?" Valentine asked.

"During Archangel," Lambert said. "But I don't know if it counts. Our column came under fire at night. I bailed out and started blasting away at the gun flashes with everyone else. Turned out we were shooting at our own men. No one was killed, but two of our men ended up in the hospital."

"It happens," Valentine said.

"Post said when you were young, you lost someone close by accident like that."

"True," Valentine said.

"I'm sorry; was he not supposed to talk about it? He only told me to make me feel better about that night."

"I didn't know you two were that close."

"Oh, I might as well tell you. I facilitated his adoption of Moira's daughter after her plane went down. 'Facilitated' isn't quite the word. Stole, maybe. She was supposed to go to that special school where they're bringing up trans-human children."

"Trans-human?"

"It's just an official designation for people enhanced by the Lifeweavers. You never ran into it?"

"I've been out of the communication loop for a while now."

"Of course."

"Well, it's better than subhuman," Valentine said. "I've met a few civilians who'd use that word."

He decided to change the subject.

"When did Styachowski and Post get so close? During the fight at Big Rock Hill?"

"You mean Valentine's Stand?"

"The history books don't call it that."

"She knew him from that, obviously. She met him again when he was assigned to the assessment staff. He gave a very thorough report, and . . . Moira said she had a thing for the older, fatherly-looking guys. I was a little surprised: She never said anything about an interest— Well, that's neither here nor there. But I understand the appeal. He is good-looking. I got to know Post better through her. He told me some interesting details about life in camp with General Martinez, by the way. He knew Moira and I had been close and he said he wanted me to have her gun the last time we— I mean, the last time we met."

Valentine didn't know the extent of Post's injuries that confined him to his chair, didn't know how his marriage had been put back together or under what terms. None of his business.

Lambert was blushing. Valentine couldn't ever remember seeing her blush before.

"Does Gail know . . . about Will's connection with Jenny's real mother?"

"No. Moira said they ended it after you brought Gail back. It took them a while to figure out who each of them was and who the other was in the marriage. Will told me Gail had changed a lot out there, through her experiences. But he was determined to take care of her."

Valentine decided to pry. "Who's Jenny's father?"

"I—I . . . Moira said it was a man she met after the Razors broke up."

"None of my business. I wonder if Jenny's got a little Bear in her—or a lot. Some of the Bears get very randy after a fight."

"I've heard that," Lambert said.

"Whatever Moira had in her blood might have been passed to her daughter."

Lambert opened a little gear bag and began to clean the submachine gun. Valentine did the same with his rifle.

"But Bear parents don't always pass on their tendencies, I'm told," Lambert said. "Sometimes the kid's just a little feistier than most or heals bumps and bruises faster. Also, she's a girl. Don't female Bear fetuses miscarry?"

"I was told that it's adult women who tend to have heart attacks or strokes when the Lifeweavers try to turn them Bear," Valentine said. "I don't know about the children."

"Southern Command is still doing that breeding program. Because there are so few Lifeweavers."

Valentine nodded. He'd been part of that breeding program. Strange stuff. "I haven't spoken to one in ages."

"Knowingly, anyway. They're operating in secret these days, with so many Kurian agents around."

Boat trips leave you a lot of time to think. As Valentine played with his new rifle's butt and balance, trying to decide if he should add another inch to the butt, he thought about his friend.

Old Will. Well, not that old; he had a decade on Valentine at most, whatever his personnel file said. In the Kurian Zone you always falsified your birth date whenever you had the chance. Valentine pictured Styachowski running her quick fingers through Post's salt-and-pepper hair. So there was some hot blood beneath that cool countenance.

"Patrol boat signaling to board," the ship's speaker announced, breaking in on his thoughts.

Mantilla had warned all of them to expect this. The Southern Command soldiers were to go down and wait in the engine room.

Valentine filed down behind the rest of the hatchet men, new rifle and an ammunition vest ready—just in case.

Lambert hurried to catch up to him. "Mantilla wants us ready to go up top. He says he doesn't know this patrol boat. There may be a problem."

Valentine wished there was time to go forward into the cargo barge and get some of the explosives. No time.

He warned the young doctor and the old nurse to be ready, just in case, and had the hatchet men arm themselves and wait in the engine room. Orders given, he went up to the cabin deck just under the bridge. The portholes were a good size for shooting.

Valentine took a look at the patrol boat. Valentine didn't see the usual blue-white streamer of the Mississippi's river patrol, so he suspected it was from one of the Kurian towns. Maybe they were in search of bribes. But the craft had official-looking lights. It was a low, boxy craft and looked like it had a crew of three—sort of a brown-water tow truck.

He had a height advantage from the cabin deck.

The patrol craft suddenly sprouted a machine gun from its roof. The barrel turned to cover the bridge.

Valentine tipped a bunk and shoved it against the porthole wall. He didn't do anything as stupid as shoving the barrel out the window; he just kept watch.

The boat pulled up and lines were passed.

Valentine, flattening himself against the wall beside the porthole, watched two men and a dog come on board. The senior officer, judging from the stars on his shoulders, kept his hand on his pistol as he came aboard. He had a squinty, suspicious look about him, like an old storekeeper watching kids pick over candy tubs.

Captain Mantilla came down to greet them. The older of the two men looked shocked, perhaps at the captain's slovenly appearance. Suddenly, the officer threw out his arms and embraced Mantilla like a long-lost brother.

Valentine couldn't understand it, but it seemed like the crisis had passed. He watched the search team go forward.

He wrapped the gun in a blanket and stowed it and the ammunition vest in a locker. He didn't need to change clothes; like the rest of the passengers, he'd been wearing crew overalls so he could move around on deck freely without drawing attention from the riverbank.

Curious, he went out to the rail on the port side and watched Mantilla with the search team. They were doing a good deal of animated talking and very little searching. Even the dog looked bored and relaxed, sitting and gazing up at the humans, panting.

The patrolmen debarked. Valentine waited for the inevitable bribe to pass down to the senior officer, but a square bottle full of amber-colored liquor passed up to Mantilla instead.

The patrol craft untied and proceeded downriver. Mantilla's tug gunned into life.

✝

As it turned out, they were boarded from the other side of the river an hour's slow progress from where they had met the patrol boat.

Valentine saw some soldiers, probably out of Rally Base, signal with a portable electric lantern and wave them in. By the time anchors had fixed their drift, a little red-and-white rowboat set out from a backwash, fighting its way through some riverside growth.

Two men were in it, a big muscular fellow at the oars who had the look of a river drifter who made a little spare money watching for enemy activity, and a magazine cover of a man with slicked-back hair.

"Permission to come aboard, Captain?" slicked-back hair called.

"Granted."

The baggage came first. A big military-issue duffel hit the deck with a whump, tossed up by the muscular man in the rowboat. It was followed by the would-be passenger. On closer inspection Valentine saw that he had a pencil-thin mustache, precisely trimmed to the edges of his mouth.

Which was smiling, at the moment.

"Good God, I was afraid I'd missed you. My river rat swore to me that your tug had passed yesterday. I thought a very bumpy ride had been in vain. Broke records getting to Rally Base.

"Let's see. Transport warrant. Letter of introduction, and permission to be on Southern Command military property. That's the lot. I was hoping to hitch a ride."

"This trip is chartered by Colonel Lambert," Mantilla said. "You'll have to ask her."

"Who are you?" Lambert asked from her spot at the rail.

"Rollo A. Boelnitz, but my friends call me Pencil. I'm a freelancer with *The Bulletin*. My specialty is actually Missouri but I'm eager to learn about Kentucky."

The Bulletin was a minor paper published near the skeleton of the old Wal-Mart complex in Arkansas. It was new—post Archangel and the UFR anyway. Valentine had never read it.

"Why Pencil, Mr. Boelnitz? Because of the mustache?" Lambert asked.

"No, at school. I always lost my pencil and had to borrow. It just stuck."

Lambert glanced at Valentine. "You wanted reinforcements. One pen a mighty army makes."

Valentine disliked him, maybe simply because of the way

Lambert had perked up and thrown her chest out since this young icon came aboard.

"General Lehman suggested I join you," Boelnitz offered. "I was talking to him to get a retrospective on his tenure. He said a bit of publicity might help your cause in Kentucky, and the Cause on top of it."

Lambert examined his paperwork. "That's Lehman's signature. The permission to be on Southern Command property might have been overkill. Kentucky's neither fish nor fowl at the moment."

"Do you know what you're getting yourself into?" Valentine asked. "There's no regular mails between Kentucky and the UFR. No banks to cash expense vouchers."

"I was hoping for the traditional hospitality of Southern Command to members of the press. As to my stories, one of your men can transmit via radio. General Lehman said you are in radio contact twice daily."

That settled any issue about this being a put-up job. Radio security was about as tight as Southern Command could make it, involving scramblers and rotating frequencies. Lehman must have passed that tidbit on. Standard Southern Command procedure for brigades in the field was three radio checks a day. As theirs had to be relayed through Rally Base, they found it easier to do just two.

Valentine shrugged and gave Lambert a hint of a nod.

"Welcome aboard, Pencil. I hope you find the situation in Kentucky interesting," she said.

"But not too interesting," Valentine said. "We all had enough interesting this summer to last us till pension draw."

Boelnitz shook hands all around. It was hard to say which version of Pencil Boelnitz was more handsome: serious, expletive Boelnitz or grinning, eager-to-befriend Boelnitz. Valentine couldn't tell whether Lambert had a preference, either.

†

The bottle their patrol boat had given them contained some seven-year-old bourbon. Mantilla shared a glass with Valentine that night.

They sat in the captain's day cabin. Valentine supposed it was meant to be an office too, but the ship's records seemed to take up one thick sheaf of paper in various sizes, stains, and colors attached to a rusty clipboard.

A single bulb cast yellow light on the cabin deal table. Mantilla and Valentine sat with their legs projecting out into the center of the cabin as the captain poured.

"This is even better for your cold than honey," Mantilla said.

"It makes being sick a little more relaxing. The inspection today—what was that about?"

Mantilla leaned back and put his chin down so the shadow of the cabin light hid his eyes. "A formality, as it turned out."

"Thought you said you didn't know the boat."

"I didn't. But I turned out to be an old friend of the officer in command of the patrol boat."

"Were you?"

Mantilla chuckled. "For a little while. Today anyway."

"I thought you hadn't met him before."

"I never saw his face in the whole of my life. And you would remember a face like that. Like an asshole with pimples."

"What does that mean?"

"You know how a shitty bunghole seems like it's winking at you—"

"No, you never met him, but he knew you?"

"Major Valentine, let's just say that I'm an expert in letting people see what they want to see."

Valentine finished his glass of bourbon and tapped it. To be friendly, Mantilla tossed back his own, gave a little cough, and re-filled them both.

"Let me tell you a secret about people, Valentine. They're really good at fooling themselves. They go through life jerking themselves off, complimenting themselves that they're seeing things as they are. Really it's wishing, like a little boy on a skate-board pretending it's a jet airplane. Some *chocha* says *no, no, no* but the prick she's with hears *yes, yes, yes*."

"Or she's hearing wedding bells and he's thinking bedsprings. But I don't see how that gets a sealed bottle of bourbon out of a local river cop."

"He didn't want to come on board and find trouble. He was hoping for a friendly face. I gave him one."

"Just how did you do that?"

"Allow me to keep a few secrets, Major. I will say this. All it takes is the tiniest bit of a nudge. A shape in the shadows turns into an old friend. A crumpled old diner check turns into a valuable bill." He pointed to the sheaf of paper on the wall. "An old spread-sheet becomes a transport warrant."

"Sounds like magic."

"With magic, people are looking for the trick that is fooling them. What I do is give them a little help fooling themselves."

"Go on," Valentine said, interested.

"You're walking down a dark street and you hear someone following. *Merde!* When you turn around, would you rather see a policeman or, better yet, your neighbor following behind? But of course. As you turn, you hope, you pray, it is not a thug or worse. These men on the river, even the patrols, they do not want trouble.

They like to meet bargemen they know, friends who bring the good sweet liqueurs of Mexico and Curaçao, gold even, or silks from the Pacific Rim and Brazil that they have obtained in New Orleans."

Valentine took another mouthful of neat bourbon. Was the captain presenting him with what he wanted to see? Did he want to see an unkempt, out-of-shape boatman with a sweat-yellowed cap and grease stains on his knees and chest?

Valentine supposed he did. Older, weathered, an experienced man who'd lived long on the river and attended to his engines even at the cost of some mess, Mantilla had Valentine's respect. Even a little flab added to the secure image; Mantilla enjoyed his food. Then there was the keen, roving eye from the face Mantilla never quite turned directly toward you. Canny, with part of his mind on you, part of it on ship or river or weather. "Handy trick," Valentine said. "I don't suppose you could teach me the knack."

"When you work up the guts to look into your own mind and come to terms with what's living there, then you can come to me and speak of venturing into others' minds."

†

Valentine saw two more examples of Mantilla's trickery at a Kurian river station near Memphis when the captain stopped to pick up a few spare parts for his barge and some diesel for the motors, and then again outside Paducah, where their ship was inspected again. Two men went down into the barge hold ahead, and Valentine held his breath until they emerged, yawning.

Half a day later they approached Evansville and Henderson across the river. No bridge spanned the river anymore, but there were plenty of small craft on both sides. They scattered as the tug approached.

"Your boys close the river? Do I have to worry about artillery gunning for me?" Mantilla asked Valentine, who was standing with him on the bridge.

"No. Not a lot of traffic up and down the Ohio except food. We don't want to starve anyone. But I'd better go first in your launch and send some people down to the landing, just in case. We'll need all our motor resources to unload the cargo."

†

Valentine was met by a pair of Wolf scouts who took him up to an artillery spotter with a field phone. They'd made some progress with the communications grid in his absence. Perhaps his old "shit detail" had done the work. They didn't fight like Bears, but they had an interesting skill set. He called operations and reported the arrival of supplies from Southern Command. The hatchet men weren't worth calling reinforcements, so he called them specialists.

With that done, he returned to Mantilla's tug.

"We have some odds and ends needing transport back," Valentine said. "Sick and lamed men." Also a few who wanted out of it and were willing to take a dishonorable discharge to get away as soon as they could.

"Some might have to ride in the shell if there are too many. I'll need food for them, if there are many."

"That can be arranged."

"Then I'll be happy to offer transport back. In Paducah they will be surprised to see me again so soon."

"Captain Mantilla, once more I'm in your debt," Valentine said.

Mantilla pushed his hat back on his head. "It's my pleasure to aid a Saint-Valentine."

"It's just Valentine. As you can probably tell, I am about as Italian as I am Afghan."

Or does he know my mother was named Saint Croix? Valentine wondered.

"I've one more favor to ask. Do you know anyone on the river who can get a message up to St. Louis? There's a big church there that tends to the human population and the Grog captives. Slaves, I guess you'd call them. I have a friend near there that they help now and then."

"I'd be honored to bring a message to Sissy."

"Sissy?"

"Isn't that what you call Narcisse?"

"Do you know her?"

Mantilla dropped his chin so his eyes fell into shadow again. "Almost as well as you do, Major Valentine."

CHAPTER FOUR

*F*ort Seng: Javelin landed and set up housekeeping within earshot
of its victory against the Moondaggers on the banks of the Ohio.

In the hills just outside of Henderson, which is now mostly a ghost
town, a thickly wooded old state park is now more state than park.
Named after the naturalist, the Audubon State Park has changed hands
several times in the past year.

Briefly used as a headquarters by the Moondaggers, the park was
captured by Javelin almost intact, complete with supply depots and
communications gear.

They were attracted by the clean water, space, cabins, and utility
buildings. Just off the highway, near the entrance of the camp, is a set
of impressive stone buildings constructed from the plentiful limestone
of the area's land.

The biggest building is reminiscent of a French château, a former
museum complete with turret and gardens, broad patios all around, and
decorative walls. Though long since stripped of its valuable Audubon
prints, it still has pleasant, sun-filled rooms. The Moondaggers, hurrying
up from Bowling Green to cut Southern Command off from its escape
into Illinois, used its comfortable rooms as a headquarters and relocated
the powerful Evansville Quisling who'd occupied the place to one of
the two guest homes behind the pool patio. He and his family fled to the
Northwest Ordnance as Colonel Bloom's columns approached.

*Southern Command occupied the building with very little altera-
tion. Of course the prayer mats and Kurian iconography had to go—
unless the former were clean sheepskin or made of precious metals in
the case of the latter. Southern Command set up a permanent hospital
in the old staff quarters: The cooking area and numerous small rooms
fitted for two were ideal for the purpose.*

*The flagpole now bears Southern Command's five-pointed star
and the stylized white-and-red handshake of the Kentucky Alliance—
UNITED WE STAND.*

*Behind the estate house is a parking lot with an oversized lime-
stone gatehouse. That became the unofficial duty office and clearing
center as Javelin reorganized itself after their losses on the long retreat across Kentucky and the battles with the Moondaggers. The rich
Quisling's driver and mechanics once lived at the gatehouse, and he
expanded the place to add overnight accommodations for his friends'
drivers and a small canteen for staff. Javelin turned the canteen into
a recreation club and also a grill where any soldier could get a quick
bite, on duty or off.*

†

Valentine noticed the improvements to the camp as soon as he led
his party up past the small organized mountains of debarked supplies on Henderson Landing. He checked in Lambert, his hatchet
men and medical staff, and Pencil Boelnitz under the watchful
eyes of the sentries on the western side of the main highway's
pared-down bridges into Evansville. They walked up past artillery positions shielded by hill from direct fire from the river, and
communication lines strung to observers ready to order fire down
on river traffic, but the Ohio was empty that day.

As there was plenty of daylight left, Valentine sent the hatchet
men and medicos under gate-guide to their appropriate headquar-

ters and borrowed some horses to take Lambert and Pencil Boelnitz on a tour of the battlefield where they'd attacked the Moondaggers. He showed them were the guns were sighted, where the Jones boy had swum the river, the spot where Rand had fallen.

Rand had to be remembered somewhere. Valentine described him in detail to Boelnitz. Such promise, lost.

From the site of Rand's death Valentine could still see in his mind's eye his old company's heavy weapons Grogs, Ford and Chevy, gamboling forward with one long arm to add speed to what looked like an unbalanced canter, the other carrying their support weapons the way regular soldiers tote automatic rifles.

"We saw them run," Valentine said, pointing out the final Moondagger line. "After all the tough talk about reprisals, roads lined with crucified, blinded, tongueless prisoners, men who'd be burned alive in cages, they ran. They wept when they surrendered too, begged, wiped our muddy boots with their beards."

"What did you do with the prisoners?" Boelnitz asked.

Valentine smiled. Perhaps his reputation had preceded him again. "Exchanged the foot soldiers for some of ours. The Moondaggers lied in some cases and handed over dead men— one or two still warm—in exchange for theirs. According to their philosophy, we're a 'gutter people' who can be lied to if it'll help defeat us. I think they forgot how much we gutter people enjoy kicking the asses of those who label us gutter people. Evansville is keeping a few more in their county lockup for trial. There are a lot of murders and rapes in Kentucky to be answered for. Still, wish we'd bagged a colonel or two. No offense, Colonel Lambert."

Lambert just turned up the corner of her mouth, lost in the hazy sunshine. Her eyes weren't interested, her questions perfunctory and polite.

The trees were as brown and bare as a tanned stripper gearing up for her big reveal.

"The big bugs got away, as usual," Valentine finished. He noticed that even the husks of the dead Moondagger vehicles had been hauled away. Probably melted down for scrap after every ounce of conductive metal had been torn out.

Valentine led them over to the old highway running south out of Evansville. Some of the buildings on the double-laned highway showed signs of occupation. A grease pit and a bar had opened up, and some mule wagons were parked in front of an old store. Valentine's ears picked up sounds of construction from within.

He wondered what the soldiers of Javelin were using for money. They'd probably picked up a lot of odds and ends on the retreat across Kentucky, or had looted watches and rings from dead Moondaggers—Southern Command turned a blind eye to some of the more ghoulish habits of her soldiers, especially after a victory. Valentine had seen ashtrays made out of Grog hands and rocking chairs with stretched, gray, fuzzy skin stapled to the supports, date and place of the former wearer's death inked discreetly into a corner of the leather.

After the tour of the battlefield, they turned east of the road and into the shadow of tall trees. Just outside the roadblock at the sentry post, with a fresh-painted sign identifying everything behind the gate as belonging to Southern Command and notifying all that trespassers may be treated as spies, a curious little vehicle stood. It was a cross between a chariot and a station wagon. The odd sort of tandem motorbike had a stiff bar leading back to a hollowed-out shell of a station wagon, its engine compartment hoodless and filled only with cargo netting.

A man in a rather greasy black suit, his white dog collar frayed and holes at the knees and elbows, gave them a halloo. He had a pinched look to his face, like someone had grabbed him by the ears and given a good pull.

"Free doughnuts, fresh made today. Come right over—all are welcome."

Valentine glanced at the sentry pacing the gate barrier who'd pricked up his ears at the singsong greeting. The corporal shrugged.

Valentine's eyes picked up lettering on the side of the souped-up go-cart: NUCM-I.

"What do the letters stand for?" Valentine asked.

"I'll tell you as soon as you give your opinion of this batch. Ran out of my own flour so I'm using the local stuff."

The doughnut he offered on a piece of wax paper was tasty. He'd dipped it in honey.

Valentine had read somewhere or other that the Persians had given the Greeks honey specially made from plants with pharmacological effects. He hoped that wasn't the case here.

"It's delicious," Valentine said, swallowing.

"I have iced tea to wash it down. Sorry it's not sweetened—the honey's scarce enough—but a dunk or two will sweeten her up." Valentine noticed that the pastry giver addressed himself more to Boelnitz than either Valentine or Lambert, despite the insignia on the uniforms. In the Kurian Zone, it rarely hurt to favor the best looking, best fed, and best dressed.

Lambert and Boelnitz each accepted a doughnut as well.

"You going to tell me about those letters?" Valentine asked.

"I'm with the New Universal Church Missions—Independent."

Lambert made a coughing sound. Boelnitz eyed his doughnut, hand frozen as though the pastry had magically transformed into a scorpion.

"Don't worry, friend. I call all brother, whatever their affiliation or uniform. My dunkers are wholesome as fresh milk."

Valentine guessed that the man had been living off of dough-nuts, fresh milk, and maybe a little rainwater and nutritious sun-and-moonshine for a little too long. His skin had a touch of yellow about it, and the greasy skin on his brow was blotchy. But it just made the eager stare in his eyes more authentic.

"I don't want to sound like I'm threatening you," Boelnitz said. "But aren't you afraid of, uh, street justice, so to speak? Some soldiers don't like Universal Church lectures."

"A missionary must be prepared to take a blow. Die, even, as an example of sacrifice."

"What, you give out pamphlets with the doughnuts?"

"No, though I have some literature if you'd like to read it. I have some good stories, written as entertainment, but they contain valuable lessons for today's questioner."

"Today's questioner is tomorrow's dinner, if he's not careful," Valentine said.

The missionary's face slid carefully into neutral. "Every potter's field has its share of broken shards. The just have nothing to fear. All this violence is wrong, wrong, brother. You Arkansas and Texas boys are a long way from home. Why not go back? The only land in Kentucky you'll ever claim is a grave if you continue down this path."

"Thanks for the doughnut," Valentine said. "It was delicious."

They checked in at the sentry post. Valentine nodded to the effusive "welcome backs" and signed in Boelnitz as an unarmed civilian. They issued the reporter a temporary ID. The men looked like they were willing to issue Lambert something else entirely. She was fresh and bright rather than thin and road-worn like the women of Javelin who'd made the long round-trip.

Lambert spoke up. "As a civilian you'll have to stay out of headquarters unless escorted. If you've written stories you need to transmit, just give them to me or the acting exec."

"I know security procedure," Boelnitz said. "All I need to be happy is a bed with a roof over my head. I hate tents."

"We'll see what we can do."

Lambert passed her reassignment orders to the corporal on duty to inspect.

"You have seniority on Colonel Bloom, sir," he said, tapping her months-in-rank line item.

"I'm not here to turn the camp upside down."

The pleasant walk through the woods to the headquarters building was fueled by a sugar rush from the honey and dough. Valentine's pack felt lighter than it had all day.

"Speaking of security," Boelnitz said, "that fellow outside the gate seems like a security risk. He's positioned to count everyone going in and coming out."

"The Kurians aren't usually that obvious," Valentine said. "I think he's just a nut, convinced that if he does something crazy enough long enough, the Kur will reward him with a brass ring."

"No harm treating him like a spy," Lambert said. "Best thing in the world is an agent with blown coverage who doesn't know he's unmasked. We can feed him all sorts of information. Low-grade stuff that's true for a while and then, when we really need it, false data to cover for a real operation."

"Voice of experience?" Boelnitz said. "Your operations in Kansas and the whole Javelin thing didn't work out that well."

"You don't know about the ones that were successful," Lambert said, shooting a wink Valentine's way.

The wink put a spring in Valentine's step. Lambert had been sullen and listless during the walk up. He'd been wondering at her state of mind, seeing herself cast into one of Southern Command's ash heaps. The river trip was just that, a trip. Now she must have felt like she'd washed up in a forgotten corner of the war against the Kur.

Seeing her energy and good humor return relieved him. Perhaps she'd just been anxious at having nothing to occupy her mind, the way a mother duck without any active ducklings to line up didn't quack or fuss.

†

A trio of soldiers on their way out of camp met them on the road. They straightened up and saluted in recognition of Lambert's eagle. Valentine could see that they had questions, but he waved them off at the first, "Excuse me, Major, is there any truth—"

"Can't talk in front of our new press representative," Valentine said.

"*Battle Cry* finally got around to sending a man over the river?"

"Not yet. Men, this is Mr. Boelnitz from the *The Bulletin*. You can call him Pencil if you like."

One of the soldiers asked what *The Bulletin* was.

"It's a small paper, new," Boelnitz said, looking a little abashed. "Published out of Fayetteville."

"Speaking of pen and paper . . . good news, men. I've brought the first mail. I'm bringing it to the all-call at the canteen for the company clerks to distribute."

The younger soldier looked at the other two.

"I don't want to wait," the senior said.

They turned around and fell in behind Valentine.

The first thing he did was stop at the big gatehouse and hand off the mail. His oversized carrier held nothing now but official correspondence for Colonel Bloom and a few small presents for his own staff.

†

With the mail delivered, Valentine's first duty was to report to his commanding officer.

Lambert turned up her collar and lowered the flaps on the hat. "Give Colonel Bloom my compliments, Major. I'll pay a call on her shortly, but I'd like to walk the grounds in mufti for the afternoon."

Valentine saluted and left her to her solitary tour. He gave orders to see to Boelnitz's quartering, and left him with a promise for a dinner where the reporter could meet some of the other officers.

The main building hadn't changed much on the outside since he'd last seen it. The comfortable-looking former museum and educational center, later an estate house, was designed to look like a cross between a mountain lodge and a small château. But once through the doors, he noticed new details. There was proper signage everywhere, a new map and roster behind a glass case, a duty desk instead of an officer making do with a bench and an entryway table that had been more suited for hats and gloves, and a proper communications center, probably servicing the new high mast rigged to the decorative gazebo behind the mansion.

"What happened to the face, Valentine?" Bloom asked after Valentine was escorted to her office.

"A difference of opinion in a brothel," Valentine said.

"Over a girl, I take it."

"My favorite there was old enough for false teeth."

Bloom chuckled and took from him her envelope of orders. The good humor bled away from her face as she read.

Colonel Cleveland Bloom took the news with professional grace. Or maybe it was just her instincts for good sportsmanship.

"I'm being benched," she said.

"Not benched, recalled. Someone has to bring the men home. They followed you most of the way across Kentucky. Southern Command must have figured you were the one to see them home."

"You'll stay?"

"They're giving me permission to orchestrate a guerrilla war."

She flipped through her written orders, found an attachment, scanned it.

"With what? They're not leaving you much. A communications team and a few hospital personnel to care for the wounded and sick who can't be moved. That Quisling rabble of yours will need more than that to be anything more than glorified POWs."

They'd had this argument before. Like most officers in Southern Command, she had a low opinion of the kind of men who the Kurians used to fill out the bottom ranks of their security and military formations. Thugs, sycophants, thieves, and bullies, with a few out-and-out sadists peppering the mix.

Valentine reminded her, "The shit detail used to be Quisling rabble. They made the round-trip with the rest of us. I don't recall the column ever being ambushed with them acting as scouts, at least until we bivouacked in the Alleghenies outside Utrecht."

"I'll leave you what I can, in terms of gear."

"Can I have a favor? I'd like to ask for volunteers to stay. I need gunners, technical staff, engineers, and armorers especially."

Bloom, when faced with difficulty, usually got a look on her face that reminded him of a journalist's description of the old US Army General Grant—*that he wears an expression as if he had determined to drive his head through a brick wall, and was about to do it.* "Don't know how Southern Command will react to that. You're talking about prime skill sets."

"They'll list them as Insurgency Assist. They'll still draw in-country pay. One day counts as two toward pension."

Bloom's mouth writhed as though she were chuckling, but she didn't make a sound. "By volunteers, you mean . . ."

"Real volunteers, sir. No shanghais or arm-twisting."

"Then good luck to you."

"Will that be all, sir?"

She looked at her orders from Southern Command. "They leave it to my discretion over exactly when I turn over command of this post to Colonel Lambert, though I'll maintain operational command of the brigade even while it's based here until it returns across the Mississippi. Seems to me there's just enough wiggle room for me to keep the troops here until you're convinced the base is functioning properly, from hot water to cooking gas to master comm links."

"I'll have a list tomorrow, sir."

"Anything else for me, Valentine?"

He had to choose his words carefully. "I told the truth about what happened, sir. I argued that we won an important victory, even if it wasn't the victory they expected. Southern Command's looking for a scapegoat. I expect they'll make Colonel Lambert and General Lehman take most of the blame. Lehman's being sent to a quiet desk and Lambert's out here. Be ready to answer for us, and for yourself."

"Thanks for the warning."

"Anything else, sir?"

"Is Colonel Lambert in the headquarters?"

"She's walking around . . . incognito, I suppose you could call it. She wanted to get a feel for the men and the place unofficially, before she takes an official role."

"I understand. If you come across her, please ask her if she'd like to have dinner with me tonight."

"Yes, sir. I'll pass the word."

Bloom sat back down to reread her orders, saying a few more words about hoping Lambert wouldn't mind eating late.

†

As Valentine walked toward his new formation's billet, he saw his hatchet men inspecting the vehicles in the motor pool. Of the long column of vehicles that had started out with Javelin, only one battered old army truck had survived the entire journey out of the large vehicles. The rest had been cannibalized to keep others going or lost to wear, Moondagger rockets, artillery, and mines, or accident. A few civilian pickups, Hummers, and motorcycles remained, looking like candidates for a demolition derby thanks to the knocks and cracks.

"Master Sergeant Brage," Valentine said, pronouncing his name as *Braggy*.

"It's *BRAY-zhe*, Major," Brage said, as irritated as Valentine hoped he'd be.

"Sorry, Sergeant," Valentine said. "Why the interest in the motor pool?"

"Orders, sir," Brage said, tapping his chest pocket. "We're to determine what's worth taking and what'll be left behind. My staff and I have final word. Our decisions are final and unalterable."

"I've seen my share of alterations to unalterable. May I see the orders, please?"

He handed them over with the air of a poker player laying down a straight flush.

Valentine read the first paragraph and then went to the next pages and checked the signatures, seals, and dates. He recognized the hand at the bottom.

"My old friend General Martinez. You're on his staff?"

"I have that honor, sir." With a wave, the rest of his hatchet men returned to work.

"Martinez has been honoring me for years now. I hardly feel it anymore," Valentine said.

"I'm sure you mean *General* Martinez, sir. Of course, whether I make the GHQ staff depends on my success with this assignment. I intend to leave no stone unturned."

"I wouldn't advise you to turn over too many stones in Martinez's staff garden. Not a pretty sight."

"I have to get back to work, Major. I'd advise you not to hinder me."

"Or what, Sergeant Bragg?"

"*BRAY-zhe*, sir. Anyone caught red-handed in the act of taking or keeping Southern Command property from its proper allocation, right down to sidearms, may be dealt with summarily," Brage said, sounding as though he were reciting. "That only applies in combat areas, of course."

"Of course. And if you want to see a combat area, Sergeant Bragg, I suggest you try to take a weapon from one of my men."

†

Javelin stood on parade, a great U of men. It reminded Valentine of his farewell to the Razorbacks in Texarkana, when they retired the tattered old flag that had waved over Big Rock Hill and been bomb-blasted at Love Field in Dallas.

Valentine read out the list of commendations and promotions. The men stepped forward to receive their medals and new patches and collar tabs from Bloom.

A delegation of civilians and officers of the new city militia from Evansville sat in chairs, watching. Valentine hoped they were impressed. All they'd seen of Southern Command's forces up to now had been files of tired, dirty, unshaven men lining up to receive donations of food, toiletries, and bedding from Evansville's factories, workshops, and small farmers.

Valentine had juggled with the schedule a little to get as many excused from duties as possible, but it was worth it.

He stepped forward to the microphone when she was done. "Colonel, with your permission I'd like to add one more name. If you'll indulge me, sir."

Bloom beamed. Her teeth might not have been as bright as Ladyfair's, but her smile was better. "With the greatest of pleasure."

Valentine spoke into the microphone, which put his voice out over the field amplifier, a device that turned your words into power-assisted speech that sounded a little like aluminum being worked. "Javelin Brigade, I have one more promotion. At this time I would like to recognize one of my oldest friends in the Cause.

"Top Sergeant Patel, would you step forward, please?"

Patel hesitated for a moment and then handed his cane to his corporal and marched out into the center of the U of formed ranks. Valentine couldn't tell if he was wincing or not. He marched without any sign of weakness in his old, worn-down knees.

"This man has been looking out for me since I was a shavetail lieutenant with his shoes tied like a civilian's. He helped me select and train my company, the shit detail."

The term was a badge of honor now, ever since their action at the railroad cut in Kentucky.

"Top Sergeant Patel performed above and beyond, crossing Kentucky and back on a pair of legs that are hardly fit for a trip to the latrine.

"I recommended, and Southern Command granted, a commission for Nilay Patel, elevating him to the rank of captain, with its attendant honors and benefits. He's been breveted over lieutenant so that our Captain Patel will never have to salute a sniveling little lieutenant with his laces half-undone ever again."

"You could have given me fair warning, sir," Patel said quietly. "Would have paid for a shave and haircut across the highway."

"Surprise," Valentine said out of the corner of his mouth. The amplified speaker popped out the *p* but nothing else. He spoke up again. "So be sure to save a seat for him on the barge home. He'll ride home in a comfortable deck chair, as befits a captain."

"Excuse me, sir," Patel said. "I'm not leaving before you and the company."

"We'll argue about it later, Captain." Valentine reached into his pocket. "These are some old insignia of mine. No branch on the reverse. They don't do that for Cats, or they put in a false one." He handed them to Patel, feeling paternal, even though his old sergeant major had almost twenty years on him. "Wear them in good health."

"Thank you, sir," Patel said, leaning over to speak into the microphone. Then, for Valentine's ears only, he continued: "It's good to feel useful again. Even if it comes with a little pain."

†

The fall weather turned colder and rainier. Through it all Southern Command's forces improved Fort Seng, rigging lighting and plumbing and communications throughout the fort. A double perimeter was laid out, though they didn't have the mines, lights, or listening posts to cover the entire length.

Valentine saw Boelnitz mostly around headquarters. He had a knack for finding something interesting going on and observing in the company of whoever was doing it, asking questions but keeping out of the way. The men felt flattered to be interviewed, as did some of the women—Valentine saw one long-service veteran giggling like a coquettish schoolgirl as they chatted. A couple of others looked at him with naked hunger, the way she-wolves might eye a dead buck strung up for dressing.

In the meantime, Valentine reintroduced himself to Bee, one of the three Grogs in camp. He'd rescued her and two others from the circus of D.C. Marvels before Javelin entered Kentucky, and he'd also known her years ago when she'd traveled as a bodyguard to a bounty hunter and trader named Hoffman Price. Big as a bull, she had arms long enough to go around him twice when she sniffed and touched and remembered who he was.

She'd apparently forgotten his existence but was equally delighted to reacquaint herself with him, and she soon fell into her old habit of trailing along somewhere in his wake with a shotgun and an assault rifle, both cut down to pistol grips, in holsters on her wide thighs, with plates of bulletproof vest serving as loincloth, vest, and mantle.

Each morning, Valentine visited the headquarters bungalow for his Quisling battalion. He had to split his time between his Quisling recruits and the main headquarters building, where Lambert needed him as she oriented herself to western Kentucky and Evansville.

His ex-Quislings were losing their baby fat, or their paunches, under Patel's double-time training. During the day, the mixture of tenting and barrack that housed his ex-Quislings—the men were building their own accommodations as part of the shake-down training—lay empty in the field behind the bungalow.

He'd chosen the bungalow not for its size or plumbing or available furniture—he liked it because it had a huge social room, a sort of living room–dining room–kitchen combined. He lined the walls of the big room with couches and stuffed comfortable chairs. Judging from the remaining books, the house had belonged to a gardener or a gamekeeper who'd worked for the estate's owner.

Valentine liked to hold meetings comfortably, with everyone seated and relaxed, usually in the evening.

This particular morning he found it in the hands of Ediyak— once a lieutenant but now a captain thanks to Rand's death. When he'd returned to Fort Seng she'd been across the river attempting to wrangle more supplies out of the Evansville leadership. She was a delicate-looking young woman, doe-eyed and usually buzzing with energy, who'd defected from the Kurian Order. The defection had been harder for her than most; she'd been involved in communications and intelligence, so she'd lived on an access-restricted section of her former base. She'd played a Mata Hari trick and arranged to date a general, slipping away from a resort hotel as her aged paramour slept. *I defected thanks to two bottles of wine and beef Wellington*, she was fond of saying.

Valentine liked his former company clerk, who'd first come to his notice when she came up with the gray denim utility-worker uniforms that allowed his company to roam Tennessee and Kentucky without attracting notice. Some of his command he respected, some he dealt with as best as he could, but he liked her as a person and found her company rewarding beyond the necessities. She was a little weak on assertiveness—she'd risen from private to corporal to sergeant to lieutenant and now captain thanks to assorted emergencies in the trek across Kentucky, and handled the detail work of each station with ease, but she seemed in a permanent state of finding her feet thanks to the constant promotions. She needed decent NCOs under her or the men would get away with murder, but she was bright and—well, "creative" was the word, he supposed. She sensed what he wanted with very few words of explanation from him.

"How's the organization going?" he asked her.

There was something theatrical about Ediyak. Maybe it was the big eyes in the thin face or her size. She made up for her small physical presence by moving constantly and gesturing. "After cutting out the unfit and the idiots, we're down to a hair over three hundred fifty," Ediyak said, swiveling on her chair and taking the roster off the wall for Valentine to examine. "The brigade's artillery stole some of the best and brightest, by the way. The culls are in a labor pool."

She rose and pointed to the large-scale local map. "Right now they're working on getting a better ferry in place between Henderson and Evansville. As you directed, I broke up our old company and made them NCOs over the new formations, five men to a platoon. So if you add them in, you have the makings of a decent battalion."

"Now tell me what's happened in the interwhiles," Valentine said.

"For a start, we're broke," she said, making a gesture that gave Valentine a pang for his mother: the *cassé* of French culture, a little motion like breaking a stick. "Evansville is a rat pile, and everyone's hoarding: food, fuel, everything from sewing thread to razor blades. Bloom asked, in her darling vigorous way, for the men to sacrifice 'valuables' or they'd have to do a thorough search of the camp to gather non–Basic Order Inventory that might be traded or sold. Of course the implied threat was that if they didn't contribute some gold and whatnot that they'd picked up on the marches, she'd search thoroughly for all of it.

"We had a few of our recruits go over to Evansville in search of a good time. Vole and a couple of his cronies. They never came back. I don't know if they deserted or the Evansville people quietly strung them up in some basement. I think the latter's more likely."

"Any good news?"

She slipped back to the desk. "Not much. Supplies are running short—food and dispensables anyway. The leg shavers among the women are sharing one razor between us."

"Opposition?"

"The Moondaggers are long gone. Kentucky doesn't have a Reaper east of Lexington, from what the Wolves tell us. Memphis sent up a couple of armored trains from the city, evacuated what's left of the Moondaggers and prominent Quislings in eastern Kentucky. The rest are holed up in the bluegrass region with what's left of the Coonskins. But anything that rides legworms is settling in for winter quarters, with the nights getting colder and their worms egging and piling up.

"Can I ask, sir, what's going to happen with us?"

"You're going home."

"We'll see about that."

"Just between you and me, Southern Command has written off Kentucky. They're sending some NCOs and transport to decide what's worth salvaging and what isn't."

"Lovely. There go our guns, sir."

"We'll see about that. By the way, Ediyak, where'd you pick up the *tschk* gesture?" Valentine asked, making the *cassé* breaking motion with his hands.

Ediyak's eyes widened. "The . . . oh, that."

"You grew up in Alabama, right?"

"Yes, sir. I grew up poor as dirt in a little patch of kudzu called Hopper where a girl was expected to be married at fifteen and nursing her way through sweet sixteen," she said, her accent suddenly redolent of boll weevils and barbecue.

"So you picked that up after you got out?"

"Yes, sir. Why so interested?"

"How did you get out?"

"Church testing. They had this extraordinary idea of putting me on the public broadcasts," she explained, her hand fluttering about her breast like a dove looking for a perch. "A sagging old Archon with my picture said I had the perfected look. If by 'perfected' they meant half-starved and iron-deficient, I'm guessing they were right. I went to school for two years learning about lapel microphones and makeup and phonetic pronunciation, a dusty duckling among graceful swans, learning to dress and talk and give the appearance of being cultured even if I was to the outhouse born. Then they decided I didn't look right next to the other news broadcasters because I was too small. I tried out for *Noonside Passions*, rehearsed with a few of the principals, but didn't get a continuing role. I did six episodes before they had me die in childbirth, giving my poor daughter to sweet little Billy, who'd only just learned to shave himself. They told me she'd grow up in no time and fall in love with him. They do get a little ripe on that show, don't they? But I'm getting away from the story of my brush with fame. I left the show and let myself be recruited into military communications."

"Is that where you saw the gesture? On the show?"

"I believe it was from a friend, a very good friend I made on *Noonside Passions*: one of the writers, a Frenchman. He'd gone to an *école* something-or-other and was in New York picking up some tips for the French version of the show."

Relief washed down Valentine's spine like cool water. Ediyak didn't seem like the Kurian-agent type, but then Kurian agents that penetrated Southern Command spent years working at not being the Kurian agent type.

She had seemed discomfited about the mention of the show, though. Or the gesture.

†

At their first evening meeting after Patel's promotion that had leaped him all the way over lieutenant in a single, overdue bound, they held an informal party. Congratulations flowed along with some bottles of bourbon of mysterious provenance.

Alessa Duvalier appeared in the middle of the chatter and pours.

She didn't look agitated, just tired and with that pained look she wore when her stomach was bothering her. Valentine took her long coat anyway, noting the mud smears and the river smell on her. The waters of the Ohio didn't need a Wolf-nose to detect.

"Where have you been?"

"Bloomington," she said.

"All that way. By yourself?"

"I hitched a ride with a good old boy who trains fighting dogs. He was on the way to a match in Indianapolis. His truck got me there and back."

"You went to a dogfight?" Valentine asked.

"No, I skipped it. So did the dogs. But they weren't in fighting shape anyway. They'd just eaten about two hundred sixty pounds of asshole after I took the wheel."

"Why Bloomington?"

"We received an underground report that the Northwest Ordnance moved into a new headquarters, and I went to check it out."

"How did it go?"

"Maybe nothing; maybe not. Headquarters was for the Grand Guard Corps' Spearhead Brigade from Striker Division. From what my old Ohio boyfriend told me, that's the best of their best, unless you count their marine raiders on the Great Lakes. Armored stuff that usually is deployed at the Turnpike Gap in Pennsylvania against the East Coast Kurians. They may just be training, from what I could pick up in the bars. It may just be exercises to impress the Illinois Kurians and the Grogs."

"Where did you get the idea to go up there?"

"Brother Mark," she said, referring to the ex–New Universal churchman who was the UFR's main diplomat, more or less, east of the Mississippi. "The underground got word to him, Kur knows how."

"Where is he now?"

"Oh, back at Elizabethtown. The wintering clans are all sending delegates to this big conference to decide what to do next. There's talk that they might declare against the Kurians; others say they're listening to a peace delegation."

Valentine retrieved his mailbag and passed out a few precious gifts he'd picked up in the UFR for his officers and senior NCOs. He couldn't bring much, considering all the personal mail he'd had to carry for Javelin's survivors, but he had a new lipstick for Ediyak, aspirin for Patel, a clever chessboard with folding cardboard pieces for one of his corporals who was a chess enthusiast, and matching Grog scar-pins for Glass and his two gunners, Ford and Chevy. And, of course, the tin of talcum powder for Duvalier and her boot-sore feet.

"Where'd you pick up the diaper bag?" Duvalier asked.

"This?" Valentine asked, looking down at the bag as though he'd never seen it before. "They said it was a mail pouch."

"It is, but even Southern Command doesn't take nine months to deliver," Patel said.

"Val, that's a diaper bag. I've seen plenty of them," Ediyak said.

"Diaper bag?"

"Southern Command, for use of," Duvalier said. "They gave one to Jules when she got out of the hospital after you inflated her."

"It's a messenger bag, Ali."

"No, sir, she's right," Ediyak said. "I saw plenty of them back at Liberty. It's a diaper bag. They came in cute pink and baby blue. You got green if you had twins."

"Doesn't say anything on the inside about diapers," Valentine said stubbornly. "Just a pattern number."

"Well, look it up in a supply catalog. It's a diaper bag."

"It's not a diaper bag," Valentine grumbled.

The women exchanged a glance and a smile.

†

Valentine continued to see Fort Seng's fixtures and equipment dribble away, allocated for return to Southern Command by the hatchet men, who were loading up the trucks as though they were Vikings loading their ships on an English beach for the trip back to the fjords.

He decided to make his stand at the artillery park when a little redheaded bird he'd put in charge of keeping track of their activities told him that was on the agenda for the next day. Valentine dressed in a mixture of military uniform and legworm leathers, complete with Cat claws, sidearm, and sword.

Bee, seeing how he dressed, took the precaution of adding a trio of double-barreled sawed-off shotguns to her array, thrust through her belt like a brace of pirate pistols.

With that, he headed over to the artillery park. Duvalier, who'd been lounging around headquarters on an old club chair in a warm, quiet corner, threw on her overcoat and followed him out the door.

Valentine fought yawns. He'd had a long night.

A copper fall day greeted him as he followed the marking stones and path logs serving as steps to the north side of the former park, where the emplaced guns squatted in a quarrylike dugouts area tearing up the ground around a trio of chicken-track-like communicating trenches linking the guns to their magazines.

Duvalier fell out of the procession as Valentine descended into the dimple in the natural terrain that served for the artillery positions.

Valentine saw Southern Command's artillerymen lounging around the fire control dugout.

Brage clearly wasn't the expert here; he stood apart while one of his hatchet men went over the guns.

"Good morning, Sergeant Bragg," Valentine said.

"That joke never gets old, does it?" Brage said. "What kind of getup is that?"

"New model Kentucky uniform."

Brage ignored him and looked over the guns. The three big howitzers were Moondagger heavy artillery that had been captured at what was now being called the Battle of Evansville Landing. The old Moondagger iconography had been filled in and modified with black marker to make a winking happy face—the dagger made a great knowing eyebrow.

Someone with fairy-tale tastes had named the big guns by painting the barrels: Morganna, Igraine, and Guinevere. None of the knights were present. Perhaps Arthur had led them off searching for the Holy Grail.

The squinty hatchet man artillery expert tut-tutted as he inspected the guns.

"Can't use these howitzers," decided the sergeant, whose name tag read *McClorin*. He gave Igraine a contemptuous pat. "Half the

lug nuts are missing. Tires are in terrible shape. You'd swear someone had been at them with a knife. Can't have the wheels falling
off. What are we going to do: drag them home, put furrows in this
beautiful Kentucky grass? The state of these guns . . . You should
be ashamed of yourself, Major—beg your pardon, sir. Those soldiers of yours playing cards all day?"

The grinning gunners looked abashed.

Valentine's oversized satchel pulled hard on his shoulder. Naturally enough, it was full of lug nuts and sights. They didn't clink,
though. He had taken care to wrap them in pages torn out from
the New Universal Church *Guidon*.

"Thank you, Sergeant McClorin. Thank you very much," Valentine said. "I will remember your name."

"Big-caliber guns are more trouble than they're worth. Need
special trucks to haul them and a logistics train a mile deep thanks
to those shells. Our factories would do better to crank out more
sixty mortars instead of trying to hit these tolerances. A good reli-
able sixty's what you need to hit-and-run in the field, or an eighty-
one if you're looking to make life miserable for the redlegs in some
Kurian post.

"Besides, it never fails: We just set them up to cover the highway coming down out of Memphis and the Kurians get word,
and next thing you know harpies as Hoods are coming out of the
night like mosquitoes. No, sir. Fixed fortification guns are plain
stupid."

Brage made a note on his clipboard. "Think you've put one
over on us, Major? Southern Command needs shells just as much
as it needs tubes."

You petty, petty bastard, Valentine thought. Good thing he
hadn't brought Chieftain or one of the other Bears along. Brage
would be tied into a decorative bow right about now.

Valentine pointed to Bee, who was digging for fat, winter-sluggish worms in the wet soil at the top of the wood steps leading down to the ready magazine.

"We keep the magazine under lock and key. All that work with concrete and reinforcing rods—we don't want it wasted with carelessness. She's in charge of the key. Hate to think where she hides it."

"I can see the stories about you are true, Major," Brage said. "You'd start a pissing match with a camel."

Duvalier was suddenly in the gun pit. She'd swung in on one of the barrels like a gymnast and landed so lightly nobody noticed her.

The master sergeant reached for his pistol.

"Keep that weapon in its holster, Sergeant Bragg!" Valentine growled.

Brage lifted the gun anyway and Valentine slipped in and grabbed his wrist, getting his body between Brage and the butt of the gun. The master sergeant was stronger than he looked and put a leg behind Valentine, but as Valentine went down he twisted, getting his hip under Brage's waist so the two touched earth together, still fighting for the gun. Valentine somehow kept the barrel pointed at dirt.

Another hatchet man drew his gun. And watched it fall to the dirt, his nerveless hand dropping beside him, twitching not from muscle action but from blood emptying from the severed wrist. Duvalier's sword continued its graceful wheel as she pinned the next sergeant with the point of her knotty walking stick. She brought the sword up, edge crossing the wooden scabbard with Brage trapped between as though his neck were lard ready to be worked into biscuit batter.

Sergeant McClorin put his back to the gun he'd condemned, aghast.

"This is—" another hatchet man said.

The gun crews were on their feet.

"Shut up, Dell," the man with his neck scissored between Duvalier's scabbard and razor-edged sword blade said.

The sergeant who'd lost his hand had gone down to his knees and had picked up his appendage. He pressed the severed end to his bleeding stump, pale and growing paler.

Valentine put his knee into Brage's kidneys. "Call off your dogs and I'll take care of my Cat."

"Fuckin' trannies!" one of the hatchet men said. "Save it for the enemy."

Bee loomed from the top of the sand-and-slat wall, assault rifle pointed into the trench.

"Graaaawg?" she asked.

Depending on circumstance, the word might mean *help*, *need*, or *distress*. Bee put the barrel between the two unengaged hatchet men.

"Good, Bee. Safe," Valentine said, releasing Brage. "Medic! Call a medic," he shouted toward the fire control dugout. One of the audience ducked back inside.

"Beeeeee!" Bee agreed.

"I'll have you both on charges," Brage began.

"You drew first, Sergeant. I was defending a member of my command who posed no threat to anyone."

Duvalier looked Brage in the eye. "Just try it. Throw your weight around. Someone else'll be carrying that clipboard by the time a Jagger gets here, and you'll be scattered across the countryside in easy-to-carry pieces.

"You all heard me," Brage said, looking around for support. "She threatened me."

"Let it go, Brage," McClorin said. "Goebler's about to go into shock."

"I'm fine," the one-handed man said. "Should I put my hand in ice or what?"

"Keep pressure on the stump and put it above your head," Valentine said, ripping the field dressing he had taped to his weapon belt off. He picked up Brage's dropped pistol and tossed it up and out of the trench and then moved to help the wounded man.

Duvalier released her captive. He had a sizable stain running down his right leg. "You," she said, taking a quick step forward and holding her blade pointed like a spear. "The one who called us trannies. Come over here and lick your friend clean."

"Stop it, Ali," Valentine said. He turned his attention back to Brage. "I think you all might want to return to Southern Command now," Valentine said. "Colonel Bloom is perfectly capable of organizing a retreat."

"Not a retreat," Brage said. "A reallocation of assets."

†

As it turned out, there was no immediate fallout from the blood shed in the dirt next to Igraine. Valentine had a half-dozen witnesses ready to swear Brage threatened Valentine and pulled his gun first. All the rest that followed was necessary to prevent the death or injury of Southern Command personnel.

Only Pencil Boelnitz, who'd heard about the scene one way or another and regretted missing it, brought it up after Colonel Bloom's query was closed. Lambert shrugged and told him: Service with David Valentine gives no end of future anecdotes—but rest assured he's even tougher on the enemy.

Valentine kicked Duvalier's information about the new Northwest Ordnance movements up to headquarters at the next, and what turned out to be final, staff meeting.

"Not my problem anymore," Bloom said. "We'll be gone in a few days."

"Thank you for seeing the work to the fort through," Valentine said. The brigade had worked hard at finishing setting up Fort Seng as a working base—and, in a typical military irony, wouldn't be around to take advantage of the comforts they'd installed.

"Now that word's got out that we're doing a last dash home, everyone wants to get going as soon as possible," Bloom said. "You sure you don't want us to bury half that Angel Food around the joint, just in case you have to blow it up quickly?"

"We'll be able to handle that. Did I get any volunteers to stay?"

"Aside from your devoted shit detail, you have a couple skutty types who know they'll do time in the brig as soon as we get back to the Jaggers. Wouldn't trust them any farther than I could smell 'em."

"The Bears are staying, suh," Gamecock, the officer in charge of the three four-man Bear teams, said. "I took it up with the boys. Consensus is the Kurians are going to hit you as soon as the rest of the brigade leaves. They figure it's the quickest way to get back to fighting."

"How about the Wolves?" Valentine asked Moytana, the captain in charge of the Wolf company that had scouted for Javelin.

"I'm under direct orders to return," Moytana said. He had the slow, assured drawl of a long-service cowhand.

"What can you leave us?"

"That's up to the bone pickers," Bloom said, referring to Valentine's grim-faced hatchet men who'd been inspecting captured vehicles and gear since they arrived, sorting the salvageable wheat from the chaff that would be left to Valentine to make of what he would.

Valentine rubbed his fresh-shaven chin. "Since this is the last meeting of this particular staff, I feel like we should have something."

"A cake?" Bloom asked.

"I was thinking some of our friend's doughnuts."

"The nut at the gate?" Bloom's clerk asked. "They're good doughnuts, but you have to hear his sermonizing about Kur and the elevation of mankind."

"Might want to roust him for a few days, so he can't count us walking out," Moytana said.

Valentine and a corporal went to get doughnuts. They took bicycles down to the entrance to the base. Bee loped along behind. Some idlers were watching the Kentuckians build small, heat-conserving homes on the other side of the old Evansville highway running west of the base.

"Mind if we take a sack?" Valentine asked the missionary.

"One to a customer, sir. Did you read that literature I gave you?"

"Fascinating stuff," Valentine said. "I have eight friends. One to a customer means I need eight doughnuts."

"Oh, that makes sense," the missionary said, reaching into a shelf in his bakery van. "Did you get to the part about the select gene rescue and propagation?"

"No."

"A well-formed man like you would do well to try out. And don't worry. Less than three percent end up castrated."

"That must have been in the fine print."

"You know, this is an evil land. Best leave it to escape what is coming. The punishment."

"Punishment?"

"I take no joy in it. It's heartbreaking. But the fools will persist in their folly."

"True enough. How long will you keep handing out doughnuts?"

"Until it begins. There will be a sign, a sign from the sky. Beware the evil star! Take it to head and heart, friend and brother. There's a shadow of death over this land. It's flying closer and closer." He handed Valentine a bag so greasy that the paper was next to transparent and went back to scanning the sky.

"I don't suppose you know what direction the danger is coming from."

"The worst dangers blossom in one's own bosom. Look to your heart, friend and brother. Watch the skies, my friend and brother. Watch the skies!"

†

Lost in the sleep of the exhausted that night, Valentine dreamed he was back in Weening.

The last time Valentine had stopped in Weening, they were using the Quickwood tree he'd planted as a maypole, dancing around it every spring. One of the local preachers accused the family who organized the event of being druids.

Valentine had placed the seed there years ago. What Valentine wanted were some specimens of Quickwood tucked away here and there throughout the Ozarks, just in case—a Johnny Appleseed of resistance to the Kurians.

The tree he'd planted in Weening would be mature in another year or two, if what Papa Legba had told him on Hispaniola about the tree's life cycle was correct. It would be producing seeds for others to distribute.

That was the essence of his dream. The young coffee bean–like Quickwood seeds were dropping off the tree and rolling into the brush while he and Gabby Cho stood waist deep in the nearby stream. The seeds turned into scarecrows, and the scarecrows divided and turned into more scarecrows, all of whom stood in the fields and woods around Weening, all subtly turned toward himself and Cho as they shivered, naked and exposed in the river.

CHAPTER FIVE

"*Repurposed.*" *Southern Command doesn't call it a retreat, or abandonment, or evacuation. Word has come down from on high: What's left of Javelin is being "repurposed."*

General Martinez calls it a part of his "new approach" to the war against the Kurians.

Admittedly, General Martinez was, is, and continues to be a controversial figure. What the precise proportion of malfeasance, malpractice, and misjudgment went into his tenure as the Southern Command chief general is the object of some dispute. There are still those who maintain that Martinez's only fault was to see to the welfare of the men under his command first and foremost, only fighting when it was absolutely necessary.

But a wise man knows that in life, absolutes vanish like a desert mirage, receding into an unknown distance before it can be quantified.

At Fort Seng, the men don't reveal much of their thoughts. They carefully pack souvenirs picked up on the march—both the conventional, like some of Karas' old Kentucky coin or one of the short, curved ceremonial knives of the Moondaggers, and the odd: buttons, bits of coal slag, commerce stamps with elaborate imagery, Kurian newspapers with their jumbled and misleading accounts of the fighting, bar coasters from the rail towns outside Lexington, even bits of legworm leather with dates of battles stitched into them. One musically inclined soldier has an entire portfolio full of sheet music. He was struck by how many of the same popular tunes were sung in Kentucky, with altered lyrics or harmonies to give the ditties a local tone.

"Gone-a-homer," an Arkansas tune reworded in Kentucky, was adopted by the troops and reworded again to capture the bittersweet nature of defeat—a defeat that meant you'd live to go home to spouses and sweethearts. Beat, whupped, kicked out: These words weren't spoken aloud but found their way into the song.

†

They were making vests and long johns out of the polyester felt Valentine had brought. It was good-quality material, warm even when wet and so light you hardly knew you were wearing it. They had some doubts about durability, so they were adding coverings and liners made out of old uniforms or Evansville tenting.

The workshop was churning out bush jackets and fatigue pants in "Evansville timber"—a mottled camouflage that was a light bleach wash of the dark uniforms the Evansville militia wore. Then they dabbed it with two colors of camouflage in a vaguely leopard-spot pattern. Of course there were variations that came from a small group of people working long hours at a fast pace. Sometimes it streaked and ran into tiger stripes; other times the pattern was so tight and tiny it resembled a sort of houndstooth.

The end result might not have impressed a discerning Old World eye, civilian or military, but Valentine was oddly proud. Once again, the uniform was one of Ediyak's designs. A big overcoat with drawstrings at waist and sleeves hung to midthigh. Beneath it was a padded riding vest of the insulating felt and canvas with plenty of utility pockets, and beneath that their uniform shirts. Trousers had reinforced knees and seats and a removable felt liner, but it turned out the buttons meant to secure the liner weren't comfortable, so they were removed and replaced by hook-and-eye loops.

Boots were still a problem. Most of his recruits had come over in civilian duty shoes, fine for the streets of Evansville but no match for the tough field exercises in wet fall weather that Patel put them through.

Hobbled men were no use to anyone. Bad feet made men even more miserable than bad teeth. Southern Command had little in the way of spares after the retreat across Kentucky, so Valentine had to settle for tire rubber "retreads" cobbled together with rawhide lacing, scraps of webbing, and heavyweight canvas for breathability.

The men called them "Kentucky galoshes" and suffered through the inevitable blisters and abrasions, but the footwear protected ankles and kept off trench foot.

†

Valentine spent long hours recruiting from the soon-to-depart brigade.

A few NCOs volunteered to stay because they wanted to finish the fight in Kentucky. Many were the best of Javelin, and Bloom crossed a few names off Valentine's list, as she doubted she'd be able to make it back to the Mississippi without them. Others accepted the extravagant promises Valentine made. One or two old soldiers elected to stick because they understood the devil in Kentucky and only God knew where they might be sent when they were "repurposed." Might as well spend the remaining time until land allotment or pension, riding herd on ex-Quislings.

Of course, beggars can't be choosers, nor can they expend much mental effort determining the motivations for those willing to help. Valentine was content to take names, get them approved by Bloom and Lambert, and then work out his battalion's order of battle—without having any of his volunteers "demoted," so to speak. He did this by creating an on-paper staff company.

One benefit of the rumors in Evansville about the departure of much of Southern Command's forces was a near panic about what might happen if the Kurians returned, especially with rumors about forces massing in Illinois, or Bloomington, or outside of Louisville for a dash down the old interstate.

So he had volunteers looking to join Fort Seng in any capacity—on the condition that their families would be able to come along if Fort Seng were abandoned. With food running short, Valentine couldn't accept all the volunteers, and even with enough to feed them he wouldn't be able to arm them, but he was able to fill out his uneven companies by taking, for once, the cream of the overflowing pail.

†

Bloom and Lambert both agreed that Southern Command needed some kind of send-off. The only point of contention was whether the piece that remained still be known as Javelin, or if the designation belonged to the brigade proper.

Bloom finally relented, mostly because Lambert had organized the whole party to begin with. If Fort Seng became a monument to the Cause's attempt to create a new Freehold east of the Mississippi and south of the Mason-Dixon, the tombstone might as well bear the proper name.

The headquarters staff kept the news of the celebration quiet to avoid raising expectations and just in case word traveled to the Kurian lengths of the river, either toward Paducah or in the direction of Louisville. No telling what the Kurians might choose to create in the way of their own farewell.

They detailed a few cooks to roast a pair of pigs and a lamb. Valentine spent the day in the field with his new battalion, returning to see beautiful paper lanterns lining the patio before the great estate house.

"The basement's full of that sort of crap," Bloom told him. "The guy who used to live here loved to throw a party."

Valentine's recruits stayed off to the side as Southern Command's soldiers occupied tables and chairs and benches. The two groups tolerated each other. Valentine's men oddly matched each other in the redyed uniforms they'd crossed over to wearing. Southern Command's troops had their patched fatigues, spruced up with their new medals and odds and ends picked up in Kentucky, mostly raccoon tails and legworm claw feet.

A band filled the chilled night air with noise. It was a merry-go-round collection of musicians as the players stopped to eat or drink and rejoined as the mood and tempo suited them.

Valentine listened to some soldiers warming themselves around a fire pit with even warmer spiked punch.

"Hope we get repurposed to Oklahoma or Texas—some kind of steer country," a corporal said. "If I never swallow another mouthful of those caterpillars, it'll be too soon."

"You're forgetting the good lean Kentucky horse meat, Corp. Meals fit for a dog."

A private leaned back, fingers interlaced behind his head as he reclined. "Soon as I get home to the wife, my johnson's being repurposed from peeing, that's for sure."

"Good woman, that. Puts up with that wood tick of a dick for more'n one night."

"What do you say, Williams?" one of the group called to a woman idly tossing cards into her helmet. "You think the bride said, 'I do,' knowing the triple-A battery Dalrymple here's sporting?"

"Size is for sluts. Give me a man with a quick tongue."

The men laughed, even Dalrymple. She added, "I meant interesting conversation, you lunk."

"Glad we're getting out of here. Only tongue you're likely to see otherwise would be out of a Reaper."

"Home alive in 'seventy-five."

"Worn-down dicks in 'seventy-six."

The chatter stopped when they noticed Valentine watching from the shadows.

"I miss the two-for-one whores of 'seventy-four, myself," Valentine said. Valentine headed for the barbecue spits, purposely altering his course so they wouldn't have to rise from their coffee and rolls and salute.

He found his old company headquarters staff passing a bottle of homemade wine, with vanquished soldiers tucked out of the way beneath their chairs.

Valentine wasn't feeling social. He passed in and out of the conversing groups, shaking hands and wishing well, never lingering to be included in a conversation.

He danced once with Bloom, who found his clumsy steps quietly amusing, and once with Lambert, who did her best to hide his offbeat lurches by holding her body so erect and stiff he had to move with her to avoid looking like he was trying to pull down a statue.

The Evansville group—"Valentine's Legion," some were beginning to call them, though Valentine himself corrected anyone who used the phrase—had an uneasy relationship with the Southern Command regulars. The average soldier had a low opinion of Quislings—they either ran from danger or knuckled under it when the Reapers hissed an order—and the soldiers preferred to keep thinking about them in familiar terms: as targets to shoot at or prisoners to be counted. So the ex-Quislings were relegated to the "back of beyond" at Fort Seng, a chilly field far from hot water.

If the goal of the celebration was to reconcile the two groups, the party was an unmitigated failure. But the two groups each ate well, albeit separately.

Brother Mark returned in the darkness. The man had a curious sixth sense about when to show up. If there was plenty of food and drink to be had, he was there. Yet he wasn't a social man. Like Valentine, he seemed to prefer hanging about the edges.

Valentine addressed a long table filled with his old shit-detail company. Many of them were wearing their new stripes and insignia for the first time.

"Be a lot more room for us once the others leave," Valentine said. "More hot water for everyone. We'll stick new recruits in your tent-shacks."

"Be good to have a home at last, sir," Glass said. His heavy-weapons Grogs were on guard duty while the men celebrated.

It was an unusually optimistic statement from Glass, but odd. He'd grown up in the Free Territory.

"We don't fit in," a corporal said. "Across the Mississippi, they put us in camps. Had to display ID all the time, wear prisoner clothes. Deep down it ain't life under the towers, but on the surface it wasn't that much different."

Valentine nodded. "You're changing that here and now. After you complete your hitch, you'll be as good as anyone else in the Republics, in the eyes of the law. You can settle wherever you like."

"Can we get our land in Kentucky?" Glass said. "Better land in some ways than Arkansas. People here aren't so hung up on where we came from."

"Not for me to promise," Valentine said. "There's Brother

Mark. Ask him. He can go to the local government and see what they have to say. But they've been plenty helpful to us up until now, haven't they?"

"Reward's always over the next hill," Glass said. "Be nice if we could get something on paper."

Getting back across the river was much on the soon-to-depart contingent's mind. Valentine had men step up to say good-bye, shake his hand, or say a few hopeful words about wishing him success in the coming winter.

They gave him a present or two as well. One soldier gave him a flexible horsehide case for the new Type Three, having seen him practicing with it on the shooting range. Another gave him one of Karas' coins, the back carefully polished and re-etched with the brigade's designation and the dates of the Javelin's operational activity in beautiful copperplate hand.

As everyone settled down into groups after the eating and drinking, to smoke or play cards or show off valuables they were contributing to Bloom's "hopper" to buy supplies for the trip home (and for which they would receive a chit in return that, in theory, would restitute them once they returned to Southern Command, probably in near-worthless military scrip), a guard sergeant with the support staff loosened her belt and exchanged a few words with the musicians. Valentine didn't know her—she was one of the replacements—but he recognized the song as soon as the soldier with the fiddle began to draw his bow.

She sang:

> *The water is wide, I cannot cross o'er*
> *But neither have I the wings to fly.*
> *Build me a boat, that will carry tow,*
> *And both shall row, my love and I.*

A ship there is, and she sails the sea,
She's laden deep as deep can be,
But not so deep as the love I'm in.
I know not if I sink or swim.

The soprano had a rare voice, sharp glassy tones that carried through the night air. Valentine was reminded of the teenage thug who loved Beethoven in *A Clockwork Orange* who described a "sophisto" woman's singing like a rare bird who'd fluttered into the dive.

A huddled figure caught Valentine's eye. Alessa Duvalier was listening from just outside of the splashy colorful light of the paper lanterns, perched on a wall with her legs drawn up and clasped to her chest.

Valentine slipped across the party, moving in her direction, while the musicians played the refrain, allowing the singer to catch her breath and more listeners to gather. Even Valentine's own battalion broke off from eating.

I leaned my back on a proud young oak,
I thought it was a trusty tree.
But first it bended, and then it broke,
And so my love proved false to me.

He joined her on the limestone wall.

Oh, love is fair and love is fine,
Bright as a rose, when first it's new;
But love grows old, and sometimes cold,
And fades away like the morning dew.

"It'll never work, you know, Val," Duvalier said. "I thought you were smart about this sort of stuff."

She had that pungent, slightly cloying smell of liquor about her.

"Which 'it,' my friend?" Valentine asked.

"If you think I'm making another drunken pass at you, I'm not," she said. "I've sworn off men."

"Switching to women?"

"Ugh."

"You never could hold your liquor. You want some seltzer? The local stuff's pretty good. It'll settle your stomach."

She pinned him with her foot. "I haven't finished with you, Valentine. I figured when you recruited all these Quislings, it was just to have them make corduroy roads or clear brush or what have you. You really want to turn this bunch into a chunk of Southern Command? Quisling scum like that?"

Valentine switched to sign language. They could communicate in sign. They used to do it on their long assignment together as husband and wife on the Gulf Coast when Valentine had been working as a Coastal Marine. He could still use it but had slowed considerably. "Keep it down; some of the scum can hear you."

"I know their kind," she said louder than ever. "They're whipped, so they'll cringe and lick your boots for a while. First chance they get—*schwwwwwpt!*" She made a throat-cutting gesture with a sauce-smeared finger.

"It's my throat."

"Women fall for crusaders. It's a chance to be part of something big and good. That day out in Nebraska when you convinced me to go help the Eagles . . . I think I fell a little for you that day. A little. Lots of people get twisted by war, turned into something

that's all sword and no plowshare. I like how you think of them."
She waved her hand, gesturing vaguely to the northeast.

"But sometimes," she said, "you get all messed up about who
the victims and the victimsizer . . . victimizers are. These bastards
were stealing and busting heads of anyone who objected a couple
months ago. Now you have them in Southern Command uniform.
You told me once you spent two years hunting down the rapists of
some girl you knew, or of the sister of some girl you knew. How
many rapists are you feeding tonight?"

"None," Valentine said. He wondered if he should stick close
to Duvalier tonight. Some of the men had heard her. While they
wouldn't loop a noose around her and beat her up, they were perfectly capable of waiting until she passed out and then playing
some sort of physical prank that would just make matters worse,
especially if Duvalier woke up while someone was inking her face
or filling her shoes with manure. "That's part of the deal I offered.
Whatever their old crimes, they get a new identity the day they
sign up."

"Like you're baptizing. Maybe the people who deserve a new
life are the ones in Evansville, not these bastards."

"Maybe Evansville is happy to have them gone."

She didn't respond for a moment, and then she slumped against
him. "Oh, Val, I'm so tired," she said, nuzzling his shoulder. "I'm
more tired than I've ever been in my life. I want to sleep forever."

"Were you across the river again?"

"Yes. Checking some roads around Evansville in an old pickup.
No sign of that armored Spearhead. But I can't shake the feeling
something's going to happen as soon as Bloom marches her people
out of camp."

"March out with them," Valentine suggested. "Take a break.
You've been going hard for as long as I've known you."

"Can't. Every time I leave you, you do something stupid and I have to claw you out of it."

"I'd do the same for you," Valentine said.

She yawned.

"You'll sleep tonight. Where do you bunk these days?"

Duvalier had a habit of sleeping in strange spots: chicken coops, dog runs, little scraped-out hollows under rusted-out cars quietly going to pieces on the roadside. It was an act of security gained from long habit in the Kurian Zone: to not be where a Reaper might be poking around, looking for a victim.

"That's what death is, right? Just going to sleep forever. Unless a Reaper gets you. I wonder if the Kurians can mess with you, you know, even after death. Like it's hell or whatever."

"That's silly." Actually, it wasn't. Valentine had seen living bodies, suspended in tanks in a death that wasn't death, in one great, skyline-dominating tower in Seattle.

"They almost got me this trip. You think my luck's used up, Val?"

Maybe that was at the heart of her dark mood, drinking, and odd talk. "You're too smart for 'em," Valentine said.

Valentine escorted her up to his room at headquarters. Though the room had his name on a piece of cardboard taped next to the door, he rarely slept there, preferring to be in the little bungalow by the battalion.

"Remember crossing Kansas?" Duvalier said as they went up the wide stairs with big corner landings. "You were always up making breakfast. I woke up and there you'd be, frying eggs in a pan in bacon fat. Then you'd pour in some flour and make breading."

"It was to prevent you from dining out of garbage bins. The food's healthier when you cook it yourself. I suppose that's why I always fried it to hell. Fear of microbes."

"I thought it was delicious," Duvalier said, slipping out of her clothes. Which took a long time—she clothed her slight frame in multiple layers.

"Father Max used to say my cooking was made for Lent," Valentine said. He watched her undress. Not for pulchritudinous reasons; he wanted to make sure there was flesh on her ribs. She was a wanderer afoot, and the long miles left her scarecrow-thin. Valentine admired her knife-cut good looks, but wished she looked a little more like the sleek general's plaything she'd been during Consul Solon's occupation than the bony adolescent raising the sheet next to him.

"Make me breakfast, Val. Make me some breakfast."

"Okay. You stop talking nonsense and get some sleep."

"Next to you. Like the old days."

"Sure."

Valentine climbed into the bed. The queen-size mattress seemed extravagant, but then the estate owner considered anything under king fit only for the hired help.

He'd not lain naked next to a woman since the erotically mobile, lusty Tikka had gathered what was left of the Kentucky Alliance and harried the Moondaggers across Kentucky. Tikka had run through his inventory of sexual tricks, many acquired from an older Ohio doctor of highly specialized obstetrics, in a few marathon sessions that left her energized and Valentine exhausted but both happily relieved of the burdens of the Kentucky retreat during their few hours together.

Last he'd heard she'd returned to the Bulletproof. He hoped she was one of the delegates in Elizabethtown.

He felt some faint stirrings below the waist as Duvalier pressed her slight body against him, sighing contentedly. But the easygoing intimacy he and Duvalier shared wasn't physical, though they took comfort in the body heat and natural comfort of each other's frames when traveling together. Their intimacy might be compared to that of a brother and sister, but outside of black-cover gothic erotic romances, few sisters slept next to their brothers with pubic thatch tickling his thigh.

No, they were more like a veteran married couple, finding reassurance in each other's bodies, knowing that they'd wake up together or not at all—save that they'd skipped the sex that usually led to such complacency and gone right to physical reassurance.

†

The party went on until dawn and beyond.

The next day he accompanied Lambert across the emptied camp to headquarters. The trampled-down, dead grass where the tents had been set up turned the parkland into something resembling a chessboard.

They passed through to the CO's office. Bloom stood there, her files tied up in three big waterproof binders by her adjutant. She walked a little stiffly but kept the cane as more of an affectation than because she needed it for moving about the office.

They exchanged the necessary salutes.

"Fort Seng is yours. What's left of it, anyway," Bloom said. She turned a bit pensive. "Still wish I knew what they did to me when I got all scared," Bloom said. "I never once the whole time felt my mind was not my own. I was just dark and depressed about everything. Doubtful. That ever happens to you, tell somebody right away."

"How were you to know?" Valentine said. Lambert walked over to the east-facing windows and looked out at the Kentucky woods.

"Helluva way to fight: Make someone get so beat up about themselves they start thinking about taking their own life. I'd rather be shot at some more."

"I understand that," Valentine said.

"What ifs—you know. What if I could have been stronger, or figured out something was wrong with me. Does it make you not crazy if you recognize that you're sick in the head? I remember knowing I felt different. I thought I was just cracking under the strain."

"You did better than anyone would have expected."

"It was beautiful for a minute, wasn't it? When we showed up and found the Green Mountain Boys there. Colonel Lambert, you know you did all that. Too bad you couldn't have seen it. Oh, that was a good day."

Lambert turned back to face Bloom. "They fooled me just as much as they fooled you. Wish I'd been a little more careful."

Valentine wondered if his repeated requests to Southern Command for assistance to be sent to Ahn-Kha's coal-country guerrillas figured into Lambert's calculus when she'd decided on Javelin as Southern Command's next venture into the Kurian Zone. She knew Valentine, trusted him. Had he let her down? Maybe that's why she'd been so formal of late.

"I think the Green Mountain Boys were happy to see Southern Command arrive too," Lambert added.

"It's still the spot Javelin landed, as far as I'm concerned. I think we'll be back, one day." Bloom focused on Valentine. "I'm sorry, Val."

"Not your doing. I know you'd have stuck."

Bloom took a deep breath, brightened. "At least everyone's rested and refit. We'll make it the rest of the way . . ."

"Easy," Valentine said.

"I'd settle for hard. One twist away from impossible, even, just so long as I get them home."

†

Valentine stood flanking Lambert, watching the brigade walk out of camp under an iron gray sky. The soldiers moved in step—a rarity for the men of Southern Command, unless they were moving as part of a graduation class or parade review or under a general's nose.

Valentine expected the Kurians would let them return across the Mississippi. The Kurians liked to see defeated men live to tell their tales. It was the ones who'd beaten them they went after.

Men like his father.

It was hard watching the men he'd come to know on the long advance and the longer retreat file off down the road.

Of course, the few volunteers stayed on: some technical staff, communications people, and trainers helping transform the Quislings into something that could stand up to the Kurian Order. Even Galloby, the agronomist, had remained, waxing enthusiastic about learning more about legworm husbandry. He had some kind of idea about putting a special bacteria in the legworm's digestive tract and getting concentrated fertilizer from the other end. But while he put droplets into petri dishes and ran chemical tests, he advised Evansville on how they could do a better job growing their own food without the rest of Indiana to rely on.

Pencil Boelnitz also stayed, and Valentine wasn't sure how to feel about that.

The supply train left, and then some of the artillery Southern Command had brought in and were now towing out, and finally the rear guard departed, pushing burdened bicycles. Red Dog dodged in and out of their wheels to the turn into woods leading to the gate, then plopped down in the sun to pant.

"You ready for this, Dots?" Valentine asked Lambert, using her old military college nickname in an effort to lighten the mood.

"No," she said, looking around as if she were seeing the tree lines of Fort Seng for the first time.

Valentine chuckled. "Too bad."

"You're helpful."

"I'd be a lot more worried if you were more confident. What's my first order, sir?" Valentine asked.

Bloom's command car came roaring back into Fort Seng. Bloom hopped out before it even came to a stop, hauling with her a Kentucky "vol"—short for volunteer: a local who served in the loosest, most disorganized militia imaginable. Their only common element was a dark blue band around their baseball-style caps. Valentine smelled blood on him.

"The Kurians moved already. They didn't waste time. We aren't even out of camp yet," Bloom said. "I'm sorry I've got to leave passing you bad news. Evansville just hauled this guy out of his boat."

"Where?" Lambert said.

The vol spoke up. "It's lights-out for Evansville and Owensboro. A bunch of flying whatsits have taken over the power plant, and some Reapers and Moondaggers are holding the technical guys hostage."

CHAPTER SIX

*T*he banks of the lower Ohio: The Greenwater Infrastructure Support Plant—the former Elmer Smith Power Plant—on the Ohio River dominates the skyline for miles around. Or rather its smokestack does, a weathered, two-color pillar that resembles a Louisville Slugger (once produced a few score miles upriver) from a distance.

It is a quiet plant, generators thrumming away and a faint wind tunnel sound from the smokestack. The plant is active and confused only on days when thundering mountains of coal are unloaded. Once carried by barge, they're now brought by Kentucky's dilapidated railroad on captured trains, and irregularly at that. The Kentuckians break out the old joke that "these colors don't run anything but short."

The river is much changed since 2022. First called by the Frenchmen who explored it "La Belle Rivière," its banks are now coated with arteriosclerosis of trash and industrial waste. In more prosperous days the river carried a weight of cargo equal to that which passed through the Panama Canal: coal barges, oil, mounds of chemicals white or gray or sulfur-colored, grain, corn, soy, tobacco, and of course steel returning from the coal-fired furnaces of Pittsburgh.

The Kurian Order still dredges the river, off and on, to its usual main channel depth of nine feet. It maintains the locks that control the river as it descends the five hundred or so feet from Pennsylvania to the

Mississippi junction at Cairo—where the few local Grog-traders are careful to correct your pronunciation to "Care-oh."

Now, in the warm-water outflow of the plant, tough carp and cat-fish survive the acidic, polluted river. The bass keep to their willow roots, stumps, and snags in their cleaner stretches of bank.

At this time of year, with the temperatures sinking lower and lower at night, fog runs along the river most mornings, sending querying fingers into the riverside ravines. The foggy wall represents the new state of affairs along the river. Much of the north bank outside Evansville belongs to the Kurian Order; the south bank to the Kentuckians. When once they exchanged jokes about wool-headed Hoosiers and barefoot Kentucky hillbillies, now the locals steal and shoot.

But around the power plant, the fog seems to cling extra thick, a shroud that suggests the unwary would do well to keep away.

†

They took the vol, who was named with a string of three personal names for first, middle, and last—John Robert Nicholas—into the main building, where members of Valentine's battalion were lugging boxes and setting up duty stations. Lambert escorted Valentine and the vol into her bare office, where a single box sat on her desk waiting to be unpacked.

"I want you to get them," Nicholas said, ignoring the bare decor. "You Southern Command people know how to deal with critters like that. We can make the soldiers jump when we have to, but this is beyond anything we can do without tanks and cannon and such-like. Don't belong on God's green earth, them things."

Nicholas shuddered. He raised his eyes to Valentine. "You'll kill 'em, right?"

"Private, Colonel Lambert's in command here," Valentine said. "Tell her how you ended up here."

Nicholas checked the insignia on their clothing. "That bird outranks that palm tree, right. I forgot. Our big bug is a senior sergeant."

"She outranks everyone on the base, Private Nicholas, so you're speaking to the right woman. Tell us what's going on."

Valentine went to the coffeepot, an expensive-looking plug-in model with silver handles and gold rings at the top and bottom that had probably been found in the house. Lucky it wasn't sitting in someone's knapsack. Or maybe it had been, and Bloom rescued it. In any case, she'd left it full of hot, delicious-smelling coffee for her successor.

The building had a pair of emergency generators, a portable gasoline-powered one and a fixed propane model, but Valentine couldn't hear either running. The power plant must still be putting out the juice, then.

"I'm to tell you that ya'll have a safe conduct pass out of Kentucky and back to the Mississippi for the next forty-eight hours, after which the skies themselves will fall on you. Those were the Tallboy's exact words, sir."

Valentine and Lambert looked at each other. The corner of her mouth turned up and Valentine shrugged.

"Now that you've passed the word," Valentine said, "tell us what happened at the plant and what exactly attacked you. We need to know as much as you can tell us about what and how many and where they are."

Lambert called in a young man she'd selected as her clerk to take notes. When he was seated, she let Nicholas begin:

"Six I saw. They came in over the fence like— No, I should start at the beginning. I was part of the ten-man security team. We do three days on, then switch and get four days off, then four days on, you know—"

"Yes," Lambert said.

"Just there to keep an eye on the river, you know. We had an OP up the smokestack. We could see the Owensboro bypass bridge on one side—only bypass bridge still up west of Louisville, I suppose you know, sir—and Evansville on the other. Luckily it wasn't my shift to be up in the wind this morning. At dawn everyone got called out to look up because there were these big things, like birds or bats only bigger than any turkey vulture you could even imagine. They were circling around the top of the stack. I think they drove Berk out. He started climbing down the outside ladder and they just harried him and harried him and he fell before he got to the first perch-rest. He fell and made a mess—spun as he came down and hit headfirst. We all ran inside after that and were looking out the windows to see what they were up to when the Tallboys came over the fence.

"Now that the plant's mostly automated, the people who work it just do maintenance on the machines and watch the load—never as much as the plant was designed to make, at least these days. That, and they work the loaders that keep the coal flowing—several people on that full-time. But those big fellers just came in and killed two of us right off the bat, and another jumped on Sergeant White, who was just trying to get away. The others herded us like dogs into the cafeteria and closed all the shutters. We just crowded in the center of the room while they circled. You ever had one of those things nipping at your heels, ma'am?"

"No," Lambert said. "All the Reapers I've seen have been dead."

"Let's hope that record remains unbroken," Valentine said.

"Then for no reason, one just reached in and grabbed a fuel man. At least I think he was—he was covered in coal dust. It fed on him. Got blood everywhere. I'd seen finished-up bodies a couple times, but this was the first time I'd seen one eaten in the flesh. Horrible sight. Most of us turned away. Figure I owed the poor soul that, you know? Someone said his name was Dewey," Nicholas added, looking at the clerk who was writing down his words.

"How did you get the message to give us?"

"After the one ate that poor coker, he grabbed me. That's where these bloodstains come from, his hands. The big pale bastard held me close, like he was going to dance with me."

The last dance, some called it.

"So the Reaper looked me in the eye and spoke, splattering flecks of blood on my face. I washed it off in the river, of course. Told me that you had time to quit Kentucky, forty-eight hours to leave with the rest of them. Of course, they had a message for the Evansville folks too. Then he carried me out like I was a toddler and chucked me in one of the commute boats the power plant workers use, and I got to Evansville as fast as the motor would take me."

"What are their demands to the Evansville people?"

"An exchange, they call it. Evacuation of Evansville. Anyone who wants to leave will be free to go into Kentucky. Then the south Illinois Kurians move in."

"I thought Evansville belonged to the Ordnance Kur," Lambert said.

"Must be some kind of deal they worked out," Valentine said.

"I don't know politics," Nicholas said. "I just wanted out of there."

They spent a few more minutes questioning him about numbers, and then they had him sketch out a map of the plant to the best of his ability. With that, they sent him to the small base hospital to be examined.

Lambert called her first staff meeting in the dining room of the big house. Moytana was there for the Wolves, waiting with the remaining platoon until Southern Command could send a replacement, Gamecock represented the Bears, and Captain Ediyak the rank and file of Valentine's battalion. Patel had charge of the base in the operations room. There seemed no getting rid of his former sergeant, for which Valentine would be everlastingly grateful. The door opened, and Brother Mark slipped in, looking tired and a little wild-haired. Valentine wondered if he'd been sleeping the previous night's party off.

"I was hoping to make this a friendly get-together," she began, ignoring Brother Mark, who was neither fish nor fowl in Southern Command but knew more about the Kurian Order than even the experts in the Miskatonic. "But the Kurians had other ideas. Word's probably gotten around the camp that they've moved against us already."

"Yes, terrible bombing," Brother Mark said.

"Bombing?" Valentine asked.

"The conference in Elizabethtown," Brother Mark said. "All the legworm clans sent representatives from the big towns to work out which way Kentucky's going to go. Franklin, Lexington, and Paducah aren't represented there, except by members of their underground. The town's been hit twice already, so you might say Kur is being represented after all. We're not sure if the planes should be part of quorum call or not."

"There wouldn't be a flying rattlesnake on the planes, would there?" Valentine asked.

"How did you know?"

"I ran into them in Dallas and again when I was out west. They're a remarkable organization. They can fly everything they need to a location, set up a small airport, and operate for as long as you can feed them fuel and munitions. They even can build simple bombs and so on if you give them high explosives and scrap for bomb casings."

"Brother Mark," Lambert said, "we're dealing with a separate event. The Kurians have seized the power plant that supplies Evansville."

"Which Kurians?" Brother Mark asked.

"Illinois, south of Chicago," Valentine said.

"Why should that matter?" Gamecock asked.

"I'm surprised you don't—," Brother Mark began.

"It's a binary problem with me, suh. Kurians are either dead, and therefore not a problem, or alive, in which case I try to make them dead."

"There's more to it than that," Brother Mark said. "To the Ordnance Kur, their Illinois cousins are practically enemies of the same degree as the people in Kentucky. To their minds, they're handing the city over to some 'neutrals.' The Ordnance wants the traffic on the river flowing free again. The Ordnance doesn't have much in the way of brown-water craft on the Ohio. They have boats from the Great Lakes, but they couldn't bring such substantial vessels to the Ohio without cutting them up into sections and reassembling them. And the rivermen in Memphis and Louisiana don't feel like raking the Ordnance's nuts out of the fire."

"Who's dumb enough to stick their nuts in a fire, I want to know," Moytana said.

Brother Mark harrumphed. "*Chest*nuts. It's a phrase going back to—"

Lambert rapped the table. "Let's get back to the situation at hand."

"Southern Illinois's no threat," Moytana said. "What forces they have are busy guarding against Grog raids out of the hills between the Ohio and the Mississippi, and the rest keep an eye on

St. Louis. We could do worse. If the Ordnance decides to send that armored column that redhead wildcat claims is assembling and training there into Evansville, we wouldn't be able to stop them any more than the local leek cutters."

"Evansville has a hospital, workshops, manufacturers, horse farms, refineries for both ethanol and coal oil, factories even, never mind the agriculture—we need all that," Valentine said. "I'm not inclined to give it up."

"All those hospitals and factories and whatnot won't be much good if they blow up the power plant," Gamecock said. "You don't just pick up megawatt generators, you know."

"All the more reason to get them back," Valentine said.

"How do we do that against dug-in Reapers?" Moytana said.

"With enough covering fire, we can blow them out," Gamecock said, looking at the map.

"No, my guess is, despite wherever the hostages are, most of the Reapers will settle in near the generators or electronics— something we can't replace easily," Moytana said. Moytana's gray hair had turned a little whiter in the year Valentine had known him. "According to your vol, they're holding all the hostages in the workers' cafeteria."

"Logical." Gamecock put in. "Easy to feed them. Big enough for everyone to stay in one room, under observation. Warm and cozy."

"Packed in like that, a Reaper or two could kill them all in under a minute," Valentine said, remembering a "sporting event" he'd once attending in Memphis where a single Reaper executed ten men before a basketball shot-clock expired. Without the use of its arms.

"One problem. All those windows. We could put six Bears in that room in less than a second through those windows."

"Wolves can keep the gargoyles and harpies off of our backs. Bears take care of the Reapers. Power plant is back in our hands."

"If we can trust the map," Moytana said. "Someone needs to make a close reconnaissance before we plan anything. For all we know this is an elaborate trap—get all the Bears inside the place and blow it to hell. I think they want us to hit it," he continued. "They've probably got the whole place rigged. A ton of dead technicians, lights out in Evansville and Owensboro, and the resistance takes the fall."

"They're not that clever," Ediyak said.

"It doesn't hurt to act as though they are," Valentine said. "I'll ask Smoke about getting over there and taking a look tonight. She'll need transport."

"Better get her over here," Lambert said. "Where is she?"

"My quarters," Valentine said.

Lambert picked up the phone atop the table and gave instructions.

Most of those at the table found something interesting in the woodwork.

"My Wolves will drive her," Moytana said. "Light-duty truck, something inconspicuous."

"Any way we can get a twist on them?" Gamecock asked.

"Put the Whirlpool plant to work making generators," Brother Mark said.

"Something more immediate."

"There might be an easier way than assault," Valentine said.

"Head back to the Mississippi with the rest of the brigade?" Ediyak asked.

"No. Who's running those Reapers? We need to find the Kurian. Take the mastermind out of the equation and the whole thing will fall apart."

"He could be anywhere," Gamecock said. "We know there's no tower around, so it's probably hiding. When a Kurian wants to stay hidden, they're next to impossible to find."

"I don't think so," Valentine said. "He has to be near enough to the plant so he can control his Reapers day or night. Their range is limited to a dozen or so miles by day, maybe less. Kentucky is thickly wooded and hilly. He needs a high perch for good transmission."

"And one well guarded. Let's not forget what chickenshits they are, suh," Gamecock said.

Duvalier knocked and entered the room. She was wrapped up in one of Valentine's field coats. The table greeted her and she plopped down in a corner.

"Where on the river on the Ohio side is there a garrison?" Valentine asked the table.

Duvalier spoke up. "That's a pretty empty stretch, especially with Evansville in revolt."

"I say it's in a boat," Moytana said. "All it has to do is go over the side."

"In this weather?" Lambert said. "Kurians don't like cold. I think it would kill 'em. No, it's holed up. Brother Mark, could it be in the river somewhere? They look aquatic."

"That I don't know," Brother Mark said.

Lambert continued. "I was in a sort of a park that re-created their home planet—not Kur, which I think is warmer. It was quite warm, with shallow water."

"Boat still seems likely," Moytana said. "Mobile."

"No, it's high up," Ediyak said. "If it gets in trouble, it just launches itself into the air. They can glide for miles."

"How do you know?" Lambert said.

"I heard . . . before I defected over," she replied. "A friend in the underground told me he'd seen one glide away from a fire they'd started in his tower. He sailed off like he was in a glider."

Moytana was studying a map on the wall. "The bridge," Moytana said.

"Bridge?" Lambert said.

"New Bridge, the people in Owensboro call it. Just east of the city. Suspension bridge with two high pylons."

Lambert shook her head. "Too easy for us to get to."

"Not necessarily. Both ends are guarded."

"I've crossed it, a couple weeks back," Duvalier said. "North to south. I had a picture of a Moondagger and some letters, claimed I was looking for him. Smugglers bribe their way across all the time. One of the smugglers told me that it's actually harder to go north to south than the other way. Going north, they just check to make sure you aren't bringing weapons and ask about your business."

Moytana nodded. "The Kurians don't want their Ohio populace slipping across the river any more than they want Kentuckians visiting Ohio. That Kurian can get high enough so it's got a clear view of the power plant. The bridge and power plant can't be more than ten miles apart, I don't think. Clear line of sight, that is—not by road. Escape by air. Escape by boat. Escape by highway. It's perfect."

"Just guesswork," Gamecock said. "You know how many old cracking towers and water tanks and cell towers we've hit because somebody theorized that a Kurian just had to be there? All we came away with was a lot of rust on our gloves and birds' nests. I still say we wait for good, strong daylight and take out the Reapers. A Kurian's just a big bucket of ugly without his walking teeth."

"Not guesswork," Moytana said. "Our scouts have seen some new uniforms on that bridge recently. We've been paying attention because of this armored column reputed to be up from Bloomington way and it's the only intact bridge within sixty miles of Evansville. We keep a close watch on it through a telescope. There are some troops in big woolly overcoats that have showed up. All tall men in winter duty hats. They don't do anything; they just keep an eye on the Ordnance regulars. They look like high-level security types. Be easy for a Reaper to look like one from a distance, especially at night. He'd just pull his hat down and turn his collar up. We thought they might be there to clamp down on desertions or make sure smugglers aren't bringing necessities into Kentucky. But maybe not."

They worked out the details of Duvalier's reconnaissance, and Moytana took her out to find a pair of Wolf drivers for her. The nights were coming earlier and earlier, and they wanted to get her to the power plant by nightfall.

†

While Duvalier was off scouting the plant, Valentine spent an hour with his rifle and a weighted satchel on his back, training in an old grain elevator in Evansville. It had a similar-loading escalator that Valentine thought similar to the suspension cabling on the bridge, though the bridge's was larger and more graceful looking. He did a good deal of climbing on the inside of the elevator in the dark, getting used to the feel of hanging and climbing and resting. Then, when his muscles couldn't take the load anymore, he practiced balance work, using the gun as a balancing pole.

Duvalier returned the next morning while Valentine was sleeping. She was exhausted and smeared with coal dust and rust streaks. After everyone had gathered again, she gave a somnambulistic report, correcting a few details on the vol's map and delivering the unwelcome news that a platoon of Moondaggers now occupied the power plant as well.

"How do we get at the Kurian without it getting away?"

Gamecock said. "In the time it takes my Bears to fight their way onto the bridge, it could escape."

"We don't even know it's there," Brother Mark said. "And even if it is there, it will in all likelihood be presenting itself as a garbage can or a loose wire hanging from a floodlight."

"Not in this weather, I don't think," Valentine said. "It'll be inside where it's warm."

"I might be able to find it," Brother Mark said. "There's just one difficulty, however. It would have to be communicating with its Reapers. Or even better, feeding."

"Is that all?" Duvalier said. "You let me in to the plant again, and I'll arrange that."

"How?" Valentine asked, unaccountably nervous at the idea.

"I'll know that when I get there."

"When will we attack the bridge? Strong daylight?" Lambert asked.

"No," Valentine said. "We'll need dark, with no moon. The bridge is too well-guarded for anything else."

"I don't like breaking up my Bears," Gamecock said. "They're too used to working together as a team."

"You won't have to," Valentine said. "That bridge is a job for a whole regiment—which we don't have—or one man. If he's there, I'll get him."

Duvalier stiffened. "Val, the last time you went off on your own wildcatting, it took me and a town full of Grogs to go get you back. Let me go."

"No, you're going to be busy at the power plant, getting it back in once piece."

They worked out a plan involving Duvalier, the Wolves, and the Bears creating a diversion at the power plant, while Valentine and Brother Mark made a try for the Kurian on the bridge.

†

The big basement in the Legion House—as the men were beginning to call it—was something of a treasure trove. Besides a spare generator and the new communications room (inhabiting what had been before then a wine cellar; the precise climate control equipment was kind to the electronics—and the operator), it had an old bar that was now filled with boxes and odds and ends of the previous occupants, arranged like sedimentary layers in an archaeological dig. There were a few holdovers from when it was a nature center: glass cases and displays. Valentine planned to empty them and return them to the "lobby" behind the main doors, where they could post Javelin memorabilia. Above that were the stored clothes from the owner and his family, elegant suits and dresses too delicate for his men to make much use of. Then above that were piles of Moondagger clothing, uniforms and slipperlike footwear and odd Kurian icons, the most artful of which was a wooden frieze of the curve of the Earth's surface in near-silhouette, as though drawn from a picture taken from orbit, with a great nail like a railroad spike driven through it. The spike had curious etchwork in it. Valentine would have to have Brother Mark take a look at it when things calmed down and see if he could make anything of it.

Valentine found an interesting, richly woven Moondagger outfit that looked part prayer robe and part dress clothes and part military outfit. It must have belonged to some high-ranking Moondagger, judging from the beautiful knitwork around the collar and seams and cuffs. It had an attractive cummerbund or waist-wrap—he wasn't sure of the word—of a flexible material like a bandage that had numerous zip pockets. Inside, Valentine even found a little Ordnance currency.

Valentine had sought find some decent attire from the ex-owner's wardrobe, an outfit suitably impressive and redolent of status, but the Moondagger robe-uniform might serve even better.

Luckily it didn't smell—some of the Moondagger stuff was now rank and musty beyond belief.

With his clothes selected, Valentine and Brother Mark worked out a rough timetable. It was a cloudy night, as had become usual as November wore on.

He and Brother Mark put together a small truck and a canoe, tying it in the bed and on the roof and looking for all the world like they were departing for a fishing trip.

Then it was a bumpy drive with Valentine, Brother Mark, and a Wolf corporal at the wheel. He knew the roads, trails, and railroad cuts for miles around and promised to get them to the other side of Owensboro—a town that was still more or less neutral. Wolf scouts had gone into town, overcoats thrown over their uniforms but weapons carried openly, and eaten at a diner with Ordnance soldiers at another table. They both paid their bills with Ordnance currency. Kentucky might be semi-free, but it was still integrated with the Kurian Order economically.

Discussion about the quality of the apple pie available in Owensboro or the amazing coffee at the Hitch had to be curtailed when they parked above the river. Valentine and the Wolf scouted and decided they were near enough to the bridge to make it a quick trip but far enough to avoid observation from the guards. Valentine and their driver set about untying the canoe while Brother Mark set out food and thermoses. They were all in for a long, cold night.

†

"Cold night," Brother Mark said. His breath steamed on the riverbank in the shadow of the bridge on the northeast side. They had left the Wolf back with the truck. "So much for our In—long-lingering summer."

"Indian summer, you mean," Valentine said. "Indian summer's a good thing, especially up among the lakes in Minnesota."

The Quisling guards didn't have any dogs on this side; Valentine was thankful for that. He'd heard barking up on the bridge at the guard change and briefly worried about patrols.

The bridge itself was elegant, a delicate-looking road bridge. Two tall pylons, one at the north end, one at the south, supported the bridge with a series of cables. They looked rather like a pair of matching spiderwebs, Valentine thought. The cables weren't tied to bigger main cables such as in more famous suspension bridges such as the Golden Gate. Instead they all linked to one of the two supporting pylons.

"You near enough?" Valentine asked.

"There's a Kurian on that bridge. That's all I may determine."

"What does it feel like?" Valentine asked.

"How do you mean?"

"The mental impression they give. Is it a voice, or thoughts?"

"It's like a chill. An open window on a still winter day in an otherwise warm room. Like the heat is leaving my body and flowing toward—it."

Valentine thought it odd that Brother Mark might be describing the cold tingle that sometimes came over him when he passed close to a Reaper.

"I just need to know where to go."

"Somewhere high, is my guess. They can sense longer distances that way without the clutter of animal and vegetable life."

Valentine looked at the riverbank. The Ohio was lined with refuse, mostly bits of plastic: bags, cracked bottles with blocky lettering advertising energy and stamina, cartons that looked like they were meant to hold eggs, chunks of foam clinging together like the chunks of ice Eliza hopped across to escape slavery.

There'd been a saying among the workers at Xanadu in Ohio—he'd learned it while digging ditches: *Flush it in Ohio, and it washes up in Indiana.* Valentine had taken it to mean that the less competent of the Northwest Ordnance were given duties in Indiana, but it appeared the phrase had a literal truth to it as well.

Owensboro, across the river, slumbered. There were burned-out ruins on the north side near the older of the town's two bridges. The closer of the two had long since collapsed—or been destroyed to simplify the border between Kentucky and the Indiana portions of the Ordnance. The "new" bridge was a little over a mile to the west, linking a bypass road that ran around the edge of what had been the suburban part of the old river town.

The Wolf had told him that Owensboro was a lively little town, popular with shady traders who brought Kurian Order products into Kentucky and returned with legworm hides, crafts, tobacco, bourbon, and marijuana. The big conference center practically in the shadow of the old bridge was still intact, the site of a bustling flea market on "Market Saturdays" every other week.

Valentine searched the bridge. He found what he was looking for even without Brother Mark—a little cocoonlike structure high on the north pylon of the bridge.

"There," Valentine said, pointing.

Brother Mark squinted. "I am afraid my vision is not what it once was."

Valentine handed him some binoculars. There must have been enough light for him to see, for he followed the delicate cabling of the bridge up to the north pylon.

"Temporary," Brother Mark said. "That, my daring Valentine, is the Kurian equivalent of a hammock-tent. Or the Kurian is very small and very young, a new bud off an old sire. Where else would he get multiple Reapers?"

Brother Mark muttered something else about budding in secret or an authorized increase.

"Is he there?" Valentine asked.

"I'm—I think so. There's some activity. As I said, it may be young. But it's able to control multiple Reapers at once. It must be a prodigy."

"All the more reason to kill it when it's young."

Brother Mark lowered the binoculars. "Savage."

"It's the truth, savage or no."

Brother Mark reached into his pocket and extracted a bandless watch. "Better get on with it, then."

Valentine changed into the black Moondagger robes and thick wool socks. He didn't have a beard, but if he tousled his hair right, it gave him a mad, Rasputin-like air that went with the Moondagger apparel. He didn't have the little curved knife many of them carried either; they were prized trophies for Southern Command's soldiers.

The robes had plenty of room in the sleeves to hide his Cat claws on their breakaway twine.

"Go back to the boat," Valentine told Brother Mark. "If you see a lot of shooting without the flare going off, just head back for the other side. If they loose the dogs in the woods, head back to the other side. If I'm still alive, I'll figure some way back, hopefully through Evansville. I'd rather not swim in this water if I don't have to. We'll have a frost by morning, judging from this wind, and I don't want to die of hypothermia thanks to wet clothes."

Brother Mark's lips writhed. "I'll do what I can to confuse matters."

"You'll do nothing. The Ordnance bridge guards are professional soldiers. I broke through a sentry point once and they chased me across half of Kentucky."

"No, I was referring to our friend in that oversized wasp nest. I have some . . . abilities where our Kurian friends are concerned, and if it's an inexperienced mind, I may be able to keep him occupied so you can approach with him unaware."

"I'm glad I decided to bring you along," Valentine said.

"Further proof that I'm good at what I do," Brother Mark said. "Hurry along now, daring Valentine."

Brother Mark was a man of deep waters—if he was a man. Valentine was beginning to wonder if he was in fact a Lifeweaver.

But he didn't have time to think about it. The Bears were scheduled to hit the power plant in two hours—or when Valentine sent up a green flare.

He took his Type Three out of the horsehide sleeve, checked the action, placed a magazine inside it, and tucked his Cat claws into the wide sleeves of the Moondagger uniform-robe. With that, he set off up the riverbank.

†

Valentine considered trying to bull his way through with his brass ring and the Moondagger outfit, but it looked like the sight lines for the guard posts covered the entire bridge. If he passed one they'd be able to see him all the way to the other.

Plus, there was a shadowy figure in the middle of the bridge that Valentine knew, without a doubt, was a Reaper. Undoubtedly there to guard its master Kurian in its nest high above.

So the easy way was out.

A Reaper, when alert and aware, was the most dangerous thing on two legs walking the earth. The eyes, ears, voice, and appetite of their Kurian, the avatars lived off of the blood of their victims.

Terrifyingly strong and juggernaut tough, they were almost impossible to sneak up on, as they could sense a sentient mind nearby. As they fed, they passed vital aura, spiritual energies Valentine only half understood, to the puppet-master animating them. After feeding, the Reaper sometimes lapsed into a half-awake state. Some believed the Kurian became either insensible in the manner of a drunkard or preoccupied with savoring the vital aura—that was the time to strike. Or during daylight, when the sun's energy interfered with the connection between Kurian and Reaper.

If I can't go up from the top of the bridge, I'll take the bottom.

Valentine heard a dog growl up on the bridge as he approached. He froze.

There weren't sentries patrolling the base of the bridge on this side. But up by the lights there were guards pacing here and there, checking the approach to the bridge.

Damn, he'd have to get wet after all.

The Kurians and their poor habits when it came to keeping roads, bridges, and utility lines in repair served them badly at the new bridge. They'd strung power lines along the side of the bridge to bring electricity into southern Indiana from the Kentucky plant. Valentine took his shoes off and tied them around his neck, and then waded out into the river and took advantage of cracks in the cement bridge pilings to climb up to the power lines.

Luckily the high-voltage lines were well insulated.

Valentine dangled from the line by his gloved hands, swaying in the funneled breezes under the bridge as he moved out over the river a few inches at a time. It was exhausting business, and soon his fingers, forearms, and shoulders burned and screamed. He hung, rested, caught his breath, and went on.

Once well out of the security lights around the roadblock at the north end, he swung up his torso and quickly rolled across the pedestrian wall on the bridge and dropped to the side, pressing himself into the shadows, and lay like a dead thing.

He quieted his mind. The only way to get past one was to camouflage yourself, body and brain. The first thing he'd been taught after becoming a Wolf was how to box up much of his consciousness and tuck it away for safekeeping. Breathe in, breathe out, letting go of worry. Breathe in, breathe out, giving your fear to the air. Breathe in, breathe out, breathe in, breathe out, your body is nothing but a puff of air, flowing invisibly across the landscape. Valentine lost himself in half-remembered poetry, gone where all things wise and fair descend, moving toward "that high Capital, where kingly Death keeps his pale court in beauty and decay."

Breathe in, breathe out.

He watched the Reaper. There was something robotic about its motions. Was the Reaper idling? Perhaps the Kurian was concentrating on his Reapers at the power plant and ignoring his guard below.

The Reaper passed, and none of the bridge guards was eager to approach its perimeter. Valentine noted that in its passing, the Reaper's foot slapped the pavement of the bridge. One of its boots was missing the sole; on the other the heel was flapping.

This Kurian didn't take very good care of his avatars. Or it had just moved far, fast.

†

The guards left the center of the bridge to the Reaper. It paced like a trapped tiger, from the north side of the bridge to the south, crossing right lane to left, and then back from south end to north.

He looked up at the Kurian's nest. There it was, like a spider's egg sac in a hayloft, high and tucked out of the weather.

Sometimes it pays to take the hard way, Valentine thought.

Valentine got the rhythm of the Reaper's route around the center pylon. When it turned its back on him and began to walk away, he jumped up to the suspension cable junction with the bridge proper. He went to one of the suspension cables, looped a utility worker's harness over the cable, and began to climb hand over hand with wool stocking feet wrapped about the cold steel.

He moved up the cable like an inchworm. The belt harness enabled him to rest when he needed to catch his breath.

But it was a cold, bad climb. Numb fingers, couldn't feel his toes, aching arms and back . . .

He rested at the top, arm looped around a defunct aircraft warning light. Now it smelled like bat guano.

Off to the east he could see the power plant, lights illuminating the smokestack.

Valentine had seen Kurian cockleshells before. All he knew about them was that the paperlike material they were made of acted as both structure and climate control. For all he knew it was living cell material, some creature with no more ability to move or alter shape than an orange.

This odd bubo on the tower was about the size of compact car, perhaps the smallest such residence Valentine had ever seen.

He had considered bringing explosives on the venture, but the Angel Food was tricky stuff to work with, and Southern Command had departed with the good electric detonators. He might have to climb both ways only to have his bomb not work.

Valentine fixed a length of climbing line to the protective grid on the pylon-topping light and lowered himself to the Kurian's enclosure, rope looped around one leg and his waist.

The Kurian's nest was also a work of suspension. Two corkscrews of the odd material anchored it to the top of the pylon.

Valentine slipped on one of his Cat claws and slashed at one of the supports. The material was much tougher than it looked; it was like trying to cut wet nylon with a butter knife. Finally it gave way with a crackly groan.

Vision, air, sound—all cut off in an instant.

It was like someone had put a wet leather bag over his head. Seeing stars from it pressing against his eyes, he realized it must be the occupant.

Valentine had never been this close to a Kurian before.

He couldn't fight it without letting go of the rope and plummeting into the Ohio. If he reached up with his Cat claws, they'd go right through the Kurian, and he'd wind up scalping himself, or worse.

Consciousness filled with gluey sludge, he felt himself go dizzy and light-headed. The Kurian was taking over, denying him the use of arms and legs—

He settled for banging his head against the pylon over and over, hard.

OUT OUT OUT! Valentine ordered the confusion.

Seeing stars, hardly knowing which way was up, Valentine felt his stocking foot slip, and he found himself upside down, suddenly free of the clammy, cold bag.

Something below spun as it fell through the night: the Kurian, looking a little like a torn scarf with sewn-on legs as it dropped lifelessly toward the river, pushed by the wind rather than riding it.

And then he realized he was dangling by one lucky loop around his leg, enervated and confused, a hammering sound in his ears.

Valentine found purchase on the Kurian's cocoon and dropped on it like a man poleaxed. The texture of the surface against his cheek felt like a dried, oversized spitball.

Except he'd done a little too good a job with his claws—the structure fell away. It fell slowly and silently, like a Japanese paper lantern might, catching air within. Or perhaps the material was a substance engineered to be near lighter than air.

The rope around his leg whipped this time like a startled snake. Valentine lashed out and grabbed one of the severed struts that had held up the cocoon. He plunged his Cat claws into it.

Hanging there, Valentine swung his leg, retrieved the rope, and hung again by two supports. Where were the damn rungs? Other side. Valentine didn't so much swing as roll to the other side, feeling with stocking feet for purchase. Finally the steel rung was in his hand and he could think again.

Valentine wondered what the goddamn thing had done to him. It felt like it was still hanging there. He waved his hand behind his back—nothing.

Despite the ladder, getting back down wouldn't be so easy.

Valentine was caught in the horns of what Duvalier had called "the assassin's dilemma." Early on in his training, she said that any fool could walk up and kill a target, provided you learned enough about its habits and grounds. The pro knew how to get away clean, or if not clean, at least alive.

If he fired the flare from here it would certainly be seen by the observers at the power plant, but the troops on the ground would wonder who'd fired it and why. But he couldn't delay until he could creep away; it gave more time for the hostage-takers at the power plant to figure out why the Reapers were acting so oddly and react.

No, Gamecock's Bears had to strike, and soon.

But Valentine had an unexpected ally. The Reaper, suddenly undirected and fearful, froze, looking this way and that. Did its master Kurian's final mental state—assuming they felt anything so prosaic and human as fear—remain in its brain psyche the way a flash left a white echo on the retinas?

The Reaper rushed toward the guards on the Indiana side of the bridge. Unfortunately for the men there, they were the closer contingent.

The first man it reached it just knocked aside with a sweep of the arm that left its victim turned around like a broken doll and twitching. It grabbed a man seated in a small, triangular armored car—was Valentine's crouched image, the last thing its master Kurian saw, reminiscent of the guard's position?—and pulled the man's arm out.

Valentine could hear the screams even high up in the wind.

It took a pull or two, but the Reaper got the man out of the car. The window wasn't big enough for the purpose, so the door had to come off, with the man's torso used as leverage.

Valentine checked his equipment and began his descent. Equilibrium and energy slowly returned, and he dropped the last ten feet to the base of the bridge.

Soldiers from the south side of the bridge were nervously peeping over the lane divider, watching the Reaper hunt their comrades like a loosed dog in a chicken run.

Valentine snuck up next to an Ordnance officer.

"Are you just going to stand here and let your men get shredded?" Valentine demanded.

The officer turned on him. "Waiting for— Who the hell are you?"

"I'm with Vengeance Six," Valentine said.

"What the hell's Vengeance—"

"Moondagger special operations," Valentine said.

"Then where's the beard and dagger?"

"It interferes with the disguise," Valentine said, hoping the man would see only a scarred man with dark hair and features.

"That's a nice Atlanta Type Three," an Ordnance NCO said.

"I thought all you Moondagger types were issued Ordnance Columbus Assault—"

Valentine wanted to quit answering questions, and the best way to do that was to start questioning himself. "Captain, have you ever dealt with a rogue? They're unpredictable and very dangerous, worse than any rabid dog you've ever imagined."

"Glad to have you, but I'll need to—"

"Almighty, man, the thing's killed one of your men already. Let's work out who's subordinate to whom later. I need some light. A sudden burst of light always confuses them." Valentine passed him the oversized plastic derringer that served as his signal gun. "Send up a flare, would you?"

"Sir, where did you come from?"

"New Universal Church School, Utica," Valentine said, giving the name of one of Brother Mark's alma maters. "When I point up, fire the flare."

"Who are you to be—"

Valentine whipped off his glove and flashed his brass ring.

"If you want to try to corral it, be my guest," Valentine said.

"After you," the captain said. The wild Reaper was carrying around the unfortunate driver's head, hissing at it like Hamlet speaking to the jester of most excellent fancy.

"Where the hell did he come from?" an NCO asked a lieutenant in an undertone that Valentine heard easily as he walked toward the Reaper.

"I hate these special operation types," the captain said. "They never let us know anything until we start catching hell."

Valentine trotted up the side of the bridge toward the north side, which was like a disturbed anthill as the Ordnance soldiers ran this way and that. Only three men stayed at their station: a group at a machine gun covering the roadblock on the bridge. They swiveled the muzzle of their weapon to aim it at the Reaper.

Valentine put his Type Three to his shoulder. He knelt and braced against a pedestrian rail between the bridge side and the traffic lanes.

He raised his left hand and waved his pointed finger skyward.

When the flare exploded into a green glow, the Reaper froze in its activities for a second, startled. Valentine, positioned so that even if he missed he wouldn't strike one of the few remaining Ordnance troopers on the other side of the bridge, squeezed the trigger.

The heavy round struck the Reaper squarely on the butt. Valentine doubted the bullet penetrated more than one layer of the strong, unearthly weave the Reapers used in their robes.

Reapers can scream when they want to. It's a high-pitched sound reminiscent of sheet metal tearing. The men at the crew-served gun, seeing Valentine shoot, opened up with their weapon as well.

Their target, probably frightened by the sudden light, pain, and noise, flattened itself under the fire and scuttled north like a crab and sprang off the bridge with an uncanny jump.

The men with the machine gun tracked it, spraying tracer off into the night. It cleared nine feet of Indiana-side fence topped by three foot loops of razor wire, landed, and disappeared into the darkness.

Leaving behind a heel from its boot.

"You're in a helluva lot of trouble, buddy!" Valentine yelled at the gunner. "I was about to put a round down its throat when you startled the bastard into fleeing."

"Thing was going nuts. What—"

"Now I have to chase it down in the goddamn woods. You know

how dangerous that is, going into the woods after a wounded, pissed-off rogue like that?"

The green light began to pulse as the flare drifted down.

"You want us to sic the dogs on—" a corporal began.

"No, they'll just scare it. I'll have to hope it calms down enough so I can get a decent shot. And for Kur's sake, keep your men out of those woods. We've had enough bled for one night."

"Yes, er—"

"Get that gate. Unlike Jumpin' Jack Slash, I can't drop sixty feet and take off running. Is that a box of defensive grenades? Give me two. There's a good man. You never know."

Valentine hung the grenades on the Moondagger cummerbund and trotted off down the road. A pair of Ordnance medics went to work on the human wreckage left behind.

"Keep those dogs out of the woods," Valentine yelled at the officer, pointing.

He confused the officer just enough to get him to turn, and in that moment Valentine hopped over the rail of the bridge and dropped the twenty feet to the riverbank. Valentine took off into the Indiana woods.

He felt strange pity for the Reaper. What it remembered of its existence as a puppet of the master Kurian, Valentine didn't know. Would it be worse to awaken, confused and pained as a newborn, to a world of bullets and explosions all around and instinctive hunger that needed feeding, or to suddenly have control over your body again? Or was it something in between, where the Kurian gave his avatar ideas, needs, and desires, and let it carry them out with a little nudge now and then or a few words bubbling up out of the subconscious?

Valentine and Brother Mark rowed back across the river, fighting the downstream current that threatened to carry them within sight of the bridge. It would be light soon. There was a little high-way stop with a good roof that the Wolves used to keep an eye on the bridge. They could warm themselves there and have a hot meal that would refresh them for the slow, bumpy ride home.

"What's that?" Brother Mark asked, pointing behind them.

Valentine put the oar across his thighs and looked over his shoulder. Something like a turtle's back was cutting through the current. Valentine saw a face come up for air.

"That," Valentine said, "is a Reaper head."

It wasn't swimming hard to intercept them; it was just following.

Valentine put his oar in the water and took six vigorous strokes while he thought. Then he set the oar in the bottom of the canoe and carefully turned around.

He took up one of the Ordnance hand grenades. It was the more powerful of the two used by their military, designed to be thrown from cover at an advancing enemy. Javelin had captured plenty from the Moondaggers, who used them to clear buildings.

"Hold up for a moment," Valentine said.

After a quick read of the yellow letters on the side to double-check the instructions, Valentine stripped off the red safety tape and pulled the fuse pin. The grenade whispered like a snake.

He knew better than to stand up in a canoe, so, kneeling and bracing as best as he could, he hurled the grenade at the following head.

It was a poor throw. It plopped short and detonated in a fountain of water with a rumbling roar that sounded like an oversized toilet flushing.

"Well done, my man," Brother Mark said.

"We'll see," Valentine said.

The last of the water fell and the head was still there, though it had halted and drifted with the current. It took a cautious stroke or two toward them again, letting the current put more distance between them.

"Not easily discouraged," Brother Mark said.

"Row hard," Valentine said.

Paddling hard enough to froth the river, with Valentine steering and Brother Mark puffing with the effort of providing power, they beached the canoe on the little brush-overgrown spit that they'd used to cautiously launch it a few hours before.

The Reaper scuttled up and out of the water sideways, like the crabs Valentine had seen on the Gulf Coast.

"Lord, oh lord, the thing's stalking us," Brother Mark said.

It had killed before but not fed. Valentine saw the yellow eyes, bright with something that was probably hunger in this cold, fixed on the slower-moving Brother Mark.

Valentine no longer felt sorry for the creature. The easy sympathy that came when he pictured it wandering the woods, confused and hungry, had been replaced by pale-skinned, black-fanged reality.

"Anything in your bag of tricks that lets you suggest something to a Reaper? Like going back across the river and trying the hunting in Indiana?"

Brother Mark closed his eyes, opened them, and then closed them again, this time firmly. "No, Major, nothing, I'm afraid. I get no sense of a mind there, not even a human one."

Valentine put his sights on it and it froze. It retained enough knowledge, then, to know what a pointed gun meant.

That made it more dangerous.

It slipped behind a tree with a swift step that cut the air like the sound of an arrow in flight.

"Shit," Valentine said.

He had one hope left.

A predator has a stronger survival instinct than most people credit it with. To the hunting cat or the pursuing wolf, serious injury is synonymous with death. If not defending young or scrapping with a challenger for territory, a predator will usually shy away from an aggressive display, especially if you can overawe it in size and noise.

Of course this isn't the case with all meat eaters. A wolverine or a bear will often welcome a fight.

He handed his remaining grenade to Brother Mark. "If it gets its tongue in me, toss this. They get lost in the act of feeding. You could run up and hang it off its back."

Valentine had lost a comrade in the old Labor Regiment that way near Weening, the night he killed his first Reaper. Weening still had the skull nailed to the town gate. The kids sometimes chalked words under it that appealed to a teenage sense of humor.

Valentine rolled up the Moodagger sleeves and slipped into his old, comfortable Cat claws. He advanced on the Reaper, arms spread wide.

It peeked from around the bole of the tree at him.

"Ha!" Valentine shouted. He swept one outstretched arm against winter-bare branches, stripping bark and crackling twigs.

"Ha!" Valentine shouted again, pantomiming a lunge as he approached.

"HA!" he tried again, stomping hard with his good leg.

If it came at him, he might still live. A good swipe across the nose might blind it.

The Reaper was dripping water from its robes but not moving. Nothing to do but go all in.

Valentine ran at it with a scream, and its eyes widened. It sprang away, running hard to the east up through the riverbank brush.

Valentine pursued it for as long as he could keep up the sprint and then lobbed a rock in its direction. His aim was better this time. The stone struck it in the leg and it jumped, crashing through some low-hanging branches and falling. It picked itself up and kept running.

"Yeah, you do that," Valentine puffed.

Valentine wasn't looking forward to the walk back to the truck. He'd have his rifle up and his sphincter tight the whole way, leading Brother Mark in wide circuits around anything big enough to hide the Reaper.

He had the funny feeling they hadn't seen the last of this fellow. And he'd have to pass the news to the Kentucky volunteers that there was a wild Reaper loose on their side of the river.

Just what the remaining Wolves and Bears would want to hear after the action at the power plant—assuming some catastrophe hadn't left the grounds of the power plant strewn with bodies.

†

They drove back Fort Seng at a crawl, the vegetable-oil-powered diesel banging away in first and second gear over the broken-down roads. Valentine, exhausted and half-asleep in his seat, had the driver take them to the power plant first.

He was relieved to see a pair of Wolves step out and halt them on the last turn before the plant. They had to carefully go off road and route around a roadblock the Wolves had cut, unsure of the possibilities of a counterattack from the bridge and wanting to hold it up long enough for the Bears and Wolves—and one unpredictable Cat—to escape.

They found the power plant in Southern Command's hands and only lightly damaged in the offices, where explosives had been used to drive out the confused Reapers.

Valentine felt dwarfed by the immense architecture of the

power plant and the towering smokestack. It seemed like a monument that would stand forever, like Independence Rock in Wyoming or the great Kurian tower in Seattle.

"Made angel food out of 'em, sir," Chieftain, the senior Bear NCO, said. He liked to decorate his uniform with feathers of various raptors—and a vulture or two.

Silvertip, another Bear who loved Kentucky and had decided to settle there and become a dealer in legworm leather, was partially undressed, sitting in the chill air and carefully scrubbing blood out of his studded leather with an old toothbrush. "Six," Silvertip said. "Don't remember ever taking so many in one day before."

"The Ghost did that," Chieftain said. "Shut down their master. Wolves saw the flare, certain enough, and got word to us. We went in and found the whole place in a tumult."

"Where's Ali?" Valentine asked. There were several leather-winged harpy bodies in a pile near the gate. Not enough for Valentine's taste, but they'd picked off a few.

"The Cat? I think she's sleeping in the kitchen."

There were Wolves near the exterior door, all asleep with bits of a meal scattered across the floor except one sergeant in deer-skins quietly putting a freshly cleaned Remington back together. He pointed Valentine in the direction of the cafeteria.

The cafeteria had blood and black Reaper tar on the floor and a good deal of damage to the walls from bullet holes. The windows were broken where the Bears had come in.

Valentine found Duvalier in the kitchen, curled up between a steaming stove and a basket of potatoes. One of his Wolves was opening cans of tomatoes and pouring them into a vast soup pot.

She was sleeping cradling her sword stick, looking like a little girl snuggling with an anorexic doll. Valentine nudged her with a toe.

"Good job," he said as she blinked awake and yawned.

"You found the Kurian."

"Where we thought he was," Valentine said. "Just a little one."

"He was hungry enough."

"How did you feed him?"

"With the Moondaggers," Duvalier said, pouring herself some coffee from an urn. "It was like one of those *Noonside Passions* episodes I used to watch in New Orleans. I pretended to be a girl looking for her brother who was being held in the power plant, and this sergeant promised to get him back for me. The name I gave was for a dead man. Lying bastard. So he slobbered on me for a bit and then fobbed me off on a private to take me back to the gate where other family members were waiting, trying to shout messages to the men in the cafeteria.

"I played up to the private a little, the sergeant saw it and got jealous, and the next thing you knew they were fighting. Some officer-priest broke it up, took me away for 'counseling' and he started groping me five minutes later. I screamed bloody murder and the next thing you know half the Moondaggers were fighting with each other. I'll admit, I egged it on a bit by snatching a dagger and sticking it in the priest's kidney. The Reapers broke it up and killed two of them and hauled the bunch of us into the cafeteria. Then they lost it and started running around like a chickens with their heads off. Next thing I knew the Bears were coming in the windows."

"Your feminine wiles have lost nothing over the years," Valentine said.

She snorted. "Dream on, Valentine. I think they put Chope or one of the other Church aphrodisiacs in that syrupy fruit juice they drink. I tell you, Val, there isn't enough hot water in the world to wash off the grubby fingerprints."

CHAPTER SEVEN

O wensboro, December: Kentucky's third largest city, though a little smaller than nearby Evansville, has a vaguely Bohemian air to it. Long a riverfront town, Owensboro had its moments of fame: Its courthouse was burned by Confederate raiders during the Civil War, and once, at the turn of the twentieth century, it had been shaping up to be one of the pivot points of the new automobile industry before being eclipsed by Ford in Detroit. It was also notable for being the site of the last public hanging in the United States, that of Rainey Bethea for the rape and murder of a septuagenarian named Lischa Edwards in the 1930s.

If Lexington is more bustling thanks to its status as a transport hub linking the Georgia Control and the rest of the middle and deep south Kurian Zones with the Ordnance and others to the north, and Louisville more industrious because of the huge legworm-rendering plants that turn quasi-insectoid flesh and a corn syrup sauce into WHAM!, Owensboro is proud of its cultural heritage. It prides itself on barbecue and bluegrass and, even in the reduced circumstances of the Kurian era, still manages to hold a few festivals a year dedicated to food and drink.

Now it is a popular watering hole for wealthy members of the Northwest Ordnance visiting from their vast homes and ranches in the delightful hills of southern Kentucky and the bluegrass outside Louisville. They enjoy the nominally illicit thrill of a visit across the river to dine and shop. The backdoor and under-the-table nature of the commerce along Owensboro's main street is the sizzle for goods that are often counterfeit, courtesy of the wily Kentuckians. The "Greek" olive oil is from Georgia, the "Colombian" coffee from Alabama, and the "Swiss" chocolate could be bought ten times cheaper in Pennsylvania. The gold in the quarter bars allegedly taken from Fort Knox is real enough; the identifying stamps aren't.

The bourbon, musical instruments, and barbecue sauce is real, however, as is the Kentucky weed. For some reason, plants that have been grown from seeds that passed through the digestive tract of a legworm are considered more valuable.

The giant sassafras tree—according to the locals the largest in the world—is still standing. It was recently the site of another public hanging, that of one of the Moondaggers from the nearby power plant who'd gone over the fence only to be run down by the city's impromptu militia, mobilized to render aid to Southern Command in the return of their plant workers.

The city is quieter than usual this December. Though often subdued in the winter, this time around the city is in lockdown. It's not the troubles at the power plant, or the revolt in Evansville, or the proximity of the forces of Southern Command that has closed the bridge and wharf to Kurian Order traffic. It is the great groups of strangers of all varieties coming in, from long-haired legworm ranchers to statuesque urbane females with gleaming leather courier bags and attractive wool suits.

There's a good deal of speculation about who the strangers are. The locals, for all their guitar picking and hurdy-gurdy cranking and trucks with smuggling compartments over the axles, are keener observers of Kentucky politics than it might seem. They suspect that they're playing host to the Kentucky Assembly but are willing to let history be made before they start talking about it in the main street's many cafés and bandstand joints.

†

The Crucible Legion, as it was now being styled, had its first field operation providing security on the streets of Owensboro. Valentine had a standing order to put anyone who called it "Valentine's Legion" to work filling potholes, and it didn't take many days of punishment with wheelbarrow and shovel before the name disappeared.

Both the informal name and the formal request to go to Owensboro had come through Brother Mark, who'd decamped without a moment's rest to the Assembly at Elizabethtown and engineered its move to Owensboro.

Valentine and Lambert allocated two companies to the security detail, one to provide a presence on the streets in town and a second in reserve just to the west, ready to move to the west bridge or travel on the Owensboro bypass as needed. Valentine gave the street detail's command to Ediyak, and Patel's company had the reserve duty. Ediyak had an intelligent charm about her that would mix well with civilians, and Patel could be relied upon to get his men from A to B in a hurry if it became necessary.

Valentine had little to do but get to know the town and keep his men from talking too much in the bars or being too high profile on the streets. The soldiers of the legion had the unusual orders to keep out of the establishments of the downtown they were guarding.

He felt odd patrolling a town not in Southern Command control, but as the Owensboro Emergency Council explained it, the delegates didn't trust some of the hotheads in the more vociferous clans not to try to storm the convention center and force the vote their way at gunpoint.

While the forces of Southern Command couldn't be called

"neutrals" in Kentucky politics, they were famous for letting the civilians carry out votes without anything more than a soldier's fatalistic interest in the events of elected officials.

All Valentine's soldiers could do was provide an illusion of security. They stood in pairs and trios on the street corners and walked through the old town square and along the rusted, broken river walk. But if a file of Northwest Ordnance gunboats came chugging down the Ohio, all they could do was point the delegates to their designated bombproofs.

Of course, an illusion could be a powerful thing, as Valentine had learned at substantial pain in the Kurian Zone.

Owensboro had a police force, of sorts, who appeared to have one law for the town's residents and another for strangers and transients. Valentine had to keep in the good graces of the local police captain, his deputies, and his "detectives"—who, as far as Valentine could tell, were in charge of extorting money from the shadier local establishments.

The Kentucky Assembly met at the waterfront conference center that played host to Owensboro's famous flea markets. Instead of socks and shoelaces and genuine Japanese electric razors, they traded votes during the day and drinks at night.

Valentine set up his command post in the old town welcome center right on the main street, with a good view of his observation post on the old severed bridge over the Ohio that ran into the center of town. The welcome center had become a sort of lounge for restaurant and accommodation touts and cabdrivers. The touts and drivers were so busy with the Kentucky Assembly in town, they had no need of a place to sit out of the weather and swap lies about their clients, and Valentine had moved in without any protest.

Brother Mark came in on a coal train with a few other delegates, including Tikka, now dressed in an impressive mix of cotton, legworm leather, and riding boots that made Valentine think of a dashing flying ace of the First World War. She looked Valentine levelly in the eye and shook his hand before excusing herself.

"That bright young woman's building an army for Kentucky. Or an Army of Kentucky, though they haven't settled on a name," Brother Mark said in admiration.

"I hope word doesn't get out."

"Kentucky is turning into the proverbial tar baby for the Kurian Order," Brother Mark bubbled. Valentine wondered if he was drunk. Perhaps it was the stimulation of so much social intercourse, running from faction to faction, picking up on the queer electrical currents that run through political assemblies. "They're like Br'er Fox, getting stuck in the tar."

"I think the version I heard had Br'er Rabbit getting stuck. Br'er Fox wins one for a change," Valentine said.

"Well, either way the analogy is sound. Every time the Kurians try to attack Kentucky, they only get themselves stuck in worse trouble. They sent the Moondaggers in after us, and they perpetrated outrages against a people that tend to pick up their guns and let the lead fly until the point of honor is settled. Just when matters were beginning to calm down, they tried their gambit at the power plant. Now all of Kentucky is talking about that over their back fences and cracker barrels."

"I've yet to see a cracker barrel my whole time in Kentucky," Valentine said. Brother Mark had a city man's habit of cornpone clichés to make his points about the rural folks.

"Yes, yes, well, you know what I mean. But they're stuck in worse now. The bombing of Elizabethtown is another example. It united the delegates just as it chased them out of the city. Half were ready to break off and go home until the bombs started falling."

"And delivered them right into our lap," Valentine said.

"You're a victim of your own success, my daring Valentine," Brother Mark said. "All Elizabethtown spoke of the way you handled the power plant difficulty, and that smothered the idea of moving to Bowling Green or Danville. When planes hit the conference center unexpectedly again in a night raid, they decided to relocate in secret to Owensboro. We picked up two more legworm clans and several of the towns in the south. The only major holdouts are the towns in the Cincinnati-Louisville-Lexington triangle, but you can hardly blame them, practically in the shadow of all those Kurian towers."

There was still a pretense of an assembly going on in Elizabethtown, complete with press notices. A radio broadcaster calling himself Dr. Samuel Johnson—Valentine had no idea if that was his real name or not, but he felt as though he should know the name—continued to report jumbled details and play recorded interviews allegedly obtained in Elizabethtown over what was probably Free Kentucky's only computer–telephone line hookup. Of course Kurian agents were hunting all around Elizabethtown for the site of the assembly, probably so it could be targeted for bombing again, but for now the decampment to Owensboro and the new swearing in of delegates at the high school basketball court had remained a secret.

They kept an "underground special" radio in Valentine's city headquarters for listening to Dr. Johnson's daily report. Valentine, who was right in Owensboro with the Assembly meeting only around the corner from him, knew more about how the debate was progressing from a transmitter in Elizabethtown than he did from local reports.

Odd world. But he'd noted that before.

There didn't seem to be much for his security team to do. In the end, his one great contribution was to take Pencil Boelnitz off the hands of the Assembly security team. He snuck into the Assembly once, was warned off, and was escorted out. When he got in again the very same day, the Assembly sergeant at arms demanded that he never see Boelnitz's classic profile again.

Valentine had the journalist put under guard and walked back to Fort Seng.

Even Brother Mark wouldn't update Valentine on the real progress of the debate. Valentine plied him with food and had Ediyak cut and style his hair—strange duty for someone with captain's bars, but she was as curious as Valentine about the progress of the debate and was willing to play sort of a Mata Hari with comb and straight razor.

"Sworn to secrecy, I'm afraid," Brother Mark said, wincing at the amount of gray exposed at his temples. "Everyone's afraid of an opinion getting back to the Kurians. There's a rule, until the actual Assembly vote, that none of the voting on motions and so on is to be recorded or reported."

"But Dr. Johnson's sources keep giving him a 'sense of the Assembly,'" Ediyak said, applying a little Macassar oil (Owensboro style—probably cooking oil with a little dye).

"Dr. Johnson is not necessarily accurate in his reports," Brother Mark said. "Remember, he's also reporting that they're meeting in an 'undisclosed location outside Elizabethtown.'"

"Well, that's true after a fashion," Valentine said. "About eighty miles outside Elizabethtown."

"Why didn't they do this last summer?" Ediyak asked.

"Karas was operating on his own hook with his own allied clans," Brother Mark said. "But some of Kentucky supported him and started putting together a democratic assembly, on paper at least. The Assembly is almost feudal, going back to the traditions of the Magna Carta. This is a collection of powerful and influential men and women. Kentucky's nobility, you might say."

"You wouldn't know it by how they're spending in town," Ediyak said.

"They're afraid to show their faces. If you see a man hurrying down the street with his collar turned up and his hat pulled down, I guarantee that's an Assembly member."

Brother Mark was willing to brief them on general parameters of the debate. There were three broad factions in the Assembly, the Old Deal Caucus, the Militant Independents, and the All-Ins. According to Brother Mark, the future of Kentucky would be determined by which way the Militant Independents voted.

"Hard to say what'll tip the balance," Brother Mark said. "The Kurians seem to have finally figured out that threatening Kentucky is causing more problems than it's solved."

The debate was raging among the people as well. Dr. Johnson, when he had no news to report, read letters and notes from a few phone calls and even news reports from overseas. Of course there was no knowing just how much the good doctor was editorializing, but the vast majority of the messages he read were in favor of Kentucky declaring itself against the Kurians, though there were mixed feelings about whether they should join the United Free Republics or no.

†

The United Free Republics, as it turned out, suddenly developed a diplomatic interest in the situation in Kentucky.

A civilian of Valentine's acquaintance named Sime arrived with more than a dozen security men and aides dressed in the ordinary buttoned, collarless shirts and denims, corduroys, and moleskins of the Kentuckians.

Valentine could only gape at the motorcade. He hadn't seen vehicles like this since driving Fran Paoli's big Lincoln out of the Ordnance on Halloween night. The one at the front was marred by a big brush cutter. The passenger van at the rear bore a medical red cross. All were excessively dirty, however.

Sime checked in at Valentine's security office on a blustery afternoon. At the moment, Valentine didn't have anything but oatmeal and hot apple cider to serve his elegant visitor.

Valentine wasn't sure how he felt about Sime. In some ways they were similar: in age, melting-pot heritage—Sime a dark chocolate and Valentine a native bronze—and general height and build. There were contrasts: Sime was smooth-skinned, Valentine scarred; Sime bald, Valentine long-haired. Valentine found Sime's usual scent of sandalwood and gentleman's talc appealing.

More important, every time Valentine became involved with Sime, Valentine seemed to end up in deeper difficulty. Now Sime was giving him the additional headache of keeping tabs on one of Southern Command's bigger political bugs.

Sime idled in the lobby, after requesting the Kentuckians for an opportunity to speak on behalf of Southern Command. Perhaps for power-play reasons of their own, the Assembly put him off for a day.

"You wouldn't have a shower in here somewhere?" Sime asked Valentine. He had an entourage of sixteen, personal security types and drivers and communication staff.

"There's hot water in the washroom. Best I can do. You're going to have difficulty finding accommodations in town, unless you want to squat in a rat run or take charity. You're welcome to stay on base, but it's a two-hour drive to Fort Seng."

"We can sleep in the vehicles. They're rigged for it."

"I don't suppose they're rigged to carry medical goods and antibiotics. We could really use some."

"Yes, we'll spare what we can. I've brought you the latest ravies vaccine too."

"New strain loose?"

"You'll have to ask the doctor. I believe it's just this year's booster," Sime said.

"We could really use a doctor at the post."

Sime pursed his lips, and Valentine knew the man well enough to know when his patience was wearing thin. "I thought you had support from Evansville."

"It's a small manufacturing city, and even that's not much good without raw materials. I don't want to strip the town of what little they have for their own people. And it helps to have a doctor who has to obey orders."

"Personnel isn't my specialty. Remember, I'm not here to support your guerrillas or *légion étrangère* or whatever you're running here."

"What are you going to tell the Assembly?" Valentine asked.

"What do you think I'll tell them?" Sime asked.

"A rousing speech promising the friendship of the Free Republics, as long as that friendship doesn't get measured in bootheels over the river," Valentine said.

Sime had a good poker face. No tells gave away whether he was angered or amused. "I may just surprise you. I hope you come and hear it."

"I'm afraid they won't let me in."

The lips tightened again. "The man handling security for the town? I'll see what I can do."

"Seems to me everything you've been involved in has been a disaster for Southern Command," Valentine said. Sime's smooth exterior made Valentine want to stick a pin in him just to see if he would pop. "Kansas, Javelin . . . what about the offensive in the Rio Grande Valley? Your handiwork too?"

"You earned your dislike, Valentine. Maybe one of these days you'll grow up and realize I'm in the same fight as you. I can't swing a blade and I shoot like a cross-eyed man and I'd be dead in a week if I had to eat preserved ration concentrate and WHAM! But I know people and I can read my audience."

"Bet that comes in handy when a Reaper tears the roof off your house."

"Maybe I'm better equipped for fighting the kind of battles the Kurians wage. They don't put—what's that phrase?—shit on target. They'd rather make their target give up and go home, or do a deal that swaps a few lives, a few towns, for a generation's security."

He stared at Valentine. Valentine recognized the challenge and tried to meet his eyes, held them for a long moment, and then found an old lighting fixture over Sime's shoulder suddenly of great interest.

Perhaps he had been unfair to Sime.

"Like you, I'm ready to make sacrifices for victory," Sime continued. "I was ready to give you up to get Kansas. And if I could trade your life for a different outcome in Kansas, I would, like a shot."

"The feeling's mutual."

"Would you, now, if it came to it?" Sime said. "If you could get the high country of Kansas back for us by just putting that pistol to my head and squeezing the trigger, would you?"

Valentine took his hand away from his belt and crossed his arms.

"It's never that easy," Valentine said.

"Your father would have."

"You knew him?"

"Not firsthand. But I know the history. He was what we called a plantation burner. Left a lot of scorched earth—and scorched bodies—behind. But it made the Kurians pull out of most of Missouri. I won't argue the results. I'm sorry if he told you different, but that's the truth of the matter."

"He never told me anything at all."

"You a fan of football, Valentine?"

"I know the basics, but I never had much time to follow it."

"I'm a big fan. We have some fair mud leagues running the spine from Little Rock to Texarkana. I'm a Buzzsaw man, myself."

Valentine had overheard enough sports talk to be conversant. "I've heard of them. I think they won the championship a few years back."

"Two seasons ago. Every good team needs what I like to call a hatchet. With the Buzzsaws, it's a linebacker. It's the crazy mean player, the guy who puts people down for a game or two. So instead of covering assignments, the opposing team's eyeing the hatchet, wondering who's going to be broken next. Bad sportsmanship? Maybe. But I've learned something before I started shaving my gray hairs. Most good organizations have a hatchet or two to do the dirty work."

"I see."

"You'd make a pretty good hatchet. You have the right name, anyway, thanks to your father's, well, fierce reputation."

Valentine shrugged. The gesture made him feel like a hypocrite— a shrug from a subordinate always annoyed him—but he was only too happy to use it himself with the slippery Sime. "I always thought of myself as more of a screwdriver. Always being used for jobs other than the one I'm designed to do."

†

Sime was good to his word. An Assembly ID showed up for Valentine the next day. Though he had to report to the Assembly's own sergeant at arms to get his picture taken with a Polaroid and have a card made.

The Assembly itself was run by the Agenda. That office was held by a woman, thin and wan and brittle-haired; she looked like a cancer victim. Brother Mark introduced Valentine to her. She greeted him gravely, made a polite mention of the power plant and said she hoped Kentucky would support his command in the manner of allies who'd bled together, and then she moved on to other business.

Her handshake was a frail one.

"You are no doubt wondering," Brother Mark said. "Some kind of cancer, but it's not public knowledge. She's doing her best to get through the Assembly before it claims her."

"Brave woman."

"From a great old family in Lexington," Brother Mark said. "Our good Agenda believes that however this goes, the Kurian Order is going to extract their revenge on whoever leads the Assembly. She intends to die quietly this winter and deny them the satisfaction."

Once the formalities were taken care of, Brother Mark showed him around the pre-22, poorly lit convention hall, which smelled like musty carpet and popcorn to Valentine's sensitive nose. A lectern platform stood at one end, with most of the folding chairs around more-or-less arranged to face it. On the platform was a lectern with its own podium and a small desk just above a discreetly placed recorder's station.

The Kentuckians, a smattering of representatives from the

Evansville area, and even a delegation from the rebels in West Virginia—he'd hoped Ahn-Kha would be among them but the golden Grog would have stood out among the men like an elk in a goat herd—had gathered into three distinct groups.

As Brother Mark explained it, the biggest faction in the room was the Militant Independents. A mixture of legworm clans and burghers, these Kentuckians believed that Kentucky now stood in a position of strength to negotiate with the Northwest Ordnance north of the Ohio and the Tennessee Kurians and the Georgia Control to the south. They had a provisional charter drawn up that declared Kentucky a self-governing territory with a promise not to engage in operations outside its old United States borders, nor to shelter fugitives or guerrillas.

"The fugitive law is the real sticking point," Brother Mark said. "Almost everyone in the legworm clan has a relative or an in-law who fled the Kurian Zone. They'd be grandfathered in, of course, but there's sympathy for escapees."

"How do they know the Kurians will go along with it?"

"I suspect there's already been some back-and-forth. Rumor has it a top-brass ring fixer has been negotiating in Louisville."

Valentine had heard of "fixers" before: trusted human intermediaries who handled difficulties between the various Kurian Zones. Without their intervention, the Kurians would eliminate each other in the snake-pit world of high-level Kurian politicking.

Was there a conference going on in, say, Chicago or Cleveland or Atlanta, with Kurian representatives meeting to determine what to do about the chaos in Kentucky? He hoped some stealthy Cat had managed to worm her way in to listen. Or better yet, plant a thermobaric bomb.

Next in size among the groups at the Assembly was the All-Ins. These delegates represented the legworm clans gathered under

"King" Karas last summer for Javelin and their supporting towns, the thinned-down remainders of the Kentucky Alliance who'd done much of the fighting in the destruction of the Moondaggers. They'd already beaten the Moondaggers and were expecting the other delegates to join them in a rebellion well-started, to their minds.

The Old Deal Caucus was the smallest contingent but, not surprisingly, the most polished and best turned out. They represented Kentucky's Kurian-occupied cities and those with financial interests in the Kurian system. They had their chairs in a circle in the far east corner, mostly talking among themselves.

Of all the delegates, these men and women from the Old Deal Caucus may have been the most courageous, to Valentine's mind. Their lives, and probably those of their families, would be forfeit if the Kurians learned of their presence here. The more hard-line rebels considered them only a baby step away from being open collaborators, and Valentine's sharp ears picked up one of the All-Ins saying that they should hang the lot of them.

Whichever way the Assembly ultimately voted, Valentine suspected that these delegates would suffer the most.

Maybe it was just ego, the desire to show Valentine that there were victories to be won in the political arena as well as on the battlefield, but Sime had facilitated Valentine's credentialing on the day he was scheduled to address the Assembly on behalf of Southern Command.

†

Sime, looking like a walking advertising poster for skin toner, stepped to the podium as the Agenda introduced him from her little desk. Sime's aides had cleared away the Styrofoam cups and the scribble-covered scraps of provisional resolutions and vote-counts littering the podium and the stagelike platform. Much of the audience quieted—not just hushed voices and close-together heads, but true attention. Evidently all were interested in what he had to say.

"Thank you, Madam Agenda," Sime said.

"I come before you as a friend of liberty and an open enemy of the Kurian Order.

"This Assembly is now addressing the most vital question in human history. What is the future of our species?

"There are those who counsel for surrender. Certainly, deals may be struck with relative ease. Either the Northwest Ordnance or the Georgia Control would be happy to hand out a few brass rings, sign elaborate guarantees, and offer the usual Kurian promises of better food, housing, and medical care in exchange for the Kurian Order policing of criminals and troublemakers. Are there any voices who consider this their preferred option?"

The Assembly didn't produce so much as a cough. Had it been night, Valentine suspected he could have heard crickets outside.

"The next option is an understanding with the Kurians such as you lived under these past decades: the emasculated autonomy trading produce for peace before your martyred hero, Mr. King Karas, declared himself against our oppressors."

Several members stood up and began to applaud. Valentine recognized them as members of Sime's entourage, sprinkled about the assembly. The others who joined in on the recognition of the dead hero's name looked enthusiastic enough, but Valentine felt a little sickened by the planted enthusiasm.

Sime nodded solemnly, looking toward the circled chairs of the Old Deal Caucus. "The rightness of his decision, I think, is not questioned by anyone in this Assembly, even if the outcome was not all that we in the Free Republics hoped would come of our alliance.

"Are there any who think that all the blood shed across Kentucky between the Alliance clans and Southern Command's forces was wasted?"

"Madam Agenda," a delegate said, upon being recognized and permitted to speak. "The representative from through the woods and over the river forgets that Kentucky is more than just legworm ranchers. There are farms, mines, towns, and cities. Not all of us suffered reprisals. Even with the troubles up north, the Nashville Kur left us in peace, and the Georgia Control even pulled back from the borderlands."

A white-haired oldster cleared his throat. "Maybe the vamps don't know which way we're jumping, or even whether we're gonna jump, and they don't want to startle us. It's the sitting frog that's easiest to catch."

The Agenda pounded her gavel at her own small desk at the edge of the stagelike platform. "The delegate from Bowling Green will keep order."

Sime asked for permission to continue his address, and she nodded.

"There is a third alternative, one pursued by the Ozark Free Territory throughout its history, though we have recently been joined by Texas and much of Oklahoma and part of Kansas into the Free Republics. It is both the hardest and the easiest course: that of resistance.

"I say hardest because it means fighting, funerals, constant vigilance, loss of precious blood and matériel. Empty bellies in winter and blistered hands in summer. It has long been said that freedom is not free, but in the United Free Republics we've learned that those who desire freedom pay a bill more costly than the alternatives of supplication or cooperation. Freedom is a more exacting taskmaster than any Kurian Lord."

Sime had worked up a good head of steam. Valentine realized why he survived as elected leaders came and went. "Yet it is also the easiest choice, for we can meet the terrible reckoning with a clear conscience that we remain human beings, dignity intact, our births and deaths ordered only by our Lord on his Eternal Throne.

"We will not be chickens in a coop or pigs in a pen. No, we're the wolves in the forest, the bears in their caves, and those who would have pelts made from us must beware.

"While our cause is yours, I must tell you that for the moment, all that Southern Command can promise is that we will tie down as many of the enemy forces as we can on our borders. We've suffered grave losses recently. We need a few years' respite to catch our breath before taking the offensive again. All I can offer the Assembly is moral support and what our forces near Evansville are able to recruit and train."

The Assembly hid their feelings well, but Valentine could see consternation in the All-In faction.

They applauded, politely, and Valentine could only imagine the reception Sime would have received if he'd promised a whole division of Guards, complete with an artillery train and armored-car support.

"I'm glad you didn't overpromise," Valentine said later as he and Sime watched Brother Mark go from group to group to exchange a few words with the faction leadership.

"It's the New Realism, Valentine."

"Putting 'new' in front of anything as tenuous as a word like 'realism' sounds like an excuse rather than a strategy."

"Nevertheless," Sime said coolly, "I have to work within the parameters of the possible, just as you do."

"And you agree with this New Realism?"

"Of course not. We can't beat the Kurians playing defense."

Either Sime was an unusually artful liar or he'd finally revealed something of himself beyond an official presence. "Something's been bothering me for years," Valentine said. "I hope you don't mind if I ask."

"Shoot," Sime said.

"I've met a lot of men who shave their skulls, but your head looks . . . polished. What's your secret?"

Sime's face broke into a wide smile. He flicked his forefinger down his nose. "I'll loan you my razor and we can go over to a washbasin—"

"On you it looks distinguished. I would look like a mental patient."

"If I let my real hair grow, I'd look much older. Be proud of yours. Not enough gray yet to dismay the twenty-year-olds."

"I never had luck with twenty-year-olds, even when I was twenty," Valentine said. "Where will you go next?"

"You know that joke the Denver Freehold tells about the UFR, don't you?" Sime asked.

"What's that?"

"*Too near for a penal colony, too big for an insane asylum, and too fractious to be a nation.* I heard a similar joke in the Mexican desert, just not so family friendly in language. I'll return to our insane penal colony nation."

"Can't say that I like you, sir. But I'm glad you're with the team," Valentine said.

"The feeling is mutual," Sime said. "By the way, did you enjoy that soap?" The first time they'd met, when Valentine was sitting in prison awaiting trial for the murder of some Quisling prisoners, he'd complimented Sime on the unique smell of his sandalwood soap. Sime had presented him with a supply before the launch of Javelin. Valentine found it's aroma relaxing, especially when worked into a fragrant lather in a steaming field-tub of water, and had used it frequently during the retreat whenever they paused long enough for a hot bath.

"Sadly, yes. Used it up last summer."

"I've a spare bar. I'll drop it by your fort on the way out. Oh, I'm taking Moytana back with me. The new broom wants a large reserve of Wolves ready to be shifted at need, and Moytana's due for an important promotion. Besides, his replacement has arrived."

†

Rumor had it the Assembly would vote before the first day of winter. Valentine found a reason to hang about the convention hall, hoping to run into Brother Mark in one of his circuits.

Valentine enjoyed the late fall air, chill but sunny. It reminded him of the Octobers of his youth in Minnesota. He wondered if the chill was characteristic of Kentucky this time of year.

A rather decrepit legworm stood facing the river. It was bare of all baggage, of course. Even the heavy saddle chair had been stripped off, and sheets of plastic tarp protected the legworm from the wind. Battle pads were on the side facing the street, with VOTE FOR FREEDOM = VENGEANCE painted on the mattresslike panels in Day-Glo colors.

Valentine felt for the legworm. In cold weather, their instinct was to gather in big heaps, forming domes that warmed and protected their eggs as living nests.

This dilapidated old creature had hide hanging off every which way and looked clearly uncomfortable on asphalt, glistening probes out to smell the air.

Valentine marked an ancient plastic refuse container holding a mix of leaves and refuse, probably from the quick cleanup of the convention center. Valentine picked it up and dumped it under the legworm's front end.

Where was the legworm's pilot? He could at least feed his beast.

"Wonder which end is worse, sometimes," a delegate said as he puffed politely nearby on a cigarette.

The legworm happily sucked up the refuse. Paper would be digested as regularly as the crackling leaves.

Valentine looked down its torn, perforated side. Skin was falling away in patches from—

Nature abhors regularity, and something about the pattern on the legworm's side facing the building disturbed Valentine.

Valentine quit breathing, froze. Sixteen holes in the legworm's side. He lifted a piece of loose skin, saw stitching in the legworm's hide.

He looked around, kicked some more refuse under the legworm's nose. He marked rings around the light sensors that passed for eyes. The creature wasn't old; it was ill cared for and badly fed. It had clearly been ridden on very little feed recently.

The legworm's anchor detached with a casual press to the carabiner attaching the drag chains to the fire hydrant serving as a hitching post.

"You!" he called to the smoker on the corner of the main drag. "Get everyone back from this side of the building. This worm's a bomb!"

When is it set to go off?

Valentine unsheathed his knife and prodded the creature in its sensitive underside.

Valentine crept along, keeping low in the gutter, moving the legworm along with shallow stabs. Clear fluid ran down the knife blade, making his hand sticky.

The legworm angled left, drawing away from the building as it slowly turned from the conference center, tracing a path as gradual a curve as an old highway on-ramp.

Duckwalking made his bad leg scream with pain. Valentine waited for the cataclysm that would snuff his life out like a candle in a blast of air.

The hungry legworm hit some of the overgrowth at the end of street. What had once been a pleasant river walk had largely collapsed into brush and small trees. The starving legworm settled into a hurried munch.

Valentine, launching off his good leg, used a saddle chain to swing up and over the beast and dashed for the convention center.

Whoever had spread the alarm didn't do a very good job. Several delegates, their ID cards whipped by the wind, ran out the doors on the worm's side.

"Not that way," Valentine yelled, waving them toward the main street.

Koosh! Koosh! Koosh! Koosh!

Valentine had his face in the pavement. Later, he was told by witnesses that some kind of charges had fired out of one side of the beast like cannons firing in an old pirate movie. Most of the charges fell in the Ohio, detonating in white fountains like a long series of dynamite fishing charges. Valentine, deafened, felt the patter of worm guts all around.

When the thunder stopped, he stood up. The worm had been opened messily, mostly in the direction of the river. Part of the northwest corner of the conference center looked like it had been struck by artillery fire.

Troops, police, and citizenry were running in from all directions. Valentine went to work getting help to the figures knocked off their feet or staggering around in a daze, turning chaos into order.

Valentine felt something squish and slip underfoot as he directed the confusion. He glanced down, expecting a brown smear of dog feces, and realized he was standing on a length of human intestine.

†

Incredibly, within a few hours of the blast the Assembly had reconvened.

"They are ready to vote," Brother Mark said. "They've excluded all non-Kentuckians from the Assembly."

Valentine saw the Evansville delegates decamp en masse for the beer halls and wine gardens of Owensboro—if you called a wood-paneled interior with a couple of potted palms a garden, that is.

"Which way do you think it'll go?" Valentine asked.

"Our, or rather, freedom's way, praise God. You know, that bomb ended up being ironic. It was obviously meant to blow the Assembly apart, but it ended up pulling them together. Another foot stuck well into mouth on the part of the Kurian Order. The one man killed was named Lucius F. B. Lincoln, by the way—a delegate from Paducah. A good name for today's entry into Kentucky history. He ended up doing more for the Cause by dying than we'll ever do, should we both live out our threescore and ten. The Assembly's all talking to each other again. I think they know those shaped charges would have torn through the Old Dealers or All-Ins without discriminating according to political belief."

"That's a hard way to put it," Valentine said.

"It's a hard world. I tell you, Valentine, that bomb couldn't have worked better if we planned it and one of our Cats had done it herself."

"You don't think we did, I hope," Valentine said.

"I don't know that we're that clever."

"I'd say ruthless," Valentine said.

"Oh, mass manipulation isn't all that hard," Brother Mark said. "I had whole seminars devoted to it. We're herd animals, Valentine. One good startle and we flock together. Then once you get us going, we all run in the same direction. There's a lot of power in a stampede, if you channel it properly."

"Perhaps. But it can also send your herd right off a cliff," Valentine said, "the way our ancestors used to hunt buffalo. Saved a lot of effort with spears and arrows."

"You're a curious creature, son. I can never make out whether you're a shepherd or a wolf."

"Black sheep," Valentine said.

"No, there's hunter in you."

Valentine nodded to some relief sentries, and said to them, "When the post has been turned over, head over to the diner and get some food. Kentucky is buying our meals, for once."

He turned back to the old churchman. "When I was inducted into the Wolves, the Lifeweaver warned me I'd never be the same. I'd be forever sundered from my fellow man, or words to that effect. I was too keen to get on with it to pay much attention."

"It's a bargain most of the men in your profession make, and it's a very, very old one. War changes a man, separates him from someone who hasn't seen it. You're both exalted and damned at the same time by the experience."

"What about you?" Valentine asked. "You've seen your share of fighting."

"Oh, I was damned before I saw my first battlefield."

†

Valentine was organizing his soldiers to block nonexistent traffic two blocks away from the convention center, using old rust buckets dragged into position as roadblocks.

Mr. Lincoln, the only man killed, had been running to jump in the river when the charges in the legworm went off. There was some bickering when his underage daughter, who had accompanied him to the Assembly, was given his place in the voting. Some said her sobs swayed a few critical votes.

He heard the commotion, the yells and firearms being discharged after the vote was tallied.

Some security. There weren't supposed to be firearms in the conference center. Well, Valentine's men were responsible for the streets; it was the sergeant at arms of the Assembly who'd been negligent. That, or after the bomb attack, they'd allowed the delegates to arm themselves.

Valentine sent a detail under a formidably tall Texan to get the delegates to unload their pieces and opened up a line of communication to Lambert at Fort Seng, which could radio relay to Southern Command.

Tikka herself was the first out of the convention center. She had a red streamer tied to the barrel of her rifle. The streamer matched the flame in her eyes.

"The vote was 139 to 31!" she said, leaping into Valentine's arms and wrapping her hard-muscled legs around his back. Her lips were hot and vital. "Five blanks in protest," she said when she was finished kissing him. "Cowards."

"For the Cause?" Valentine asked.

"I wouldn't have run otherwise," she said. "I want to fuck, to celebrate. You had a hand in this."

"That's all I can afford to put in at the moment. I'm on duty."

"Isn't part of your duty to maintain close contact with your Kentucky allies?"

"The closest kind of cooperation," Valentine said. "But we've just had a bomb explode, and no one seems to have any idea who brought a forty-foot legworm into town and how it was parked next to the Assembly."

She slipped off. "Too bad. May I use your radio? I want to communicate with my command."

Energetic Tikka. Denied one piece of equipment, she'll requisition another.

Valentine nodded and led her to his radio operator. Tikka almost bodychecked him out of his chair in her eagerness to put the headset on. Valentine knew he should really get it confirmed and look at an official roll count for his own report, but he trusted Tikka.

Valentine noted the time and vote on his duty log, and carefully covered the page so the cheap pencil (taken from the narthex of a New Universal Church, where lots are available to write "confessions," which were, in practice, accusations against a relative or neighbor) wouldn't smear. You never know what might end up in some museum case.

"Yes," Tikka said over the radio. "Put Warfoot into effect and open up the training camps." She pressed her earpiece to her head. "Oh, that's a big affirmative. Couldn't have gone better. Lost one delegate, but every cause needs a martyr."

Valentine, when he later considered her words over the radio, wondered just how large a role Tikka had in Mr. Lincoln's martyrdom. He hoped Tikka was just being her usual, brutally direct self. What he'd seen of the birth of the Kentucky Freehold was bloody enough, without adding deliberate political murder to the tally.

CHAPTER EIGHT

*T*he *Kentucky Freehold: Births are messy endeavors, biological or political.*

Even the name "Kentucky Freehold" could be considered a mess, because the territory under control of the Assembly didn't include her two most populous cities, but it did include a few counties in Tennessee between the Big South Fork and Dale Hollow Lake and the chunk of Indiana around Evansville.

In that winter of 2076, the Kentucky Freehold voted into existence by the Assembly was a name only. There wasn't even a cohesive idea behind the name. There was no constitution, no separation of powers, no way to raise money nor legitimate channels in which to spend it. In the weeks after the vote, the Assembly adjourned to their home clans, towns, estates, and businesses to work out quick elections of delegates to the new freehold legislature.

The one piece of business the Assembly did manage to conduct was to vote into existence an Army of Kentucky. The A-o-K, as it came to be known, was to receive all the "manpower or material necessary to effect a defense of the Kentucky Free State," but who was to give what was left to the parties concerned.

As to the Southern Command forces in Kentucky, the Assembly reasoned that forces at Fort Seng were installed to help Kentucky—and help, to the Assembly's mind, would flow like water through a pipe from Southern Command's little force to Kentucky.

†

Fort Seng was full of new arrivals.

Valentine thought he was dreaming when he met the first of them as he led his companies back from Owensboro. A handsome young black man in Wolf deerskins emerged from cover at a good overwatch on the highway running east from Henderson to Owensboro.

"Frat," Valentine said. "You can't be— You're Moytana's replacement?" It wouldn't do to hug in front of all the men, so he settled for an exchange of salutes and handshakes.

Valentine hadn't seen him in years, since he'd discovered him in Wisconsin living with Molly Carlson's family. Though they'd never served together beyond the events in Wisconsin, Valentine's recommendation had won him a place in the Wolves.

The commission Frat had earned on his own.

"Major Valentine. Welcome back. We've heard the good news about the vote," he said in a deeper voice than Valentine remembered. He wore lieutenant's bars, and had dark campaign stripes running across the shoulder fabric on his ammunition vest.

Valentine hopped out of the truck, tossing his diaper bag on the seat. He'd decided he liked the bag; he always seemed to be carrying paperwork, and it also comfortably fit a couple of spare pairs of underwear and an extra layer or two in case it turned colder.

Frat eyed the bag. "Heard you were dead, Major."

"I heard the same about you," Valentine said. "Frat," Valentine said again. It wouldn't do to stand dumbstruck, so he fiddled with his glove as he pulled it off. "Lieutenant Carlson, I mean."

"Good to see you, sir."

"Wolf replacements arrived, then?"

"My platoon, from the reserve. We were part of the regimental general reserve. We scouted for the Rio Grande operation, came home dog-tired and thinking, *Job well done.* Got the bad news once we reached Fort Smith. Men still wanted to go back and volunteered—but they sent us here instead."

"Moytana was a good officer. You can learn a lot from him, even if it's just by a quick changeover briefing and by reading his paperwork. I'll see if I can get a few of his Wolves to remain behind to orient your Wolves."

"Thank you, sir. Actually, I was glad to hear I'll be serving with you. Not exactly again, but . . ."

"I know what you mean. It's good to see you too, Lieutenant."

Valentine wondered why Frat was still only a lieutenant. Of course, he was very young, and the Wolves had nothing higher than colonel, so there were only so many spaces on the rungs to climb.

"I stopped in to see Molly on my way to Jonesboro," Frat said. "She sends her regards. I have a letter from Edward, but, well. . . you know."

"I know." Valentine found himself looking forward to reading it. Strange, that. He had a biological connection to a girl who barely knew he existed, and an invented fiction connecting him to another man's son. Life liked playing jokes with his feelings, rearranging relationships like an old magnetic poetry set.

"I'm not the only new arrival. My platoon guided in some civilians. Well, quasi-civilians, but I'll let herself explain it to you."

Valentine and Frat swapped chitchat the rest of the way back to Fort Seng. Frat made a few inquiries about Valentine's command. There were the most incredible rumors floating around Southern Command about his organization: They were all convicted criminals under death sentence, choosing service instead of the rope, or Valentine had an all-girl bodyguard of legworm-riding Amazons,

or he was building a private army of freebooters who were stripping Kentucky like locusts of everything from legworm egg hides
to bourbon.

"Southern Command scuttlebutt," Valentine said. "How I
miss it."

†

Back at Fort Seng, Valentine observed some new vehicles in the
well-guarded motor lot. The vehicles were an ill-matched set compared to Sime's quick-moving column and looked better suited for
extensive off-road operation. They had extra tires and cans marked
"diesel," "gas," and "water" mounted on them.

He reported to Lambert first, who only told him that they had
a new set of headaches for the battalion but that it might work out
to the benefit of the Cause in general and the battalion in particular. Then he drank a large, cold glass of milk—it was goat's milk;
cow milk had run out—and went out to observe the arrivals.

They were equally interested in meeting him. Frat offered to
introduce him to the visitors.

The gathering looked like a small, well-armed gypsy camp
filled with people in neatly mended surplus uniforms that had a
sort of broken double ring stitched on the shoulders.

If Valentine had been forced to describe the woman following
the corporal walking up to him, he would have said "statuesque."
Her face, under a bush hat with the brim stuck up on the left with
a jaunty feathered pin, might have been molded alabaster. He put
her age as fortyish or a very youthful-looking fifty, though her eyes
danced with an ageless sparkle, blue ice on fire. She wore a long
leather skirt and steel-tipped jodhpur boots with thick canvas half
chaps, and she evidently knew enough about uniforms to pick him
out as the ranking officer.

"Visitor in camp, Major," the corporal reported. "Mrs. O'Coombe, with a Southern Command travel warrant."

As Valentine introduced himself, she shook his hand. The almost challenging grip and steady eye contact marked her as a Texan.

Valentine knew the name O'Coombe. The family owned the largest cattle ranch in the United Free Republics—some said it stretched beyond the official borders. Now that he had a name, he even recognized the emblem on their fatigues, the Hooked O-C. They were said to be fabulously wealthy. At least as such things were measured in the Freehold.

"Mister Valentine. I've read about you on several occasions, as I recall. You're just the man I want to see about my venture into Kentucky."

She said the word "Mister" with such polite friendliness, he had no business correcting her. But her use of the word "venture" put Valentine on his guard. Was she some kind of wildcatter with an eye toward opening up a trade in legworm leather?

"I have here, Mister Valentine, a letter from the president himself. President Starpe was a good friend of my late husband's. He dined on our ranch on three occasions while in office and was a frequent visitor before."

She reached into her hacking jacket and removed a folded manila envelope. The letter within had a foil seal over a red-and-blue ribbon, with the outgoing presidential signature and a notation indicating it had been transcribed by his personal secretary.

After noting that it was simply addressed to "Officer, executive, or mariner commanding" and contained some polite words of thanks, Valentine read to the meat of the letter.

Please offer whatever aid and assistance to Mrs. Bethany
O'Coombe you consider practical. The retrieval and return

of any and all of our wounded left behind on last summer's
retreat would be, in my opinion, invaluable to our cause as
well as the morale of the forces of Southern Command.

Mrs. O'Coombe is a personal friend of mine. She can be
trusted with Southern Command information and matériel
relevant to her plans, and her signature would be accepted on
any equipment voucher if she requests the use of any device or
machine. I would consider it a singular favor for you to offer
her any assistance that does not materially endanger your
other duties.

A crusader. Valentine had seen a few in his time, dedicated to relieving Southern Command of the evils of drink or the dangers of professional women and syphilis. This woman was clearly here to do more than give a few speeches, take a few oaths, or show some slides of tertiary cases. Were these vehicles a specialized medical train to care for the few wounded that remained in Fort Seng's small hospital?

"I would be delighted to accommodate you, Mrs. O'Coombe. Please tell me, how may I be of service?"

She looked around before answering. "I understand that during the battles of this summer, some wounded were left behind with such of our Kentucky allies who could be trusted with their safety. I would like to help recover them. From what I understand of your expertise, Mister Valentine, you have a good deal of experience going in and getting people out of difficulty. I've hoped that you could aid me from the first I heard."

"Why here, Mrs. O'Coombe? As a Texan, I'd think you'd be more interested in the Rio Grande Valley. More troops were involved in that action, I believe. I suspect there are more wounded scattered around southern Texas than we have here. We had the advantage of legworms, you see. All but our worst cases could be moved while remaining in their beds—or hammocks, rather."

"I have a personal interest, Mister Valentine. I recently learned my son was among those left behind as your column retreated from the mountains." Her gaze wavered a little, and Valentine saw what he suspected to be tears. "I have come to get him back. I should like you to guide me across Kentucky. As you're the one who left our soldiers scattered across the Cumberland, I expect you would be the one best able to help me retrieve them."

Frat stiffened a little at that.

"I would suggest that you speak to my commanding officer, ma'am," Valentine suggested.

†

Lambert heard Mrs. O'Coombe out and invited her to enjoy what hospitality Fort Seng could provide while she considered the matter. Could she perhaps return this evening, for dinner, and there they could discuss the matter in detail?

Mrs. O'Coombe was much obliged and said she'd be delighted.

Valentine was curious, a little aggravated, and anything but delighted at Lambert's response.

"You're not considering sending me across Kentucky as a tour guide for that stack of grief, I hope, sir," he said once Mrs. O'Coombe had left the building.

"I'm certainly inclined to let her have you," Lambert said. "Apart from wanting our wounded back and safe, the gratitude of the Hooked O-C is well worth having. I expect she'll be as influential with the new president as the old."

"I didn't even know her son was with us," Valentine said. "Usually Southern Command tells us when we have to deal with a scion of the carriage trade. Quietly, but they tell us."

"Someone slipped up," Lambert agreed. "Noble of him to volunteer. Mom passed down something besides Texas sand."

Valentine didn't have a number one uniform worthy of a formal dinner with Lambert and their important guest. His least-patched ensemble was the militia corporal's uniform he wore when traveling in Southern Command, but that had bloodstains on it now, and no effort of soap or will could eradicate them.

He settled for the Moondagger robes he'd worn the night he knocked the young Kurian out of its tree, with his leaf clipped on the collar and a Southern Command tricolor pinned to the shoulder.

David Valentine wasn't one to stand in front of a mirror admiring himself, but he had to admit the Moondagger robe-uniform suited him. The various shades of black complemented his skin and dark hair and made his perfectly ordinary brown eyes look a little more striking when set in all that black. His old legworm boots gave him some dash and swagger with their silver accents. The scars on the left side of his face had healed down to not much more than big wrinkles and a pockmark, and the old companion descending his right cheek looked more like the romantic scarring of a dread pirate than the stupid souvenir of nearly having his head blown off.

The dinner was held in the conference room, complete with a white lace tablecloth and candlesticks.

It turned out he needn't have worried about his appearance. Colonel Lambert had invited an eclectic company to her dinner.

Mrs. O'Coombe was there in her same field skirt and little lace-up boots, only now garbed in a silken blouse and a— Valentine couldn't find the word for it. Stole? It was a leather half vest that went around behind her neck and hung down in two narrow pleats in front with bright brass emblems. All Valentine could think of was sleigh bells on a horse.

Fort Seng's three Logistic Commando wagon masters were there as well, two western Kentucky specialists and one more they'd hauled all the way to the Appalachians and back. They smelled faintly of stock animals and sweat, but they'd combed their hair and flattened it with oil. Patel wore his new legion-style captain's uniform and had polished his two canes. That was a bit unlike Nilay Patel; he was more the type to grit his teeth through an evening of aching knees and retire with a bottle of aspirin. Lambert looked trim and neat as one would expect, her hair brushed and shaped by a dress clip for the use of female officers. And finally Alessa Duvalier stood next to the fire, warming her backside and dressed in a little black outfit that must have been liberated from the basement, perhaps from some formal ball of the great man's daughter. A red bra peeked from behind the low-cut front. Valentine vaguely thought it was a sartorial faux pas, but Duvalier's red hair, spiky and disarrayed as usual, made it work.

Odd assortment. If Lambert wanted to impress Mrs. O'Coombe, why not invite Captain Ediyak with her model-cheekbone looks and polished Eastern manners? Why not Gamecock, who had a courtliness all his own behind the braids and scars, smooth as his rolling accent, that showed off some collective unconscious vestige of the grace of old South Carolina?

Brother Mark, the other obvious candidate, was off on a junket with the Agenda from the late Assembly. Or, more correctly, the soon-to-be-late Agenda. They were arranging for the establishment of a temporary government in Kentucky, and the ex-churchman wanted to plead for an office devoted to relations with allies in the Cause.

Valentine joined Duvalier at the fire.

"What the hell is that, Val?" she asked, fingering the finely patterned knit trim on the top robe.

"It's the nicest thing I have that fits me. Some Moondagger's dress-up outfit."

"I've seen those before," she said, her voice hardly more than a whisper. "That's what they wear when they have a date with a Reaper. They treat it like a wedding."

Valentine searched her eyes for some hint of a joke. She did sometimes put him on.

"No joke," she supplied.

"Well, it's still an attractive ensemble," Valentine said. "I like how it looks, so what the hell."

"Your funeral," Duvalier said.

Lambert finished making her introductions, and everyone sat. Valentine sat opposite Lambert with Patel on one side and Duvalier on the other, with the Logistics Commandoes near them. Mrs. O'Coombe was in the place of honor to Lambert's right.

Patel fiddled with his array of silverware. "Which is the one to clean the grease from one's lips, Major?" he asked quietly.

"You can dip your fingers in the fingerbowl and touch them to your lips when you're done eating," Valentine said under his breath.

Lambert, as host, got the Logistics Commandoes talking about their difficulty finding even food staples, with Southern Command currency worthless here and what was left of Colonel Bloom's booty pile diminishing rapidly.

"They want gold, or Kurian bank guarantees, or valuables for trade," one of the Kentuckians said. "We're out of all the usual stuff we trade. Our depots don't have dynamite or two-way radios; not even paper and ink or razor blades."

"The vote didn't change nothing," his friend added.

"We could send a few Wolves with the LCs on their next run, sir," Patel said. "Give them a choice of Southern Command scrip or lead."

Valentine was tempted. "No."

"Been done before, Major," Patel said.

The dishes came out. It was a meager dinner, "ration beef" and seasoned patties made from falafel and corn that would probably be allocated to the pigs on Mrs. O'Coombe's ranch.

Lambert spoke up. "We're trying to teach these recruits that just because you've got a uniform and a gun, whatever you can grab is not yours for the taking. We have to set an example. Tighten our belts."

"We'll be eating our belts before winter's up, at this rate," the third Logistics Commando said.

"Mister Valentine," Mrs. O'Coombe said. "I couldn't help overhearing your conversation regarding the supply difficulties. I'm traveling with a substantial amount of gold and Kurian Bills of Guarantee."

Duvalier choked on her apple juice.

"I've dealt on both sides of the border often enough to know that one needs hard assets and negotiables to overcome certain bureaucratic difficulties."

"Excuse me, madam, but where did you get bills?" Valentine asked. Bills were certificates guaranteeing "employment, useful or otherwise" for a set period, usually five or ten years. They were extremely difficult to forge. Some said the seals acted in much the same manner as a brass ring, and they were very valuable in the Kurian Zone. Many an old-timer would trade his entire life's accumulation for a five-year certificate.

She read Patel's scowl. "If you think I trade cattle on both sides of Nomansland out of greed, you're wrong, sir. I sometimes find it useful to bribe for or buy what I cannot obtain in the Free Republics."

If she was in a giving vein, Valentine did not want to spoil her mood with accusations. He tapped Patel in the ankle. "Of course we'd be grateful for your assistance. What can you spare?"

"I can give you six thousand C-coin in gold and six Kurian five-year bills. You will, of course, sign a promissory note that I may redeem back at Fort Smith for their cash value, assessed per Logistic Commando fair market pricing of whichever month is current when I turn them in."

Southern Command, perpetually starved for precious metals, would be thrilled to have Mrs. O'Coombe show up demanding hundred-dollar gold coins by the roll. Frontier posts kept gold on hand for smugglers coming out of the Kurian Zone with antibiotics or computer chips or hard intelligence, and they'd be loath to part with it for nothing but a promissory note from a written-off outpost.

How would the loan change the status of Mrs. O'Coombe on the post? The men would learn she was buying their cornmeal and chickens and bacon, one way or another. Suppose she started issuing them orders, as though they were her bunkhouse cowpunchers?

"Dangerous to be traveling with that much gold, ma'am," Patel said, breaking in on Valentine's thoughts. Obvious thing to say. Perhaps Patel was buying him time to think it over.

She smiled, dazzling white teeth against those pink lips. "More dangerous than Reapers, Mister Patel?"

The men had to be fed, one way or another. The only other option would be to go in and take it at gunpoint, and they weren't pirates. At least not yet.

Valentine weighed his options. Once Kentucky got itself organized, Fort Seng would petition for support from the Assembly. Though Valentine wondered if his forces, being neither fish nor fowl, so to speak, would find themselves divested of support from both the rebels in Kentucky and his own Southern Command, especially once General Martinez took over and instituted his new "defensive" policies.

Mrs. O'Coombe waited, her hands clasped decorously in her lap. She'd only nibbled politely at the meager fare.

"Madam, I accept your very generous offer on behalf of my men," Lambert said, her train of thought arriving at the decision platform.

"Always willing to help the Cause, Colonel," Mrs. O'Coombe said. "Now, Mister Valentine, perhaps you will attend to the matter of facilitating me in the effort of finding my son. I would like your advice on routes and what sort of personnel we should bring."

"A complicated question, madam," Valentine said. "It depends on supply capacity in your vehicles, what sort of fuel they need . . ."

Duvalier hummed quietly:

The choice tan, the bought man,
Prisoner 'tween golden sheets . . .

It was a pop tune from just before the cataclysm in 2022 and had been prominently listed on most barroom virtual disc-jockey machines.

Patel let off an explosive fart and excused himself, but it stopped Duvalier's quiet amusement.

Well, if Valentine was going to take her gold, he'd get more for it than butter and eggs. Valentine hemmed and hawed his way through the conversation about the trip to recover her son—and others, of course—and as usual struck upon an idea while his brain was busy fencing with Mrs. O'Coombe.

†

Valentine escaped Mrs. O'Coombe the next day, pleading that he had to go into Evansville to see about purchasing supplies.

Evansville had an impressive city hall thanks to the region's ample limestone, but it reminded Valentine of a church with long-dead parishioners. Most of the offices were empty.

They should have used the empty rooms for the overflowing waiting room. Luckily, his uniform brought him right to the attention of the city's governor.

How they arrived at that title Valentine didn't know then, but he later learned that since Evansville considered itself a different state than Kentucky even though it was now part of the Kentucky Free-hold, by definition it should have a governor as chief executive.

In this case the governor was a former member of the underground named Durand. Professor Durand, actually; he ran a secret college devoted to preserving classical Western education from the tailoring, trimming, and alteration of the Kurian Order.

He reminded Valentine a bit of Trotsky in his dress and glasses, minus the brains and the talent and the vigor.

"Can I help you, Major Valentine?" Durand asked. He was sorting papers into four piles on his desk, and he glanced up at Valentine as he stood before his desk.

Valentine would have sworn in court that he recognized some of the documents from his last visit three weeks ago, before the action at the power station, when he unsuccessfully pleaded for the Evansville provisional government to purchase supplies for Fort Seng.

"You've done so much already, Governor," Valentine said. "I'm simply here to pay my respects before we depart. A last duty call before I plunge into getting the camp relocated."

"Depart?" Durand asked, looking vaguely alarmed and suddenly less interested in the paperwork on his desk.

Valentine examined the walls of the office. A few corners of torn-off Kurian NUC enthusiasm posters remained between the windows. "Yes, the fort will be relocated. For security reasons I can't disclose our destination, but the town's leadership has made a most generous offer, and strategically it makes sense—we'll be closer to the center mass of Kentucky, able to operate on interior lines. . . . You know the military advantages."

"But . . . the underground has word of an armored column north of here. Cannon, armored cars, riot buses, gunabagoes . . ."

"Yes, how is the city militia progressing in its training? The key is to brush back the infantry support. Then it's much easier to take out the armor."

"You've made so many improvements to your camp, I understand. Hot water, electricity . . ."

"Perhaps your militia can relocate and take advantage of all our hard work. True, that would mean a longer response time if you needed them to deal with, say, some airdropped Reapers."

"What is this other town offering you?"

"Offering? I'm doing my duty, Professor, not engaging in bid taking."

"Surely Evansville has its advantages. The textile plant, the appliances, our phone system . . ."

"All are superior to central Kentucky, I grant you," Valentine said. "But my men are running short on eggs and dairy and fresh meat and vegetables. The new town has offered to supply us amply. I have to consider the health and fitness of my men."

Valentine took out some of the gold coins Mrs. O'Coombe had so generously offered. "Of course, we'll have more difficulty purchasing building materials, tenting, plumbing supplies, munitions, uniforms, and such in Kentucky. After I've finished here, I will visit the marketplace and see if I can't have a selection packed and ready for transport."

Durand's eyes watched the jingling coins. "We've had something of a food crisis here, as well," Durand said. "It appears to be easing since the vote to declare openly against the Kurian Order. We've been neglectful of our protectors across the river. Now we could easily restart the flow of foodstuffs. I expect a boat full of chickens and eggs could be put across in no time."

Valentine took out a piece of paper. "We'll need this every week." He passed the grocery list to Durand.

"Basic staples shouldn't be difficult. But chocolate?"

"Some of my soldiers have a sweet tooth, but I imagine most of it will end up in the stomachs of Evansville's beautiful young women."

"You drive a hard bargain, Major. Is this quite ethical? Extorting the people you promised to protect?"

"Evansville's delegates voted to support the armed resistance to the Kurian Order in men and matériel. I've most of the men I need. My material needs are small compared to the army they're trying to build outside the Kurian Triangle. You might consider yourself lucky."

"It appears we are bound to be symbionts, Major. I'll see to the deliveries of your foodstuffs."

"Then we shall be happy to remain in our comfortable and beautiful surroundings, with the congenial company of Evansville and Owensboro," Valentine said.

"I'm sure," Durand said. "I feel as though I've been played like a harp."

"If that column comes roaring south out of Bloomington, you'll be glad we stayed, or you might end up playing your own harp, sir."

†

He didn't want to go on Mrs. O'Coombe's expedition. He wished Moytana were still present; it would have been a much better assignment for a group of experienced Wolves.

It took a direct order from Lambert to get him to agree to do it.

They talked it over across her desk. Lambert had a policy that in private, when seated, you could talk to her without military formalities and treat her as a sounding board rather than a commander. It was a tradition Valentine had always followed with his own subordinates. Valentine remembered picking it up from Captain LeHavre. He wondered if Lambert had acquired it from Moira Styachowski.

Or did it come to Lambert from Valentine, in a roundabout way?

"Take whoever you like, just none of my captains," Lambert said, signing a blank ad hoc special duty personnel sheet and passing it to him.

Damn. So much for Patel. He could have ridden the whole way.

"I was thinking two Bears. Ali." As a Cat, Duvalier was considered a captain in rank, but Valentine suspected Lambert didn't need to hold on to her. "A Wolf scouting team."

"Medical staff?"

"They have enough to do here. Our patroness said she has her own medical team."

"Why don't you take Boelnitz too," Lambert said. "He's been making himself a nuisance here. I don't know if he's filed a story yet."

"Maybe he's working on a novel," Valentine said. He observed that Lambert's desk was as clean as an Archon's shaving mirror. Lambert managed to do a tremendous amount of work—she was in the process of reorganizing Fort Seng from the top down—but there was no evidence of it except for a three-drawer file cabinet and a brace of three-ring binders. Her clerk was always buzzing in and out like a pollen-laden honeybee, keeping the binders updated.

"I'd hate to be away if that column moves south," Valentine said.

"We'll just call you back," Lambert said. "Mrs. O'Coombe can delay them with a pillar of fire, and then spread her arms and part the Tennessee for us to get away."

Valentine couldn't say why he didn't like the idea of leaving Fort Seng. How do you put disquiet and restlessness into words? Normally he'd look forward to picking up his men and getting them on the road home—that sort of thing left a better aftertaste than surviving a battle.

One more thing bothered him. Red Dog had appeared a little nervous of late, always looking around with the whites of his eyes showing and hiding under tables and stonework. He'd even been dragged out from under the defunct hot tub in the estate house's garden gazebo.

Red Dog had been a tool of the Kurians in the retreat across Kentucky, when one Kurian had somehow linked through the dog's mind to Javelin's commanders at headquarters. If Red Dog was nervous, Valentine was nervous.

"Nice work at the dinner," Valentine said. "I think when Mrs. O'Coombe had to eat what we've been living on, it encouraged her to part with her gold."

"I just think she's a deeply decent person," Lambert said. "You don't often meet one of those."

"I met one back at the war college in Pine Bluff," Valentine said. "A little stick of a thing, always dotting *i*'s and crossing *t*'s."

"And I remember a shy young lieutenant who was always

looking at his shoes and talking about the weather when he should have been asking me to a dance," Lambert said.

"We were both too busy, I think," Valentine said.

"And now we're in a fort where Southern Command rules on down-chain, up-chain, and cross-chain fraternization will be strictly observed. And not 'strictly' in the fun, blindfold and handcuffs sense, either."

"Dirty Bird Colonel," Valentine laughed. "Hands off."

"That goes for your captain, too, Major."

"Nilay Patel and I share a love that cannot—"

"You know who I mean. I don't want Boelnitz returning to his paper with an episode of *Noonside Passions* ready for action."

"Yes, ma'am. But rest easy: Ediyak didn't earn that rapid rise the hard way."

Duvalier waited a beat. "You're impossible, Valentine. Anyway, let's keep it zipped up for once, shall we?"

"As long as you restrain yourself with Boelnitz. You've made time for how many interviews?"

"I don't recall him being in the chain of command," Lambert said. "And if he were, I'd just have my clerk make a new page minus his name. But point taken, Valentine. Honestly, the only thing I want to get intimate with is that hot tub, if Prist and Toyonikka get if functional again."

CHAPTER NINE

*C*ivilian *and military relations: Southern Command has a long
history of "turnouts" to offer assistance to civilians in need. Their ethic
might almost be described by the words "protect and serve."*

*Bases always serve as a temporary haven for the lost, dispossessed,
or desperate. The men and women in uniform know they depend on the
civilian populace for food and support. There are endless tales of whole
camps going hungry to share their rations with hard-up locals and their
children.*

*In return, civilians do what they can to provide for soldiers on the
march, act as spare pairs of eyes and ears, and put in extra hours as poorly
paid labor levies doing everything from laundry to garbage burial.*

*Especially in frontier areas, the soldiers are the only law and order
around. While they can't treat criminals as combatants, they do have
the power to hold someone until they can be turned over to civilian
authorities—and the farther out the base, the longer the wait for a mar-
shal or judge riding circuit to appear.*

*More important for this period in the turbulent history of the Middle
Freestates, they can provide escort for vehicles, trains, and watercraft.*

*For all Valentine's reluctance to join Mrs. O'Coombe's famous
and tragic trek to recover her son, the rest of Fort Seng worked like
demons to prepare her group and vehicles for their journey. "Home
by Christmas," the men said to each other, hoping that ten days on the*

road would suffice to recover the men Javelin had left scattered across Kentucky.

Each soldier could picture himself left behind somewhere. They provisioned and checked and armed the already well-equipped vehicles. For the average man in the ranks, letters from the president and connections in the general headquarters staff were remote facts, like the Hooked O-C straddling much of southern Oklahoma and northern Texas. What they understood was that the cots bolted to the inside of the trucks and vehicles would bring home those who'd been left behind—at least those who survived their injuries and the sweeps of Javelin's trail by bloodthirsty Moondaggers.

✝

He met O'Coombe's team on a warm December day. Valentine hadn't seen vehicles like these since the drive on Dallas, and these specimens were in much better condition.

They sat there, not exactly gleaming in the sun but looking formidable in their grit and mud streaks.

Mrs. O'Coombe introduced him to her right-hand man, an ex-Bear named Stuck. Valentine hadn't met many ex-Bears. It seemed you were either a Bear or you were a deceased Bear; the ex-Bears he'd met were all so badly damaged they couldn't stand up or hold a gun.

Stuck had all his arms and legs and sensory organs intact. All that seemed to be missing was the bristling, grouchy Bear attitude. He was a big, meaty, soft-spoken man with a wide, angular mustache.

Stuck took Valentine down the line. He introduced Valentine to the wagon master, Habanero, a tough older man, thin and dry and leathery as a piece of jerky. He had a combination hearing aid–radio communicator that he used to issue orders to the drivers in the column.

"Ex-artillery in the Guards," Stuck explained as they left to inspect the vehicles. "Used to haul around guns. Deaf as a post but knows engines and suspensions and transmissions."

First, there was Rover, the command car. It was a high-clearance model that looked like something out of an African safari, right down to a heavy cage around the cabin. Extra jerricans of water and gasoline festooned the back and sides, spare tires were mounted on the front and hood, packs were tied to the cage, and up top a pair of radio antennae bent from the rear bumpers and were tied forward like scorpion tails. The command car had a turret ring—empty for now.

Stuck said there was an automatic grenade launcher and two bins of grenades in the bay.

Then there was the Bushmaster. The vehicle was a beautiful, rust-free armored personnel carrier, long bodied with a toothy grin up front thanks to heavy brush breakers. An armored cupola sat at the top, and firing slits lined the side. Valentine saw canvas-covered barrels sprouting like antennae.

"Teeth as false as Grandpa's," Stuck said.

Stuck glanced around before opening the armored car's back.

The vehicle was under command of a thickset homunculus. The man looked like he'd been folded and imperfectly unfolded again. Scarred, with a squint eye and an upturned mouth, his face looked as though someone had given his unformed face a vigorous stir with wooden spoon. Even his ears were uneven.

Valentine recognized him. "I know you, don't I?"

"Yes, sir, thanks, sir," he said as they shook hands. "March south to Dallas. We was just ahead of your Razorbacks in column with the old One hundred fifteenth. I drove a rocket sled."

A vicious-looking dog that seemed mostly Doberman sniffed Valentine from next to the driver.

Hazardous duty, since the rockets had a tendency to blow up

in the crew's face. Southern Command had any number of improvised artillery units. Crude rocketry was popular because the howling, crashing projectiles unnerved even the most dug-in Grogs. Someone said it was because the rockets made a noise that sounded like the Grog word for lightning strikes.

Valentine suspected it might be the other way around—that the Grogs started calling lightning strikes after the sound effect from the rockets.

"Dover—no, Drake. Your crew pulled my command car out of a mud hole outside Sulphur Springs."

"That we did, sir."

"Serves me right for taking the wheel. I never was much of a driver."

Stuck spoke up. "Drake here is on her ladyship's— Well, we call them the ranch's sheriff's deputies. He keeps law and order among the hands and their families."

"Not popular work, sir, but it pays well," Drake said.

"Quite a dog you have there," Valentine said, looking at the beast's scarred muscle. "Can I pet it?"

"You can, sir, but I wouldn't advise it. I don't even pet him."

"How's she drive, Drake?" Valentine asked.

"Like steering a pig with handlebars shoved up its ass, but it'll get there and back," Drake said.

"Riot control platform, isn't it? I've seen these in Illinois."

"That it is, sir."

Stuck opened the small access hatch in the larger back door. "We've got it rigged out to carry injured in comfort."

The tunnellike inside was full of twelve folding bunks attached to the walls of the vehicle, as well as seats along the walls: cushioned lockers. The bunks blocked some of the firing slits but not the cupola.

The machine guns looked more frightening from the outside, thanks to the big barrels. Inside, they were revealed to be assault rifles rigged out with box magazines. Still, firepower is firepower.

"What's up top? A broomstick?" Valentine asked.

"Oh, the gun's real enough," Drake said. "Twenty millimeters of lead that'll turn any breathing target into dog meat, from a Reaper to a legworm."

"Dogs know better than to eat off a dead Reaper," Stuck said.

Next in line was the Chuckwagon. It was a standard military truck with an armored-up cabin, a mounted machine gun at the back, and a twin-tank trailer dragging behind. The paint job and new tires made Javelin's venerable and road-worn Comanche look like the tired old army mule she was. The Chuckwagon towed a trailer with two big black tanks on it.

The hood was up on this one, and a plump behind wiggled as a woman in overalls inspected the engine.

"Ma," Stuck shouted. "There's someone needs meeting."

"Busy here."

"You're never that busy. Come out of there."

A plump, graying woman hopped down from the front bumper. She wiped her hands and gave a wave Valentine decided to interpret as friendly gesture instead of sloppy contempt.

"This is Ma, one of the ranch's roving cooks. Ex–Southern Command and ex–Logistics Commando, she's our expert on Tennessee and Kentucky."

"Really only know it to the Tennessee River, but from the Goat Shack to Church Dump, I've been up and down her. My specialty was likker, of course, but I traded in parts and guns too."

Valentine nodded. "I'll put you to work on this trip. We need medical supplies and—"

"'Scuse me, sir, but I don't know medicinals; never had much of a mind for 'em. Too easy to get stock-shuffled or wheezed or lose it all in the old Bayou flush. Easier to spot a true rifle barrel or bourbon from busthead."

Finally, there was the Boneyard, a military ambulance truck. It had the same basic frame as the Rover, with a longer back end and higher payload bay. A bright red cross against a white background decorated its hood and flanks.

"Doc and the nurse are helping out in your hospital," Stuck said. "The driver's name is Big Gustauf, old Missouri German. My guess is he's eating. Never was a Bear as far as I know, but he's got the appetite of one."

Valentine paced back up the column and found the matriarch who'd assembled all this to bring her boy home. "I'd like to congratulate you on your column, Mrs. O'Coombe."

She offered a friendly tip of the head in return for the compliment. "When we were young my husband and I ranched right into Nomansland," she said. "Hard years. Dangerous years. I knew what to bring on such an expedition."

"I hope your care obtains results."

"That's in God's hands, Mister Valentine. All I can do is my best."

"God usually fights on the side of the better prepared," Valentine said.

"I don't care for your sense of humor, Mister Valentine, but as an experienced soldier I suspect you've earned your cynicism."

"Your son didn't serve under the name O'Coombe, did he?" Valentine asked.

"No, he didn't want to be pestered for money or jobs for relatives," Mrs. O'Coombe said. "He served under my maiden name, Rockaway. Sweet of him, was it not, Mister Valentine?"

Valentine made a note of that. He'd have to check the roll call records and medical lists to learn which legworm clan ended up taking care of him. They had left only a handful of wounded behind who seemed likely to survive, and even then only in areas controlled by their allied clans.

"How much do you know about Kentucky?" Valentine asked.

"My sources say there are many off-road trails thanks to the feeding habits of the legworms. I wanted vehicles that could use poorly serviced roads and even those trails."

"How did you get vehicles like these together?" Valentine asked. When he'd first seen her, he wondered if she'd hired mercenaries. They knew about moving off-road with a column of vehicles. They had plenty of tow chains and cables ready to offer assistance to the next in line or the previous. He noticed the various trucks' engines had cloth cowlings stitched and strapped over them. The cloth had an interesting sheen. Valentine suspected it was Reaper cloth from their robes.

"Get them? Sir, they're from our ranch. We control property that covers hundreds of square miles. The ranch wouldn't function without range-capable wheels."

"Where do you ride?" Valentine asked Stuck.

He lifted a muscular, hairy arm and pointed to a pair of heavy motorcycles with leather saddlebags and rifle clips on the handlebars. "Me and Longshot are the bikers."

"Where's Longshot?" Valentine asked.

"Up here," he heard a female voice say.

Valentine looked up and saw a woman in old-fashioned biker leathers sunning herself atop the Bushmaster. She zipped up her jacket. "I'm the scout sniper."

She had strong Indian features, dirtied from riding her motorcycle. There was a clean pattern around where she presumably wore her goggles. You wouldn't necessarily call her "pretty" or "beautiful." Striking was more like it, with strong features and long black hair that put Valentine's to shame. "Comanche?" Valentine asked.

"Hell if I know. Tucumcari mutt: little bit of everything. You?"

"North Minnesota mix," Valentine said.

"Hey, want to see me feed these beasts?" Stuck asked.

Valentine nodded.

He walked over to the Chuckwagon's trailer. It had big twin tanks that Valentine had assumed were powered by gasoline or diesel or vegetable oil.

Longshot hopped down, and Stuck opened a latched cooler strapped on a little platform between the tanks. Two buckets rested inside. A ripe fecal smell came out, so powerful it almost billowed. Valentine watched Stuck and Longshot, apparently oblivious to the odor, each lift a bucket and pour it into one of the tanks.

"Everyone pisses and shits in the old honeybucket," Stuck said. "Food scraps are good too, especially carbohydrates."

Stuck took a leather lanyard from around his neck. Valentine noticed a Reaper thumb on it, interesting only thanks to an overlarge, pointed nail capping it. The lanyard also had two keys. Stuck used one of them to open a locked box on the tanker trailer and took out a plastic jug of blue-white crystals with a metal scoop sunk in.

"This is my job. I check the test strips and seed."

He extracted a long dipstick from the fragrant tank, wiped it on a piece of paper about the size of a Band-Aid, carefully placed the test paper in a clip, and held it up to a color-coded, plasticized sheet. Nodding, he made a notation on a clipboard that rested on the box's hinged cover.

"The Kurians guard this stuff like the Reaper cloth factories,"

Stuck said, leveling and dumping three roughly teaspoon-sized portions of the granules into the larger scoop.

"I've seen those factories," Valentine said. "Or one of them, anyway, in the Southwest."

"This tank's just about done," Stuck said. "Takes about thirty-six hours to do three hundred fifty gallons. Then we refill off this tank while we fill the other with waste, or pig corn, or melon rinds, or what have you. In a pinch, these engines can run off of kerosene, regular diesel, or even waste cooking oil, but this stuff's easier on 'em, and Habby doesn't bitch about changing gunked-up fuel filters."

Valentine watched him dump the crystals into the conversion tank.

"Always makes me wish I'd learned more science and chemistry and stuff, instead of just getting good at taking Reapers and Grogs apart," Stuck said.

"So where did you get that stuff? I've never even heard of it," Valentine said.

"The Great Dame is friends with some big bug in Santa Fe. He's playing both sides of the border, scared there'll be a reckoning if Denver Freehold and Southern Command pair up and hit the Southwest. He's a honcho in transport. Keeps trying to propose, but she shoots him down."

"What's your story, Stuck?"

"I was never cut out for military life, even as a Bear. Hurry up and wait, hurry up and wait. Drove me crazy. Stand here, look there, turn your head and cough, bend over and pull 'em apart. Not my lifestyle at all. Mrs. O'Coombe keeps me busy out in the open where I'm alone, riding from post to post checking security. No one to piss me off that way."

He looked up from the mix. "Longshot, get over here," Stuck said. "What do you think of this color?"

"More water," she said.

"That's what I thought. Thanks."

She hopped down and bumped into Valentine.

Valentine found himself looking into the reversed-raccoon eyes of the girl. The face mask had left an odd pattern on her features. Dusky and dark, she reminded him a little of Malita, save that Longshot was a good deal shorter.

"You must love your bike," Valentine said.

"I was out scouting east of here this morning," she said.

"Longshot gets bored easily," Stuck said, watching her grab a washcloth and towel and head for the camp's showers. "She's a retired guerrilla from down Mexico way. Met her during Operation Snakebite. She's ridden at my side ever since."

"Full partnership, or limited liability?" Valentine asked.

"Nah. A Reaper yanked my gear off when I was captured in 'sixty-six. Didn't hurt as much as you'd think, but about all she does is keep me warm."

†

Valentine had a hard decision to make, and after consulting Lambert, he presented it to Mrs. O'Coombe the night before their scheduled departure.

"I'm afraid I'll have to commandeer your doctor for Fort Seng, Mrs. O'Coombe. Our remaining doctor is exhausted. He's worked seven days a week for over a month now."

"And just who do you suggest will look after my son or any wounded we recover?"

"We'll take our nurse. If they've lived this long, I doubt they'll need any more care than that."

"I'm sorry, Mister Valentine, but this is one time I must tell you no. I don't like the idea of traveling with wounded without a doctor."

"A nurse should be sufficient for travel," Valentine said. And that was that. He had rank, after all, and it would take months for Mrs O'Coombe to get her friends to exert their influence for or against him. And by then he hoped to have her son back.

†

Valentine passed the word and names for an officers' call and then arranged for food to be sent up to what was now being called the map room. Next to the communications center, it had formerly been a game room. Lambert had altered it so it featured everything from a large-scale map of Kentucky to an updated map of the Evansville area, river charts, and even a globe Lambert had colored with crayons to reflect resistance hot spots against the Kurian Order.

Lambert was a whirlwind. Somebody had a screw loose if they had just cast this woman aside as part of a political housecleaning.

Gamecock was there representing his Bears, Frat for the Wolves, and Duvalier just because she saw the others gathering and wanted to grab a comfortable armchair. Patel was present, of course, and Colonel Bloom's new executive officer, a Guard lieutenant who'd distinguished himself at the bridge where Bloom had been wounded on Javelin's retreat.

"You looking forward to your trip, suh?" Gamecock said.

"We won't be touring. I don't care how well equipped and crewed she is. If she's recovering Southern Command forces, we need Southern Command along. I think she's sailing into trouble."

"Isn't she a bit old for you, Val?" Duvalier asked.

"You can come along and keep an eye on me," Valentine said. He hadn't yet told her that he wanted her to as part of his command.

"No walking, I hope," Duvalier said, with a light laugh that did Valentine's spirits good. She'd been so moody lately. "Twice back and forth across the state is enough for me."

"Who would you like to bring, sir?" Patel asked.

Valentine looked at his notes. "I'd like to take two Bears—Chieftain and Silvertip—four Wolves, and a nurse."

"Who's bringing the beer and barbecue?" Duvalier asked.

"Do I have to remind you that this is an officers' call, Captain?" Valentine said, using her titular rank.

"Then I'll join the tour," Duvalier said.

"Call it a survey, call it a reconnaissance in force, call it a recovery operation. Call it anything you like. It's my intent to have a mobile force of some strength who knows how to deal with Reapers. With the legworm clans encamped for the winter, they'll be so many sitting ducks for whatever vengeance Missionary Doughnut is talking about."

"Goodwill tour it is," Lambert said. "Our friend out front has never made much sense. Seeing some Southern Command forces in Kentucky's heartland will do the Cause some good, in any case. And let's not forget our outgoing president's letter. If I go myself, I'll consider my duties discharged."

"Can I go with my Wolves, sir?" Frat asked. "I'd like to see a little more of Kentucky."

Valentine looked at Lambert, who nodded. "Glad to have you along, Lieutenant. Thanks for volunteering. You'll save me a lot of legwork."

Duvalier snickered at that. Valentine wondered why she was so merry this morning.

†

Alarm.

Valentine came out of his sleep, heart pounding, a terrible sense that death stood over his pillow.

The Valentingle.

He hadn't called it that at first. If he thought about it, he might have remembered that he once called it "the willies" or "the creeps." The name came from his companions in the Wolves, who learned to trust his judgment about when they were safe to take refuge for the night—what hamlets might be visited quietly, whispering to the inhabitants through back porch screens.

Whether it was sixth sense, the kind of natural instinct that makes a rabbit freeze when a hawk's shadow passes overhead, or some strange gift of the Lifeweavers, Valentine couldn't say.

But he did trust it. A Reaper was prowling.

Valentine slipped into his trousers and boots almost at the same time, tying them in the dark.

He grabbed the pistol belt hanging on his bedpost. Next came the rifle. Valentine checked his ammunition by touch, inserted a magazine, chambered a shot. He slung on his sword. Oddly enough, the blade was more comforting than even the guns. There was something atavistic in having a good handle grip at the end of an implement you can wave about.

Duvalier would say that it wasn't atavism. . . .

Valentine hand-cranked his field phone. "Operations."

"Operations," they answered.

"This is Major Valentine. Any alerts?" He swapped hands with the receiver so he could pull on his uniform shirt.

"Negative, Major Valentine."

"Well, I'm calling one. Pass the word: alert alert alert. I want to hear from the sentries by the time I get down there."

The communications center lay snug in the basement.

Valentine looked out the window. The alarm klaxon went off, sending black birds flapping off the garbage dump and a raccoon scuttling. Emergency lights tripped on in quick succession. They

226

were perhaps not as bright as Southern Command's sodium lights that illuminated woods on the other side of the parking lot, but they had precise coverage that left no concealing shadows on the concentric rings of decorative patio stones. The old estate house had quite a security system.

A shadow whipped across the lawn, bounding like a decidedly unjolly black giant, covering three meters at a stride, a dark cloak flapping like wings.

Reaper!

Could it be their old friend from the Ohio? The clothing was different, it seemed. The other one hadn't even had a cloak and cowl when he'd last seen it, and it seemed doubtful that a wild Reaper could attain one.

Valentine, in more of a hurry to throw off the shutters and open the sash than ever any St. Nick–chasing father, fumbled with the window. He knocked it open at the cost of a painful pinch to his finger when the rising pane caught him. He swung his legs out and sat briefly on the sill like a child working up the nerve to jump, rifle heavy across his thighs.

Valentine had no need to nerve himself, but he did want one last look at the Reaper's track from the advantage of height. Would it angle toward the soldiers' tents or the munitions dugout? Kurians had been known to sacrifice a Reaper, if it meant blowing up half a base.

It did neither. It headed straight for the woods south, toward the river.

Valentine jumped, felt the cool night air rush up his trouser legs. He landed on his good leg, cradling the rifle carefully against his midsection as though it were a baby.

With that he was off, settling into his old Wolf lope, the bad leg giving him the port-and-starboard sway of a tipsy sailor or perhaps an off-balance metronome.

He cast about with a coonhound's frantic anxiety at the edge of the woods. The tracks were there, hard to see in the deep night of the woods. Only the Reaper's furious pace allowed him to find the tracks at all.

Valentine searched the woods with his hard ears. The wind was smothering whatever sounds the Reaper made—if it was in fact running and not just trying to lure him into the woods.

Deciding on handiness over firepower, Valentine slung his rifle. Drawing his pistol and sword, he tucked the blade under his arm and began stalking into the woods with the pistol in a solid, two-handed "teacup" grip, searching more with his ears than his eyes.

His footfalls sounded like land mines detonating to his nervous ears. Of course, anyone venturing into thick woods after a Reaper would be a madman not to be nervous.

Motion out of the corner of his eye—

Valentine swung, the red fluorescent dot on the pistol's foresight tracking through wooded night to . . .

A chittering raccoon, blinking at him from a tree branch.

Valentine lowered the pistol barrel.

In a cheap horror movie, this would be the moment for the Reaper to come up behind. Valentine turned a full circle. The woods were empty.

†

A half hour later he'd traced the tracks to an old road running along the bank of the Ohio River above the flood line. Above what was technically the flood line, that is; the road showed evidence of having survived at least one flood. The Reaper could have continued on to the river or headed down the road in either direction. It might even have stashed a bicycle somewhere—a Reaper could reach a fantastic speed on two wheels.

Now all that was left was the grim accounting. Perhaps the Reaper had grabbed some poor sentry and terrified him into giving an estimate of their reduced strength once Bloom had departed. There'd be a name to report missing and fear in the camp.

Such a loss would be worse to take than an ambush or a firefight, where at least the men could feel like they shot back. A single man's death after so many weeks without a casualty worse than a broken ankle would loom all the larger over dinner conversation.

It took three hours for word to come back to the alarmed operations center: all in-fort personnel present and accounted for, from the most distant sentry to the cook stocking potatoes in one of the basements against the winter.

One other person had caught a good look at the Reaper, and Valentine and Lambert heard the story from a shaken-up mechanic named Cleland, brought in by Frat, who'd found him in crouched on the unpleasant side of a board over a pit toilet and helped him out. Cleland was up late winterproofing a pump, went to the cookhouse for a hot sandwich and coffee, and saw a tall figure standing silhouetted against one of the security lights.

"Just looked like he was trying to keep warm, wrapped up. Didn't notice how tall he was right off as I was headin' up the hill, you know."

Valentine's nose noted that Cleland hadn't done the most thorough job cleaning up before giving his report.

"Standing in the light?" Valentine asked.

"Turned toward it, more like. I saw something in its hand."

"He needed light," Lambert said, looking at Valentine. "It's a dark night."

"Could you see what it was?" Valentine asked.

"Piece of paper, maybe. It shoved whatever it was into its cloak when it heard me. Damn thing looked right at me. Yellow eyes.

Nobody ever told me how bright they were. A man doesn't forget that. Don't think I ever will."

"What then?"

"I ran like the devil. Or like the devil was after me, more like. Dodged through the transport-lot and jumped into the old latrine."

"You can go, Cleland," Lambert said. "Get a drink if you like at the hospital. Medicinal bourbon."

"What do you think?" Lambert asked Valentine after Cleland left.

Valentine looked at the alert report. "They found a garbage can overturned by the cookhouse. Could be raccoons again."

"A Reaper snuck onto the base to go through our garbage? Not even the garbage at headquarters; a can full of greasy wax paper and coffee grounds?"

Valentine had the same uncomfortable feeling he'd had on his first trip into the Kurian Zone, when he learned that one of his charges had been leaving information for Kurian trackers.

"A message drop," Valentine said.

"Possibly. People go to the canteen at all hours. It's a good spot. Almost everyone's there once a day."

"That means—it could be anyone."

"In a camp full of Quislings," Lambert said.

"Not anymore . . . at least I hope not," Valentine said.

Lambert lowered her voice. "They turned on their superiors once. We have to consider the possibility that they'll do it again. How many of them are above going for a brass ring and an estate in Iowa?"

†

"Will you take tea with me, Mister Valentine?" Mrs. O'Coombe asked as Valentine passed through her mini-camp on a blustery afternoon with blown leaves rattling against the Rover's paneling. "You look chilled."

Valentine had no need to be anywhere. The column was waiting for a report from the Kentuckians about the status of their wounded left behind, not to mention offical permission to move through the new Freehold with an armed column. "Yes. I would like to talk to you."

"Tea elevates any social interaction," she said, placing an elegant copper pot on the electrical camp stove running off the generator. Valentine admired the long spout and handle. The decorative top had elaborate etching.

She opened a tin and spooned some black leaves into the holder at the top of the pot.

"You'll forgive me—I make some ceremony of this," she said. "Teatime was always my time on the ranch. Even my husband, God rest him, didn't disturb me if I closed my library door."

She poured.

"Tea is the smell of civilization, don't you think?"

Valentine sniffed, briefly bringing the old mental focus to his nostrils. Not a strong scent, even to his old Wolf nose. Just wet leaves and hot water.

"Not much of a smell." Valentine said. "I've heard people put, er, that oil, berge—"

"Bergamot," she corrected. "Yes, Earl Grey. A classic. Not that hard to make. Are you a fan of teas, Mister Valentine?"

"I used to drink some good stuff in New Orleans. Lots of trade there. I had sage tea in Texas. I trade my whiskey and tobacco rations for tea, the Southern Command stuff."

"Dusty mud," she said. "These are real leaves, from China and India."

They drank. Valentine sniffed again, letting his Wolf's nose explore the pleasantly delicate aroma.

"No, it's not a strong smell," she said. "But then civilization isn't a strong presence either. The whole idea is the sublimation of coarser practices. Yet when it disappears—just as when your cup is empty—you'll notice its absence more. Receiving mail is an ordinary experience until it doesn't show up for a week; then its interruption is keenly felt."

"We'd like nothing better than weekly mail out here."

"How is the bond tour going, Mister Valentine?"

"Poorly, I'm afraid. These Kentuckians keep their gold close. We've had some donations of whiskey, boots, and craft goods that we might be able to trade for butter and eggs, if we come across a farm wife in a patriotic mood. You'll see that on the road."

"I am anxious to get started. I wish to see my son again."

"You know, there's a chance we may never find Corporal O'Coombe." Valentine thought it better not to list all the reasons—sepsis, an illness, discovery by Moondaggers sweeping across Javelin's line of retreat looking for those left behind to take and torture . . .

"I've prepared myself for that eventuality, Mister Valentine."

"You seem like a woman used to getting her way. I hope we'll be able to complete our sweep and bring back a few more of Southern Command's own."

"My staff and their vehicles are entirely at your disposal, sir. Our agreement still stands. I am allowed to search for my son; you are allowed to bring back any you have left behind. If we cannot find news of my son, all I ask is a finding that he's been killed in action so that his memory may be honored accordingly."

Valentine would be glad to have Mrs. O'Coombe's crew out of his graying hair. Her precious doctor was always asking for better water, more sanitizer, more hands to pick up shifts changing bandages and bedding.

In the end, Mrs. O'Coombe's doctor came along after all, but only after the remaining Javelin doctor personally spoke to Valentine and explained that having a doctor along might mean the difference between a continued recovery and a setback as they moved the wounded.

Though Valentine wondered how much of a specialist Mrs. O'Coombe's doctor really was. He went by the unimaginative moniker of "Doc" and seemed more like a country sawbones than an expert in difficult recoveries, though his nurse, a thick-fingered Louisiana-born woman named Sahita, had the serene, slightly blank look of an experienced caregiver. Sahita looked at the entire world through narrowed eyes and seemed naturally immune to chitchat, responding only in monosyllables if at all possible to any conversational efforts.

Valentine and Frat did a final inspection before boarding the vehicles. Food, clothing, gear, guns. Everyone a first-aid kit, everyone a tool for finding food or making shelter.

Frat had a big shoulder bag over his arm as well, stuffed with maps and battered old guidebooks to Kentucky. Valentine was rather touched by the imitation, if that's what it was rather than coincidence.

Though Frat had avoided choosing a diaper bag for his miscellany.

Inspection complete and vehicles pronounced ready, they boarded their transport and put the engines in gear. Despite his misgivings, Valentine was relieved to be on the move at last. The sooner they started, the sooner he could return.

The vehicles rolled out of Fort Seng in column order the next morning.

The motorcycles blatted out first, followed by Rover with Valentine riding shotgun and Mrs. O'Coombe in back, looking for all the world like an annoying mother-in-law in a comedy of the previous century. Duvalier slumped next to her, head pillowed on her rolled-up overcoat, already settling in to sleep. Bee had reluctantly taken a place in the Bushmaster behind but soon amused herself by unloading magazines, cleaning the bullets, and reloading the magazines.

The rest of the camouflage-painted parade followed.

Valentine had a big, comfortable seat, and there was a clip for his rifle in the dashboard. A clever little map or reading light could be bent down from the ceiling, and there was even a little case in the seat for a pair of binoculars or maps or sandwiches or books or whatever else you might desire on a long trip.

For such a wretched, ungoverned, miserable place, the Old World sure put a lot of thought into conveniences, Valentine thought ironically. Of course a New Universal churchman would counter that the conveniences applied to only one half of one percent of the world's population.

Habanero the wagon master controlled the wheel and gearshift in Rover, his earpiece in and a little control pad on his thigh that allowed him to radio the other drivers. He gave Valentine an extension so he could plug in to listen—and to speak if he had to.

In the cabin of Rover, Valentine felt his usual isolation from the outside world when riding in a vehicle. While he enjoyed the comfort and convenience, you lost much of the appreciation of landscape and distance, proper humility before wind and weather.

Of course he couldn't overlook the advantages an engine and wheels gave when you had two hundred miles to cover in search of your scattered wounded. The pleasant, ten-minute walk to the gate took but a moment in Rover.

"Slow here," Valentine said as they approached the gate and the doughnut-selling missionary.

"You need to install a drive-up window," Valentine yelled from his rolled-down window. He'd been saving up the jibe all morning.

"Wise of you," the missionary said. "Oh, it's you, my brother and friend. I'm glad you've decided to bow to the inevitable. But time runs short! Hurry! Go like Lot and his wife and do not look back."

"Sorry to disappoint," Valentine said, getting out to claim a final doughnut for the road. "We're not leaving. We're just off to do a little touring. Would you recommend the Corvette museum in Bowling Green or the Lincoln birthplace?" Behind, he heard Duvalier get out, yawning.

"I weep for you," the missionary said. "You're all dead, you know. A reckoning is coming. Weeds have sprouted in Kentucky's green gardens, and it is time for the gardeners to replant. But first, the scythes and the cutters. Scythes and cutters, I say."

"They better be sharper than you," Duvalier said. "It's a sad—"

"Wait a moment," Valentine said. "What's this about, you? What scythes, what cutters? I don't believe in visions unless they're specific."

"Oh, it's coming, sir. Sooner than anyone expects." He looked up and down the column. "You have one final chance to repent. Turn west and follow the sun. If you turn east, by your actions is Kentucky doomed. You sow the seeds of your own destruction."

"Shut up, you," one of the Wolves yelled from the Chuckwagon.

"Want us to gag him with his own pastries?" Frat called to Valentine.

Valentine held up his hand, halting the Wolves in their tracks. "How does a man like you come by such intelligence?"

The doughnut missionary grinned. He passed a finger down

his nose. "I prayed and I learned over many long years. But I too had faults: pride and greed and lust. I was cast out to make my way among the heathen. But they did not take all my gifts. I still have my vision."

"False prophecy. I've seen no portents. Red sunsets before the Kurians ever move, my mother always told me. Long red sunsets and dawns, with blood on the clouds."

"Whispers on the wind, you poor soul. That's how I know. Whispers on the wind."

"Would that the wind were a little clearer."

"I hear voices, you poor lost soul. See visions. Visions! Oh, they break the heart."

"I'm sorry you're so burdened. How long have you carried that cross?"

"Had them since I was little. Born in a Church hall, the New England Archon's own retreat it was, but a grim place and nothing but lessons from the time I took my first step. That's no way to serve the gods, no sir, not for me. I ran away as soon as I could climb over the wall and never looked back. Took up with some relief and reassurance workers and then signed up for the missions, first in group and then alone and with only faith and my poor wit. Been warning souls away from folly and death ever since."

Valentine took out his pocket notebook. "How long before our day of judgment? I'd like to make some preparations. Will, disposition of assets, and so forth."

"That I can't tell you. Soon, though, sir. Soon. This will be a cruel winter, and many won't live to see the spring. I say again: Repent now and leave Kentucky!"

Valentine decided he'd heard all the detail he'd ever hear from the doughnut missionary, and he climbed back into Rover.

"Why do you let that thing carry on so, Mister Valentine?" Mrs. O'Coombe said. "It insults every faculty of taste and reason."

"The men like his doughnuts," Valentine said. A few had hopped out of the column to claim theirs. Valentine saw Frat hurl his into the man's face as they pulled away.

Mrs. O'Coombe snorted. "I heard a little of him on the way in. I wouldn't give one of his clots of dough to one of my dogs. Sugar and lard. Mark my words, Mister Valentine, he's trying to clog their arteries or give your men diabetes. Now, tell me, should we turn east immediately, or should we go south and pick up the old parkway?"

CHAPTER TEN

T

he Discard Run: Winter is the quietest time of the year in Kentucky. The locals retreat to the hearth and their livestock to barns (or to great intertwined piles, in the case of the legworms), and the frequent rains and occasional snow accumulation keep people close to home unless emergency forces them to travel. It is a time for neighbors and small towns to get together and enjoy the indoor pursuits of the season: the final steps in the canning and preserving of the harvest, pursuit of courtship or friendship, sewing circles, and hand tool swap meets.

The column was sped on its way east by two factors. First, they did not have to forage for food or fuel, though where it was available, they were able to buy more with Mrs. O'Coombe's gold. Second, the Kurian Order no longer existed outside Louisville, Lexington, or the crossriver suburbs of Cincinnati—none of which the column was interested in visiting. There were no checkpoints to route around, unwatched fords to find, or patrols to look out for. The only thing their motorcycle scouts had to do was report the condition of the roads or cuts or trails ahead.

Valentine, always willing to see a glass half empty when anything having to do with the Kurian Order was being discussed, maintained that the ease on the eastbound leg would just mean that much more difficulty on the westbound.

Luckily, he couldn't imagine just how right he was.

†

Lambert had sent word to the clans through Brother Mark of the proposed route tracing the retreat of Javelin, with instructions that any of Southern Command's surviving wounded be made ready for travel and certain frequencies be scanned for radio contact.

They hadn't left many behind, at least many who were expected to live more than a day or two. Valentine doubted they'd need half the bed space that had been allocated in the Bushmaster. Either the soldiers would be recovered enough now to sit, or they'd be beyond medical attention.

Once in the Nolin and Green River Valleys, in this manner they picked up three of their wounded who'd escaped death by their wounds, secondary diseases, or the vengeful Moondaggers who'd followed in Javelin's wake.

The soldiers they picked up, eager to thank Valentine for their collection, were introduced to Mrs. O'Coombe, the true sponsor of their deliverance.

Valentine decided he liked her a little better when he saw her attend to the soldiers they were accumulating. It wasn't an act for the benefit of anyone, especially Valentine, who seemed to have as natural a knack for aggravating her as a piece of steel has for striking sparks when struck by a sharp piece of flint or quartz. She tended to them in a mix of Christian compassion and patriotic fervor. Nothing was too good for those who'd lost so much in the pursuit of the Cause.

He began to enjoy the trip. The cold weather invigorated him, if anything, and apart from delivering anecdotes about the retreat or advice on routes, he had little to do. Mrs. O'Coombe made all the strategic decisions for the column, and the mile-by-mile operations were handled by wagon master Habanero.

Frat was a superb scout, though Valentine was beginning to see why he was still a lieutenant. He wanted to do everything on his own. Run every risk, shoulder every burden, scout every town, be the first through every door. Valentine was impressed with his courage.

Had LeHavre ever said anything like that about his own eager young lieutenant out of the wilds of northern Minnesota? Of course, LeHavre had brought Valentine along differently, keeping him back rather than sending him forward until he found his feet among the men and in the responsibilities of his platoon.

Bee slept outside, snoring softly, her head pillowed on her shotgun. She'd arranged her mane—Valentine could never decide whether Grog hair should be called "mane" or "fur"—into a star to show off the wound she'd received when the Coonskins turned on the Kentucky Alliance.

She was proud of her wound, issued at his side like a stamp of bravery. Valentine wondered just when whatever debt Bee decided she owed him for freeing her would be paid off. She was mysterious about her loyalty, and Valentine's rough-and-ready Grog gutturals weren't up to discussions of intangibles.

But Frat could hold up his end of any conversation. The boy, who'd once possessed a wary, quiet intelligence, had turned into a well-spoken man.

Valentine waved Frat in, heard his report, and then had him sit on one of the tiny camp stools. His long legs made him look a little like a frog ready to give a good loud croak.

"What's with the big bag, son?"

"Saw yours and sort of admired it, sir. All these maps are a hassle."

"I used to carry them rolled up in a tube."

They chatted for a while. Valentine asked about his officers' training, and they shared memories of Pine Bluff. Frat accidentally mentioned a brothel that was either new or had escaped Valentine's notice in his days as a shy, studious lieutenant.

They laughed at their mutual awkwardness. Frat, for admitting that he took a trip upstairs as a rite of passage (always on the house for a Hunter on his first visit, it seemed), and Valentine for living so sheltered a student life that he was unaware of its existence.

Sometimes, their conversations turned serious.

"You ever heard the theory that the Kurians keep the Freeholds in business? That they have allies at the top of our military and government?" Valentine said.

"Well, sir," Frat said. "I think this might be a conversation that wouldn't stand an Honor Code examination."

"The 'sir' stuff only counts when we're standing up. I want your opinion. Disparaging and doubting our superiors is a fine old American tradition."

Frat thought for a moment. "It's something men like to shout after a defeat. They cry, 'Betrayed,' and run. Makes them feel better about running way, or keeping out of it to begin with. If the game's fixed, there's no sense putting any skin into it."

"You've put some thought into this already," Valentine said.

"There was the exact same argument when we got back from Kansas all bloodied, kind of. What's that saying? *Never attribute to malevolence what can be explained by stupidity.* Something like that."

"I heard it as *malice*. Interesting that we agree on that. Of course Kur has a few agents in the Free Republics; they'd be fools not to, and we're not fighting fools. Where'd you get that cry, 'Betrayed!'?"

"Those Shelby Foote books you gave me about the Civil War when I signed up."

"Ah, I'd forgotten about that." Valentine had thought the volumes would teach Frat some useful lessons about leadership in adversity.

"If you ask me, Kansas wasn't malice or stupidity. They just got lucky. The whole Moondagger army was training for a run at those Grogs in Omaha. But you know that."

Valentine had a lot of former friends there. Last he heard, after a big battle the Grogs had retreated up the Missouri River Valley and were now finding friends among the Nebraska ranchers he'd met when looking for the Twisted Cross with Duvalier.

"Actually I don't. I was out of the country at the time."

"Kansas was bad. One of the places I was reported killed, as I recall. My platoon was ambushed and I made it away with only two men. I think the others were captured. We tried to follow and see if we could help them escape, but—they were the Moondaggers, you see. Someone told me that Moondagger priests can channel aura to a Kurian just like a Reaper, and in return they get special powers, just like Wolves do, kind of. That's one of the reasons I volunteered to come out here, to get another crack at them."

"What's left of the ones that operated in eastern Kentucky are back in the Bluegrass region, licking their wounds, last I heard, under the protection of a clan called the Coonskins, who betrayed the Kentucky Alliance. The ones who chased us across western Kentucky have been scattered. Not many survived the massacre on the road to Bowling Green. I would have liked a few officers as prisoners, personally, but the legworm clans had women and children to avenge."

"We're heading near there, right?"

"Yes. Corporal O'Coombe was dropped off in the Rolling Fork Valley southwest of Louisville. But we don't want to tangle with them or the Coonskins. Not with two motorcycles and four transport vehicles."

"Isn't the size of the dog in the fight—," Frat began.

"Why aren't you a captain, Frat?" Valentine asked.

"Most of the fights I've been in since Archangel have been losing ones. In Kansas I lost a platoon. Rio Grande was a disaster, or turned into one a long time after I left. Maybe third time's the charm. Seems to me if I'm in charge of a permanent group of Wolves operating in Kentucky, I oughta be a captain at that."

"You're at the damp and sticky part of the bottom of the barrel in Kentucky, you know, Frat. Southern Command has written us off."

Frat listened to the wind for a moment and poked the center of the fire. "They wrote your boys off on top of Big Rock Hill too. They asked me to contribute to a memorial service for you and those Razorbacks when we lost communication when that big gun started blasting you. We got a big speech about how you bought us time and we had to make it count."

Valentine remembered the earth quaking with each fall of Crocodile's monster shells. The poor, maddened dog who had to be shot; the numbed, desperate man who wandered out into the churned earth to seek disintegration in one of the blasts.

"Let's forget that for now," Valentine said, taking his map out of his diaper bag. "Here's where I'd like you to scout tomorrow. . . ."

With that, they lost themselves in operational details until it was time for Valentine to check the sentries before turning in.

†

A clear, cold night on the banks of the Rolling Fork with the temperature dropping enough for men to sleep curled up with a fire-warmed rock . . .

The Valentingle came hard, so hard that Valentine thought he was ill until he recognized the familiar prickling on his scalp, the feeling that every molecule in his body was lining up to be counted. Valentine was almost nauseous with the alarm.

What the hell is approaching camp? What from hell, make it ...

Valentine fumbled at his pocket, found the chain, and put whistle to mouth. "Alarm! Take your posts," Valentine yelled.

Something wicked this way comes.

Valentine heard the engine on the Bushwhacker come to life. Clicks and clatters of magazines being sent home sounded all around like crickets.

Valentine found his Type Three and put in a red-striped Quickwood magazine.

"Frat has a visitor. He's coming in with a parley," one of the Wolves said, shining a flashlight on himself as he approached through the brush. "It's a freak-Reaper—with a flag of truce."

†

Valentine recognized what he saw prodded along by Frat, a forage bag over its head. It was taller, more spindly than most Reapers, and its tightly wound apparel had tufts of fur at the edges. Great wings were folded at its side so they stuck out behind like a pair of curved swords, and it paced with torso bobbing and head bobbing, knees reversed like a bird.

He'd seen something like this before, perched on a limb, watching him load his column back onto boats after their gun raid into Kentucky.

A big scallop-shaped pouch hung from its waist, loose and empty, but apart from that it bore no weapons or other obvious gear.

"Ranks only, please," Valentine said to the gaping men. He glanced up at the clear sky, looking for other fliers, and then addressed the newcomer. "I will keep you blindfolded. No reason for you to look around."

"It is in your nature to quiver in fear." The creature had a high, faintly squawking voice, as though a goose were talking, rather than an ordinary Reaper's breathy whisper. Though softly spoken, the high-pitched words carried through the night like the notes of a flute.

"He knows how to get things off on the right foot," Chieftain said, his twin, gracefully curved forged-steel tomahawks at the ready.

"Those wings give me the loosies," Ma said. "I hate a bird you can't eat."

Bee brought up her big Grog gun and used a tree branch to rest it on with the sights lined up on the Reaper.

Valentine guessed that her gun wouldn't kill it, but it'd tear off an almighty big piece on the way through. The Reaper looked fragile. He wondered if the Kurians had built it to be proof against Quickwood, and was tempted to test it. Give Boelnitz something colorful at last: gunning down an emissary under its flag of truce.

Valentine looked at Mrs. O'Coombe, who had drawn herself up to her full height, hand resting on a pistol belt she'd strapped on. She nodded to Valentine.

"What do you have to say?" he asked.

"We are—how would you understand it?—an important branch of a larger tree concerning itself with affairs in North America. We of like mind are fond of you humans—such a mix of greatness and folly, with your charming notions of assistance to those outside your name. They call us the Jack in the Box. We've done our best to research the source and are somewhat confused, for we have nothing to do with hamburgers and French fries or a winding musical toy."

Its speech had an uncanny sound to it, as though the words were being forced through a vocalization apparatus ill-suited to English, yet it was easy to comprehend the words. Valentine wondered of the bird thing was making noises of the appropriate length, and the Kurian was speaking directly to their brains.

"Let's hear him whistle 'Pop Goes the Weasel,'" Silvertip said quietly to Chieftain.

"Still, there," Valentine called over his shoulder. "Lieutenant, wrap a handkerchief over that bag. I get the feeling he's looking right through it."

Frat threw his rain poncho over the Reaper's head.

"That's better."

"Indeed. We can't smell you anymore, just this musty fabric. What do you use for waterproofing, apart from grotty, bacteria-gathering mammal oils?"

"Reaper blood," Chieftain said.

"What is your real name, Jack in the Box?" Valentine asked.

"Silence, renegade. Return the brass ring you so ill-advisedly carry or we will say no more."

They all stood in silence for five full minutes—Valentine timed it with his watch.

"Perhaps we should start breakfast," Valentine said.

"Return the ring!"

"I earned it fairly. If you want it, try to take it."

"This is one of your flags of truce!" Jack in the Box's avatar said.

"Then speak your piece," Valentine said. "Do you want to surrender to us?"

"I come to offer a bargain. I like the people of this land: their independent streak, their enjoyment of hearty meals and entertainments, their work ethic—but most of all their adaptability. From a few escaped legworms running wild they have built an entire civilization, using them alternately as a food source and transportation and warcraft. They even use the skins of the eggs. No Grog dared penetrate a legworm nest with fresh spawn wriggling about, yet they send teenagers in to snatch the material from under living scythes."

"So you admire the state," Longshot said. "So do I. But I'm not making demands of people who never did me or my kind any harm."

"It is for the superior to arrange the affairs of the inferior. I only choose favorites to improve."

"Leave if all you want to do is argue and waste my beauty sleep," Duvalier said. "I don't have time for this."

"Quit arguing with the thing; it gets us nowhere," Valentine said. "Let's hear it, then."

"That Kentucky be placed under our protection. We will not take one life from your Alliance lands. Not one. No tribute, no flesh of worm or cow or goat—all we will ask is that it remain strictly neutral in the contest between civilization and progress on one side, and atavism and greed on the other."

"Civilization and progress—" Frat began.

"Oh, you only lack the experience of years, boy."

"You lack the experience of who you should be calling boy," Frat said, reaching for his parang.

"Are we done here?" Valentine asked. "You're giving your offer to the wrong people."

"Mankind has always been a herd. Well, two herds. The larger of the two are the dullards, the grotty masses with their simple pursuits of sex and drink and sport. They are easy to keep and thrive with a minimum of animal husbandry. But among you there is an elite, who appreciate art and culture. It's only the passions of youth that seek the physical gratification rather than the mental that has kept your race from progressing out of its current stage. A little more selective breeding and you would have made the leap to thought-energy manipulation on your own. We will fulfill that potential. But we have the time to see it through. Give us a few more generations."

"Baloney," Valentine said.

"You've been among our better vanguards of the new *Homo sapiens lux*, David Valentine. Have you not seen it with your own eyes?"

Valentine thought of Fran Paoli—no, that made him too uncomfortable. What about the officers Solon collected? Even at the time Valentine admired them. Intelligent, energetic, committed, organized. Cooperative as ants, brilliant as artists—they came so close to establishing their order in rebellious territory captured only a few months before. . . .

Yes, Valentine had admired them.

How had Valentine's memory latched onto Consul Solon's team so quickly? He'd spent years in the Kurian Zone, and his more recent time with, say, Pyp's Flying Circus was more pleasant to consider. Did the Kurian know what mental cards he was holding? Captain Mantilla had said that one's opponents were almost too eager to give the game away, seek the most comfortable mental path.

Was the Kurian putting a few illuminated markers on that path?

"We would almost take it to be universal," Jack in the Box continued. "On the Grog's world they became two distinct races, the golden and the gray, in their terms."

"Eloi and Morlocks," Chieftain said. "Only you feed on both."

"Does the same apply to your *Dau'wa?*" Valentine asked, using the old Lifeweaver name for the renegades who practiced vampirism.

"On Kur, the weak and the stupid were consumed long ago," Jack in the Box answered. "The most resourceful of us survived. Then they went after each other. But it provided the necessary lessons. We are all sprigs of a few hardy family trees, tested and tested again."

"Tested or twisted?" Valentine asked.

Who are you, Jack? Some Kurian who came off worse in a contest, looking for a safe place to hide? Valentine played music in his mind as he listened, mental chaff against the Kurian exploring his mind. Childhood nursery rhymes worked well, like the one employed by the Bears in the northeast to calm themselves down. *The itsy-bitsy spider . . .*

"Where would you put your tower?" Duvalier asked.

"We had in mind the Lincoln birthplace. The architecture is pleasing, the location central yet out of the way. It would suit us."

"How many 'us' would that be?"

"We are the only one. For now. But if the time comes, I may have others of my kind take refuge with me. The deal would remain the same. All we ask is to be left alone and for this land to remain neutral."

"Is there an 'or else' attached?"

"There always is. We have intimations of what our brethren are planning. Only my intervention can stop the whirlwind that is about to sweep across this land."

"This isn't for us to decide," Valentine said. "You need to speak to the Kentuckians."

"Events are not altogether in my control, either. I came to you in the hope that you would have that apostate who goes by the name Brother Mark persuade them into wisdom rather than folly. Our brethren are disappointed in the foolish gesture your cousins made in Owensboro. Tell your Brother Mark that Gall has been specified for Kentucky."

The creature reached inside its robes, and Valentine saw fingers shift all around from trigger guard to trigger—save for Duvalier, who's sword appeared with a *snick*. It produced a white, capped cylinder about the size of a dinner candle high for all to see, and then dropped it at its feet.

"You men like to have matters set down on paper. I give you paper."

"Thanks anyway. We've rolls of it," Duvalier said.

"Perhaps that's for the Kentuckians to say," Mrs. O'Coombe said. "It's their land."

"So entertaining a discussion," Jack in the Box said. "We almost forgot to offer a compliment. Brilliant gambit in Owensboro. You are worthy of your name after all."

"Gambit?" Valentine asked.

"Yes. The bomb. Blowing up some of your own. You won your goal, but the herd you stampeded is heading for a cliff. Keep your workmanship in mind in the coming days as the bodies pile up and this beautiful, rich land becomes a waste."

"We'll take you along to meet the Assembly," Valentine decided.

"No, I know that trick as well. You think you'll use our avatar to locate us."

"Maybe we won't give your avatar a choice."

"All I have to do is have it hold its breath. These flying forms are frail. Their hearts explode if deprived of oxygen for long. But that would be a shame. You will have no way to give an answer."

Valentine hated to admit defeat. "How shall we answer you, then?"

"We will be in touch. But if you ever wish another audience, simply tie a bedsheet on top of one of these vehicles. They will be observed. We will send a messenger."

So, the Kurian knew all about their vehicles. They hadn't seen its silhouette flying around in daylight, so it must search for them at night. Well, there were ways to hide vehicles and disperse lifesign.

"Be vigorous, Valentine. Do not delay even one day. We do not make empty threats; we choose the time and the place of their being carried out. The seeds of the destruction are already planted. My brethren only need to give the signal for them to sprout. You, Valentine, shall be the agent of this land's destruction. It will be your responsibility. The question is, of course, can you handle the responsibility? Can you handle responsibility?"

"You talk too much," Frat said. "The major's under orders, like the rest of us."

"Negotiating such an arrangement, even if the Kentucky Assembly is interested, would take a lot of time," Valentine said. "If this whirlwind is as imminent as you claim, you had better delay it, or you'll find yourself taking refuge in a wasteland."

The bird thing cocked its head. "Keep in touch."

Valentine nodded to Frat, who gave it a vigorous turn. He walked it out of camp.

Valentine turned to Habanero. "Wagon master, see if you can raise Fort Seng on your radio. We need to find out where Brother Mark is."

He turned to the owner of the biggest property in the Free Territory. "Mrs. O'Coombe, I'm sorry, but the needs of Southern Command and Kentucky will have to delay finding your son."

She tore her eyes from the strange strut of Jack in the Box's avatar. "But you said tomorrow we will be in the territory where he'd been left."

"We'll get there. Just not tomorrow."

She drew herself up. "Mister Valentine. I equipped this convoy with the best communications equipment I could find. The transmitter alone is worth one of my barns and its resident livestock. Are you telling me it is not adequate to pass along a message that may or may not be an empty threat?"

"Brother Mark may need transport to whatever responsible parties can decide what to do about this."

"Are you giving me an order?"

"If I have to," Valentine said, careful to keep his rifle under his arm as the camp began to line up behind their respective leaders, the Bears and Wolves with Valentine, the drivers and mechanics and security men and medical staff with Mrs. O'Coombe. Stuck just stood up and stared at Valentine.

Duvalier hopped up on top of the Bushmaster. "Cool off, all of you. I don't know who or where this Jack-in-the-off is, but we start throwing down on each other, he'll be laughing until the robins come back."

The camp broke into a dozen separate arguments over the reality of the threat:

"If a Kurian told me my dick was on fire, I wouldn't look down and give him the satisfaction."

"They always give you a last chance."

"So this Kurian makes peace with Kentucky. What about the rest of them? It's all well and good to be neutral, but others gotta respect it or it don't mean jack."

"It's like a game to the Kurians," Stuck said to Valentine's Bears. "Sometimes their threats are empty; other times they are carried out to the last degree and beyond. They keep us guessing and on edge."

"Just good poker," Chieftain said. "Sometimes you can win a pile on the cheap, if you know how to bluff."

"I have Fort Seng, five-five," Habanero said from the radio.

Valentine walked over to the parked Rover. So much for sleep. "Tell them to get Colonel Lambert on the line. Wake her up if they have to. We need to talk."

✝

You never knew how much of a Kurian threat was illusion and how much was steel. They were like magicians, always diverting attention from the operating hand.

Valentine put a steadying grip on Chieftain's arm. The Bear's hair had risen on top of his head. Valentine had known Bears who turned purple when readying for a fight, or whose eyes lit up like a pair of flares, or who turned into snorting, steaming, turf-tearing bulls. He'd never seen one give himself a war headdress before. Valentine had always assumed that Chieftain's name came from the Bear's characteristic tomahawks.

"Eloi and Morlocks?" Valentine asked, by way of calming him down.

"I could never much stand reading, Major. But I liked that H. G. Wells guy. Except for *Food of the Gods*; that one was just too weird."

"But maybe the most topical, considering tonight's conversation," Valentine said. But to be honest, he'd skimmed it too when he was thirteen.

"I read my share of the stuff when I was a boy," Valentine said, remembering the long winters in Father Max's library. He'd once thought it profitless idling, but it gave him a truer picture of the world before the cataclysm in 2022 than he received through bits and pieces of the reworked histories of New Universal Church photo-studies children in the Kurian Zone received.

Valentine had sat in any number of New Universal Church lobbies, waiting for free cocoa or bread issued in exchange for attending a short lecture. He'd paged through photograph after photograph of poverty, devastation from war, death by starvation and disease, every horror imaginable and most of them featuring children as victims.

In the Free Territories most of the history the kids learned had to do with the post-2022 resistance and the crimes perpetrated in the Kurian Zone. It was taken as a given that the Old World was a pleasant idyll. One side showed ugly pictures of a hell; the other painted fair, vague portraits of a heaven.

Valentine believed the reality to be a blend. Perhaps whether you lived in heaven or hell depended more on your mental attitude than anything.

Back to the present. *One of the drawbacks of aging*, Valentine thought from his venerable age of having recently turned thirty, *is a tendency to dwell on the past.* Living in many of his memories would mean a waking nightmare. Better to think about the future.

With that thought firmly in mind, Valentine examined the baton the flying Reaper had brought. Mrs. O'Coombe's crew was already calling it "Mothman."

The baton case looked like polished bone, possibly a femur from a preadolescent human. Valentine didn't know bones well enough to determine. Besides, the joints were sawn off where the tube had been threaded and capped.

He buried the cylinder and its caps. No telling what the Kurian might have planted in the baton in the way of location devices. For all he knew there could be an audio-video transmitter.

The offer itself took up only one paragraph. There was no signature or date. The paper had a watermark that looked vaguely like a stylized depiction of an eclipse—a ring of faintly red fire, offering just enough of a glow to read the letters in darkness. Perhaps that was the Kurian's version of a commitment.

Valentine touched it with a first-aid kit's tweezers.

A FAIR OFFER OF A SECURE FUTURE

—it began, and went on to outline the same deal the Reaper had spoken of. Autonomy for Kentucky save for the Kurian bridgehead at Louisville—a fair exchange for Evansville—provided it remained neutral in the war.

Frat returned, looking thoughtful, and stowed his rifle and gear. Valentine waved him over to the radio, where he was waiting to see if Lambert could make contact with Brother Mark—then perhaps he and the old churchman could have personal communication.

The lieutenant looked like he'd aged a year since Valentine had last seen him. Had the Kurian figured out a way to siphon off a little aura? He'd decided some time ago that that was what had happened to him at the Owensboro western bridge.

"How'd that thing ever find you, Frat?" Valentine asked. "Did it just flap down?"

"I thought I heard an engine—aircraft, maybe—and went up a hill so I could find a better listening spot.

"It gave a chittering sound from a tree above. I looked up and there it was. I thought my number was up. But it had a white hand towel in each mitt and waved them."

"You shouldn't go poking around alone," Valentine said.

"What, some good ol' boys around here will bend me over and make me squeal?"

"That's a dream date compared to what a Reaper might do to you."

Frat shrugged.

"Frat, one more thing. Did it have anything in that bag?"

"I searched it. Nothing but dog hair and stank. I think that was a ration pouch. Maybe some toy poodle got packed as its lunch."

"Didn't seem like the kind of creature that could fly far to me."

"Maybe the engine noise was from an aircraft, dropping the thing off."

Valentine nodded. "We had a little argument over the management of the column while you were gone. We're going to get Brother Mark."

"Before we get Mrs. O'Coombe's son? Hope you know what you're doing. She seems like a useful woman to know, if you ever decide to turn civilian and take up private employment."

CHAPTER ELEVEN

*C*entral Kentucky, January: The locals have a saying: "You have
to come here on purpose." This is the fastness of Kentucky, the region
that stretches southeast from Louisville to the Tennessee Valley. It is
a bewildering maze of knobs, gullies, streams, ridges, choked at the
swampy bottoms and backwaters, breezy and cool and clear atop the
region's many ridges.

The meadows, breathing in the shadows of the ridges, are the gut
of the country. So rich in blackberry bramble and cherry, with grasses
that grow indefatigably in summer and only a little less lushly in the
brief winters, the meadows support dairy cattle for the landholders and
such an abundance of deer that even the region's skilled hunters hardly
trim the population.

Winters here pass mild; snow blows across several times a year but
melts quickly. Even the songbirds seem to be resting between mid-
December and February; all the greens and browns fade and blend together and everything looks washed-out and dull.

The water is the same, winter or summer. The hills are rich in
wells and springs, all flowing with clean, crisp, limestone-filtered water
tastier than any city tap could produce. Underground flows and seeps
have worn away the region's limestone, honeycombing it with sinks and
caves famous, dangerous, and unknown.

The people are clannish in the best sense of the word. Interlocking *circles of families spread news, offer support, celebrate marriages, and mourn deaths at the many little churches dotting the region. They are fiercely independent, even from their fellow Kentuckians: the city folk outside Cincinnati and Louisville, the flatlanders of the more gentle hills to the west (not that they don't range their legworms there and maintain good relations with the Jackson Purchase locals), or the Appalachian mountain folk. In past decades some were moonshiners and marijuana growers; later they ran Internet start-ups and were artisans. They were the first in Kentucky to learn how to wrangle legworms, to study their herds and breeding cycles, unafraid to learn from even the smattering of Grogs in southern Indiana, becoming elderly veterans of the battles following the cataclysm in 2022 in worm riding and harvesting.*

They use the many caves and holes to hide their weapons, their precious machine tools, their spare radios, and even explosives.

This is the heartland of the old Kentucky Alliance that accompanied Southern Command's Javelin into West Virginia. Now what's left of that fellowship is reorganizing itself into the Army of Kentucky—at least that's the formal name on the documents coming out of the government. The worm riders, wintering their mounts in the protective heaps they form around each year's eggs, are now a group called the Line Rifles and organized into three troops: the Gunslingers, the Bulletproof, and the Mammoth.

Men like to have something or someone to follow. Sometimes it's nothing but a favorite song; other times a bullet-torn flag. In the case of the Mounted Rifles of the Army of Kentucky, their standard is a warrior queen.

Young and beautiful in her full bloom, with a mane of hair flowing and alive as a galloping horse's tail, she wears her authority the way another woman might wear a favorite hat, only taking it out for special occasions and drawing all the more eyes because of it. She's a natural atop a legworm or a horse, and she designs and sews her own uniform from egg skins she's harvested herself, bearing a pistol that belonged to her father and a pair of binoculars presented to her by the old Bulletproof clan chief she grew up calling her leader.

Her words were the ones the Kentucky Alliance listened to on the long retreat back from the Appalachians, when many were discouraged and wished to go home. Her voice gave the order for the counterattack on the banks of the Ohio that sent the Moondaggers running. Under her leadership they chased the bearded invaders all the way to Bowling Green.

She has her hands full at the moment. There's a white-hot blood feud with the old Coonskin clan, who betrayed the Kentucky Alliance on the long retreat, dividing cousin against cousin, uncle against niece. What's left of the Coonskins have taken on the Moondagger faith, and members of the Mammoth troop are forever disappearing for weeks at a time while they avenge some sister or cousin.

As if that's not enough, the newly constituted government of Kentucky is still getting itself organized. Volunteers come in unequipped, untrained, and irregularly, hungry and in shoes with old pieces of tire serving as soles, adding to the food supply problem even while they wait for a rifle.

†

Valentine's luck was in. As it happened, Brother Mark was also in the Karas' Kentucky Alliance heartland. They managed to get a fix on each other over the radio and agreed to meet on Gunslinger clan ground.

What was left of the old alliance welcomed them into the Gunslinger camp squatting for the winter in the ruins of a megachurch near a group of their worm piles outside of Danville. If not cheering, exactly, there were shouted halloos and greetings and excited children rolling around and bumping like marbles.

The camp was unsettling in one manner, though. It seemed to be devoid of men between fourteen and forty. All Valentine saw were boys and old men. He knew the Gunslingers had suffered losses during the summer's fighting, but he had no idea they were this grievous.

There were plenty of horsemen and vehicles and guns in camp, however. Tikka was there with a column of her all-Kentucky army, and Brother Mark had arrived with a few members of the Assembly and their staff.

"Lots of mouths to feed, mouths that didn't do any planting or weeding or varmint shooting this summer," one of the cooks grumbled as he spooned soup into variegated plastic containers.

Valentine presented Mrs. O'Coombe to the temporary leader of the Gunslingers, an old woman who'd long served as an advisor to their clan's leader. Mrs. O'Coombe quivered like an excited horse as she asked about her son.

The Gunslinger leader asked the camp doctor, who stepped up and cleared his throat. "I have good news for you, madam," he said. "Your son is alive and well. I saw him not four days ago."

"May I see him, please?"

The temporary clan chief shook her head. "He is with our muster. They left to meet the Coonskins on the Kentucky river some ways north of here. Corporal Rockaway is serving with the new army's artillery."

"But—he is a soldier of Southern Command," Mrs. O'Coombe said. "He has four years left. . . ."

"An informal arrangement," the Gunslinger said. "He's still in what's left of the Southern Command Guard uniform. Settle, ma'am; settle. He's just along so we can show strength if they try another decapitation attack. Fine boy you raised."

"It's that Last Chance," Brother Mark said. "Raving about

some kind of apocalypse that's going to hit Kentucky. Sad thing is, he's getting a few converts."

Valentine fought his body. It wanted to be up and in action, chopping wood or clearing brush for kindling if nothing else.

"We've had a lot of townies flee to Coonskin territory," the clan leader said. "Mostly people who drew breath thanks to the Kurian Order anyway, so good riddance to them."

"If you would provide me with a guide—," Mrs. O'Coombe said.

"Sorry, ma'am. I hate to say no to a worried mother—I have four myself and one grandchild—but it's a clan rule. When a fighting man is away, no parents, no children, no spouses until the fighting's over."

"But there is to be no fighting," Mrs. O'Coombe said.

"We hope not. As I was saying, our people end up worrying more about their families than the enemy, and they get themselves in trouble that way. But it looks like you brought a few gunmen of your own. If you want to send them up with a message to your boy, they're welcome to join young Tikka upcountry. Until then, I'd like to offer you our hospitality."

Gunslinger hospitality was meager with all the visitors in camp and the holidays emptying larders.

Everyone was talking about the peace conference between the Gunslingers and the Coonskin–Moondaggers northeast of them in the Bluegrass proper. The idea that Kentucky might be allowed to just let the bodies lie and stop the raids and counterraids that had been going on ever since the Moondaggers marched across Kentucky, burning and kidnapping, gave everyone hope for an early spring without gunfire exchanged in Kentucky's tangled dells.

Valentine had the disquieting feeling that their hopes would be in vain. This cease-fire might be the final calm before the storm.

†

The reinforcements were already pulling out of the Gunslinger winter camp to join the others to the north. Tikka's Army of Kentucky were dressed like scarecrows in everything from denim to black-dyed sports uniforms, but most sported new winter hacking coats in a uniform deerskin brown, *A-o-K* stenciled on the shoulder. Behind them were guns and commissary wagons. Valentine hadn't seen such a mule train since the campaign in Dallas. The animals looked fresher than the men.

Tikka greeted Mrs. O'Coombe's lined-up staff and Valentine's Southern Command additions. She and a few members of her staff took a quick appreciative look at their bikes and vehicles.

"How are you keeping these beasts fed in the backwoods?" one of the men in a new-looking uniform with a coonskin on the outside of his muffler-style field-jacket collar said.

"We burn organic," Stuck said.

Someone on the staff muttered to a friend about outsiders buying corn oil when there were hungry mouths this lean winter. The comment wasn't meant for him, so Valentine didn't react.

"I don't suppose we can count on that APC up at the peace conference," Tikka said to Stuck.

"We've got a few of our own wounded to take care of. It's mostly a hospital truck."

"Then how about lending your doc and that medical wagon, in case there's a fight."

"I'll ask Mrs. O'Coombe," Stuck said, and walked off.

Habanero was pointing out modifications to the suspension as Tikka walked Valentine back toward the road north.

"You want to join us and see the fun?" Tikka asked.

"The man I'm looking for is up there already. Yes, I'm glad to accept your invitation."

Tikka faked a stumble and knocked into Valentine with her shoulder. "On duty again, I'll bet."

"I'm not sure how to categorize what we're doing at the moment," Valentine said. "Civilian liaison, I suppose."

"Figures. I wouldn't object to a quick liaison under a blanket, but this time I'm the one with a bunch of men expecting me to have my pants on at all hours. Besides, your redhead's looking at me like I'm selling New Universal Church Bibles door-to-door."

Valentine turned around and saw Duvalier sitting cross-legged on the hood of the Chuckwagon, warming herself on the engine. She threw her leg over her sword stick and rubbed the handle in an obscene manner.

"Thin little thing," Tikka said. "I remember her now; she's the one who comes and goes. You should buy her a good Kentucky ham."

"She's always looked like that, but she still puts in thirty miles a day of walking when she has to." Valentine wanted to change the subject. "You know, I don't think I've congratulated you on your new post."

"I delivered one big victory, and now I get cheered everywhere I go. They keep saying they're going to appoint a general-in-chief for the A-o-K, and I wish they'd get on with it. I'm shooting from the hip from the time I get up until the moment I pull off my boots—when I get a chance to sleep, that is. I was brought up to keep the Bulletproof's worms from getting rustled and our stills from getting stolen, not to do this commanding general stuff. Speaking of which, if the men don't see me in my command truck, they won't keep closed up properly. I'll see you on the banks of the Kentucky, David."

†

Stuck remained at the Gunslinger winter camp. Where Mrs. O'Coombe went, so did he, a hulking shadow. At the moment he sat pillowed between Longshot's thighs as she rubbed oil into his scalp and massaged his temples, looking like a monkey grooming her mate.

"What's that all about?" Duvalier asked Valentine.

"Bears get twitchy if they don't let off steam somehow. That's how brawls start: Bears with nothing to use as a way to vent."

"Like chopping wood?" Duvalier asked.

Valentine stared at her. He'd never thought of it beyond satisfying exercise.

"You sure you don't want to come up to the peace conference?" he asked.

Duvalier poked him with her elbow. "Snore. There's an interesting craft market in Danville, they say. Maybe I'll visit that. I picked up some real gold braid in Indiana. I'll skip a few days of you making goggle eyes at your bowlegged worm rider."

Valentine decided not to ask how she'd acquired the braid. "I'm not sure how to make 'goggle eyes,'" Valentine said, and then regretted it instantly. A lot of times Duvalier said nonsensical stuff just to provoke him.

"You know, Val, you're just a big plaything to her. A doll with really nice hair and a dick."

"What a shame I missed Christmas morning."

"That's it. I am coming along, if only to keep you from embarrassing us."

†

The banks of the Kentucky were thickly wooded at the slight bulge that passed for a lake designated as the border between Gunslinger and Coonskin territory. Behind the banks were the river-cut hills, scarred with limestone cuts and patched with tufts of wood like an old man's hairline.

They could see on the other side of the river the observation positions of what was presumably the Coonskin force, no doubt here to safeguard their own negotiators.

Valentine's binoculars weren't much better than his eyes at that distance, but with the help of one of the A-o-K's telescopes, he could get a look at individual figures. He recognized the dark battle dress and red dagger sheaths of the Moondaggers.

"The Coonskins have formally united the Moondaggers," Brother Mark said. "May they live to see the error of their ways and have regret come to wisdom."

Frat took a long look at the foes he'd heard so much about. "Religious nuts, huh?"

"If you call worshipping Kurians a religion," Valentine said. Frat turned the eyepiece over to Boelnitz. He turned the knob back and forth, sweeping across the camp, and then made a few notes in his leather journal.

"Some of 'em like the lifestyle, I guess," the Gunslinger observer said. "No tobacco, booze, or red meat but all the wives you want."

"They've been calling themselves the Kentucky Loyal Host lately," a Gunslinger in an officer's slouch hat said.

"Fancy-sounding word for 'traitor,'" Silvertip observed.

Their long search ended in a matter-of-fact fashion. Valentine and Frat were escorted to Corporal Rockaway, raised O'Coombe, where he was setting up mortar positions on the hillside above the river.

"Your boy Rockaway—or O'Coombe, or whatever his name is—he's involved in this. He may be on one leg and be wearing a diaper, but he's a heck of a fire director and trainer for our captured Moondagger artillery," one of Tikka's captains said as he walked them along the ridgeline.

And making a bad job of it, too, to Valentine's mind. The artillery's position could be observed from across the river.

Valentine remembered Rockaway as soon as he saw the face, but there had been changes. He limped worse than Valentine and seemed to have lost weight everywhere but his midsection. He was a rather plain-looking, freckled young man with sandy hair and a delicate chin like his mother's. He seemed lost in the big service jacket the A-o-K wore, but he still had his Southern Command helmet. Valentine was surprised someone hadn't talked him out of it when he was left behind. Javelin ran short on helmets long before they hit Evansville.

"Did you pick out these emplacements?" Valentine asked as others kept trotting up to Corporal Rockaway for instructions.

"Orders," Corporal Rockaway said. He had some of his mother's Texas accent too. "We're supposed to show our teeth so there won't be any funny business like at Utrecht. Hey, Doc. What the heck are you doing all this way?" O'Coombe's doctor stepped forward. "We've come a long way to bring you home. I'm glad to see you well. When we'd heard—"

Rockaway smiled, which much improved his face. "Hell, Doc, well's a relative term. You put my first diaper on me, and I'm here to tell, I'm back in diapers now and will be for the rest of my life. Some emergency patching to the digestive tract, they said. And I have to drink lots of water to help things along. But I can still fight; I just leak a little doing it. I like fighting these Moondagger sons of bitches. If everything— Well, tell Mom not to worry."

"You can tell her yourself when this is done. She's back with the Gunslinger camp," Valentine said.

"She came all this way too? Devoted of her. When the news came about my older brothers, she just tightened up her mouth and hung black crepe around their pictures and made big donations in their names to the Rear Guard Fund."

Valentine had no business getting involved in family dynamics. He jerked his chin at Frat, and they excused themselves.

Once they were out of earshot, Frat said, "Heart's in the right place but the kid doesn't know much about setting up a battery. If anything goes down, he's making it easy for the Moondaggers. They're not all cross-eyed and stigmatic, I don't suppose."

"Not hardly," Valentine said, remembering the sniper's bullet that had sprayed Rand's brains all over headquarters.

†

Valentine spotted Tikka emerging from a knot of hilltop woods, walking the ridgeline. Corporal Rockaway limped up to her, and they spoke for a few minutes. Tikka pointed as she spoke, both toward the ridge on the other side of the river where the Coonskins and the Moondaggers were encamped, and behind, where the rest of her train was presumably approaching and deploying.

Once again, she made a show of strength, putting some of her vehicles and horse wagons in plain view on the hill.

She was kind enough to invite Valentine to accompany her to the peace conference. All she asked was that he wear one of the A-o-K field jackets and a hat, and keep to the back with his mouth shut.

Duvalier managed to work her way into the party too. Boelnitz tried to get permission to come along, but Tikka insisted that he stay back on the riverbank.

"Remember what happened the last time we were invited to a conference?" Valentine said.

Tikka grinned fiercely. "As a matter of fact, we're very much hoping for an encore."

"Without legworms? Won't you be at a disadvantage?"

"They'll be assuming that, yeah."

†

VIPs arrived in cars and passenger trucks; the Gunslingers and Bulletproof and a smattering of other old Alliance soldiers on horseback or in wagon trains. Many arrived via old-fashioned shoe leather.

They met out on the small lake, a widening in the Kentucky River separating Coonskin land from the Gunslingers.

Valentine felt like he'd read about a peace meeting like this before, but he couldn't place the exact circumstances.

The two sides rowed out to a pontoon houseboat anchored midlake. There, on the sundeck atop the houseboat (after both sides verified that neither had filled the living quarters with gunmen), they met.

Their forces lined the tree-filled banks to either side of the river. Valentine didn't understand the fascination. There was little enough to watch.

He wasn't important enough to go up on the top deck with the Kentucky or Coonskin principals. But he could listen from the base of the ladder facing the west side of the river.

There were introductions, neither side being particularly gracious beyond the grace required of opponents who were used to shooting each other on sight. If the Gunslingers were colder in their formalities, it was because they'd suffered more outrage at the hands of the Moondaggers.

In many more words than the Reaper's avatar used, they offered the representatives of the Kentucky Assembly essentially the same status as Jack in the Box had spoken of: a neutral Kentucky, running its own domestic affairs but leaving the outside world to the Kurians. The Agenda and Tikka were no more inclined to welcome the proposal from some Moonskin mouthpiece and a few traitors than they were through Valentine's birdlike Reaper.

✝

"Glad to see you admit we whupped you out of Kentucky," Tikka said.

"We stayed only long enough to chase Southern Command out," a Moondagger responded. "Then we returned to our allies."

"Formerly *our* allies," Tikka said. "They turned on us; they'll turn on you someday. Remember that."

"You are the traitors," an educated Kentucky accent said. "The Kurians indulged you, and you paid them back by aiding terrorists and wreckers and murderers—"

"There is a reckoning coming!" one of the Moondaggers began to shout thickly. Valentine recognized the voice at once, their old blustering friend Last Chance. "A reckoning! This land, long peaceful—"

Ha! Valentine thought. Last Chance wasn't at the battle between the Bulletproof and the Wildcats a few years back.

"—needs to be cleansed of the filth that has washed into it. Intruders! Interlopers! Troublemakers! Trouble they brought, and death will be their reward—or something worse than death."

Duvalier made a fist and flicked out two fingers toward Last Chance with her thumb slightly up—the American Sign Language version of "asshole."

"That's not how you go about negotiating in Kentucky, beardy," the new Agenda for the Assembly said—the previous one was too sick to make the journey to the river. "You want to deal with us, you tell us what you offer and you let us make up our minds. You don't threaten."

Valentine liked the new Agenda already. Later he learned he was a man named Zettel, though most called him Mr. Zee. Formerly the clan chief of the Gunslingers and a friend of Karas, Mr. Zee, Valentine had been told, came from a family who'd once owned quarries and he'd grown up covered in limestone dust.

"We'll consider your offer and give you an answer tomorrow. Here, on the boat again. Shall we say noon?" Agenda Zettel said.

"There can be only one answer," the educated voice said. "The other doesn't bear thinking about. We both love Kentucky too much to see it turned into a graveyard."

Duvalier looked up at the sky, shivered. She edged closer to Valentine and stuck her hands in his pocket.

"We could go up there and kill all of them," she whispered. "Pay them back for Utrecht."

Killers who don't like killing never last long. They become drunks or careless. Duvalier liked it, as long as her targets were Quislings, the higher up in the social hierarchy the better.

Valentine had a dark part of him that liked it as well. The shadow that lurked inside him chose its time and place to be satisfied.

"The Assembly can make up its mind. It's their choice. Let's not make it for them."

A few more words were exchanged upstairs about day and night signals.

They departed. Valentine put one hand in his pocket and gripped Duvalier's with the other, making sure she accompanied him to one of the boats heading back for the Gunslinger shore.

†

They waited in line and ate like the rest of the Gunslingers and A-o-K troops. Chieftain and Silvertip were going back for thirds when Tikka interrupted and asked for a moment with Valentine. They stepped out of earshot.

"Mr. Zee's meeting with the Assembly representatives is civilians only, so I thought I'd track you down and talk to you."

Her dark good looks were suited for a chill Kentucky night. She sparkled like a bit of Kentucky's bituminous coal. Valentine knew that all you had to do was touch a match to her and she could generate a whole evening's worth of warmth.

"What reply should we give, in your opinion?" Tikka asked.

"Why should my opinion matter?" Valentine asked.

"I trust it, for one," Tikka said.

"I'm . . . uneasy. Everyone in the Kurian Order seems to be shouting 'surrender' or at least 'keep out' at Kentucky. I can't make sense of it. I don't mean to denigrate the land or the people, but it's not like Kentucky is filled with industries they'd miss and resources they can't get anywhere else."

"There's the coal," Tikka said. "And the Cumberland's the easiest route to the east coast in the South."

"Perhaps they are more worried about invasion than we thought. I can't help but feel there's something here very important to the Kurian Order."

"What? We know about what they did here; they weren't at all secretive about it. There are no big tracts of the country that are off-limits. A few towers in Lexington, a few more in Louisville. The legworm meat? The big plants up in Louisville fill boxcars with canned protein every day. I was told some of it even gets traded overseas."

Valentine tried to keep his mind on the possibilities in the Kurian strategy, rather than the possibilities behind Tikka's uniform shirt buttons. "Without food it's hard to grow your population. Maybe that's all it is: They don't want to lose their free-labor butchery."

"Perhaps its just geography. If Kentucky becomes a Freehold, the Free Territory extends from the foothills of the Appalachians to Mexico. That's a lot of people and a lot of resources, more than many countries in the world have." Tikka worked her fist into her palm. "The Assembly said that they wanted to hear from me before they make their final decision. Whichever way I go, I think the rest of the Alliance will follow."

"That's quite a responsibility."

"Well, if someone else made the decision and I didn't agree, it'd drive me straight into a froth."

Valentine smiled at her.

"I think we should tell them to make like a frog and boil. I'm sure they want us to disarm, get complacent, and then they'll give us the works anyway."

"It's happened before," Valentine said, meaning both throughout human history and in relations with the Kurian Order.

†

That night the reunited elements of the Kentucky Alliance held a celebration. All along the hillside impromptu bands started up their fiddles and guitars, or raucous parties rolled out the barrels of beer and casks of bourbon.

The locals knew how to live well. Any excuse for a celebration. The sentries and flankers were out and paying attention to their duties, so it wasn't all revelry.

Valentine didn't join in. He was tired from the trip and worried about what the Kurians were hatching in their towers, and he was in no mood for carousing—especially with negotiations at an impasse and an enemy army just across the river.

Chieftain and Silvertip were content to load up with food and settle down by Valentine and Duvalier.

"In another time," Duvalier said, "all we'd be worried about now is keeping New Year's resolutions. High-carb or lo-carb diets." Duvalier had the pinched look of someone on a no-food diet, but then her stomach gave her difficulty under the stress of field cooking.

"I've plenty of resolve. I just hope I'm granted the strength to see it through. Then another generation will get to worry about their carb intake," Valentine said.

"I don't know about that," Silvertip said. "I don't think the old world's ever coming back. Good riddance to it."

Chieftain stood up. "Not this speech again. I'm going back for seconds. I'll have fourths by the time he's done."

Silvertip gave him an elaborate double-index-finger salute. "You just don't know wisdom when you hear it. I say it's all got to come down. Everything: Kurian Order, the Free Territories. Let's say we beat the Kurians—we're not just restoring the United States as it was. There's Grogs settled all across in their bands from the swamps in North Carolina through Indianapolis, St. Louis, the Great South Trail and then up Nevada and out to Oregon. We just going to put them on reservations? Exterminate them? The Kurians have ruined half of mankind and impoverished the rest. Southern Command's handed out land right and left. Suppose some relations show up with old deeds saying it's theirs?

"It's all gonna get burned down, and then maybe the decent folks will rebuild civilization. The honest and diligent and talented will find others of like mind and start setting up again. It'll be ugly for the Kurian herds, but maybe their kids or their grandkids will be human beings again. That's why your legion's bound to fail, beg your pardon, Major.

"In the end, we'll be thanking the Kurians. They gave us a challenge and we'll end up better for it, the way a forest fire helps the trees thrive. Gotta burn away the rubbish once in a while."

Valentine disagreed but knew better than to get into a heated argument with a Bear. Most of Valentine's command would be "rubbish" in Silvertip's taxonomy. Time would tell.

Chieftain returned with a piece of newspaper filled with honey-dipped apple slices. "He give you the *world's got to burn down* speech?"

†

Valentine bedded down with the sounds of music and celebration still echoing from the hillside.

Duvalier shook him awake in the predawn.

"There's something brewing across the river. Can you hear it?"

Valentine went to the riverbank. There was still enough night air for the sound to carry; his Wolf's ears did the rest. A steady crunch and soft clatters and clanks like distant, out-of-tune wind chimes sounded from the screen of growth and trees across the river.

Frat was already at the riverbank, on his belly with a pair of binoculars to his eyes.

"You thinking what I'm thinking?" Valentine asked.

"We're about to get served by the Host," Frat said.

"Run to the A-o-K headquarters and tell Tikka that they're coming."

Frat passed the binoculars to Valentine and took off.

Flashes of light, like distant lightning, lit up the eastern riverbank ridge. Valentine saw the red lines of shells pass overhead.

They landed among the mortar tubes and wagons parked on the hillside.

"Those rotten bastards," Silvertip said, roused by the smell of action. "May they all rot in Kurian innards, or whatever happens when they dine."

"I have a feeling it's about to become unhealthy in these trees. We'd better fall back to the hill," Valentine said.

He made sure of Duvalier and his weapons and pulled everyone out of the woods, turning them south so they moved parallel to river and hill until they made it outside the box of artillery.

The Host executed their attack well. Valentine grudgingly granted them that. Artillery shells exploded in the vehicle park and all along the artillery line, sending up plumes of black-rimmed gasoline explosions. Smaller secondary explosions from readied mortar shells added to the dirt in the air.

Branches and undergrowth up and moved on the opposite bank, as though the Birnam Wood suddenly decided to move a few yards toward the Ohio.

Boats shot through the gaps in the riverbank growth. Lines of the Host—it looked as though most were Moondaggers—splashed into the water and then fell into the boats, where they picked up paddles and began to paddle madly across the river.

The pontoon boat seemed to spark, and suddenly smoke began to pour out of its windows and lower doors. Strange gray smoke, to be sure, but it did its job obscuring the river.

"I know that smoke," Valentine said. "Ping-Pong balls and match heads. Like ten thousand or so."

The smoke billowed and spread under the influence of the wind, advancing toward them at an angle like a flanking army.

Valentine was of the opinion that many battles were won or lost before the first shot was fired. One side just did a better job of getting more force into a position where it could strike than the other. Such was the case here.

The Kentucky Alliance could see it as easily as he could and decided to get while the getting was good, as a few of their own artillery shells fell blind into the mass of smoke.

"Let's get out of here!" Frat shouted.

"Bastards. Let me at 'em," Chieftain said.

"You'll fall back with the rest of us," Valentine said, grabbing the giant by the shirt collar and dragging him back.

Silvertip, not yet full of battle fury and able to think, yanked Valentine so hard in the tug-of-war with Chieftain's anger that the potential daisy chain broke. Valentine had to check to see if he left his boots behind. Bee did a three-limb galumph up and into the smoke.

As Silvertip dragged Valentine up the riverbank slope, he observed that the Moondagger artillery fire must have been heavy and accurate. The smoldering Alliance vehicles had been burned beyond belief.

With a scattering of fleeing Gunslingers, Valentine joined the route away from the riverbank, running as though hell itself followed.

Another Kentucky disaster to add to his list. At least Southern Command wasn't involved with this one, and at best it would be a minor, two-paragraph notation in the newspapers.

Valentine made it over the hill, and suddenly the trees were thinner and he was into pasture.

He pulled up. A long line of foxholes and headlogs and machine-gun nests stood before him. Behind there were piles of logs and the A-o-K's few armored cars.

This was no slapdash last line of defense but a prepared position. It was obviously quickly done. The fire lanes were imperfectly cleared and the knocked-over trees didn't have their branches trimmed as they should have, but it provided ample if imperfect cover for the reserve.

An A-o-K sergeant took Valentine back to Tikka's headquarters. Valentine heard regular reports of strength and direction coming in from observers on the ridge—she'd scared up a field-phone system from somewhere. Probably captured Moondagger equipment.

The Host came over the ridge in three attacking waves with a skirmish line trotting hard out in front, whooping and yelling. Their cries of victory as they drove the last few Alliance members like rabbits turned into confused alarm as they realized what they'd just stuck their head into.

An old trainer had once told Valentine that firefights won by just putting more SoT—shit on target—than the other guy. With the lines of riflemen backed by machine gunners, who were backed by light cannon and .50 calibers on the trucks and improvised armored cars, the Kentucky Alliance was throwing a pound of shit for every ounce hurled back by the dismayed Moondaggers.

The Gunslingers and Tikka's A-o-K had a deadly effect. Valentine saw limbs of trees and entire boles fall in the holocaust sweeping across the Kentuckians' front. What it did to the enemy could only be imagined.

They fell in rows, replaced by more men pouring up and over the hill.

"Get on up there," an Alliance captain shouted, pointing at the advancing Moondaggers.

"Go on then," Valentine called to Chieftain.

"About fuckin' time. Aiyeeeee!"

The Bear ran forward, spraying with this double-magazined

assault rifle. When he emptied both ends of ammunition, he planted the gun on its long bayonet and drew his tomahawks.

Valentine settled for employing his Type Three. Duvalier, hugging a protective tree trunk like a frightened child gripping its mother, used Frat's binoculars to spot for him. Valentine squeezed shot after shot out, picking out officers for the most part.

Duvalier also seemed to be going by beard length.

They weren't men; they were funny targets in dark uniforms and hairy faces. A beard on a field radio fell. A beard firing a signal flare—down. A beard setting up a machine gun on a tripod to return fire—knocked back into the grass.

Shouts and whoops started up from the Gunslinger and A-o-K lines, and a second wave of riflemen went up and forward, passing through and over the first wave, who covered them with fire laid down on the retreating Host.

Chieftain raged among a group of Moondaggers who'd found a wooded dimple in the landscape from which they returned fire. Pieces of men flew this way and that as he swung and stomped and swung again.

The forward motion stopped at the crest of the hill. The Kentuckians threw themselves down and began to pick off retreated targets.

"Let 'em have it," yelled Rockaway into his field radio from his new hilltop post.

Mortar shells whistled down into the trees at the riverbank, detonating in showers of splinters or foaming splashes of water.

A Kurian machine gun opened up on Rockaway's position, guided by his antenna. Valentine dropped to a knee and returned fire with the Type Three.

"Silvertip, try to do something about that gun" was the only order Valentine gave that day that had anything to do with the progress of the battle. He felt like a bit of a fraud, watching shells detonate on the western riverbank among the Host's boats. Maybe Southern Command needed Kentucky more than Kentucky needed Southern Command.

"Pre-ranged fire missions," Rockaway said. "Hope they brought a lot of tweezers."

The Kentuckians ended up with a few prisoners and a lot of big canvas-sided motorized riverboats.

As the battle sputtered out, Valentine found Tikka.

"Brilliant retreat and counterattack," Valentine said.

"Oldest trick in the book," Tikka said.

"I didn't know you'd studied Scipio Africanus, Tikka."

She frowned. "I'm not big on astrology. No sir, I learned all my tactics reading Bernard Cornwell. It's an old Wellington maneuver: Get on the reverse slope out of the line of fire, and then blast away when the Frenchies come over the crest, and advance to throw them back. We just didn't blast them quite as much as they approached; we wanted them to scatter a little bit as they advanced."

"So you swapped out the artillery and vehicles last night during the party," Valentine said.

"Too noisy for you? That was the idea. To cover sound while we were building the fortifications. We parked old wrecks and set up black-painted fence-post mortars to replace the real ones."

"Would have been nice to be let in on the secret. I might have been able to offer a few suggestions. We have some experienced snipers in our group. They could have trimmed the Moondaggers down by a few more."

"I'm sorry, Valentine, but after Utrecht I'll never trust Southern Command's security again."

†

Valentine must have had an air of command about him, because all through the day members of the Gunslingers who'd fought with Javelin across Kentucky kept coming to him for orders, probably out of habit more than anything. Whether to bind prisoners or just march them with their hands up. What to do with captured weapons and equipment. How to organize a search party for a missing officer. Valentine issued advice rather than orders and sent a constant stream of problems to Tikka's headquarters on the ridge.

For just being an observer, he had an exhausting day.

That night he found Boelnitz scribbling away with the remains of a meal around him as Chieftain and Silvertip told war stories about the fighting in Kentucky.

"You should know better than to ask Bears about a fight," Valentine said to Pencil. "To hear them tell it, the rest of us are just there to keep the fried chicken and pie coming while they do all the fighting."

Boelnitz chewed on his pencil, apparently not hearing.

"So, how's the story coming, Boelnitz?"

Valentine had to repeat himself before the journalist looked up from his leather-covered notebook.

"Story? Not the one I was expecting, Major."

"You're getting some good tall tales out of these two, I hope."

"Kentucky's been interesting enough, but I don't know if my editor will want travelogue. I wish I had the guts to go inside one of those legworm tangles and get a few pictures, but the locals say that until the worms are born, it can be dangerous."

"That's right," said a nearby Gunslinger who'd plopped down to listen to the Bears spin their yarns. "Make any kind of disturbance and they'll snip you in half easy as you might pull a weed."

"To be honest, Major Valentine, I was expecting you to be a little different, more of the legend and less prosaic. Where are the raids into the estate homes in Indiana? You haven't even interrogated any of those Moondaggers or the Kentucky Host or whatever they call themselves to see what's in store for Kentucky."

"The Kurians never tell their foot soldiers their plans. They like to keep everyone guessing, including the other Kurians. I wouldn't be surprised if the reason they're so desperate is because they're afraid Atlanta will just end up taking over Kentucky the way they have much of Tennessee.

"Besides, if you were expecting a war in Indiana, you need men for that kind of job. Our ex-Quisling recruits need training. Most of them are experienced in handling weapons and vehicles and equipment due to a smattering of law enforcement or military duty, but they've got to learn to act as a team somewhere less predictable than a city street. More important, learn to trust each other and their officers. Trust doesn't come easy to someone brought up in the Kurian Order. They're so scared of making a mistake that they all stand around waiting for orders, and then for someone else to go first. There's a story for you."

"Problem is," the neighboring Gunslinger said, "they ain't even human in anything but shape. All the spunk's been bred right out of them, the way a team horse reacts different from a Thoroughbred lead mare or a wild stallion."

Valentine spent the next forty-five minutes on and off the radio. Frat had returned by then, having volunteered to scout across the river, looking thoughtful. After he secured his rifle and gear, he sat down by Valentine, eager for news.

"Where's the Kentucky Host?" Valentine asked. "Run out for more ice?"

"Left the party early," Frat said, milking the joke. He became serious. "Are we going down an evolutionary blind alley, sir?"

"Where does that come from?"

"They left some of their literature behind. There was a magazine I hadn't seen before, comparing various kinds of testing before and after the Kurians came. Of course the article proves there's been improvement in human mental acuity after their arrival."

"An article saying it doesn't make it true. Don't read Kurian intellectual porn; it's all lies anyway."

Frat dug around his satchel and tossed the magazine at Valentine's feet. "Well, I thought it was interesting.

"We're more moral than the enemy, right?" Frat continued. "Isn't that a hindrance? They'll do anything to win. We won't. Doesn't that make them the 'fittest' in a Darwinian sense?"

"Fittest doesn't mean strongest or most brutal. Loyalty confers an evolutionary advantage. So does sacrifice. You get all this from those traditional morals the brutes dispense with. Mountain gorillas trample strangers. That's about as brutal as you can get. For all I know, mountain gorillas no longer exist."

Frat looked down. For a moment he seemed to be summoning words, but they never made it out.

†

They convinced Rockaway to leave his guns and return to the Gunslinger camp. Now that the A-o-K had arrived, there were some experienced artillerymen to take over the mortar sections in any case, but he was still strangely reluctant, even though he admitted he hadn't seen his mother in years.

Tikka finally ended up ordering him to leave. "Show some consideration for your poor mother," she said.

So they rode back with Doc and his nurse in the Boneyard. The medical workers were more exhausted than even the Bears, having worked on the wounded of both sides in the late Battle of the Kentucky River.

They were not the first to arrive back at the Gunslinger camp, so the news of the victory on the riverbank, and the losses, had already been absorbed, celebrated, or mourned.

Valentine, wanting to be a bit of a showman, had the driver back the overloaded Boneyard back toward the little circle of Mrs. O'Coombe's convoy. Valentine and Duvalier hopped out of the cab, and he opened the doors for the assembled Hooked O-C staff.

"Mrs. O'Coombe," Valentine said, "your son."

The effect was spoiled somewhat by the fact that Chieftain and Silvertip were dressed only in their rather worn-through underwear.

"We've come some way to find you, Corporal Rockaway," Valentine said. "I've brought a familiar face."

The corporal jumped down out of the back of the ambulance medical truck.

"What's the matter, Mother?" Corporal O'Coombe said. "Sorry to see me still breathing?"

†

It wasn't the reunion between a son who served under his mother's name and his devoted parent that Valentine had imagined.

Mrs. O'Coombe stiffened. "You know I'm pleased to see you alive, Keve. Please be civil in front of your fellow men in uniform. Don't disgrace the uniform you wear."

"Respect the people beneath the uniform too, Mother."

"If you're going to be this way, perhaps we should talk in private."

"Do you have something you want me to sign, Mother, now that you've recovered from your disappointment that I'm still alive? Produce it. You know I'm not interested in running a ranch, however large."

"I'm glad your father isn't alive to hear this."

"Yes, yes: *The good sons died, the bad one lived. God must have a plan; all we can know is that he gives burdens to those strong enough to handle them.*"

Rockaway turned to Valentine. "My mother probably left out a few details. Like that the ownership of the ranch was willed by my father to his sons, and Mother only would own it if we were all dead. What is it, Mother? Do you want to sell off some of the land, or riverfront, or water rights?"

She extracted some surveys and a blueprint from her bush jacket. "I am building a home for the disabled in the Antelope Hills, on the Canadian River. I need to deed the necessary acreage to Southern Command."

Rockaway didn't even look at the papers.

"I'll do you one better, Mother. I'll sell you the whole ranch—lock, stock, and the old man's cutest little whorehouse in Texas—for a grand total of one dollar. I'll accept Southern Command scrip if you aren't carrying your usual smuggler's gold."

"That's very generous of you, Keve, and I am happy to accept. The problem is that you'll have to do this in a UFR courtroom, in front of a judge. My beloved husband's will was most specific on points of ownership."

She turned toward Valentine and the others. "You probably think I'm a grasping, conniving woman. Nothing of the sort. It's just extremely hard to run a business interest of this size when you can't enter into contracts without the owner's approval, and the owner is seven hundred miles away from a lawyer, a notary, and witnesses. My son, as you can see, is uninterested in a business that provides a quarter of all Southern Command's meat and that employs a permanent staff of over a thousand and seasonal help three times that."

"I'm only sorry I didn't sign it over to you two years ago," Rockaway said. "But I was seeing Arbita and she didn't want me to give it up, and for my sins I listened to her. But I'll sign it over to you now, Mother."

"So you'll return to the UFR with us?"

"If that's what it takes for me to be able to live my life in peace, do my job, and marry who and where I choose, I'll take the trip."

So the happy reunion wasn't quite so happy, at least as far as Mrs. O'Coombe and her son were concerned.

†

Brother Mark needed a ride back to Fort Seng. A wounded Gunslinger named Thursday was also going that way, as he wanted to recover over the winter at home with his family in a town called Grand Junction on the road back. His brother-in-law was supposed to drive out to the Gunslingers and pick him up, but his brother-in-law had flaked. Again. O'Coombe and Valentine's command had passed near it on the way up, and Thursday promised it was just over a ridge from their route home, on an old federal route in reasonably good condition.

They packed up the four vehicles. Valentine made sure Bee had all her odds and ends. Traveling with a Grog was a little like taking a child or a pet on a journey: You needed to make sure you remembered favorite toys, snacks, and clothing.

Thursday wasn't much of a guide. He spent a lot of time examining map, compass, and map again before giving instructions that proved to be guesswork. Valentine could have done just as well with an old road atlas. Thursday's wound was a piece of shrapnel to the buttock, or so he said, and he rode on a special pillow. Valentine wondered if he wasn't really suffering from aggravated hemorrhoids.

His instincts improved once they crossed a small river and he claimed to be in home territory.

"Grand Junction's not even an hour away, now. Three more big ridges and we're there. We could use a garrison of you Southern Command boys, now. There's a marketplace and even a bank that trades Karas' old currency for the new government scrip. Some riders came in a while back and tried to rob the town, but we shooed them off."

Valentine said, "Most of Southern Command's back across the river. All that's left are some training and technical personnel."

"That's Southern Command all over. They claim they swing the biggest dicks but always come up short when belts hit the floor."

A flake struck the windshield like a bug. A big piece of almost-sleet, it sledded down on its own melt.

"I guess winter's here," Valentine said, by way of breaking the tense silence.

In his winters south of central Missouri, Valentine had softened in his attitude toward cold weather. Winters weren't a matter of life-or-death survival, with desperate, predawn to postdusk fall efforts to stock up on enough fuel, food, and fodder to get yourself and the livestock through to spring—an almost unimaginable span of time away. Winter was a season of rest, refit, and relaxation.

The horizon closed in as the real snow started, following behind the big flakes like a wall of Napoleonic infantry advancing behind their pickets.

Valentine didn't like the look of the big, soft flakes. When they first appeared they fell idly, spinning and drifting in the wind, but minute by minute they thickened, aligning themselves in a single, southeasterly direction.

"Better slow down," he told the driver. "Turn on the running lights. I think we can quit worrying about aerial observation."

"Hope we don't have to do too much off-roading in this," the driver said. "Wish the locals took better care of the roads."

"Legworms make their own roads," Thursday said. "We like it nice and run-down. The Ordnance doesn't risk their axles bothering us." He chuckled. "This is Kentucky. We just don't get that hard weather. Even the sky takes it easy here. This'll blow over in no time."

CHAPTER TWELVE

*T*he Storm, January, the fifty-sixth year of the Kurian Order: Though *rare, heavy winter weather sometimes burdens Kentucky. Blizzards have been known to dump enough snow to form formidable, chin-high drifts where the snow is pushed and channeled by wind and terrain, and once in place, the snow is surprisingly tenacious when protected by hill or tree from the sun.*

The storm that winter of 2076 became a byword for bad conditions for generations after. To anyone who survived it, nothing that hit Kentucky in the future could compare to those wild weeks in January when the sky seemed determined to alternately freeze and bury the state.

The Moondagger prophet from the houseboat on the Kentucky River might have smiled in satisfaction as white judgment fell. Some said the real reason for the bad weather was the Kurian desire to see Kentucky's populace gathered together yet isolated, the better to be stationary targets for what bloomed like Christmas cactus in the thick of storm and gloom.

†

The storm and the night dragged on.

The snow waxed so heavy that night that they couldn't see more than fifteen or twenty feet in front of Rover. The headlights reflected back so much light from the snow they did more harm than good, so they drove using the service red guide lights. The motorcycles were useless in this weather, so Stuck and Longshot stopped and hung them up on the side of the Bushmaster. Fortunately, Thursday had put them on the right road for once, and all the driver in the cramped Rover had to do was stay on it.

With the storm raging outside, reaching Grand Junction became not just a matter of convenience but a necessity. If they pulled off and camped, everything would take three times as long thanks to the weather, and no one would have a comfortable night.

"Still can't believe about the Coonskins," Thursday said. "They were good men. Had many a meal with them when we all rode for Karas. The Moondaggers must have threatened them with something awful."

"Haw," Habanero said. "I'll bet every head in my share that no one threatened them with anything more than having to come home to six wives."

"That's how the Kurians get you," Longshot said. "Giveaways. That's how they took over in the first place, my old man always said. They showed up—and, sure, they offered food and fuel, but there was more than that. They offered structure and freedom from having to think for yourself."

"I'm sure that's just what people in an earthquake-hit city wanted," Thursday said. "What the hell you talking about, Habby?"

"It's like that story about how to trap swamp pigs. Ever heard it?"

"No," Thursday said.

Valentine had. Habanero had all of five parables, and the pig one wasn't nearly as good as his story about the frog and the scorpion. Mostly because that one was shorter.

Mrs. O'Coombe read her Bible by map light.

"Well, seems that down in the Congaree swamp in South Carolina there was a whole passel of pigs running wild. Now, pigs are smart. Every now and then a hunter would go in and try to get one, but most came back empty-handed, the pigs were so wary and wild.

"Well, a stranger feller came into town and said he was going to get them pigs. Of course all the locals about laughed him out of town, but he ignored them. Instead he went and bought himself a couple fifty-pound bags of corn.

"Every day he went into the swamp and poured some corn on one of the pig trails in a nice woodsy spot. Well, of course the pigs came along and ate the corn. It was free, after all. Easier than rooting up grubs and tubers.

"After a few days, with the pigs showing up regular for their feed, he put a few beams down in front of the corn, and he watched them eat from a distance. Just wood on the ground, easy for a pig to hop over, and none of them minded making that jump to get at that corn. Then he started building a fence for a stockyard. He always made sure there were plenty of ways in and out for the pigs. They were a little nervous of the construction—one or two hightailed it right back into the swamp—but the rest were getting really used to that corn, so they went in.

"Now gradually he shut off the entrances and exits, kept watching them from nearer and nearer, and made it tougher and tougher for the pigs to go in and get the corn, till all they had was a little gap to squeeze through. But darned if they didn't squeeze through and gobble till every last bit of the corn was eaten.

"Only one time, when they were done, the pigs saw that there was no way back out of the pen. He'd blocked it up.

"They got their free grain still. 'Nother day or two, anyway, before a big ol' livestock trailer pulled up, and they used sticks and dogs to herd them pigs right into the trailer. Didn't cost him much: a few big bags of corn to convince them pigs there was such a thing as a free lunch."

"So that's what they're doing to us Kentuckians, you think?" Thursday asked.

"I don't know if the Kurians are smart as that man down Congaree way. But the Kurians are big on advertising their wares as free, aren't they? Sometimes I think the scariest words in the American idiom are 'no obligation.' Of course, sometimes they stick in an 'absolutely' 'cause that one more lie just pushes people right over the edge into stupid."

†

They only knew they entered Grand Junction once buildings appeared on either side of the road.

"I know just where you should park, Habby," Thursday said to the wagon master at the wheel. "There's a grain mill just the other side of town. Not one of those claptrap corrugated iron things—real stonework. Abandoned now because of the lack of juice. We grind grain with a couple oxen these days, the old-fashioned way."

Valentine looked out the window. He was used to seeing gutted storefronts, but one of the buildings that had a hole in the front looked like it had received recent damaged—the splinters in the door were white and fresh.

"I wonder how long we'll be snowed in here," Duvalier said from the bench she had to herself at the very back of Rover. "Charmingly dead."

"What's that?" Habanero said suddenly into his mike.

Valentine plugged his own headset in, uneasy. "What happened?" Mrs. O'Coombe said.

"Ma in Chuckwagon says she just hit a person."

"Good God," Mrs. O'Coombe said.

Valentine's earphone crackled: "—maybe it was just a big dog. But he came leaping, trying to get on the back of Bushmaster, and slipped. Under my wheels before I knew it. We bumped over him."

"We should stop," Mrs. O'Coombe said.

"What kind of fool runs into a line of trucks in this weather?" Thursday said, his face unholy in the dim light of the console.

"Must have been a dog," Habanero said. "Shadows are weird with all the reflections."

"Here's the mill," Thursday said. "I'll get it open for you, and then I'll check in with our sheriff and let him know you've arrived. As long as that wasn't him Ma ran over."

He laughed at his own joke, but no one else did.

The mill looked like a staggered tower, in levels going back from the street rising to a sloped roof on the top floor like an old ski jump.

"Always thought this building would be great to live in if you could gut and rebuild like they used to. Left just here, Habby," Thursday said. "Don't think you can get more than the first two vehicles parked inside. The loading dock's only made for one truck, really. There's plenty of space around the side with the train tracks."

Habanero turned on Rover's lights. A metal gate broke the pattern in the stone sides of the mill. Thursday climbed out and met his dancing shadow at a crank handle.

Turning the handle, he raised what had probably once been an electric door.

Thursday lost his footing. Mrs. O'Coombe took a sudden breath at his fall.

Or not a fall. Thursday disappeared under the half-raised gate with a scream.

"What the hell!" Habanero said.

"Wagon master, get ready to reverse and get out of here," Valentine said.

Habanero began to speak into his microphone.

Valentine grabbed his rifle out of its seat-back clip and stepped outside.

"Valen—" Duvalier began, but he slammed the door.

He ducked down, looking into the dark of the old grain elevator. Rover's lights cast beams through that were cut off by the half-closed door. A pair of hands, Thursday's, were reaching out of the darkness and clawing in an effort to crawl back to Rover—but something was holding him back.

And hurting him. Thursday was screaming like a man being slowly dismembered.

Valentine wished he had a light clipped to the barrel of the gun. He looked around at the column but could see nothing but the whirling flakes and the columns lights.

The Type Three pointed from his hip at the gate, he went to the crank for the door gate. He extended his arm and gripped the freezing-cold metal. Tendons tight, he managed to turn the wheel with one hand while he kept the barrel of his rifle pointed at the growing gap between tracked door and ground.

Thursday's hands were twitching spasmodically now, and as more and more light bled into the mill, the rest of him was revealed.

A piercing shriek in his ear. Ali was out of the car, a pistol in hand and a sword stick under her arm. Valentine had never heard her shriek like that—the noise must be coming from another.

Ragged two-legged forms appeared in the white bath of the headlights. Gore-smeared mouths testified to a recent, messy feast.

Ravies!

Valentine had encountered the disease on his first independent command in the Kurian Zone.

Ravies was a disease of multiple strains, first used in 2022 to help break down the old order, and used here and there since whenever the Kurians needed to stir up a little chaos. On his trip into Louisiana as junior lieutenant of Zulu Company in the Wolves, the Kurians reacted by gathering up some of the indigenous swamp folk and infecting them with the latest strain.

Valentine took them down with four quick shots. Red carnations blossomed on their chests and they staggered in confusion before crashing to the ground, dead.

As a member of Southern Command, he'd been inoculated against the disease, but you never knew how current your booster was. Valentine had a theory that they were sometimes injected with nothing but some colored saline solution to give them confidence before going into the Kurian Zone, so they wouldn't panic if faced with the disease, spread by bite and gouge and gush of arterial blood.

It didn't take a special shot to the brain or anything like that to kill a ravies sufferer, as some people thought—though if you wanted to live to go home and kiss your sweetheart again, you made damn sure you put some lead into center mass, for a ravies sufferer felt no pain. Indeed, he or she felt nothing but a desire to rend and tear.

Valentine realized Duvalier's scream had been answered, in a muffled and echoed manner, from farther up the street in town.

Hopefully those who shrieked the responsorial were confused by the muffling effects of the snow as to where exactly Valentine's column was.

Valentine fiddled with his Type Three, took out the bayonet, and fixed it at the front of the rifle. He worked the slide in the hilt, extending the blade to its full length.

He pounded on Habanero's window. "Alert everyone: There's ravies in this town and God knows where else," Valentine said. "Get Rover and the Chuckwagon inside. We can block the main door with the Boneyard and stuff the Bushmaster in the truck entryway. Toss me a flashlight."

Valentine took a green plastic tube handed to him and clicked on the prism of long-lasting LED light. A beam one-tenth as powerful as Rover's, but much more flexible, played around the inside of the grain mill. Nothing else was drawn out of the shadows by the bouncing light, so Valentine satisfied himself that the grain elevator was empty of everything but corpses.

For now.

Judging from the smell, the locals used part of the old grain tower as a smokehouse.

Grain mills always reminded Valentine a little of churches. They had the same shadowy, steeplelike towers, tiny staircases up to balconies and antechambers, and of course the important platform at one end. In mills, that was where grain could be ground into feed or flour.

With blood and pieces of Thursday scattered on the floor, the phrase "dark Satanic Mills" from Blake's Jerusalem floated through Valentine's mind. Valentine pulled the corpses out of the path of the vehicles and waved the Rover in.

Thursday had done them one favor before his untimely death. He had guided them to a well-built structure. Limestone gave decent insulation, and it was as strong or stronger than brick.

Mrs. O'Coombe jumped out of Rover. "Mister Valentine. If there is the ravies virus in town, shouldn't we drive on—"

"If the weather were clear, that would be my choice," Valentine said.

Habanero nodded from the window. "He's right; we're lucky to have gotten this far."

Frat and his Wolves needed something to do. Valentine sent them up a short set of steps and into the mill's office to look for messages from the town's inhabitants.

"No noise," Valentine said.

"Put Rover over there," Valentine told the wagon master, indicating a corner by the old loader equipment. "Get Chuckwagon in here."

"The medical wagon is more valuable," Mrs. O'Coombe said.

"Right now the fuel in Chuckwagon's trailer is the most important thing," Valentine said. "And we can all get a hot meal. We can refuel Rover, Chuckwagon, and Bushmaster, and then put Chuckwagon outside and bring Boneyard in."

Mrs. O'Coombe blinked. "Very well. You are thoughtful under stress, Mister Valentine. I admire that. But I still think we should hurry on, weather or no weather."

"You could make yourself useful by refueling Rover," Valentine said to Mrs. O'Coombe, urgency consuming his usual polite phrasing with the great lady.

"Snow's killing the sound," Stuck said, entering the mill. He had a skullcap of snow already. "Ravies are drawn to motion and sound. They won't see us or hear us even if the town's full of them. As long as there's no shooting."

Habanero spoke into his comm link. Valentine heard the Chuckwagon backing outside.

Bee, who was riding in the Chuckwagon to give her two-ax-handle-wide frame elbow room, hopped out and trotted to Valentine's side, sniffing the blood in the air.

"Easy now, Bee. It's okay," Valentine said. How much she got from syntax and how much from tone he didn't know, but she went to work arranging the bodies neatly head to toe. She put Thursday one way and the ravies victims Valentine had shot the other.

Stuck was at the gate entrance, a big gun in a sling across his chest. Valentine had to look twice, but he recognized it as an automatic shotgun. He wondered where Stuck had acquired it and where it had stayed hidden in their travels—the weapon in his arms was easily worth its weight in solid silver. It was one of the few weapons that didn't require a tripod and that could kill a Reaper with a single burst of fire.

With the Chuckwagon parked, its trailer well inside, Valentine had Habanero tell the driver of the Bushmaster to back up the APC through the gate and into truck dock. It would fill it, perhaps not as tight as the Dutch boy's finger in the proverbial dike, but close.

Backing up the Bushmaster was no easy matter—the driver didn't have the usual rearview mirrors. Rockaway was at the top forward hatch, passing instructions to the driver.

Figures flashed out of the darkness, barefoot in the snow.

"Get inside, get inside, get inside!" Valentine shouted to Stuck. "Habanero, Bushmaster needs to clear the gate and get in the loading dock. Have Boneyard pull forward and wait, buttoned up tight."

Valentine heard a scream. Rockaway lit up the night with his pistol, firing at the ravies running for the Bushmaster.

Another charged out of the snow on his blind side. Valentine swung to aim, but the ravie jumped right out of his sights and landed on Rockaway, biting and pulling.

"Keve," Mrs. O'Coombe screamed from the doorway.

Rockaway emptied his gun blind and over his shoulder into the thing biting him.

Chaos. Everyone shouted at once, mostly to get the gate down.

"How the hell do you shut this door?" Stuck hollered.

"Inside!" Valentine yelled to Stuck. He was fumbling around with the wheel Thursday had used to raise the gate.

The Bushmaster rumbled through the gate.

A flash of brown and Duvalier was up on the gate rails. Duvalier had leaped nine feet in the air and now hung from a manual handle, trying to bring it down with her slight weight.

Valentine finally thought to look on the side of the wall opposite the crank and saw a pawl in the teeth of a wheel. There was a simple lever to remove it.

The compressed thunder that was the fire of the automatic shotgun licked out into the night, turning snowfall orange.

"Cease fire," Valentine shouted. If the Bushmaster opened up with its cannon, it would draw every ravie for a mile. "You'll just attract more. Habanero, tell the people in Boneyard and Bushmaster to turn off lights and engines—don't fire. Don't fire!"

Habanero repeated the orders.

The smaller door on the back of the Bushmaster opened, and Boelnitz jumped out, pulling a bloody-shirted Rockaway out, and the two ran for the mill.

Panicky fool! The fear of ravies caused just as much damage as the sufferers.

A shirtless figure tore out of the darkness. It didn't so much as tackle Boelnitz as run over him. It pulled up, as though shocked he'd gone down so easily.

Rockaway fell on his own.

Stuck took a quick step from the door crank and swung with

his rifle butt, cracking the ravie across the back of the neck. It turned on him, swinging an arm that sprawled Stuck.

Valentine aimed the Type Three and put two into the ravie's back. It went down on its knees. Boelnitz, stunned, crawled toward the door and the safety of the mill's interior, lit by the headlights of Rover and Chuckwagon. Stuck picked Rockaway up by his belt and almost threw him through the door like a bowler trying for a strike.

"The hell's the matter with you?" Stuck said, kicking Boelnitz toward the mill. "Why didn't you stay in the APC?"

Valentine let loose the lever on the pawl, and the door, still with Duvalier hanging on it as she tried to force it with her leg, descended. Valentine stopped it high enough so a man could still enter at a crouch.

Stuck rolled in and sighted his gun to cover Bushmaster.

Valentine dragged Boelnitz in.

"Dumbshit didn't shut the door on Bushmaster," Stuck said, swinging the barrel of the auto-shotgun and pressing it to the thick, soft hair on Boelnitz's head.

Mrs. O'Coombe hugged her bloody son. "My God, my God . . . ," she kept repeating.

Valentine kicked up the gun barrel, and Stuck head-butted him in the gut.

Duvalier dropped from above, landing on Stuck's shoulders, and wrapped her legs around his back. She put her sword stick across his throat.

"Okay, okay," Stuck said. "Get 'er off!"

"Close the door, somebody," Valentine gasped as they untangled themselves.

Mrs. O'Coombe worked the lever and the door rattled down at last.

A pair of hands thrust themselves under the gate. Mrs. O'Coombe pushed the pawl back in, held it there.

Metal bent at the bottom of the gate as though a forklift were being used to pull it up instead of a pair of hands. The bottom of the gate groaned and began to bend.

Duvalier's sword flashed and sparked as it ran along the gate bottom, leaving severed fingertips lying about like dropped peanuts.

"The pawl, ma'am," Valentine shouted. Rockaway reached for it. Mrs. O'Coombe broke out of her reverie and extracted it.

Valentine stomped the handle hard. The door slammed shut.

"You better?" he asked Stuck.

The ex-Bear nodded.

"I'd forgotten how much I enjoy noise and danger," Mrs. O'Coombe said to no one in particular. "Very little, to be precise."

"You wouldn't have really shot me, would you?" Boelnitz said, picking himself up.

Stuck took a deep breath. "Maybe not me, but the Bear sure as hell was about to."

Boelnitz looked at Valentine. "Thank you. I owe you."

"Valentine, what the hell was that?" Stuck said, pointing at the fingers on the ground.

Valentine ignored him, tore open his own tiny first-aid kit, opened the little three-ounce flask of iodine, and poured and dabbed it into Rockaway's bites and scratches.

"Doc says they're nervous in Boneyard," Habanero reported as Valentine's heartbeat began to return to normal. "It's not exactly an armored car."

"Get Doc in here at once," Mrs. O'Coombe said. "My son's been bitten."

"I'm not opening the door until things quiet down out there," Valentine said. "This is the best we can do."

"What the hell was that?" Stuck continued, shaking his head. "Have you ever seen a ravies case like that?"

"They were . . . like Bears," Duvalier said. "I've never seen anyone bend steel like that, except a Bear."

"Maybe it wasn't human. Maybe they've got a more human-looking Reaper," Valentine said, looking at the fingers.

"A Reaper would have just torn through it," Duvalier said. "Trying to lift it is a dumb way to get in. Reapers are smarter than that."

"Everyone needs to eat as much garlic as possible," Ma said from the Chuckwagon as she sorted through her stock. "I'll make a poultice for Keve."

"That's an old wives' tale," Stuck said.

"Well, I got to be an old wife by following old wives' tales, so you'll eat your garlic."

Valentine had heard dozens of folk remedies supposed to ward off ravies. Eating asparagus was one of the stranger ones.

Getting iodine into a ravies bite right away was the only one the Miskatonic people said worked. Iodine and a quick broad-spectrum antibiotic within a few minutes. The latter was a good deal less easy to come by in the Kurian Zone.

Instead of reminiscing, he should be refueling Rover and getting the Boneyard in, and then they could take care of Bushmaster. Everyone should get a hot meal and catch some rest too, and he'd better see how the Wolves were doing battening down the office in front.

So much for the responsibility-free tour of central Kentucky.

†

As it turned out, Doc snuck in the front door with his bag, moving extremely quietly. He cleaned Rockaway's wounds and gave him two injections, one for the pain, the other an antibiotic.

"Contact with Fort Seng," reported Habanero, who hadn't quit listening to Rover's radio since pulling it into the mill.

They'd rigged lanterns in the mill. Valentine had considered running the tiny portable generator to spare the vehicles' batteries but decided against it. A storm this intense couldn't last much longer, not in Kentucky.

He took a deep breath to wake himself up and put on the second headset.

"Major, we're getting reports of ravies outbreaks all across the Mississippi plateau," Lambert's voice crackled at the other end of the radio. "Report position and status, please."

"Grand Junction. We've just had a brush with them, sir."

"Repeat, please."

"We've fought a skirmish. Two casualties." Technically they'd just lost Thursday, but Rockaway had been bitten. . . .

"Major, I'm hearing strange reports about this strain. The infected cases are unusually strong and ferocious."

"I won't vouch for the ferocious, but they are strong, exceptionally strong. Like Bears."

"Are there other outbreaks in Kentucky you know of?"

"No, sir. This is the first we've seen of it. How are things at base?"

"Quiet. No sign of it. A new patrol has just gone out to check Owensboro. We've lost contact with the town."

"Orders?" Valentine asked.

"Get back as quickly as you can. The underground has informed us that that armored column has moved south from Bloomington and is now outside Owensboro. They've been shelling the city."

"We'll be mobile as soon as the weather lets up," Valentine said.

"Good luck," Lambert said. "Report when you're moving again."

"Wilco. Signing off."

"Signing off."

"We were lucky, I think," Stuck said. "I'll bet there is only a handful of ravies left in this town—mostly ones who were torn up in scrapes with them and succumbed to the infection."

"Lucky?" Boelnitz said, looking at Rockaway, who was being tended to at the far end of the mill by Doc.

"I said we," Stuck said. "Not him."

†

With time to think and a hot cup of Mrs. O'Coombe's tea inside him, Valentine realized the Kurians had played a brilliant double cross in Kentucky.

Or perhaps it was a triple cross, if you considered the attack on the Kentucky River position a double cross. He almost had to admire the genius of it. If the attack on the A-o-K had routed the principal body of armed and organized men in central Kentucky, the Kurians would have been in the position to act as saviors when the ravies virus hit. The New Universal Church could show up en masse, ready to inject the populace with either a real antiserum or a saline solution, all the while persuading the populace of the advantages of returning to their semiprotected status in the Kurian Order.

As it turned out, the attack failed, but it also served to concentrate their enemies. With the storm raging, they wouldn't be able to spread out and contain the virus to a few hot spots. Instead, the A-o-K would suffer the agonies of men knowing their families were threatened and unable to do a damn thing about it. Given the brief existence of the A-o-K, it might dissolve entirely, like salt in a rainstorm, fragmenting into bands of men desperate to return home.

The one patch of light in the snowy, howling gloom was that Kentucky wasn't the earthquake-and-volcano-ravaged populace of 2022. The legworm clans were armed to the teeth—man, woman, and child—and were used to living and working within the confines of armed camps organized for defense. Ravies bands fought dumb. They didn't coordinate, concentrate properly, or pick a weak spot in their target's defenses—except by accident.

Valentine didn't like the look of Boelnitz. He had been pale and quiet ever since the madness between Bushmaster and the gate.

Worried that the journalist might be going into shock from stress alone, Valentine squatted down next to him.

"Something for your notebook at last," Valentine said, noticing that the paper under his pencil was empty. "Don't let it bother you."

"The wounded in Bushmaster. They saw O'Coombe's boy was bitten. They said he had to go out, or they'd shoot him. I think they meant it."

Boelnitz looked at his notebook. "When I said I owe you, I meant it. I owe you the truth," Boelnitz said. "I've been flying under false colors, I'm afraid. Here."

He handed Valentine the leather notebook with a trembling hand and opened it to a creased clipping.

"It's one thing to write about wars and warriors and strategy," Boelnitz said. "It looks very different when you're looking down the barrel of a gun. Or up one."

Valentine read a few paragraphs.

It was always a strange sensation to parse another's depiction of oneself, like hearing someone describe the rooms in one's own home, bare facts attached to memories and emotions but as artificial and obvious as plastic tags in the ears of livestock. Valentine took in the words in the *Clarion*'s familiar, sententious style and typeface with the unsettling feeling of reading his own obituary:

> The terror of Little Rock during the late rising against Consul Solon, David Valentine has created a career that makes for exciting, if disturbing, reading. Trailed by a hulking, hairy-handed killer bodyguard named Ahn-Kha, Valentine is a man of desperate gambits and vicious enmities without remorse or regret. The corpses of gutted, strung-up POWs and murder to followers like the Smalls . . .

Valentine couldn't read any more.

"I only showed that to you because I can't reconcile the figure described in Southern Command's archives, at least the ones I was given clearance to see, and *Clarion*'s articles with the person in the flesh. I just thought it was time for a little honesty. Pencil Boelnitz is a fiction; it's the name of my first editor, the English teacher who helped us run the school newspaper. My real name is Llewellyn. Cooper Llewellyn."

"You thought . . . you thought that if I knew you were from the *Clarion* . . . what? I'd run you off base?"

"Something like that."

"I have to say, I like Pencil Boelnitz better. He seemed like the kind of guy who'd observe and relate what he observed without trying to psychoanalyze a man he'd known for only a few weeks."

"You've a right to be mad. But there's a sign up at the *Clarion*: *Anyone can transcribe. A journalist reveals.*"

Valentine chuckled. "I can't see why your paper is so beloved for its editorial page, if that's the best they can do. It's easy to come up with something like that for any profession. *Anyone can disrobe. A stripper profits.*"

CHAPTER THIRTEEN

*R*avies.

One of the most terrifying weapons in the Kurian Order's arsenal is the disease that makes man revert to a howling beast, a lizard brain seeking to kill, feed, and, yes, sometimes even procreate.

How they remove all the higher brain functions, leaving the lower full of savage cunning and reckless determination, only their elite scientists would be able to say.

The fear of a ravies outbreak is one way of keeping their human herds in line. There's such a thing as civilizational memory, and the human strata of the Kurian Order have been taught that only timely arrival of help from Kur stemmed the howling tide that threatened to wash away mankind in the red-number year of 2022. They instinctively know that without the protection of the towers, the screamers might return.

Anyone who's heard the dive-bomber wail of a ravies victim in full cry has the unhappy privilege of hearing it repeated in nightmares for years to come.

Of course in the Freeholds, they know that ravies is just another Kurian trick up one of the sleeves of a determined and ruthless creature with more limbs than can be easily counted on a living specimen.

Folk remedies abound, all of them nearly useless. A bucket of ice-cold water is said to distract a sufferer long enough for you to make an escape. If you suck a wound clean while chewing real mint gum mixed with pieces of pickled ginger, onion, and garlic, you'll never catch an infection from a bite. Pregnant women are naturally immune—this particular canard leads to all manner of bizarre remedies as others seek the mystic benefits, from drinking breast milk to pouring umbilical cord blood into a fresh wound. And, of course, that the only sure way to stop a ravies sufferer from getting at you is to shoot them in the head.

Of course, anyone who's ever emptied a magazine into the center mass of an oncoming screamer knows that they go down and stay down when suffering sucking chest wounds, cardiac damage, or traumatic blood loss.

No, the only facts absolutely known about ravies is that it is a disease that affects brain tissue and the nervous system. Sufferers don't feel any pain and are hyperaware, ravenous, and irritable, and if they are startled or provoked, they will try to rend and bite the source into submission and an easy meal. Heart rate and blood pressure both increase. Most brain-wave patterns decrease, save for the delta, the wave most associated with dreams, and beta, which increases during anxiety or intense concentration.

Many wonder why the Kurians, usually so careful with lives and the aura that might be harvested, allow whole populations to be reduced by the disease.

David Valentine had two theories. One is that ravies encounters shocked and wore down professional military types—no one enjoys gunning down children and preteens who, under ideal conditions, could be easily kept away with a walking stick or a riot shield until they drop from exhaustion. It took David Valentine months to quit hearing the screams in his sleep following his first encounter with ravies near the Red River in 2065. The other is that sufferers were harvested like everyone else in the Kurian Order, with the disease simply adding flavor to the aura thanks to the unknown tortures of body and mind.

†

Stuck was right, as it turned out. There weren't many cases in town. As they switched vehicles for refueling from the trailer, only one more ravie attacked, and Frat brought her down with a clean head shot.

They prepared to leave the mill once there was full daylight.

"We're going to try to keep moving to make it back to Fort Seng without another stop," Valentine told the assembled vehicle chiefs in the mill. "We'll take on rescues of anyone alongside the road until the vehicles are at capacity."

"Isn't that dangerous, sir?" Chieftain asked. "They might be bit. And if we lose a vehicle, who'll end up walking if there's no excess capacity?"

"And what about that kid?" Silvertip put in. "He's been bit."

"He's in Boneyard, with his mother and Doc keeping an eye on him," Valentine said. "At the moment he's not symptomatic, not even trembling, so the iodine may have got it or Southern Command's last year's vaccination may work against this strain. In any case, they'll keep him sedated. As for rescues, if we lose a vehicle, we'll travel overloaded and chance the fine."

One or two got the joke and laughed.

"One more thing: Let's break out the winter camouflage. We're still soldiers, and we still have eyes in the sky watching us and enemies to fight."

†

The winter camouflage was mostly old bedsheets and fancy tablecloths cut into ponchos, and extra felt that could be wrapped around your shins and tied with twine to create extrawarm gaiters.

Valentine changed the route order. Bushmaster would go first in order to clear drifts. Rover would follow, and then Boneyard and Chuckwagon brought up the rear. The two Southern Command Bears would ride in the Chuckwagon, as they'd most likely be attacked from the rear by ravies running on foot—Valentine had never heard of a ravie driving.

They wouldn't use the motorcycles at all, not with the snow and this strain of ravies that could leap the way they'd seen at the mill gate. Longshot volunteered to ride in the open atop Bushmaster so she could stand up and look over drifts, but Valentine told her to keep warm out of the wind.

So they pulled out. Valentine chalked a rough mile marker of empty circles on one of the roof struts of Rover. Every ten miles, he'd mark one off.

As they pulled out of Grand Junction and made it back to the old federal highway, he filled in the first of the twelve circles.

†

Three circles filled.

With room in Rover thanks to Mrs. O'Coombe being in Boneyard, Brother Mark now rode shotgun and Boelnitz, desirous of keeping away from Stuck, crammed himself into the backmost seat. Valentine sat behind Habanero so he could consult his maps and speak into the driver's ear, Duvalier next to him.

The snowfall had stopped, but the wind still threw up enough snow to make visibility bad and kept the convoy to less than five miles an hour.

The heavy cloud cover made for gloomy thoughts.

"Anything from the A-o-K on the radio?" Valentine asked as Habanero worked buttons to tune it.

"No, sir. Got some CB, just some lady looking for her man. Says she's scared."

"Take her position and tell her we'll report her if we can get in touch with anyone," Valentine said.

While Habanero spoke on the radio, Duvalier nudged in closer to him.

"I wonder if this is it for Kentucky, then. How widespread is the virus, do you think? Think they hit the Republics too?" Duvalier asked.

"If it's a tough new strain, seems a waste not to do as much damage as you can. Either way, Southern Command needs to know it's here. Any luck with the radio?" Valentine asked Habanero.

"Maybe atmospherics are just bad," Habanero said.

"What do you mean, if this is it?" Brother Mark said, balling his fists on the dash. "Kentucky survived the ravies plague in 2022 when nobody knew what was happening. They'll survive this. People are more prepared for this sort of crisis now."

Valentine looked at mile markers on the truck top. "Someone told me once that the Kurians were handling both sides of this war, and if they ever became really worried about us, they'd just wipe us out."

Brother Mark sighed. "Of all people, Valentine, I'm surprised you would consider such nonsense. Why would they want the Freeholds? We run guns into the Kurian Zones, broadcast news, and give people a safe place to run to, if they get away. They can't want that."

"I don't know," Valentine said. "Having a war going on can be handy. You can blame shortages on it, deaths, tell folks that the reason the days of milk and honey are a long way off is because there's a war to be won first. And its a convenient place to send ambitious, restive men who might otherwise challenge Kur."

Brother Mark locked his knuckles against each other. "I don't think so. Unless they are keeping it even from the Church. I rose fairly high before my soul fought back against my interest, and many times I handled communications for my Archon. I saw nothing to indicate that was true."

"Maybe they wouldn't trust such an important detail to written communications."

"There are five-year plenaries attended by a majority of Archons from around the world. None but the Archons attend. They depart with masses of facts and figures—not that the thick binders of data do them much good; you cannot trust the statistics of a functionary whose life depends on pleasing the boss with the totals in a report. But when the Archons return, there are sometimes a few promotions or a new Church construction project—ordinary activities."

"I wouldn't mind dropping in on one of those and changing the agenda," Valentine said. He glanced at his map again. Two more miles and he could fill in another circle. "Where are they held?"

"The location is held secret until the last minute. Probably because of vigorous, ambitious young men such as yourself with similar ideas."

Valentine always smiled inside at Brother Mark's description of him as a wet-behind-the-ears kid.

"Let me see. . . . Since I entered the Church it has been held at Paris, Cairo, Bahrain, Rome, and Rio de Janeiro. Not that there aren't important churchmen from Indonesia or middle Africa or the subcontinent; I believe the Archons simply like to see a few sights and shop."

†

They saw their share of sights on the drive, descending from the Mississippi plateau in central Kentucky.

Valentine would rather not have seen any of them, and it took a while for him to forget them.

As the wind died down and it turned into a still winter day, they saw smudges on the horizon, barns and houses and whole blocks of towns burning.

They saw cars and trucks with doors torn off and windshields punched in, blood splattered on the upholstery and panels.

The column passed huddled figures along the side of the road, sitting in meager shelter afforded by ruins of houses and ancient, rusted shells of cars and trucks. Many of them had frozen to death, fleeing God-knew-what blind in the night. When the column saw a figure floundering in the snow, waving its arms, they slowed and shouted. If it shouted back in English, they let them climb into the back of the Chuckwagon.

If not . . .

Target practice, Chieftain called it.

For the ravies, the snow worked against them.

Valentine tried to turn his mind off, not think about the future. The old Kurian trick might just work again. If that armored column massing outside Owensboro came into Kentucky and plunged into the heartland of the state—and the Kentucky Alliance—bringing order by killing off the diseased and dangerous, the Kur might just be hailed as heroes. At the very least they'd have little difficulty seizing key road junctions, towns, and rail lines. The disease-ravaged A-o-K wouldn't be in any kind of shape to contest the matter.

His own command would be hounded out of the state, and Southern Command, instead of having a quietly neutral bunch of legworm ranchers, would have a full-fledged enemy with access to some hard-to-stop cavalry.

†

Five circles filled in . . .

"I think I've got a Kentucky contact, sir. Major Valentine, they're asking for you by name. You know somebody called Ankle?"

Ahn-Kha! Even Duvalier bolted awake.

Valentine put on a pair of earphones and cursed when they wouldn't adjust fast enough.

He heard his friend's deep, slightly rubbery tones speaking: " . . . very short of ammunition. Before I lost contact with friends in the Shenandoah, I was told they had military roadblocks in all the principal passes, and there were reports of aircraft flying in the mountains."

"How are you, Old Horse?" Valentine asked, his throat tight.

"My David, can it be that you are caught up in this too?"

"Afraid so. What's your status?"

"It goes . . . hard, my David. There are so few of us left. I sent some of the men away so they could see to their homes and families. I only hope I did not delay too long. We are— Well, best not to say too much over the radio. But a good-bye may be in order."

For Ahn-Kha, always quick to make light of burdens, to talk like this, it turned everything behind Valentine's stomach muscles into a solid block of ice.

"Don't draw attention to yourself. They seem to be drawn by light and noise," Valentine said. "You haven't been bitten, have you?"

Static came back, or maybe the Golden One was laughing and shaking the mike. "Oh, yes, many times. Fortunately I seem to be immune. I wish I could say the same for the rest of my brave men. I will not say more. We have made some hard choices, hard decisions, and more hard decisions are coming. As you said, we too are aware that they are drawn to sudden sounds and sharp flashes and—" His words were lost to static. Habanero adjusted the dial. "We've used blasting explosives to try to draw them up into the mountains, away from our populations. We have, perhaps, been too successful. One might walk across the throng using heads like paving stones. Excuse me, there is some commotion. I must sign off."

"Good luck," Valentine said, wishing for once he had Sime's tongue for a phrase worthy of his old friend.

Valentine watched Boelnitz, an earpiece for the radio in one ear, writing furiously and transcribing the Grog's words.

"Who's writing this passage? Pencil Boelnitz or Cooper Llewellyn?" Valentine asked.

"I don't know, Major. All I can do is try to be accurate about what I'm hearing."

"I hope you're getting it right, sir. That's the hulking, hairy-handed killer I know," Valentine said.

Boelnitz drew away, pencil trembling. Valentine realized he was snarling.

†

Seven circles filled in . . .

They were getting closer to the Ohio now. The land became less hilly and was filled with more old farms. Someone sprayed the column with gunfire as they passed. It caused no casualties, but Valentine wondered if the person shot because he or she suspected they were from the Northwest Ordnance, or if they shot because they suspected they were Southern Command.

Out of the hills, the drifts grew less and less and finally disappeared entirely. The snow hadn't been as heavy in this part of Kentucky. Valentine put Rover back at the head of the column, but the ice patches were still treacherous.

"Major, Doc says we should pull over," Habanero said, acknowledging a signal. Valentine had taken his headset off so he could think about Ahn-Kha.

"Why?" But Valentine could guess.

"He wants you to look at Rockaway."

Valentine didn't want to stop for anything. "He's symptomatic?"

"Doc just wants to pull over."

Valentine signaled for a stop. Everyone took the opportunity to get out and hit the honeybuckets.

Valentine went to the Boneyard. The nurse silently opened the rear hatch. A red-eyed Mrs. O'Coombe nodded to him, her Bible stuck in her lap, a finger marking her place.

"Well, Doc?" Valentine asked.

He shook his head. "He's symptomatic. Starting to shake."

"You have him sedated?"

"Yes," the nurse said.

"What's the usual medical procedure for ravies?" Valentine said.

Doc sighed. "Ninety percent of the time, they're quietly euthanized. Some are kept around to try various kinds of experimental medications. They don't feel pain, from what we can tell by brainwave function and glandular response. Oh, and early cases are important for study to develop a vaccine. That's where the booster shots come from. Too bad he missed this last series, issue date October. We should have thought to bring some."

"I want you to end this, Mister Valentine," Mrs. O'Coombe said.

"End this?" Valentine asked.

"I can't watch him suffer."

"He's not suffering, is he, Doc?"

Doc agreed, "Not while the sedatives hold out. Even when

they wear off, provided we can keep him in the bed, I'm not sure suffering is the right word for what he'll be going through."

Valentine wondered how much of the patriotic, Bible-reading charity act of Mrs. O'Coombe was real. With Keve Rockaway/ O'Coombe dead, she'd own the vast ranch her husband had built.

"Any decision about your son's health I'll leave to the Doc."

Doc said, "I work for her ladyship, I'll remind you, Valentine."

"A rich woman outranks the Hippocratic oath?" Valentine asked.

"Major," Doc said. "Please. I'm in no hurry. I'm just wondering if I'll still have a job if I ever make it back to the Hooked O-C."

"Do what you can, Doc," Valentine said. "Anything else?"

"One more thing, Major," Doc said. He took out a little powder blue case. "In my younger days, before I settled down to bring babies into the world and plaster broken bones and dig bullets out, I was a researcher.

"This is a perfectly ordinary piece of medical technology from fifty years back. Nowadays I use it for interesting butterfly pupae and leaves. It instantly freezes and preserves, like liquid nitrogen without all the fuss and bother.

"I've been taking samples of Keve's blood as the disease progressed to see how his body's fighting it, and to see just how the ravies virus is attacking and changing him. It could be useful to Southern Command in developing a serum for a vaccination." He handed the case to Valentine.

"I'll get it back across the Mississippi as soon as I can," Valentine said.

Mrs. O'Coombe caressed her son's head.

"Keep an eye on her, Doc," Valentine said.

"Understood." Doc lowered his voice. "In all honesty, Major, she does love her son. She loved all her sons. Deep down, I think she was really trying to get him back home, but make it his idea."

Valentine stepped out of Boneyard. "Hey, Major," he heard one of the Wolves call. "There's a plane flying around north of here a few miles. Two-engine job. Looks kind of like it's circling."

Valentine wondered if the plane was part of Jack in the Box's operation. How did he fit in with the divine judgment of war, famine, disease, and death to Kentucky?

Which reminded him. He called Frat over. "Frat, how are you on a motorcycle?"

"Decent, sir. I used one to get around in Kansas."

"I want you to courier something important back to Fort Seng for us. And, if necessary, get it all the way back to the Mississippi— but that'll be for Colonel Lambert to decide."

"I don't want to leave you in the middle of this mess," Frat said.

"You'll do as I ask, Lieutenant. If you want to be addressed as captain in a week, that is."

"Captain!" Frat grinned.

"A platoon of Wolves this far outside Southern Command is supposed to have a captain in charge. I hope you'll be it."

"Not as easy as it sounds. But we should get a sample back to Southern Command as soon as possible."

They gave Stuck's big motorcycle to Frat. Frat grabbed his rifle and his bag and very carefully put Doc's sample freezer in a hard case. Doc added a final blood sample and a note before packing it on the bike.

Valentine shook Frat's hand, and the young man tied a scarf around his face. "I'll get it through, sir."

Valentine wondered just where that Ordnance armored column was. Their own vehicles would be simple target practice for a real—

"Frat, even if we don't get through, these blood samples need to. They're more important to Southern Command than everything in this convoy."

"Understood, sir."

He watched the youth rumble off, trying not to think of his own misadventures as a courier. Maybe somewhere on the road Frat would meet another capable young teen, the way Valentine had long ago met Frat. Part of being in service was helping train talented young people to take your place.

By the time Frat had left, the plane had taken off too, flying back to the north—probably across the Ohio in just a few minutes.

Valentine tried to raise Fort Seng to inform Lambert that Frat was on the way, but he couldn't make contact. With one more thing to worry about, Valentine returned to Rover and put the convoy in motion again.

"See if you can find a road turning north," he told Habanero. "I'd like to see what that plane is up to."

†

"Looks like a flea market that broke up quick," Duvalier said.

Valentine wouldn't forget the sight of the body field as long as he lived.

Even as an old man he'd remember details, be able to traverse the gentle slopes dotted with briar thickets, stepping from body to body.

You had to choose route and footing if you didn't want to step on some child.

Judging from the injuries and old bloodstains on the bodies, these were ravies victims. Some had torn or missing clothes, and all had the haggard, thin-skinned look of someone in the grip of the raving madness.

"What killed them, Doc?" Valentine asked.

"My guess is some kind of nerve agent. That accounts for some of the grotesque posing. Whatever it was, it happened quickly." He knelt to look at a body. "Notice anything funny about these?" Doc asked.

"There's nothing funny in this field," Duvalier said.

"Strange, then. Look at the ravies," Doc said.

Valentine had a tough time looking close. This was like peeping into a Nazi gas chamber. Though he felt a bit of a hypocrite; he would have turned the Bushmaster's cannon on them if they'd been attacking his vehicles.

"I don't—" Duvalier said.

"The hair," Doc said. "Ears, chins, eyebrows, arm hair. Worse on the men than the women, but everyone but the kids are showing very rapid body hair growth. A side effect of this strain of ravies, perhaps?"

Valentine let the doctor keep chattering. Valentine wondered where the pilot of the little twin-engined plane was now. *Enjoying a cup of coffee at an airstrip, while his plane is being refueled?*

"I don't think they really knew what was happening," Doc said. "Ravies does cloud the mind a bit."

"Wolves found something interesting, sir," Chieftain reported, looking at a deerskin-clad arm waving them over.

The vehicle tracks were easy to find and, sadly, easier to follow. They stood at the center of the field, in an empty space like a little doughnut hole surrounded by bodies.

"Okay, they drove in, or the ravies found them here," Doc said. "Then when the ravies were good and tight around the vehicle, those inside slaughtered them all in a matter of minutes."

"This one was still twitching," Valentine said, looking at a victim who'd left gouges in the turf. "I think he tried to crawl toward the truck."

Chieftain said, "Maybe it was a field bakery van or a chuck wagon. Food, you think? Baskets of fresh bread hanging off it? They look hungry."

"Ravies does that," Doc said. "You get ravenous. It's a hard virus on the system. The body's usual defense mechanisms—fatigue, nausea—that discourage activity during hunger are overridden."

Valentine wondered what could attract such throngs of ravies, yet keep them from tearing whatever made those tracks to bits. His own column would probably have need of such a gimmick before they returned to Fort Seng.

†

Nine circles filled in . . .

Maybe it was the sun in their eyes as they drove west. Maybe it was error caused by driver fatigue. Maybe it was the speed. Valentine was anxious to move fast—there was less snow on the ground, and they had a chance to be back at Fort Seng that night.

They dipped as they passed under a railroad bridge, much overgrown, and suddenly there were ravies on either side of them and the headlights of a big armored car before them.

It wasn't an equal contest. Rover folded against the old Brinks truck like a cardboard box hitting a steamroller.

When the stars began to fade from Valentine's eyes, he heard angelic strings playing. For a moment, he couldn't decide if he was hallucinating or ascending to a very unoriginal, badly lit, bare-bones heaven.

Valentine looked out the spiderwebbed window and saw tattered ravies all around, cocking their heads, milling, either work-ing themselves up to an attack or calming down after one.

Then he saw the big armored car, and it all came back to him.

The music was coming from the armored car. Chopin or some-one like him.

Valentine prodded Habanero, but it would take more than a friendly tap to revive him. He was impaled on the steering column like a butterfly on a pin.

Duvalier opened her door and fell out, still gripping her sword cane. Brother Mark seemed to be unconscious, blood masking his face, with a similar stain on the window.

Valentine heard an engine roar, and the armored car backed up. He waited for it to rev up, roar forward, and crush what was left of Rover.

He took his rifle out of its clip and climbed out. The least damaged of any of them, Boelnitz or whatever he called himself crawled forward and out.

Boneyard came forward to their rescue.

The music suddenly died. A new tune struck up, a harsh num-ber welcoming them to a jungle with plenty of fun and games.

The ravies didn't like the sound of the music. They began to spread away from the armored car in consternation.

Boneyard's driver came out of his cab. He slammed the door as he climbed down.

The ravies heads turned, looking at him.

"Careful," Valentine said.

Boneyard's driver put his gun to his shoulder and fired at the speaker atop the armored car.

Which showed initiative but not very good judgment.

A pair of teenage ravies came running, as though the spitting assault rifle was an ice cream truck's musical bell.

Bushmaster bumped off road and gave them covering fire, Silvertip at the turret ring with the 20mm cannon.

Like sand running out of an hourglass, more and more ravies sprang into violent motion, running toward the vehicles.

Nothing to do about it now.

Valentine went around behind Rover, set his rifle on the rear bumper, and began to fire into the ravies. Machine guns and cannon tore into them.

Regular troops would have scattered or taken cover on the ground. Not these men, women, and children. Most of them went for the Bushmaster: It was the biggest and—

"Chuckwagon," Duvalier shouted in Valentine's ear, pointing.

A mass of ravies hit Bushmaster like an incoming tsunami. They tipped it, perhaps by accident, in their fury to get at the noisy guns.

Valentine pulled Brother Mark out of Rover and threw him over his shoulder in a fireman's carry. A ravie with a mustache gone mad sprang around the corner.

"Uungh!" Duvalier grunted as she opened the ravie from rib to hip point with her sword. She spun and took a child's head off behind her.

Chuckwagon pulled up next to Boneyard, forming a V by having the front bumpers just meet.

"Leave them, leave them!" Mrs. O'Coombe shouted to the Boneyard's driver. "Get me out of here!"

Silvertip extracted himself from Bushmaster's cupola. But he'd left an arm behind, crushed against the autocannon. He tottered a few steps toward the tattered crowd beating at the driver's front window, studded leather fist raised, and toppled face forward into the snow.

Valentine set down Brother Mark between the two big trucks.

He brought down three approaching ravies, clicked on empty, and changed magazines.

But there was still fighting around Bushmaster.

Longshot climbed out one of the side doors, now a top hatch on the prostrate APC. Her bike was strapped there. All she had to do was untie it and right it. Valentine watched, astonished, as she gunned the engine, laid a streak of rubber with the back tire as the front stayed braked. She released and shot along the armored side of the Bushmaster, flew off its front, and knocked a ravie down as she landed. Sending up a rooster tail of snow, she tore off east.

"That coward," Mrs. O'Coombe sputtered. "There were wounded in there."

A figure tottered out from around the back of Bushmaster, looking like a doomed beetle covered by biting army ants. Bee staggered under the weight of a dozen men, women, and children. She shrugged one off.

All Valentine had left for the Type Three was Quickwood bullets. He loaded and used them, sighting carefully and picking two off of Bee.

Bee writhed, throwing off a few, breaking another with a punch, crushing a head, removing an arm.

But there were too many, clawing and biting.

Bee dropped under the weight.

Valentine saw her agonized face through the mass of legs.

Valentine lined up his Type Three, ready to put a bullet in her head. Bee opened her mouth—

To bite an ankle.

Valentine only hoped he could end with such courage.

With the bayonet, mes enfants. *It's nothing but shot,* Valentine thought, quoting one of the heroes of the Legion he'd read of thanks to the headquarters library.

Valentine had never used a rifle bayonet for anything but opening cans since training. But he extended the one on the Type Three.

Valentine charged, yelling, his vision going red in fury and despair.

The ravies bared their teeth.

Valentine threw himself into them, lunging and wrenching and clubbing. A hand like a steel claw grabbed his arm, and he responded by giving way to the pull, throwing himself into the opponent. He clubbed the butt of his gun into the ravie's face again and again.

Another lunge and he lifted a young man off Bee like a kebab on his bayonet skewer.

He noticed Duvalier next to him, slashing like mad, killing anything that approached her like a bug zapper firing cold steel bolts.

He got Bee's arm around his shoulder and dragged her up. She managed to rise.

A storm of gunfire cut down the ravies in his way back to the V between Boneyard and Chuckwagon. Stuck stood atop the Bushmaster, firing his assault shotgun. Chieftain stood at his back, removing fingers and hands from ravies trying to climb atop the wreck.

Valentine realized he was bleeding but he felt no pain, fighting madness coursing through his nervous system.

He stumbled into the Boneyard, almost carrying Bee, rifle dangling by its sling and .45 pistol in his hand now.

"Graawg," Bee said, tears in her good eye, the other socket a gory pulp, pointing to bloody divots in her shoulder.

"Doc, you got a shot or something you can give her?" Valentine asked.

"I'll fix her up."

Valentine waved Stuck over.

"No, wounded inside!" he shouted, gesturing at the Bushmaster beneath him.

He emptied the shotgun into the remaining ravies all around. *Pkew!*

A red blossom appeared in Stuck's shoulder, and he toppled off the APC.

Valentine looked back at the musical armored car. A rifle barrel projected from a rivet-trimmed slot in the front passenger-side window.

He could see the grinning faces of the driver and gunner behind their armored glass.

"Chieftain, take out those fuckers!" Valentine shouted.

The Bear nodded and disappeared.

Stuck, despite the rifle wound, was still swinging. He had a knife in each hand and used them like meathooks, plunging the blades in and pulling his opponents off their feet.

"You want a piece of me? There's plenty left, you assholes! Reapers and Grogs left enough for yas!"

Stuck led the remaining ravies down the road, shouting and gesticulating even as his steps grew more and more erratic.

While Stuck attracted ravie attention, Chieftain was dragging something away from the Bushmaster. Valentine realized it was the 20mm cannon. The big Bear, hair bristling up like a cockatiel's, righted it, braced it with his legs, and pointed it at the armored car.

Valentine looked at the armored car. The faces in the cabin weren't smiling anymore.

Krack! Krack! Krack! Krack! Krack!

The thick glass of the armored car had five holes with little auras of cracks all around, and blood splattered about on the inside.

And still the music played on.

†

Valentine—covered in quick-and-dirty bandages and iodine, injected with Mrs. O'Coombe's expensive Boneyard antibiotics, and feeling like he'd been taken apart and put together by a drunk tinker—investigated the musical armored car.

The back door was unlocked. After the cannon fire had killed the men in the cab, whoever was back there ran off into the growing dark.

There were a lot of dials and switches and electronic equipment, a screen and a controller for a camera at the back, and a blinking little box that one of the Wolves told him held all the music the system played in digital form.

Most of the music was soothing light classical, according to the computer-literate Wolf. "I guess they were attracting those Woolies by playing calming music," the Wolf said, giving this strain of ravies a name that was soon in wide use both officially and unofficially.

"It must soothe them," Doc said.

"And attract them at the same time. Must have been what they used to gather them . . . so the plane could spray them. That's how they killed them off," Valentine said, words finally catching up to his guesswork.

They fiddled until they had music playing and put some gentle Mozart up. A few ravies, wandering back from their final encounter with Stuck, shuffled up to the truck to listen.

Valentine gave orders that they weren't to be harmed. More important, they weren't to be disturbed by any aggravating noise.

They were prevented from engaging in further speculation by the arrival of a company from the Fort Seng battalion.

They were on bikes, Captain Nilay Patel wobbling unevenly at their head.

"The cavalry's a little late to the rescue," Valentine said with an effort. He had at least three bloody ravies bites, bound up in stinging iodine.

"The cavalry is having a hard time biking on melting ice," Patel said. "It's Colonel Lambert's idea, sir. We were leading a party of civilians out of Owensboro with the full battalion in field gear. There's a whole Northwest Ordnance column of trucks and motorcycle infantry and light armor getting set to cross the bridge where you got that Kurian."

"And you were heading toward them or away?"

"Trying to keep as quiet as possible as we got away, obviously, sir. That fury on a motorcycle came roaring up and said you'd had some difficulty. Colonel Lambert sent me back for you and Captain Ediyak ahead with the dependents, and then organized the rest into a Mike Force to support either if we ran into trouble. She's a better than fair tactician, sir."

"Where'd you get the bicycles?"

"We found them in a warehouse in Owensboro. Ownership seemed to be a matter of some dispute, as they were meant for transport to a purchaser in the Ordnance, but said trader was in no mood to fulfill his end with ravies in town. Colonel Lambert made him a generous purchase offer."

"What was that?" Valentine asked, but he suspected he knew Lambert's bid.

"He could ride along with the rest of the civilians, provided the bikes came as well." Patel looked at the stuporous ravies gathered around the musical truck. "What are we going to do with this lot?"

"Give them back to the people who created them."

"An excellent idea, sir, but just how do we do that?"

"We're going to need some noise, Patel. A whole lot of noise."

"I'm sure that can be arranged. Music or—"

"I have three vocalists in mind," Valentine said. "My radio's wrecked. Can you put me in touch with Fort Seng?"

†

They cleaned out the armored car's cab and brought the engine to life. Valentine put Ma at the wheel, as she understood both the armored car's controls and the volume and direction controls on the loudspeakers. Valentine had them turn down the road toward Owensboro. According to Patel, the city had been hard hit by ravies.

Bee with her Grog gun, the techie Wolf, Boelnitz for the sake of his story, and Chieftain just in case rode in back. Valentine road shotgun, squeezed onto the seat with Duvalier, who was clinging to him like a limpet.

"I'm worried about those bites," she said. "First sign of trembling, you go into handcuffs."

Valentine wondered if the bites were taking their toll. He was so very tired. But he had to see this through before he succumbed to either exhaustion or the disease.

They passed through the beltline of the city and drove among the Woolies like wary naturalists intruding on a family of gorillas. They thronged thicker and thicker around the armored car.

Suspicious, bloodshot eyes glared at them. Nostrils flared as the Woolies took in their scent.

"A little more soothing music," Valentine said.

Ma fiddled with her thumb, rolling it back and forth across the ancient, electrical-taped device. Harsh, synthesized music blared.

The Woolies startled.

The music hushed, stopped. A big Woolie, his mouth ringed by a brown smear of dried blood like a child's misadventure with lipstick, lurched toward the speaker, head cocked.

Ma said something under her breath—Valentine had no attention to spare for anyone but the big Woolie—and a soothing cello backed by violins started up.

The speakers ratcheted up, filling the main street with noise.

More Woolies emerged from alleys and doorways, some dragging dead dogs or more gruesome bits of fodder.

"They like that," Duvalier said, peering out a firing slot.

"Just like the Pied Piper," Valentine said. "Now to teach Hamelin a lesson."

†

Soon his followers filled two lanes and the verge to either side of the highway leading out of Owensboro and to the east.

They found a slight hill from which they could see the bridge and watch the fireworks. Valentine signaled Ma to stop the soothing music.

Valentine's trio of iron throats opened up. Guinevere, Igraine, and Morganna began to sing, and their notes fell upon the highway in brilliant flash and thunder.

The ravies ran toward the bridge.

"There go the Woolies!" one of the artillery observers reported over the radio. The Wolf's moniker had spread quickly.

The forces of the Northwest Ordnance had removed their barricades and some of the fencing to allow the invasion force to rumble across the bridge, its formation undisturbed. The Woolies found no resistance to their rush.

Panic struck the soldiers of Ohio's elite force. Immunization or no, an inoculation wasn't proof against one's injection arm being yanked out of its socket.

Valentine, having seen the destruction visited on Kentucky, rejoiced at like medicine being distributed among the "relief" forces parked in a long file along the highway.

He heard the drone of an engine. A plane hove into view.

"Bee!" Valentine said. He formed his hands into wings and had them crash.

Bee grinned from among her bandages, licked a bullet, and slid it into her big Grog gun. She put the gun to her shoulder and raised the barrel to the sky, as though it were a flag. The barrel began to descend as smoothly as a fine watch hand, lining up with the approaching plane, which had turned to pass directly over the bridge so that its flight path matched the north-south span.

It was a two-engine plane. She'd have to be quick to take out both as it passed over the bridge.

The plane dove, seeming to head straight for them. It hadn't started sprinkling its nerve agent yet, not wanting to lay it on their own forces.

Bee brought the gun barrel down, down, down, humming to herself. She fired.

The plane didn't so much as wobble. It continued its pass, remorseless. Valentine waited for the fine spray of nerve agent that would lock up heart and limb—

The plane shot over their heads, wingtips still, level as a board, engines roaring and flaps down, following a perfect five-degree decline to hit and skip and cartwheel into the woods of Kentucky.

Valentine heard firing from the other side of the bridge. A gasoline explosion lit up the low winter clouds.

Valentine tried to tell himself that he was killing two birds with one stone, not slaughtering civilians to confuse a military offensive.

"I know what the editorial in the *Clarion* would be," Boelnitz said. "*Southern Command Uses Bioweapons in Indiana Massacre.*"

Valentine was inclined to agree: both that they'd use the headline and that the headline was true. But you had to give the enemy whatever flavor of hell they gave you. "Of course, you could add some picturesque color thanks to your firsthand experiences."

"Hell with them," Boelnitz said. "You know, the publisher used to tell me, 'It's always more complicated than a headline.' That's only so much bovine scat one can tolerate. Our headline here is pretty easy. 'Victory.' They should have offered, instead of threatened."

"I hope we can remember that," Valentine said. "You know, Llwellyn or Boelnitz or whatever you want to call yourself, Kentucky could use a newspaper. It's one of the building blocks of a civilization. What do you say? Want to bring the first amendment back to Kentucky?"

Boelnitz smiled. "I have a feeling that as long as you're here, there'll be no end of stories."

CHAPTER FOURTEEN

*F*ort Seng, February, the fifty-sixth year of the Kurian Order. The snow has melted and the winter has returned to normal. Old-timers are predicting an early spring, perhaps to balance the fierce January weather.

The losses of Kentucky are great and still being counted. But the damages from the ravies virus could have been much worse. As it turned out, the snow that the Kurians hoped would freeze Kentucky's population in place while their disease swept across the wooded hills worked against its spread rather than for it—the towns hardest hit by the virus were contained by the weather, rather than the reverse.

It was a meager, hard winter, but it is ending. The shortages and bitter cold are fading as new winds blow and new supply lines are created. Old, tattered uniforms are traded in for the new pattern, and equipment and weapons improve as equipment is gleaned and reconditioned from the fight near the Owensboro west bridge.

Also, there is the knowledge that they won a victory against the best that the Northwest Ordnance could muster, even if the ravies victims paid the tab on that victorious banquet.

†

Valentine never suffered even a quiver from the ravies bites.

Had the iodine and antibiotics worked? He didn't know. It

hadn't done Keve Rockaway any good. When last Valentine heard, Rockaway was an invalid on the huge ranch straddling the Texas–Oklahoma border country. His mother had retired from public life to nurse him, and the real leader of the ranch was the new ex-Bear named Chieftain. Mrs. O'Coombe had arranged for three hundred head of first-class beef cattle to be brought to Kentucky in exchange for a few legworms and men with the experience to breed them. According to her, the ranch encompassed a good deal of wasteland that might support legworms.

She even spoke of establishing a horse farm or two nearby. Southern Command always needed fresh horseflesh.

But that was trivia. Valentine wondered how Southern Command had managed to have an effective vaccine to a strain of ravies that had never been deployed. Or perhaps it was just a very, very happy accident that Southern Command's latest vaccine was also proof against the Kurians' newest weapon.

So many questions that needed answering.

"I do have one piece of good news," Lambert said one morning at a meeting with Valentine. "We're in radio contact with the Bulletproof through the Army of Kentucky. They said a certain over-sized yellow Grog of old acquaintance staggered into their camp pulling a cart full of kids. He had pink ribbons tied to his ears and a teddy bear riding between his ears."

It was the best news Valentine had heard since Narcisse's reply to the letter he'd had Mantilla deliver. She and Blake would await his instructions about joining him in Kentucky, once he arranged with a river rat for properly discreet transport. "Ahn-Kha is alive?"

"A little chewed up, they said. Their chief promised to send him here just as soon as a worm can be saddled this spring."

Valentine wondered if he was dreaming. If he did see Ahn-

Kha again, he'd send him right back to his people. The Golden Ones had been driven out of Omaha and needed a leader of Ahn-Kha's caliber.

Lambert decided to celebrate the victory with a grand review of her battalion. It couldn't be said that they'd fought a battle, but they'd performed effectively in the field, keeping the ravies off while they protected Owensboro's civilian population.

Valentine recovered fast, as he always did, and managed to stand through the whole review.

They formed the men up, four companies strong plus an almost equal number of auxiliaries in an oversized "support pool."

The Southern Command "remainders" stood in a quiet group off to one side, watching the ex-Quislings in their polished boots and fresh uniforms.

"Our new regimental flag, my friends," Valentine said, pointing to a banner flying overhead. Even though they were a smallish regiment.

The flag couldn't be said to be fancy. Valentine had worked out the design with Ediyak, now in charge of the headquarters platoon.

He'd loosely based it on an old Free French flag. It was red and blue, with a big white five-pointed star dividing it at the center and large enough to touch the edges of the banner with its top point and bottom two feet. A little black pyramid with a Roman numeral I in silver filled the bottom-center between the two legs of the star.

With the flag flying, Lambert began the speech Valentine had written, largely cribbed from a military history book he'd swiped from Southern Command's service libraries.

"Legion soldier, you are a volunteer, serving the Cause of freedom with honor and teamwork.

"Each legion soldier is your brother in arms, whatever his origin, his past, or his creed. You show to him the same respect that binds the members of the same family bloodline.

"You respect the traditions of these United States. Discipline and training are your strengths. Courage and truth are the virtues that will one day make you admired among your peers and in the history books.

"You are proud of your place in the legion. You are always orderly, clean, and ready. Your behavior will never give anyone reason to reproach you. Your person, your quarters, and your base are always clean and ready for any inspection or visitor.

"You are an elite soldier. You consider your weapon as your most precious possession. You constantly maintain your physical fitness, level of training, and readiness for action.

"Your mission is sacred. It is carried out until the end, in respect of the Constitution, the customs of war, and law of civil organization, if need be, at the risk of your own life in defense of these ideals.

"In combat you act without passion or hatred. You respect surrendered enemies. You never surrender your dead, your wounded, or your weapons.

"You consider all of the above your oath and will carry it out until released by your superiors or through death."

Ediyak modeled the new uniform. The cut was similar to his old shit detail company's utility-worker uniforms, right down to the tool vest, the padded knees and elbows (a simple fold of the fleece made for light and comfortable cushioning), and the pen holders on the shoulder. The outer shell was a thick nylon-blend canvas of Evansville tenting, the inner the soft fleece so generously supplied by Southern Command. The color was a rather uninspiring, but usefully muted, rifle green. She'd daubed hers with gray and brown and black into a camouflage pattern.

Valentine tried to read their faces. Were the men standing a little taller? He could tell Lambert's speech, the new flag, and the new uniform had their interest and attention.

†

He spent two frantic days trying to make contact with the Bulletproof. He wouldn't believe the news about Ahn-Kha until he heard his old friend's voice.

In between haunting the communications center and helping Patel and Ediyak evaluate the new NCOs, he was asked to visit Doc. Doc had stayed behind to research the new strain of ravies the Kurian Order had deployed that winter. Despite the gray hair and the bent frame, he'd been putting in long hours seven days a week. He'd spent an inordinate amount of time on the radio, mostly advising communities how to prevent cholera and deal with an isolated ravie found here and there, half-starved and confused. The challenge had reawakened the committed researcher who'd lost himself on the Hooked O-C ranch.

Valentine walked over to the hospital—formerly the servants' quarters for the estate. The patients had small, comfortable, climate-controlled rooms. They'd turned a former garage into an operating room, and the old office into an examining room and dispensary. Doc had taken one of the little patient rooms for his research. What little equipment he had, he'd brought with him to begin with.

"Major Valentine, a moment of your attention, please," Doc said. He stood in his office, rocking from the waist. Doc kept eyeing Valentine's sidearm.

Valentine was expecting another request for nonexistent microscopes or a culture incubator. "Sure, Doc. My time is yours."

"May we speak privately? I have some analysis to show you. I would not want my . . . theory—theory, mind you—to become a subject of common discussion."

"I'd like nothing better," Valentine said, and shut the office door.

Doc went to his closet and opened the door. On the inside he'd pinned up a map of Kentucky. He flipped on a bright track light that placed a spot of light on the map when the door was all the way open. The glare made Valentine's head hurt and he felt a little nauseous as Doc invited him over to look at Kentucky, covered in incredibly tiny notations.

"Doc, I've been meaning to ask: Wherever did you learn to write that small?"

"My father was a hog man, Major. He didn't like to waste good feed money on paper. So I learned to take notes in the margins of my classmates' discards. By the time I was studying biology at Jasper Poly—"

"Never mind. I didn't know you'd been tracking our trip to get the O'Coombe boy so closely," Valentine said, looking at the map.

"But I haven't," Doc said, shoving his hands in his pockets, where they went to work like two furiously digging rodents as he rocked. "This is an epidemiological study. With ravies, geography is a strong predictor. Ravies sufferers naturally seek water, whether for sustenance or its cooling effect. Given no higher attraction, such as noise or a food source, they will find water and then follow small tributary to larger river, rather in the manner one is taught to find civilization if lost in the outdoors.

"Of course, my information is sketchy and mostly based on radio reports. But the dates and places of outbreaks show a curious track, don't you think?"

Valentine did think. It followed the arc of their path through north-central Kentucky.

"Always forty-eight to seventy-two hours behind us. Grand Junction. Elizabethtown. Danville. It always started in places we'd visited. We've been a four-wheel Typhoid Mary through Kentucky, Major Valentine."

"Someone's infected but not showing symptoms? They shook hands with a Kentuckian and spread the virus without knowing what they were doing? I thought ravies didn't pass through casual contact; you had to break the skin or eat contaminated food or some such."

Doc shook his head. "Even if it had been via casual contact, it spread too fast. No, the contact network for any one of us is not wide enough, not for this kind of effect in only forty-eight hours. There were multiple infections. It had to be placed in a food source or water supply."

Valentine startled at the implication. "You're saying someone in our column spread it intentionally."

"I'm saying that is what my analysis indicates. My sourcing may be faulty. There might be a statistical anomaly, as our communications with Fort Seng relied on relays with stops behind us, so the data points are naturally skewed to cover our trail. But there were no alarms from outside, say, Bowling Green or Frankfort, as you would expect from a population center that wide."

"Why would the Kurians use us? You'd think trained harpies or—"

"I'm no strategist, Major."

The Kurians would want to use the forces of Southern Command to make sure Kentucky would know who to blame for losses. Give every family a grievance.

Suddenly Valentine knew who'd spread the virus, and where he'd got it from. The sudden realization made him so sick he staggered to Doc's sink and vomited.

Valentine wiped his mouth. Double cross, triple cross, cross back . . . Kurian treachery was like a hall of mirrors. Somewhere a vulnerable back was showing to plunge the knife in. No doubt there were Kurian agents dropping a few broad hints, revealing a few interesting details, in minds willing to believe the worst about outsiders. Bears weren't well understood even in the UFR. Many a regular citizen heard only of howling teams of battle-maddened men killing anything that moved. He could see an average Kentuckian believing Southern Command had brought a contagion into their land, probably by accident. But the dead were still the dead.

†

The winter wind blew dead leaves and freezing rain in confused swirls. Valentine didn't like freezing rain. It magically found crevices—the collar, the small of the back, the tops of your shoes—hitting and melting and leaving you wet and cold.

He'd summoned Lambert, Duvalier, Ediyak, Gamecock, and Nilay Patel to the old basement of the estate house. They'd cleaned it out and were in the process of turning it into a sort of theater that could show either movies or live plays.

It could also serve as a courtroom, if need be.

Frat stood before him, his bright new bars shining.

"Why'd you do it, Captain?" Valentine asked.

"Do what, sir?"

"Betray us," Valentine said.

Frat's eyes went wide and white. "Wha—I don't understand."

"I had that big satchel you carried, the one like mine, tested. There was some spilled preservative in there and a hell of a lot of ravies virus in the preservative fluid. What did you do? Put it in the water supply of the towns we visited?"

"We're going to have to handle this ourselves," Lambert said. "If it gets out in Kentucky that we were the vector that spread the disease . . ."

"I'll do it," Valentine said, speaking quickly as his voice fought not to break, go hoarse, choke off the words. "I brought him into Southern Command. I'll take him out."

He shoved Frat to his knees and pulled the old .45 out of its holster. A gift from another man he'd brought over from the Quislings.

Or did he hate Frat for playing the same trick he'd so often played: infiltrating, striking from within? Being better at the deadly game?

What kind of hold did Kur have on Frat's mind? They found a bright young boy, trained him, and then sent him out among decent people like the Carlsons—probably to learn more about the underground in the Kurian Zone, the mysterious lodges Valentine had heard mentioned now and again. Surely Frat was bright enough to see that life in the Freehold was better than that in the Kurian Zone. What did they promise, life eternal? Did fourteen-year-old boys even consider questions of mortality?

"It's an ugly truth, Frat. Shit rolls downhill. It's hard to stand in front of a superior and say, *We threw the dice on this one—and lost*. Someone must be to blame. You made the blame list."

Did Frat, miserable and shaking, know how like brothers they were? An accident of birth put Valentine in the woods of the Boundary Waters, Frat in some Chicago brownfield. If Valentine had been raised up in the Kurian Zone, would he have answered the bugle call of the Youth Vanguard, done his damnedest on the physical and mental tests?

Valentine stepped behind him. His .45 had never felt so heavy.

"I want my second chance," Frat said.

"What?" Lambert said. Valentine froze.

"You heard me," Frat said. "I'll put up my right hand and take the oath. Put in my years, just like the rest. Wash all this shit away."

"He's helped kill thousands in the clans," Duvalier said. "Whole families wiped out. You can't just let him walk away from that like a wet Baptist."

Valentine wondered. A highly trained ex–Kurian agent could be a valuable asset. Had Southern Command ever taken one alive? If they had, he wouldn't know about it.

But the virus Frat spread had killed thousands. Even though it had backfired on the Kurians, there were men, women, and children all over Kentucky who'd died in the madness, from the disease itself or the stress brought on by the change, or in the fighting.

"Let him live and you'll lose half of Kentucky."

Frat raised his right hand. "I freely and of my own resolve . . ."

Valentine had to make a decision. Is an ideal—a collection of words that makes everyone feel cleaner, purer—worth anything if you can just discard it at will? He'd promised every Quisling who came over a new future if they sweated and suffered and risked for the Cause.

Suppose Frat meant it and was ready to put his obvious talents to work for the new Freehold coalescing in Kentucky?

Valentine had squeezed his conscience through the keyhole of a technicality before. He pressed the pistol to the back of Frat's head, but the man who'd helped him rescue Molly Carlson went on speaking with only the briefest of pauses.

He couldn't do it. Cowardice or compassion?

He pulled back the gun.

"If you're going to take that oath, take it on your feet, Frat."

"Don't be a fool, Valentine," Lambert said.

"You want to shoot him?" Valentine asked. "Go ahead. It's not so easy to do."

"She's right, Val," Duvalier said. "Quisling snot'll turn on us first chance he gets. You can't change him no more than you can train a scorpion to quit killing beetles."

"Maybe," Valentine said. "But I'm also an officer. That little hearing we had may have returned a verdict, but it wasn't sent to headquarters for confirmation. I'm ready to suspend the execution on that technicality, barring an emergency that requires me to carry out the sentence.

"We're both hung men, Frat. We'd have nooses around our necks in civilized lands. But we're still kicking."

Frat looked off at the eastern horizon. "I'm not afraid of that gun. It's those motherfuckers who need to be afraid. They said they'd protect me."

"The piece of shit doesn't give a damn about the damage he's done," Patel said. "I'll stagger all the way to Little Rock if I have to, to get that sentence confirmed."

"I was following orders," Frat said. "Same as you all when you burned out Louisville. Or when the resistance killed every trustee on my block. Even my grandmother and my little sister. We all got sins worth a stone or two."

"He's joined up. He'll follow a better set of orders from now on," Valentine said.

†

Valentine needed air and light. He walked across the grounds of Fort Seng, Duvalier trailing carefully in his footsteps like Piglet tracking a Heffalump.

They paused on the little hill sheltering the guns and looked at the old manor house. Some soldiers were putting in new military-strength block-glass windows, yet another in the hundreds of odd jobs needed to turn an old park and former estate home into a proper military base worthy of a new Freehold.

A warm wind took over from the confused air, a fresh new gust from the southwest. The sleet fled, turning into tiny, blowing drops of rain.

"I'm ready for this winter to be over," Duvalier said, turning her face toward the wind to take in the warmth on her freckled cheek.

"Not yet," Valentine said. "There's a lot to do before spring."